Wanting to Be
JACKIE KENNEDY

ELIZABETH KERN

HillHouse Books
PETALUMA, CALIFORNIA

HillHouse Books

ISBN: 978-0-9835815-0-5
Library of Congress Control Number: 2011906887

Book design by Sandra Sanoski   www.sanoski.com
Photo of Jacqueline Kennedy by Mark Shaw
Rose photo by Diana Myrndorff, stock.xchng
Marshall Field's (Macy's) clock photo by Wendy Goeckner, Dreamstime
Chuch steeple photo by oriredmouse, iStockphoto
Happiness and *Chicago*, taken from *Chicago Poems* by Carl Sandburg, New York: Henry Holt and Company, Copyright 1916.

Library of Congress Cataloging-in-Publication Data
    1. Chicago (Ill.) – Fiction. 2. Onassis, Jacqueline Kennedy –
    1929-1994 – Fiction. 3. Middle-aged women – Fiction.
    4. Young Adult – Fiction. 5. Polish Americans – Fiction.
    6. Family Life – Fiction. 7. Catholic Church – Fiction.
    8. Nineteen Sixties. 9. Popular Culture –
    United States – History – 20th Century.

TO LEE

THE CHICAGO BOY I LOVE

*H*APPINESS

Carl Sandburg — Chicago Poems

*I asked the professors who teach the meaning of life to tell
me what is happiness.
And I went to famous executives who boss the work of
thousands of men.
They all shook their heads and gave me a smile as though
I was trying to fool with them
And then one Sunday afternoon I wandered out along
the Desplaines river
And I saw a crowd of Hungarians under the trees with
their women and children and a keg of beer and an
accordion.*

CHAPTER ONE

MAY 20, 1994

Outside O'Hare Airport, I slid into the back seat of the cab, smoothed the legs of my light wool slacks, and adjusted my sunglasses. I'd already reset my wristwatch to Chicago time. It was almost two o'clock. I didn't have to meet Joy until six—enough time to get settled, maybe take a nap. It was going to be a glorious weekend. I'd been anticipating it for months, ever since Joy and I agreed to meet in Chicago to celebrate our fiftieth birthdays. We hadn't seen each other in ten years. How could we have let that happen?

The cabdriver stowed my luggage in the trunk and slid into his seat. His dispassionate brown eyes met mine in the rear view mirror. "Where to, lay-dee?"

"The Drake Hotel on Michigan Avenue."

I could see the start of a smirk on his lips. She's one of those uppity Gold Coast women, he was probably thinking. If only he knew.

My eyes drifted from the familiar bumper-car traffic on the Kennedy Expressway to the safer environs of the cab that smelled of an exotic curry. The driver's ID card was tucked behind a smudged plastic sleeve on the back of his seat. His name was Ranjit Kalirai. He was a kid barely out of his teens, wearing a plum-colored turban and an attitude, as if he was doing me a favor by transporting me downtown.

"So Ranjit, where's home?"

"Here. Chicago," he said.

"No, I mean nationality. You're Indian, right?" If Duke were here, he'd be nudging me about now. "Don't ask personal questions, Ellie. Do you have to know everything about everyone?" I should have learned my lesson a long time ago, but obviously I hadn't. Probably never would.

"Born in India . . . came here as a kid . . . grew up on the north side."

"Me too. Milwaukee, Division, and Ashland."

"No way. That neighborhood's a dump."

His dump, my treasure, I thought. "It wasn't a dump thirty years ago. You know, all those magnificent church steeples you see off the Kennedy between North Avenue and Division—there's a lot of history there. Around the turn of the century those churches . . . St. Casimir's . . . Holy Trinity . . . St. Stan's . . . had 100,000 parishioners, all in a one-mile radius. Largest Polish population outside of Warsaw."

"Mind if I turn on the radio?"

I couldn't blame him. Why would an Indian, a Sikh, be interested in hearing the history of the Poles in Chicago? "No, go ahead," I said.

A deep-voiced female newscaster was announcing the top-of-the-hour news.

"From New York City," she said, her voice dipping, "The world mourns the passing of Jacqueline Kennedy Onassis who died last night at her Manhattan home. The former first lady was sixty-four. Her daughter, Caroline Kennedy Schlossberg, and son, John Kennedy Jr., were at her side when she died at 10:15 p.m. Senator Edward Kennedy said in a statement, 'Jackie was a part of our family and part of our hearts for forty wonderful and unforgettable years, and she will never really leave us.'"

"My God, she died." The same icy sensation I always felt when someone died washed over me. I knew Jackie was ill. I had followed her progress since she had been diagnosed with non-Hodgkin's lymphoma in January. "I hadn't expected her to go this quickly. I hoped she'd beat it . . . the cancer."

"Did you know her, lay-dee?"

"No, not personally, even though I once thought I did. You're too young to remember, but Jackie Kennedy was our first lady in the 1960s."

"She wore those hats," Ranjit said, tapping his turban.

"Pillboxes. She had an important influence on me when I was growing up. She did on a lot of young women. I followed her when she was first lady, then through her marriage to that old geezer, Aristotle Onassis. Bad judgment if you ask me. But after the assassination, I could understand her wanting to escape." My voice trailed off into silence.

"She's in a better place." Ranjit turned the radio off. "Too much bad news. Where you live now?" His voice softened, lost its edge.

"San Francisco."

"You got kids? You married?"

"Yeah, two, and my husband's a doctor," I said. I wouldn't have mentioned the doctor business if I hadn't seen the stack of medical textbooks on the seat beside him, next to a grease-stained brown paper bag that probably held his lunch, the source of the exotic aromas.

"What kind?"

"Pediatrician. Are you a student?"

"University of Illinois. Finals in two weeks. No time to study. No time to think."

We were approaching the Division Street exit close to my childhood church, St. Casimir's, one of the oldest Catholic churches in Chicago. The announcement of Jackie's death and the sight of St. Casimir's lit a tinderbox of memories inside me. I thought of the unpredictability of life and how it can be shattered in so many ways: by an assassin's bullet, a betrayal, a broken heart, even a phone call.

"Ranjit, would you please exit here?"

"We're not downtown yet, lay-dee. See those buildings? That's downtown," he said, pointing to the jagged skyline of skyscrapers in the distance.

"I know. I'd like to check out my old neighborhood. I haven't been back there in years. I'd like to see it."

He shook his head. "Okay. Where to?" he asked, straddling both exit lanes.

"Turn right and keep going." I scooted close to the window.

In a block we approached a four-story huge yellow brick building on the corner. "That's my old high school . . . Holy Family. See that brown building across the street . . . with the loading dock? It used to be the *Dziennik Chicagoski*, the Polish newspaper. And up there," I said, pointing to a narrow red brick building with a fire escape zigzagging up its face like an iron caterpillar, "that's the dental office where my mom worked before I was born."

Ranjit reached for the radio again, but a dented Ford Maverick swerved past us and honked. "Learn how to drive, raghead," the driver yelled out his window. "*Khota!*" Ranjit yelled back—Punjabi for donkey—and gave the guy the finger.

"You tell 'em, Ranjit. Turn right at Milwaukee . . . now hang a left."

Ranjit swerved left, cut off the car behind us, and boldly entered the intersection.

"Well done!" I cheered. "Now stop right here!"

"You nuts, lay-dee? I can't stop here. You want to get us killed?"

"Then slow down a little, will you? Please."

Ranjit barely braked. I rolled down the window to get a better look at the island of concrete we were passing, the triangle where the three major streets of my neighborhood—Milwaukee, Division, and Ashland—intersected. Once there was a well-kept lawn with seasonal flowers on that small island where bespectacled old men used to sit on a bench peering over their newspapers watching pretty girls enter the subway. Now only the bench remained, and beside it an unsightly row of dented newspaper dispensers. But what I wanted to see was still there—the entrance to the subway station.

"Another sign of your youth, lay-dee?"

"Yes, it is," I said, softly.

It was in that underground subway that I once pledged my heart to Jackie Kennedy. I was sixteen at the time. I was standing on the platform waiting for a train downtown. Across the tracks from me, plastered on the wall, was this oversized poster of Jackie, an ad for *LIFE* Magazine, I believe. It was shortly before Jackie became first lady. She was young then. Thirty-one.

In the picture, Jackie was standing on a balcony of a building in Washington D.C. One arm was resting casually on the railing; the other was tucked behind her back. In the distance the Washington Monument soared into an unblemished blue sky. Jackie's lipstick was coral, her dark eyebrows were impeccably tweezed, and she wore a two-piece ivory outfit that even then I knew was tailored from expensive wool that didn't itch.

I remember thinking how out-of-place that larger-than-life image of Jackie looked in our dingy subway with blue paint peeling off the walls and the floors littered with trash. Then I gazed down at my own worn winter jacket, my scarf pilled with little yarn balls that looked like cooked tapioca, and my vinyl boots, scuffed and caked with salt, and by comparison, I looked completely in place in that Division Street subway station. I was a poorly dressed kid from Little Poland in Chicago. At that moment I decided I wanted more for myself, and that if I paid attention to how Jackie dressed and walked and handled herself, maybe I'd have a chance.

"That's where I used to catch the subway downtown, Ranjit. Seven minutes to the Loop."

In his rear view mirror I caught him rolling his eyes.

"You must think I'm a crazy old lady."

His eyes met mine in the mirror. "You? You're not old. A little crazy, maybe." His voice was teasing.

I laughed and caught a glimpse of myself in the rear view mirror. Short blond hair with blonder highlights. A full smile showing white enough teeth. I guess I didn't look old thanks to my mother's genes, my hair stylist, yoga instructor, dentist, and the gobs of moisturizer I've been slathering on my face for twenty years.

"Where to now, crazy lady?" He turned around and gave me a full-tooth grin.

"Turn left on Ashland, then go straight . . . crazy driver."

Cars, delivery trucks, busses whizzed past us from every direction. In the rear view mirror Ranjit's eyeballs bounced left and right like balls in a pinball machine. Horns honked. Ranjit honked back. He was having fun.

"Make a U-ee here, please."

Ranjit rounded the triangle and executed a harrowing U-turn onto Ashland Avenue.

"Well done. Now go straight ahead and park in the middle of the block."

"Why?"

"Because that's where I used to live."

We drove slowly past buildings I hardly remembered, except for an insurance office that still had pots of spiky mother-in-law tongues in the window, and a tavern that had changed hands many times over the years. In my day it was Wacek's. Now it was Que Rico. A dark-skinned couple leaned in the doorway arguing—she waving her arms, he staggering within her orbit.

"Pull up to the huge white building," I said. "Once the *Klub Kultury* was the center of Polish culture in Chicago. There's a ballroom on the third floor that was directly across the gangway from our kitchen window. They used to have these elegant dances. The men and women would be dressed to kill in tuxedos . . . gowns . . . sparkling jewelry. On summer evenings when the windows were open, we could hear the music as if the orchestra was playing right in our living room."

Ranjit pulled up to the building, now a neglected monstrosity. He turned and looked at me like I was demented. "I do not understand you, lay-dee. You live in San Francisco on that shining hill with cable cars touching stars, and you come back to this dump. No way," he said, his high-pitched voice rising at the end of every phrase.

Then I had an idea. I fished in my handbag, pulled out a fifty dollar bill and said, "Ranjit, go have yourself a cup of coffee and meet me back here in an hour. Get some studying done. Eat your lunch. I want to take a walk." I knew he could run off with my money and luggage and I'd never see him again, but something inside told me he wouldn't do that. "Do we have a deal?"

"Yeah, sure," he said.

I flung my purse strap over my shoulder and hopped out of the cab. Just as I stepped away, Ranjit signaled me to stop. He rolled down the window and leaned across the passenger seat. "You walk, lay-dee, but I'm a nice guy. I'll follow you. Something happens, I'm responsible."

I smiled and gave him a thumbs up. Ranjit. My own personal bodyguard. How did I get so lucky?

For the next half hour, I felt like a sleuth in a time warp, meandering through my old neighborhood. Ranjit followed behind me at a respectable distance in his yellow cab. I retraced my five block walk to grade school, marking the corner of Ashland and Blackhawk where Joy and I'd met every morning at seven-thirty, noting where her house once stood. Now it was a KFC parking lot. Everything looked smaller, tighter, darker, and shabbier. There were signs of the past though—a mailbox, familiar cornice work above a doorway, a pitted marble landing at the entrance to what used to be Suzie's Cafe. On balmy summer evenings Suzie would set up a cart outside her restaurant and sell the fattest, juiciest red hots I've ever eaten. She'd line up about six red hots, bun to bun on waxed paper, and she'd squiggle yellow mustard over them in a single squeeze. Then she'd say, "Ya want piccalilli?" at the same time she'd be heaping it on.

I looked at the dark faces around me. These weren't my streets anymore. They belonged to kids in baggy jeans and hooded sweatshirts, to a new generation of mothers carrying grocery bags, admonishing children in languages I didn't understand. I tried to smile and make eye contact with the people I passed, but most of them eyed me suspiciously, as if I'd just fallen out of an airplane bound for somewhere else. I guess I did look out of place in my high-heeled boots and jaunty silk scarf, hugging a red Coach handbag under my arm, and stopping to peer into shop windows and the entryways of run-down buildings.

At St. Casimir's, I had the urge to go in—I hadn't set foot in my old church in years. I stepped up to the huge oak door and reached for the latch, a worn bronze handle with one of those thumb levers. Over the years the metal had been dulled to a smooth patina by the thumbs of thousands of immigrants, including my grandparents, Bronislaw and Stepania Manikowski. With reverence I placed my thumb on that lever and pulled. The door was locked. I stepped backward down the concrete stairs and faced the church that had once been the center of my life, and later the source of my disillusionment. Then I laughed. How preposterous of me to think that the church doors would be flung open like grandmotherly arms, awaiting my return. What did I expect? The choir belting out the Hallelujah Chorus? I turned around and there was Ranjit, leaning against his cab watching me.

"Do you believe it? My church just rejected me!" I called to him. He threw up his arms and shook his head in mock empathy.

Ten minutes later I was back where I started, on Ashland Avenue in front of my childhood home. The house I grew up in was a narrow building squished between a four-story apartment building on one side and the *Klub Kultury* on the other. My dad's funeral home was on the first floor, and above it two identical flats, each with a large front room window and a smaller bedroom window overlooking the busy avenue. My mother used to be a fanatic about keeping those windows clean and lining up the scalloped window shades. At one time, the glass sparkled like water in a crystal pitcher, now the windows were encrusted with grime and there were no window coverings at all. Once, the oak entry doors were varnished to a glossy sheen, now the wood was gray and peeling.

The building was too depressing up close, so I waited for a lull in traffic and jaywalked across four lanes of speeding cars, thinking I could rekindle memories of its pristine past from a distance. Just as I stepped onto the curb, a horn honked and tires screeched. Ranjit had made an illegal U-turn and lurched to a burn-rubber stop beside me. He rolled down his window.

"You scared the hell out of me!" I cried.

"I'll be right there, lay-dee," he said, pointing to a legal parking space a couple doors down. "Take your time. I will study for exams."

I lowered myself onto a bench outside a Mexican taqueria, pulled a half full bottle of Perrier out of my handbag, crossed my knees and stared at the building that had once been my home. I thought of my dad's funeral business and wondered how he coped with death literally at his doorstep every day of his working life. I thought of my Aunt Nina and her heartbreak and how Father Ben had "slammed through our house like a wrecking ball," as Dad once said. I thought of Duke and me fumbling with buttons and bra hooks in the dark. And I thought of Jackie Kennedy and how impressionable I was then, and how, when I felt abandoned by almost everyone in my life, she had become for me exactly what I needed her to be.

I took off my prescription sunglasses and squinted at our building. It looked softer without glasses, more ethereal, like an impressionist painting. I closed my eyes, made myself comfortable, and allowed myself to remember all that went on inside that crazy, wonderful, unforgettable house of one telephone line, two languages, a hundred opinions, and secrets that would turn the Pope's face scarlet.

CHAPTER TWO

1961

*I*t was on John Kennedy's Inauguration Day, January 20, 1961, that my predictable life started to shimmy out of control.

I remember I was sitting on a hassock in our family room watching the inauguration on our TV, a 15-inch black and white Admiral housed in a cabinet the size of a dresser. Dad had called to me from the kitchen, "Ellcha, if you sit any closer, that TV's gonna suck you in and you're going to land smack in Kennedy's lap."

"Don't I wish," I called back.

Those days I was the biggest Kennedy fan in the world. That morning I had pinned my Kennedy campaign buttons on my sweater—one of John Kennedy's smiling face on a patriotic field of red, white, and blue; the other of Jackie with her name misspelled—someone had left the c out of Jacqueline. Even then I knew it was dorky to wear those buttons, but in those days I was pretty much a dork.

Walter Cronkite was covering the inauguration from a press box that looked suspended in the air across from the

Capitol. He was a young man then, with dark hair and dark-rimmed glasses, much like the thick glasses I wore that covered my eyebrows and bumped up against my bangs. Without them I couldn't see a wall unless my nose was touching it.

Walter Cronkite's voice was reverential, not like the sardonic voices of pundits today.

"President-elect John Kennedy, who at noon today will become the nation's first Roman Catholic president, began the morning by attending Mass at Holy Trinity Church in historic Georgetown. . . . It's a brisk morning with the temperature hovering in the low twenties. But Kennedy looks chipper . . ."

"It's twenty degrees out there," Mom said from the kitchen. "Why's he holding his hat? Shouldn't he be wearing it? Where are his galoshes?"

"The Kennedys are tough," I said.

The next thing I knew, Mom was beside me, her black flats planted solidly inside two squares of speckled linoleum, a stance that told me she felt on firm footing criticizing Kennedy. In her polka dot housedress and button-down cardigan she looked like Alice Kramden of *The Honeymooners*.

"Don't you think Jackie should have been at Mass with him? I don't think she's much of a churchgoer."

It bugged me how Mom was criticizing Jackie. The world was changing and Mom just didn't get it. With the war years of Truman and Eisenhower behind us, we were entering a magical era led by a young president and first lady who had style, grace, and new ideas—and Mom was finding fault.

"Jackie's probably off having her hair done, Vera," Dad piped in. "Yeah, that Frenchie, Mr. Kenneth, is probably working on her right now, and I bet he's not doing much better than Marcie would."

"Daaad!" I groaned.

"It's true. I'd pit Marcie against Mr. Kenneth any day."

My father, Stanley Manikowski, was the proud proprietor of Manikowski's Funeral Home, with two locations on Chicago's north side—one on Ashland Avenue where we lived, the other three miles northwest on Milwaukee Avenue where his two brothers, also undertakers, and their families lived. Marcie was the beautician who worked for them. It was a family joke that whenever Dad gave Marcie instructions on how to style a dead woman's hair, in the absence of a photo, he fell back on his generic hairdo instructions: "Side part and soft curls," he'd tell her on the phone. "And put a little pink in it." That's why so many of the women they buried looked alike.

Behind me, Dad plopped himself into his Scandinavian rocker with peacock blue foam cushions. I got a whiff of the pan-fried baloney he cooked himself for breakfast along with two fried eggs—food he shouldn't have touched and Mom wouldn't have made him because of his diabetes. I turned and caught him wiping his smudged eyeglasses with the corner of his handkerchief. "Can't get the spots off," he muttered.

"By the way, Stan," Mom said, "I called Doctor Kowalski and made an appointment for you to have your eyes examined next Tuesday."

Dad's expression turned from cheery to sad. "Okay, Vera," he muttered. When he caught me staring at him, he forced a smile and pointed to the TV set.

Mom lowered herself demurely onto the brown twill couch against the wall. My sister, Marta, had followed her in, carrying her Barbie doll by a tuft of its eye-popping red vinyl hair. She was bored, which I could understand because she was only eight and had no interest in politics. She was also annoyed because on a perfectly good day off from school her favorite TV show, *Ozzie and Harriet*, had been pre-empted.

"Lookit," she squealed, "Ellie's wearing her Kennedy buttons."

All eyes shifted to me. Mom rolled her eyes. Dad chuckled. Marta smirked and clicked the sturdy heels of her Buster Brown shoes together.

In the dining room, our front door opened and rubbed against the clear plastic runner Mom had covered the carpet with to protect it from wear and tear. I could tell it was Aunt Nina by the sound of her footsteps. Nina lived downstairs in an apartment identical to ours, sandwiched between the funeral home and us. She always wore high heels to work, the higher the better, but that day she wore loafers because she also had the day off. Nina was a secretary at our parish office.

"Hi, Aunt Nina!" I said, scooting over and tapping the warm leather of the hassock for her to join me. Nina knew what that day meant to me. She tapped me on the knee. "What's happening, sweetie?"

"Well, Jack and Jackie are heading to the Capitol now, and Herbert Hoover probably won't make it because of the blizzard."

"Ask her anything, she knows it all," Dad chuckled.

"About the Kennedys," Mom was quick to add.

Then the phone rang. "Wouldn't you know it, I just sat down," Dad groused. He leapt up to answer it.

"It's for you, Nina. Some man," he said, returning to the family room.

"Oooh . . . A man." Mom arched a probing eyebrow.

It had been nearly a year since Nina's husband Al died. Nina was thirty then, and much too young to be a widow.

She and her childhood sweetheart, Al Krasznik, had only been married seven years. He grew up on Bosworth Street behind us. He was an athlete, a star baseball pitcher. They went steady throughout high school, got pinned in their senior year, and engaged after graduation. When Al joined the Marines and went off to Korea, Nina wrote him every evening. When he returned with his left leg full of shrapnel, they were married in the largest wedding I'd ever seen at St. Casimir's. Although I was only nine then, I remember them descending the steps in front of the church, arm in arm, Al limping. He was Gary Cooper handsome, and she was as stunning as Grace Kelly, smiling her dazzling smile. They were bubbling over with hopes and dreams.

Al had planned to make the Marines a career and travel around the world with Nina, and they planned to have kids. "A church pew full of 'em," Al would tease. But Korea ended their dreams, and Al had to take a job operating an elevator up and down the five floors of Wieboldt's Department Store on Milwaukee Avenue. Up and down he'd ride, from Furniture and Housewares on four, to Dry Goods and Children's Apparel on three, to Women's on two, and back to Notions, Men's wear, and Groceries on one. "I'm a vertical traveler," he used to joke. Uncle Al was a garrulous fellow, the kind of guy who always had a joke to share, some of them off-color but most of them side-slapping funny because his delivery was filled with pauses and ethnic accents, sound effects and hand gestures that few people could pull off. It was because of him that I learned the meaning of the word *raconteur*.

Then one day, Uncle Al stepped away from his elevator to tell a joke to Mitzie Semkow, a clerk in Housewares on four. After he'd told it, he backed into his elevator. To everyone's horror someone had moved his elevator car thinking it was left unattended, and whoever moved it forgot to shut the iron gate. Al backed into the elevator shaft laughing and waving and plunged to his death.

Nina and Al never did get their church pew full of kids, and Nina had to find a job. She could have worked in the family business, but our funeral home was too depressing a workplace given what she'd been through, so she branched out and took a job in the parish office. "Good thing you took typing and shorthand," I remember Mom telling her.

Nina dashed to the phone in the kitchen. At that time we had one phone line in the building. When the phone rang, it rang in our apartment, in Nina's flat, and in Dad's office downstairs. Sometimes three people answered at once. Of course, everyone ended up knowing everyone else's business. No privacy there.

The TV station switched to a commercial for Purex. A perky woman with a pageboy and a Peter Pan collar held up a can of Old Dutch Cleanser. "You'll find the woman's touch in every Purex product."

I stood up and stretched. There was just enough time to grab a glass of water, so I slid across Mom's waxed floor in my stocking feet toward the kitchen sink and stopped about a yard away from where Nina was standing with her back to me. One of her hands hugged the receiver to her ear; the other gripped the edge of the Formica countertop so hard that her fingernails were white.

I reached to open the cabinet for a glass.

Nina mumbled something I couldn't understand, but I could hear the cadence of a man's deep voice reverberating through the receiver. Then Nina said as clear as day, "You know as well as I do that we've got to stop doing this." My hand stopped in mid air.

"It's not right what we're doing," she whispered into the mouthpiece, her voice starting to crack. There was a pause, and then she said, "No good can come from it. No good at all."

I remember standing there frozen, studying the curves of Nina's body—her slim hips, her full bosom pressing against the bodice of her corduroy jumper, the color of cardboard. A sudden roll of her hips told me I'd better get the heck out of there before she turned around and caught me eavesdropping. I forgot the water and tiptoed back into the family room. What's got to stop? What's Nina doing that's so wrong? She was the most upright person I knew.

A couple minutes later, Nina returned to the hassock. Her face was pale as paper. Dad rocked his rocker forward and patted her on the back. "How's my little sis doing?"

"Day by day, Stan," she said.

"It'll be okay, Janina," Dad said, seeing her expression.

By then the dignitaries were seated in rows on the East Portico of the Capitol Building, a sea of dark coats and top hats. The camera zoomed in on their faces: Harry Truman jabbering up a blue streak; his tightlipped wife, Bess, in a grim veil that fell to the tip of her nose; handsome Teddy and his blonde wife, Joan; Bobby and Ethel. President-elect Kennedy glanced over his shoulder at Jackie, a row behind him, and he grinned. She brushed her cheek with a gloved hand and smiled back. Jackie was radiant that wintry morning in a fawn-colored coat with oversized buttons and a sable collar that matched the muff resting in her lap. Tipped slightly toward the back of her head sat a pillbox hat shaped like a marshmallow.

On a wide stage below the portico the Army and Marine Corps band struck up the first bar of *God Bless America*, and the familiar music, brimming with woodwinds and brass, sent chills down my spine. When the great contralto, Marian Anderson, broke into song, "Stand beside her, and guide her . . ." and the cymbals crashed in patriotic tribute, I slid my hand into Nina's. Her hand was trembling.

"Who was on the phone, Janina?" Dad asks.

Nina didn't look at him. "A guy selling something."

Sam Rayburn, the Speaker of the House, administered the oath of office to Lyndon Baines Johnson. I looked over at Nina. Tears were streaming down her cheeks.

"Nina, what's the matter?"

"Nothing," she whispered, wiping her face with her fingertips. "Nothing. Watch the program, Ellie." Her blond hair was pulled back into a loose French braid. A strand of blonde hair fell over her forehead and she brushed it aside.

Dad leaned forward. "Janina, you're crying."

She shook her head no. She dropped her head into her hands and mumbled.

"What'd ya say, Janina?" Dad asked.

Nina raised her head and looked at him with the saddest expression I'd seen on her since we stood as a family at Uncle Al's grave. She looked as if she could tear like a paper doll.

"Nina, don't cry," I said.

"Let her cry, Ellcha. She needs a good cry," Dad said softly. "It's been a year now and she's never had a good cry. It's Al," Dad mouthed to Mom.

I didn't know what to do, so I did what I usually did when I was nervous—I fidgeted. I adjusted the glasses on my nose. I fumbled in the pocket of my box-pleated skirt searching for God knows what. I found a rumpled tissue and handed it to Nina. Mom stretched her arm across me and handed her an embroidered handkerchief.

On TV, in his rich Harvard accent, John Kennedy was taking his oath of office.

"I do solemnly swear to execute the office of President of the United States . . ."

By then Nina's whole body was shaking.

Dad lifted himself from his chair and placed his wide hands on her shoulders. "It's okay, Janina. Al's gone, but you'll find another guy who'll love you as much as he loved ya. One of these days, you'll find yourself a good man, and you'll have a house full of kids. You want kids and you deserve to have 'em." He kept repeating this, which only made Nina cry harder.

"I don't want another guy," Nina sobbed.

President Kennedy was delivering his inaugural address.

" . . . The torch has been passed to a new generation of Americans . . ."

I'd been waiting months to hear it, but that day I couldn't concentrate. Kennedy tapped the lectern with his index finger to make a point, but my mind was on Nina. There had to be a simple explanation for what I heard.

"And so my fellow Americans, ask not what your country can do for you, ask what you can do for your country."

"Now, now Janina. We can't go back. We just have to look ahead," Dad said.

"I can't look ahead, Stan," she said, gulping air.

"You're still young. You'll find another fella. Heck, if you can't find one, I'll find one for you."

Dad held her shoulders, but his eyes were focused straight ahead—out our third floor window at a skyline of peaked rooftops capping modest two-story frame houses. Iron fire escapes supported pristine rods of snow. Red brick chimneys billowed out scarves of smoke. And in the distance, against the hazy sky, the steeple of St. Casimir's loomed over our neighborhood like a stone sentry. Its bell tower, with a commanding cross on top and a clock below, marked the hours of our lives, reminding us always to be good.

The inauguration was over and Walter Cronkite was reviewing the highlights of the morning from his press box. Behind him on the East Portico, people as small as carpenter ants exited the rows. Soon workmen would disassemble the microphones, carry away the rostrum and chairs, and remove the presidential seal and bunting.

Marta was staring into the heavy air, her eyes unblinking, clutching her Barbie doll tight. "Come sit with me," she said. I put my arm around her and pulled her close.

Eventually, Nina's sobs slowed to a whimper and her shoulders stopped shaking. She folded the hankie into a tidy damp square, and a few minutes later Mom took her by the elbow and walked her downstairs.

Thank God her crying was over. At that time I didn't know who it was on the phone. All I knew is that it had nothing to do with Al.

CHAPTER THREE

*B*ack then Joy and I had this telepathic thing about phone calls. When one of us was calling the other, we knew it the second the phone rang. When the phone rang the morning after Inauguration Day, I knew it was Joy.

"Hi. Southport/Clark at ten-thirty?"

"Sounds good. Seeya. Bye," I said.

In our house we had a three-minute limit on phone calls, and even then there was always someone listening in on our conversations. So when we'd really want to talk, we'd hop on a city bus—either the Southport/Clark line that ran north and south on Ashland, or the Number 56/ Milwaukee Avenue line that ran southeast to the Loop and northwest to the Forest Preserve. We'd pay our twenty-five cent fare, get a transfer and ride to the end of the line and back on one ticket. The buses were warm, the sights were interesting, and we had the privacy we needed.

Joy lived with her mother in a garden apartment—the basement—of a three-story brownstone across the street. I ran downstairs to Dad's office and leaned into the thick oak front door of the funeral home watching for her through the teardrop of clear glass set into a stained glass window of garnet and emerald. When I spotted Joy jaywalking across four lanes of traffic, I dashed out to meet her. A green and ivory CTA bus was heading north. Joy spotted it, and we met at the bus stop. The bus driver, a black man named Charlie, had been driving that route for years and had come to know us.

"Ah, the mortuary princesses," he said as we climbed aboard.

"That's us," Joy said in her deep monotone and slipped her quarter into the slot.

Charlie was already punching two little holes into a picture of a clock on two thin pink paper transfers. He knew our routine. "You got an hour, girls."

Whoosh. The door shut behind us and the bus began to roll. The bus smelled like diesel fuel, steam, and wet wool. We stumbled past two women in a double seat who were each reading the Polish newspaper, the *Dziennik Chicagoski*. They held the papers across their faces so only their heavy eyebrows and hats showed. Behind them, a laborer in a hooded navy blue parka was asleep with his head pressed against the smudged window; his hands, with grease under his fingernails, rested on top of the metal lunch bucket in his lap. We slid into our favorite seat behind the rear exit.

Joy's neck was wrapped in the black scarf her mother had knitted her for Christmas. Under it she wore her black woolen jacket that covered her black turtleneck and most of her peg-legged toreador pants. That year Joy had become a wearer of black. "It's hip," she'd say. "It's what the beatniks in Paris are wearing." Joy liked to be at the forefront of things.

I unbuttoned the non-hip root beer barrel buttons on my

car coat. "So what's cooking?"

"A lot." Joy shifted nervously in her seat. She cupped her hand over her mouth, sidled into me and whispered, "Andy and I had sex last night."

"No."

"Yes."

"On Inauguration Day?"

"Yeah. Why, was it illegal or something?"

"Of course not."

I gawked at her face through my thick lenses. I wanted to see if she looked any different, but she didn't. Same old Joy. Rosy cheeks. Delicate nose. Wild curly hair glinting like polished onyx against pearly skin, pulled back into a high ponytail fastened with a rubber band, probably from the Polish paper. Full lips pulled into a sly smile, or a smirk. Sometimes it was hard to tell with Joy.

"Cripe, Ellie, you're looking at me like I'm the first woman to do it!"

"Well, how was it?" I whispered.

Every since we'd reached puberty, Joy was the friend I went to with questions about sex. Once, when I admitted to her that I'd never seen a naked man's body, much less a penis, she drew one for me—in pay-attention red ink on the inside cover of my *Baltimore Catechism*, which I had a heck of a time erasing when I had to turn the book in at the end of the school year. Another time she showed me a condom. "It's a Trojan," she said, pulling the soft latex rubber out of its humpy blue package. "Guys carry them in their wallets, just in case." Now that she had first-hand experience, I felt confident asking her the big question: "How did it feel?"

She thought a second. "Like sparklers sparkling you know where," she answered too loudly. I looked around to see if anyone had overheard, but no one did. Charlie's full mahogany face was bouncing up and down in the rear view mirror, but he wasn't watching us either.

Until then Joy and Andy had been doing some heavy necking, always in the supply room of Andrzej's Restaurant, which Andy had a key to because he was the grandson of Andrew Klimaszewski, the owner of Andrzej's, the most popular Polish restaurant on the north side. Andy was majoring in business at De Paul. "They're grooming him to take over the whole shebang," Joy would brag. Her biggest dream was to become Mrs. Andrew Klimaszewski, Jr., and her biggest hope was for Andy to give her a diamond before graduation.

"Did he say he loves you?"

"No, some other things though."

"Like what?"

"Like personal. None of your business."

She loosened her scarf and gazed out the window. Her breath left an island of condensation on the window glass that began to shrink when she looked into her lap. "I think he was getting there," she said quietly. She forced a smile. "Anyway, now I have new material for confession."

I stared at her harder. Joy was a religious paradox. She drank beer, swore, and chased guys. But every Saturday afternoon at four o'clock she'd pin her black lace mantilla on top of her head and march to confession. Joy's soul was like a magic slate board. She scribbled on it hard all week and then pulled up the filmy gray sheet on Saturday, and presto, all her sins disappeared.

Joy straightened her back and folded her hands on her lap. "So, what's up with you?"

I'd been thinking about Nina, and I knew that what

happened within our walls should stay there, but Joy was almost family, so I gave her a word-for-word report of the phone conversation I'd overheard. "What do you think?" I asked.

Joy looked at me and nodded knowingly. "That's easy, Ellie. Nina's having an affair and don't keel over when I say this, but the asshole's probably married and that's why she had to call it quits."

"Nina wouldn't get involved with a married man."

"Ellie, you're so naïve. Hell, it happens all the time. Al's been dead a year. Nina's lonely. Some poor guy's probably married to a woman who's as frigid as a side of beef in a meat locker, so the two of them got together. Two lonely souls . . ."

"—In a meat locker? Joy!"

"Well, it's true," she said. "But Nina's smart and she broke it off. You heard her yourself, Ellie. She's done with it. She doesn't need that kind of crap, sneaking around and everything. So case closed, there's nothing to worry about." Joy nodded her head emphatically—the way she did when she believed she had something all figured out and didn't want to hear any arguments. "Furthermore, I think it's time you start worrying about your own love life instead of Nina's, so that's why Donna and I are fixing you up with Donna's brother, Duke. He's at Loyola. We think he's perfect for you."

"Joy, I don't need your fix-ups."

"Oh, yes you do. I'm tired of you moaning that you don't have a boyfriend, so I'm doing something about it, which is more than I can say about you."

I was just about to remind Joy of the duds—all friends of Andy's—she'd set me up with in the past. Guys with hair slicked back in a DA, a duck's ass. Guys who'd want to take off my glasses first and then my bra. But I stopped myself. It wasn't exactly easy to find guys at an all-girls high school. Wasn't a date with a college guy something I should be looking forward to?

"Why is he perfect for me?"

"You'll see, Ellie. You'll see. Here's the deal. He's going to call and you better say yes."

Funeral homes have a distinct smell. Musty flowers. Stale cigarette and cigar smoke. The acrid chemicals used in embalming. That's how it was downstairs at our place. But upstairs it was a different story. Upstairs, our hallway always smelled like a Polish restaurant: spicy *kiełbasa*, pungent sauerkraut, beef and pork roasts smothered in garlic, homemade *babka* and *mazurek* glazed with rum and almond. When I got home from my bus ride with Joy that day, Nina was baking bread. I could smell it ten steps outside her door.

We never knocked on each other's doors, so I walked right in.

"Hi Nina, it's me!"

Nina was in the pantry, so I followed the yeasty aroma into the kitchen. I leaned over the golden crusts of two braided loaves of bread cooling on her stovetop and thought about how I could talk to Nina about anything—my lovelife or lack thereof, my insecurities, my dreams for the future. Unlike Mom who would've been dialing the Pope before I finished my story, Nina would listen. She'd never jump to conclusions or judge me. And she gave great advice. There are things Nina said that I remember to this day—advice that I've passed on to my own daughter. Once, we were talking about sex and she said, "One of the most important decisions you'll ever make is whom you give your body to." Another time, she laughed and said, "Be good, but if you can't be good, be careful." That piece of advice turned out to be prophetic.

Nina joined me in the kitchen. "Bread's hot, sweetie, but go ahead and slice it anyway. I'll get the butter."

I studied Nina's face to see if she'd been crying, but she looked pretty normal. I toyed with the idea of asking her about that phone call, but in the end I decided to respect her privacy. I remember giving her an opener though.

"Anything new today?"

"Not a thing."

"Talk to anyone special?"

She looked at me with a tilted face. "Ellie, if you're worried about all the crying I was doing yesterday, don't. It's over," she said with a clip of finality in her voice. But the twitch in her eyelid made me doubt it.

Nina's eyes moved to an up-side-down issue of the *Chicago Tribune* on her side of the table. On the front page was a photo of President Kennedy looking smart in his tuxedo, grinning as if the world belonged to him, and Jackie, elegant in her classic white gown. "They make an attractive couple, the Kennedys."

I nodded. My mind was still on the phone call, but I knew I wasn't going to get more information out of her that day. So I told Nina what I intended to tell her about my fixup. "Donna's brother is going to call and ask me out."

She stared at me hard, studied my face. She had this way of seeing right through me. "So what are you worried about then?"

"I'm not worried."

She raised a questioning eyebrow.

"Well, I guess I am. I'm already a mess thinking about it, and I just found out. You know me, I'm no good at dates. What am I going to say to this guy? I'm not funny. I'm too tall

. . . just look at me."

Nina, of course, said all the right things. "You have a great sense of humor . . . you have a smile that lights up a room . . . and tall is good." She pointed to the photo of Jack and Jackie. "Jackie's tall."

"She wears a size ten shoe. That's about all we have in common. Our clodhoppers. Other than that . . . nothing," I said, making a zero with my thumb and forefinger. "This is how it is, Nina. Jackie rides horses and eats *crepes*. I ride the bus to the end of the line, maybe with a stop at Superdawg's for a red hot before heading home."

"Oh, you poor thing!"

We both sat back and laughed.

"I want a big life like Jackie's," I said.

Nina spotted some breadcrumbs on the table, wet her index finger on the tip of her tongue and picked them up one by one. "I know you do, sweetie, and I hope you have one. I hope your life is as big as you want it to be." Her lips remained parted, as if she wanted to say more.

"What, Nina?"

"Sometimes the size of a life is limited," she said softly. "I don't mean yours will be. I just mean some lives turn out to be smaller than others. Some lives are limited by circumstances. Al's was limited by Korea. Other lives are limited by money, race, education, and," she brushed her finger over her paper napkin, "by family expectations."

"You mean, Dad?"

"Uh . . . yeah. He didn't want to be an undertaker."

I nodded. "Grandpa was a tyrant, wasn't he?"

"He was stern, let's put it that way."

I'd heard the story Nina was about to tell, but I let her tell it again.

"Ever since your dad was this high," she said, holding her hand in the air about three feet above the floor, "he wanted to be an attorney."

"Then why didn't he?"

"When he asked your grandpa, all hell broke loose. Your dad was about your age and I was about seven, and it happened right here at this table. When he asked him, your grandpa glared at him with those coal black eyes of his—those eyes could have cut sheet metal. We were eating *gołąbki,* cabbage rolls. He stabbed his fork into his *gołąbek* and hollered, 'Stanley Bronislaw Manikowski, you think I built all this so you can walk away from it? This is a family business.'"

"So Dad became an undertaker like Grandpa?"

"He had no choice. That's how it was, sweetie, especially in immigrant families. Kids were grateful for what they had. They did what their parents told them to do, no questions asked. Especially the eldest. There was always pressure on the firstborn to take over the family business, or to become a priest or a nun. That's just how life was."

"Well, it's not going to be that way for me," I said.

Nina smiled wistfully. "What would a big life be for you, Ellie?"

Around that time, President Kennedy had introduced the Peace Corps. He challenged us to give two years of our lives to helping people in developing countries, to give something back to America. Of course, I wanted glamour and adventure, but in my more altruistic moments I also wanted to do some good in the world. I imagined myself digging roads, singing with children in their native languages, teaching women to bake Nina's vitamin-packed seven-grain bread. I wanted to blast into the world like a well-dressed Mother Theresa and make friends for America.

"I want to join the Peace Corps," I told Nina.

"You could do that. You could do anything if you work hard enough for it."

Then with a flourish of bravado I remember adding, "I want to experience everything in life. Love, adventure, even heartbreak."

Nina smiled sadly, and immediately I thought of Al's death and wanted to take back what I said.

"It's okay, sweetie. Go on. What else?" she encouraged.

"First of all, college. Not some fancy school like Vassar or Harvard, where I obviously wouldn't fit in, but somewhere away from home. It's not that I don't like it in Chicago—don't get me wrong—I want to leave for the experience of it . . . to branch out, you know. But you also know how Mom feels."

College had always been my dream. I was the kind of kid who lugged a stack of books home from the library when I got my first library card when I was six, and I hadn't stopped since. Books felt natural in my arms. I loved the seriousness of libraries. I loved the debates we'd have in class—about poverty and segregation and the role of women in the world—and I loved how we'd leap out of our seats and shout over one another to make our points, arguing issues like junior politicians.

For me, college was the next step. But back in the '60s, college wasn't a big deal for women. Back then, only about a third of all women went to college and in my neighborhood it was much less than that, maybe ten percent. Although I'd never said so in high school—it would have sounded snobbish—I always considered myself college material. Nina understood me, but Mom didn't have a clue.

Mom had taken a job straight out of high school as a

dental assistant with Doctor Kruk on Division Street where she worked until she got married. "I didn't need college. The doctor taught me all I know," I remember her bragging. And because of it, she believed what was good enough for her was good enough for me. "Get yourself a *nice* job at some insurance company. Then work yourself up, meet a *nice* man, get married, have a *nice* family." Back then I wanted a life bigger than our neighborhood. I would've died rather than stayed there shuffling paper in a dreary office, marrying a guy I went to grade school with, living the predictable life my family lived—in a provincial neighborhood that hadn't changed in a hundred years. "If that's how it's going to be, embalm me now," I remember telling Nina.

"We're going to work this college thing out, Ellie. I promise. Want some advice?"

"Yeah."

"Talk to your dad about it."

Just then Mom banged on the water pipes. She always banged on the water pipes with a metal spoon when she knew I was downstairs with Nina and she wanted me upstairs with her. I looked up at the ceiling. "Nuts! I was just getting started. She must have heard us laughing. Better run."

As usual, I was in a better mood after talking to Nina. I climbed the stairs hugging the loaf of bread she baked for us, looking forward to hearing from Duke.

CHAPTER FOUR

*T*he following Sunday we were late for Mass. The nine o'clock Mass was the Children's Mass where the kids sat together grouped by class with the first graders nearest the altar. Behind every class of about fifty kids sat a nun in her own private pew, looking like a dark stamp on the corner of an envelope.

Marta hurried to her third grade class, genuflected and slid into her pew. Mom, Nina, and I slunk into a pew in the middle. Dad, who'd been ushering since the first service at six o'clock, was standing in the back with the ushers. When he saw us he waved and pointed to his watch.

Mom had made us late that morning by fussing over her chicken soup. Every Sunday, we ate our main meal at noon and it was usually chicken soup with *kluski,* doughy homemade noodles that Dad called bullets for how they felt in your stomach. That day Mom had lost track of time. At eight-thirty she was still standing at the sink in her bathrobe skimming globs of chicken fat off the broth she prepared and refrigerated the evening before. "I guess my mind was off somewhere else," she said.

I knew she was worried about Dad's eyes.

Father Ben Borowczyk, the new priest at our parish, said Mass that morning. He was in his mid-thirties, but anyone looked younger than our pastor, Father Walenski, whose skin sloughed off his bones and who was so bent over that he had to lean on his acolytes for support. Unlike Father Walenski, who was always in a hurry to finish, there was a reverence about Father Ben. He looked comfortable at the altar, as if it was where he belonged.

When it came to sermons I was usually a dozer. But when Father Ben was in the pulpit, I paid attention. First of all, he was kneebucklingly handsome. He had this masculine face, with deep-set gray eyes arched by thick dark eyebrows. His cheeks and chin were peppered with shadowy stubble, the kind that looked shifty on men like Richard Nixon, but attractive on him. Secondly, he wasn't boring. He either told us a humorous story that had a spiritual point to it, or he spoke from his own experiences. As a result, we knew more about him than we did about most other priests. He grew up in Minneapolis with a younger brother, Doug, and a cousin, Steve, whom his parents had raised. He studied for the priesthood in Rome. He loved basketball, art, Chicago politics, and he played the accordion. That business about the accordion was more than I needed to know about my parish priest. At that time, especially among the cool kids trying hard to shake our immigrant backgrounds, accordions were not cool.

Father Ben genuflected before the altar and climbed into the pulpit. He studied the faces of the little ones in the first few rows and curled his lips into a smile.

"Good morning, boys and girls," he said in a robust voice.

The children said nothing because they weren't allowed to talk in church.

"Good morning!" he said louder. A few timid voices, faint as squeaking mice, spoke up. "Good morning, Father."

"Okay, you have my permission to talk in church this once, and you better take advantage of it because it won't happen again soon. Good morning!" he boomed.

"Good morning, Father Ben!" Some added the "Bo." Marta told us that the kids called him Father Ben Bo.

Our pew shook and Joy slithered in beside me. "I overslept," she mumbled in what were probably her first words of the morning. A Frenchie black beret sat cockeyed on top of her wild, uncombed hair. Her eyeliner was smeared and she smelled like stale beer and cigarettes.

"I didn't think you were coming," I whispered.

"Late night with Andy."

"At least you made it."

"Better late than sinful."

I laughed and Mom nudged me.

Taking his time, Father Ben scanned the congregation. Then he looked to the wall of arched stained glass windows to his right and tilted his head back to admire the domed ceiling above him. "This church is amazing, isn't it?"

Hundreds of heads looked around and nodded.

"I've been at St. Casimir's for six months now and still whenever I step through those doors," he said, gesturing toward the entrance, "I feel like I'm entering a magnificent cathedral in Europe."

Joy poked me in the ribs. "Do you think he's here?" she whispered.

"Who?"

"You know," she said under her breath. "Nina's guy."

"Shh, Joy," I said, cocking my head toward Nina. But Joy got me thinking, and I looked across the aisle and over my shoulder. I was trying not to be obvious. I couldn't identify a philanderer if I saw one, but that morning I was on the hunt for someone who looked like Errol Flynn with wavy hair, wandering eyes, and a pinkie ring.

"Ellie, pay attention," Mom whispered.

Father Ben's friendly gaze moved from one small face to another. "There are hundreds of beautiful churches in Europe, many of them in Poland. How many of you were born there?"

An eruption of hands including Joy's shot up and waved.

"He's asking the kids, not you," I said, yanking her elbow down.

"Well, you're the lucky ones," Father Ben said. "But for those of you who haven't been there, you can enjoy a little bit of Europe right here because your grandparents and great-grandparents built St. Casimir's for you. This church is the marvelous gift they've left you . . . an inheritance."

He turned sideways in the pulpit and stared at the baroque altar behind him. "The altar looks like a wedding cake, doesn't it, kids, with all those tiers and candles and flowers? The gold leaf is like frosting!"

"Yeah," the kids cried out.

He gripped the pulpit's railing, leaned his head back, and pointed to a mural inside the sanctuary dome that loomed above our heads like a rich blue sky—a blue Grandma Manikowski used to call *błękitny*, because of its luminosity. The mural depicted the Blessed Virgin Mary ascending into heaven. "It was painted by the artist Thaddeus Zukotynski who came to Chicago in 1888 and painted many glorious murals in our Polish churches. In his day, he was one of the world's finest painters of religious art." Father Ben pronounced the artist's name the Polish way, Ta-deusz Ju-ko-TIN-ski.

"Hundreds of masons, carpenters, and painters built St. Casimir's with the skills they learned from their forefathers. The money came from the pennies your grandparents and great-grandparents saved in jelly jars from their wages as housecleaners, waitresses, and streetcar conductors. The church took twenty years to build because they paid for it by the Polish credit plan—cash only," he laughed.

We chuckled along with him. It was refreshing to hear our voices chime like a chorus of hand bells throughout the church. This young priest was giving new life to our staid old parish.

"I don't know about you, but I love those chandeliers," he said, pointing to one of the twelve fixtures suspended from ornate brackets above the pews. We leaned our heads back and studied them—elaborate teardrops of ivory and red stained glass, adorned with gold leaf and bronze filigree.

"They look like a giant Christmas tree ornaments, don't they . . . with their tips of ruby glass?"

"Yeah!" the kids shouted.

"There's an interesting story about them that dates back to the Columbian Exposition in 1893, which was the World's Fair held in Chicago . . . on the Southside." He grinned at the little kids in the first row. "By the way, Cracker Jacks and Juicy Fruit gum were introduced at that fair!" The kids giggled.

"Pabst beer too," Joy whispered in my ear."

"Really?"

"Yup."

"The World's Fair was where world-renowned artists

gave people a look at their artistry," Father Ben continued. "Anyway, our church was being built then, and the pastor invited several of the artists to work on our church. The great Louis Comfort Tiffany designed those chandeliers. F.X. Zetter of the Royal Bavarian Institute made the magnificent stained glass windows off the side altars. The rose window above the entrance was designed by Franz Mayer of Munich."

Father Ben had our heads turning as if they were on spindles. I'd spent hundreds of hours in our church, but I'd never seen it that way. It took a newcomer to remind us that our church was a jewelry box of treasures that some of us had never noticed or through familiarity had become blind to. "Jackie would appreciate this," I said to Joy.

"You're pathetic," she mumbled back.

After splashing our minds with colors, shapes, and exotic names, he got to the spiritual point of his sermon. "There are many ways to praise God," he told the kids. "Your ancestors praised Him by using their talents as artists and craftsmen. You can do it by studying hard and learning all you can about math and history and art, and by being good competitors in sports, because you never know what vocation God has planned for you. You might grow up to build cathedrals or paint murals, invent new flavors of gum, or play heavenly music . . . maybe even the accordion," which brought a laugh. "Maybe you'll play ball for the Cubs or Bears. You never know what God has intended for you."

On the way home—we all rode together in Dad's long black funeral Cadillac Fleetwood limousine, which was our family car as well—Dad had three pairs of eyeglasses lined up on the dashboard, and in the five minutes it took us to drive home he tried out each pair. He had bad eyes like me, but his vision had been getting worse. Ever since Election Day, he'd been complaining that the newsprint in the papers was blurred and the traffic signs were difficult to read, especially at night. Everywhere I'd been finding pairs of eyeglasses he'd left about—current prescriptions, old glasses resurrected from a cigar box in his drawer, new ones of increasing magnifications he'd bought at Walgreen's. As he steered our sleek black limo with its pointed fins slowly toward home, he glanced over at Mom.

"He seems like a nice guy. Call him up, Vera. Invite him to dinner."

"Who you talking about, Stan?"

"Father Borowczyk, Vera," he said, pronouncing his name with a Polish accent, Bo-ROV-Chick.

"Yeah, Stan, sure."

We jabbered about Father Ben's sermon.

Dad said he'd heard most of it before, but had forgotten the details, so it was a good refresher. Marta said she liked to sit on the balcony and look straight into the ornament of ruby glass on the tips of the teardrop chandeliers. She emphasized the word ruby. I agreed with her. Joy said she'd dump Andy for Father Ben any day. Nina said Joy shouldn't mess with priests. Mom, who was sitting in the middle of the front seat between Dad and Nina, said nothing. She was helping Dad watch the road.

CHAPTER FIVE

⁓

Those days Jackie was everywhere. Every magazine from *McCall's* to *LIFE* to *LOOK* ran articles on her, and I wanted to read them all. When a new magazine came out, I was in line at Walgreen's with money in hand. I'd clip out the photos and articles that had special meaning to me and paste them in my scrapbook.

The day after John Kennedy was nominated, I ran to Wieboldt's and bought myself the thickest scrapbook I could find—one hundred pages with an imitation red leather cover and black pages.

The first time Joy saw my scrapbook, I was clipping a photo of Jackie out of *The Ladies Home Journal*. "Heck, Ellie, I can't believe you're stooping to such hero worship. What do you like so much about her? She's only a first lady. What's she actually done?"

"We never had a first lady like her. She's renovating the White House to be a home Americans can be proud of. She's teaching us about culture and music and fashion." In the photo Jackie was wearing a soft peach-colored shift. "Look at the simple lines of this dress. It's colorless, sleeveless . . ."

"Brainless," Joy said, rolling her eyes.

"Well, Jackie's NOT into ostentation."

"What the hell's wrong with ostentation? Look at the Pope."

From that time on, I kept my obsession to myself because I never wanted Joy to think I was getting uppity on her, and that I might want different things in life than she did—things that might separate us. I didn't tell her then or ever that I believed Jackie and I would be friends if we got to know each other. And, of course, I never told her I fantasized about meeting Jackie.

I'm on a White House tour, and a group of us are in the Blue Room, and in glides Jackie, bedazzling in an aubergine hostess gown, carrying a swatch book. She spots me in the crowd and gushes, "Ellie . . . Ellie Manikowski from Chicago . . . I'm so terribly delighted to see you!" I reply in my lowest, slowest, most sophisticated tone, "I'm so terribly delighted to see you too, Mrs. Kennedy." (Jackie preferred to be called Jacque-lene or Mrs. Kennedy, but disliked the term first lady *because it sounds like a racehorse.) The next thing you know, Jackie and I are seated side by side on a zibeline couch in her personal residence sipping jasmine tea and smoking cigarettes in long tortoise-shell cigarette holders, discussing world affairs and interior decorating. "It's important, Ellie, that you always surround yourself with lovely things like graceful furniture, fragile china and linens, softly colored fabrics, charming bibelots, laughter and fine foods, perhaps poulet chasseur and framboises a la crème served in crystal dessert dishes with a sprig of fresh mint from your herb garden. The effect is simply charming."*

"Simply charming," I repeat.

My family knew about my Jackie obsession and they ribbed me mercilessly about it. "Lookit, she's teasing her hair like Jackie Kennedy's," Marta would say.

And Mom? When I'd tried to emulate how Jackie spoke— or at least how I thought she spoke—she'd put me in my place as quickly as cleanup after supper. Once, I saw a perfect pair of high heels advertised in the *Trib* and made the mistake of saying to Mom—with a bit of attitude, I'm sure—that they were "terribly divine." She came up behind me and studied the ad. "They're nice shoes, Ellie, and we'll go downtown and buy them if they fit, but I don't like that put-on talk . . . 'terribly divine' . . . We don't talk that way around here. You must remember who you are, Ellie Manikowski."

Now I know she was trying to tell me something important: Never try to be something you're not. But back then I took it another way. It was as if I had a set station in life that I couldn't step out of, and a Polish name that would limit how far I could go. I felt she wanted me to achieve, but not too much, to be successful but only as a wife and mother.

And Dad? I thought he wanted more for me—I could see it in the twinkle in his eye when I talked about college. But sometimes I wasn't sure. As for my Jackie obsession, he'd just roll his eyes and say, "Let's hope to God she outgrows it."

CHAPTER SIX

*D*uke called the following Wednesday. Typically, I'd have been waiting for the phone to ring, but that week, with the focus being on Dad's appointment with Doctor Kowalski, my mind was on other things. So it was a surprise to hear a male voice on the phone asking for me.

"Ellie, it's Duke Dukaschewski."

"Donna's brother?"

"Yup," he chuckled. "Been my royal pleasure for seventeen years now."

We both laughed. Donna could be a royal pain in the ass, and we both knew it.

I could feel my heart thumping in my chest. Luckily, Duke was a calm kind of guy, easy to talk to. We chatted about school and our parents. His dad was a tool and die maker at A-B Dick, and his mother was a housewife. He told me he swam at the Y, and that he'd be taking the senior lifeguard test so he could be a guard at the beach that summer. "You have to pass a test swimming ten laps in a fifty-yard pool, one of them with a lifesaving hold on a drowning guy. They send in this three-hundred-pound Cyclops who fights you, and then you have to do mouth-to-mouth on him."

"Yuck!"

"No kiddin'."

Just as I was starting to relax, it happened.

There was a click on the line followed by deep breathing. Dad had picked up the phone in his office. He cleared his throat, making a phlegmy sound. "Ellcha, you've been on the line five minutes now. A funeral may be coming in." His voice reverberated like God's on a microphone.

"Who? Who's that?" Duke asked.

"It's my dad, Duke. Dad, can I have another minute?"

"ONE more minute, Ellcha."

"Wanna go out, Ellie?"

"Yeah."

"Saturday night? *Bye Bye Birdie's* downtown. Pick you up at seven?"

"I'd love to."

"Seven's too early, Ellcha," Dad butted in. "Don't ya remember? Father Ben's coming to dinner. Did ya forget?"

"Oh yeah," I said, sadly, hoping Duke would suggest another time.

"The shindig will be over by eight," Dad said.

"Well then, sir, may I take Ellie out for dessert?" His voice quickened its pace.

"It's a date," Dad said.

"You live in the funeral home?" Duke was talking fast now, as if he were on *Beat the Clock*, that old game show where contestants had to perform crazy stunts before the clock ran out.

"Above it. Enter the narrow door . . . turn left . . . go to the top." The two of them had me racing through my words.

"Got it. See you Saturday. Good night, Mr. Manikowski."
"Good night, kids."
"Bye, Duke."
I waited to hear two clicks and hung up.

What did I make of it? On any ordinary day I would have raised a fuss about Dad embarrassing me. But that day I kept my mouth shut. Dad had been to see Doctor Kowalski and he learned that he had proliferative retinopathy, an eye condition that affects diabetics and leads to blindness.

That day Uncle Frank had come to take care of business while Mom and Dad went to the Medical Arts Building downtown. When they returned, the rest of us—Nina, Marta, Uncle Frank and I, were seated around the kitchen table waiting to hear what Doctor Kowalski had to say.

"In diabetics, the new blood vessels that grow on the surface of the retina or on the optic nerve are fragile," Dad explained. "They rupture and bleed into the clear substance that fills the center of the eye and the clotted blood blocks out the light . . . and I'm going blind."

"What?" I gasped.

"—Aw shit! Stan," my uncle said. "You sure? You want me to ask John? I'll call him up," he said, pushing himself up from the chair. Uncle Frank had gone to school with John Kowalski, and I guess he thought he could get more information out of him, maybe turn bad news into good.

"No, we asked all the questions ourselves," Mom said. "Doctor John said they're starting to experiment with something called a laser where they aim a beam of light into your eye and burn out the scar tissue, but he said he wouldn't recommend it because laser's unproven and it could do more harm than good."

"You'd be a guinea pig, Stan," Uncle Frank said, sitting back down.

"Better leave well enough alone. No one wants someone shooting a hole in his eye with a laser gun," Mom said.

I was staring at Dad, trying to make sense of it. Dad slid his glasses off and rubbed the red indentations on the bridge of his nose. He had worn glasses ever since I could remember, and his face looked incomplete without them. I studied his eyes, the two watery hazel pools that had been the obsession, the worry, the object of our prayers for the past months. Deep inside those eyes globs of clotted blood were blocking out his vision. I imagined blobs of ink spreading on a blotter, joining together until everything was black. I took off my own glasses and set them beside Dad's so that the plastic temples of our glasses touched. I don't know why I did that. Maybe I was trying to give him good luck or show him love or solidarity, or tell him we were in this together—even though I didn't have diabetes and chances are I'd never go blind. Life wasn't fair. I was the one with glasses thick as a Pyrex dish and he was the one going blind. I closed my eyes and tried to imagine what blindness would be like—never again seeing the salmon and yellow pattern on our kitchen curtains, the stainless steel percolator on the counter, the crooked slant of Marta's bangs, the faces of those I loved most in the world.

"I'm sure it's not a gun, Mom, and if they were my eyes, I wouldn't give up. I'd fight for my eyes," I blurted.

Nina gave me a be-quiet-we'll-talk-later look, so I shut up. The conversation buzzed around me.

"They'll take another look in six months. . . ."

Starość nie radość," getting old's a bitch. . . ."

"Miracles happen, things change. . . ."

"All we can do is pray. . . ."

That's what our family did when someone was sick. We went to the doctor and accepted the diagnosis, then we called upon the big guns in heaven. We prayed to St. Genevieve when we had fevers. We invoked St. Apollonia for toothaches, St. Blaise for sore throats, St. Theresa of Avila for headaches, and we'd all been praying to St. Lucy for Dad's eyes.

Mom stretched her arm across Dad's back and hugged him. "Remember you're a lot more than your eyes, Stan." As her fingers kneaded wrinkles into his starched white shirt, I thought of how important the sense of touch was and how important it would become to Dad as his world slowly darkened into black. He would need to depend upon us more and more.

"We're all behind you," Mom said. "Whatever you need, Stan, we're here. None of us is going anywhere," she said, tossing the remark at me, which I took as even more evidence of how little she understood me.

Getting back to my point. How could I have made a fuss about Dad interrupting a phone call when my dad was going blind?

CHAPTER SEVEN

*S*aturday turned out to be a big deal.

In our house, when a priest came to dinner, it was like God Himself making a courtesy call. Days before, Mom would go on a rampage doing the necessary cleaning, and then she'd move into the realm of the ridiculous: ordering our underwear drawers (as if he'd look there), alphabetizing the spices in her spice rack (as if he'd notice), sweeping under the beds (as if he'd announce from the pulpit that the Manikowskis grew dust balls the size of tumbleweeds in the dark). When Father Ben came, she even washed the outside of the windows the nerve-tingling way she did—sitting on the windowsill with her fanny hanging over the street and the window shut down into her lap.

Mom thought it would be a good diversion for Dad to have the family around that evening, so she invited Nina and his brothers and their wives—Uncle Frank and Aunt Maxine, and Uncle Bruno and Aunt Mary Louise. Bruno had married an Italian woman, which Aunt Maxine pronounced *Eyetalian*, mostly to irk her. Mary Louise was the first non-

Pole in our family, which was a bone of contention among certain individuals, namely Maxine, who one Christmas when she had a few too many wines told Bruno he'd have been better off with a Polish woman, if for no other reason than to protect the purity of the Manikowski bloodline. That absurd comment had forged a silent grudge against Maxine that Mary Louise and Bruno continued to nurture.

That morning Mom had set the dining room table with her best china, silver, and stemware. It glittered atop the linen tablecloth with scalloped edges embroidered in petite green cross-stitches sewn by her own mother as a wedding gift almost twenty years earlier. As Mom fussed in the kitchen, Dad slouched in his rocking chair in the family room listening to the news on TV. Ever since his appointment with Doctor Kowalski, he hadn't bothered to angle his rocker toward the screen. He sat with his profile toward us, brooding.

A sports reporter announced that Roger Maris hit a homer at Yankee Stadium the day before.

"Ya think he's as good as Mickey Mantle? Ya think he can break the Babe's record?" Mom called to him.

Dad didn't answer.

She whispered to me. "Just look at him. It hurts to see him so sad."

That evening I was nervous about meeting Duke. I decided to wear a straight skirt and a tan sweater that wasn't too tight, and at the last minute I clipped on a fake leopard-skin collar and gold earrings embossed with tiny tiger heads. I teased my hair and tweezed my eyebrows and wondered if Duke was making any effort to get ready for our date or whether he was just going to show up like most of the guys did straight from work, smelling like the jobs they left: pumping gas, jerking sodas, bagging groceries. I studied myself in the mirror and thought I looked pretty cute—until I focused on my thick black-rimmed glasses, and then everything fell apart.

Dad rose to the occasion. He slicked his straight black hair back with Brylcreem and looked handsome in his slacks and a starched white shirt and a tan woolen cardigan buttoned over his full stomach. At the door, he gave sideways cheek pecks to Aunt Maxine and Aunt Mary Louise who carried in dishes of food, and he shook hands with his brothers and with Father Ben who was the last to arrive. Father Ben was wearing black trousers and a black shirt with a notched clerical collar, and he was carrying two bottles of wine. "Chianti," he said.

"Faaancy," Mom said.

Aunt Mary Louise carried in a pan of lasagna to be served with the filet mignon and salad Mom would prepare. When I gripped it with her potholders still attached, I about fell forward because it was as heavy as a bowling ball. We could always count on Mary Louise to produce something buttery, garlicky, cheesy, and abundant. She had this deep laugh that rose from the ebullient core of her hefty body, which was heftier then because of the baby that bulged beneath her red brocade maternity top that encircled her hips like a lampshade in a bordello. In an unspoken rivalry with Maxine, Mary Louise had the dubious distinction of being the leader in the breeding race, score six to four, counting the baby on the way. I wondered how Nina felt in the midst of this breeding competition, having by then lost her husband and her dream of a church pew full of kids.

Aunt Maxine carried in a platter of paper-thin vanilla cookies with such ceremony that you would have thought she was a priest carrying in the Holy Eucharist.

"They're extremely delicate," she whispered, offering

them to Mom. "I picked them up downtown at Stop & Shop. Made a special trip this morning." Each cookie, commercially dusted with powdered sugar, sat on the china platter, a pale island unto itself with no edges touching. Mom pursed her lips. She frowned on store-bought cookies.

Maxine blew flecks of powdered sugar dust off the sleeve of her hot pink sheath. "While I was downtown, I picked up this dress at Marshall Field's. Couldn't resist." She did a pirouette with a little hip roll to show off her new dress and slim figure. With her red hair lacquered into a beehive, she looked like a swizzle stick in a skinny Tom Collins glass.

"Va, va, va voom," Uncle Frank growled and winked at his wife.

Dad introduced Father Ben to Maxine who made a clicking sound with her tongue and said, "My, you're a handsome devil!" He smiled uncomfortably and moved on to the next introduction. When he got to Nina, they shook hands and nodded.

At dinner everyone was on his best behavior in the company of a priest. Mom made sure the conversation flowed, from discussions of the Bay of Pigs disaster, to the Russians launching a dog into orbit, to the Blackhawks beating the Detroit Red Wings four to two in the Stanley Cup. Even Dad joined in. "Why are they wasting perfectly good dogs sending them into space? I know a coupla Chicago politicians they should launch up there." Dad could never shut up when it came to the Ruskies.

I was seated at Father Ben's left, a place of honor, so in between furtive glances at my own wristwatch and at his, I did my best to engage him in conversation.

"You know Nina from the parish office?" I said.

"Um hum," he said, smiling at Nina across the table. Nina moved her wine glass around in small circles beside her plate. Ever since Inauguration Day she had been as jittery as jello. She caught me staring at her and I shifted my attention to Father Ben. "Marta says you play music for the kids sometimes. How'd you get interested in the accordion?"

"I grew up in a German neighborhood in Minneapolis where a lot of kids took lessons."

"Like Chicago," Maxine interjected. She took a slow drag on her cigarette, squinted one eye and blew an authoritative cloud of smoke out of the opposite side of her mouth. Maxine was one of those women who could smoke and eat at the same time.

"Exactly. My cousin Steve used to go to our neighborhood music store for lessons, and I'd go with. I'd be in the waiting room and he'd be hitting all these sour notes. Finally, his instructor told my mother that she was wasting her money."

"Where was his mom?" I asked.

"My parents raised Steve after his folks died in a car crash. Steve's like an older brother to me. Anyway, this accordion was sitting around, so I started playing. It was a beginner model, a diatonic German-style accordion with ten buttons . . . heavy as a TV set. I was eight then and a pretty scrawny kid. Nothing like I am now." He gave me a tongue-in-cheek grin. "I could barely lift the darn thing."

We all laughed, but Nina smiled weakly.

"I stopped playing in high school when it wasn't cool to play the accordion. We were struggling hard to be American," Father Ben told the group. Heads around the table nodded. "But I got interested later again and stopped caring what people thought."

Another conversation began at the opposite end of

the table and Father Ben turned to me. "That's a lovely painting," he said, gesturing at a painting of the Madonna and Child in a gilded frame on the wall across from us, next to First Communion portraits of Marta and me. "Correggio, I believe."

"Yeah, the original's at the Art Institute," I said stupidly— as if anyone would have mistaken ours for the original.

"I enjoy the Art Institute. Sometimes I go there just to think."

"Maybe because museums are like churches," I said, sneaking a look at his wristwatch. *Seven-thirty.* I knew I was in perilously deep water discussing art with a priest, so I followed up with a safe question. "Do you have a favorite work of art, Father?"

He pressed his lips together and thought. "It would have to be Donatello's sculpture of Mary Magdalen," he said firmly. "It's in the Baptistry in Florence on a pedestal in a small alcove near the entrance. The first time I saw her I was speechless. I can't go there without stopping in to visit her." He talked about Mary Magdalen as if she were an old friend.

I decided to speak his language. "What's she like?"

"She's about this tall," he said, holding his hand about three feet off the floor. Father Ben talked with his hands, like an Italian. They were masculine hands that moved in cadence with his voice.

"She's haggard and wasting away. Her mouth is stretched open in a kind of agony that brings tears to your eyes. She reminds me of candle wax dripping in a drafty room, only the drips are heavy slashes and shards of wood that weigh her down." Father Ben's hand chopped the air. "What Donatello was trying to show was the anguish Mary Magdalen felt over the years she spent as a prostitute." Ellie, I hope you have a chance to see her one of these days." He glanced across the table. "Nina, I hope you do too."

Nina fumbled nervously with a button on her sweater. "Maybe some day."

On the table, Father Ben's two bottles of Chianti were empty, and they were passing around bottles of the *nice* Taylor sauterne my mother bought at Szaltus Liquors to go with her *nice* filet mignons.

Father Ben leaned over to Dad and asked, "May I pour you some wine?"

"Can't drink, my diabetes," he said. "I used to sneak a drink every now and then, but with my eye problem, I can't." He gave Father Ben the short version of what Doctor Kowalski said. Father Ben listened with his elbow on the table and his chin cupped in his hand. He tapped his upper lip with his forefinger and shook his head, worry lines chiseled in his forehead. "I'm sorry to hear that," he said sincerely. "So sorry."

Dad shook his head glumly. "I see a lot of suffering in my line of work, and now it's hitting home," he said in a voice a bit above a whisper. Why do these things happen to us, Father?"

Relieved to be off the hook about art, I sat back and listened.

"As a priest, you'd think I'd have the answers, Stan, but I don't. I've come to believe that life is so profound, so deep, and so perplexing that even with all our searching for answers, we'll never fully understand. The best I can say is that death and suffering are mysteries, and that mystery is something we have to live with until the end, when hopefully, then we'll understand. For now, we have to trust that God's love will carry us through, and we have to believe that love—the kind of love I see in this family—is stronger than suffering."

An honest answer, I thought.

Mom saw Dad slipping into a funk, and, true to form, she stepped in and changed the subject. "Stan, tell Father Ben about Ignatz," she called to him from across the table.

"Nah, Vera, no one wants to hear that story," Dad said, waving his hand in front of his face like a paddle.

Father Ben took the cue from Mom. He raised his wine glass. "*Nazdrowie*," he toasted in Polish. "Here's to the Manikowski clan." He gestured toward Mom and Dad. "Here's to Vera, an extraordinary hostess, and to Stan, who I understand, along with Bruno, is a legendary storyteller. Thanks for including me at your family table." His toast was heartfelt, but he was also giving Dad a chance to collect himself, or pass the storytelling baton to his brother.

"*Nazdrowie*," we lifted our glasses and clinked them as far as we could reach.

"Stan, tell about Ignatz!" Maxine's voice soared above the rest.

"Okay, okay, I'll tell the story," Dad said, forcing a smile. He adjusted himself in his chair and took a deep breath. He lit a cigar and puffed on it. In addition to collecting himself, he was reconstructing the story in his mind so he could tell it the exact same way he always had. He scanned our faces, stopping at Father Ben's.

"There was this fellow in the parish named Ignatz Trembula. He's long gone now, so I can talk about him. About ten years ago we buried his wife, Zofia. On the night of the wake downstairs," Dad said, pointing at the floor, "poor Ignatz stops at Wacek's Tavern down the block and gets himself a little befuddled."

"He gets schnockered," Uncle Frank added.

Dad worked the cigar between his lips. "Well, Ignatz comes into the funeral home and staggers over to the casket and he starts to wail, 'Zofia, Zofia, I'll never find a woman as good as you.' Well, I look in on him and see he's crying at the casket of the wrong woman."

"We had two wakes that night," Uncle Bruno explained.

"Both women looked alike," I added, as I always did at that point of the story. "Side part, soft curls."

Dad grinned at me approvingly, then looked back at Father Ben. "So I take Ignatz by the arm and I say to him, 'Iggy, your Zofia is there, not here. Then you know what happened?"

"No," Father Ben answered.

"It's the next day. On the ride to the cemetery Ignatz says to me, 'Stashu, I think I get married again.' And he hands me Zofia's engagement ring and asks me to keep it until he needs it. Then about six months later he comes knocking on our door. 'Stashu, I think I'm in love.' I return the ring and say, 'I wish you the best of luck, Ignatz.'"

"That's sweet," I said.

"Bury, bury sweet," Maxine cackled.

"That Ignatz, he was a lady's man," Uncle Bruno laughed.

I looked across the table to see if Nina was okay, but her chair was empty.

"Where's Nina?" I asked.

"Headache," Mom whispered. "She'll be fine." The house could blow up and Mom would say, "It'll be fine." I checked my watch. *Seven-fifty-five.*

By then Uncle Bruno was telling another story, and another flowed from that, and before you knew it we all had tears in our eyes from laughing. Aunt Maxine was squealing loud enough to shatter the crystal chandelier. Uncle Frank was slapping his hand on the table, and Father Ben was tipping his chair back and laughing so hard he could have fallen over. Aunt Mary Louise was patting her pregnant belly and discharging full-bodied belly laughs that would have been alarming if you didn't know Mary Louise. Even Dad was enjoying himself.

Muffled in the commotion, I heard a knock at the door. I glanced at my watch. *Eight o'clock.*

"It must be Ellie's beau!" Maxine chirped.

"Ellie's blind date," Mom said, leaping up as if a cherry bomb had exploded beneath her chair. She headed for the door, but I got there first. My hand was shaking as I reached for the doorknob.

"Duke? Come in," I said nervously.

That's when I got my first look at Duke. He was taller than I expected, with thick black-rimmed glasses that matched my own. Beneath the dim ceiling light in the hallway his dark hair appeared curly and shiny, as if it was wet. To my relief, he was over six-feet tall.

"Hi, I'm Ellie," I said, nervously.

Duke studied me and smiled. I swallowed hard knowing exactly what he was seeing: a gawky girl with a goofy grin and glasses, and behind her a welcoming committee of tipsy aunts, uncles, and a priest, all of them shamelessly checking him out as future husband material.

Duke stepped into the dining room and confidently offered his hand to Mom who was so close behind me I could smell her Chanel No. 5 and feel her breath on my neck.

"Duke, is that your real name?" she asked, taking right over. I gave her a look.

"It's David, ma'am. David Dukaschewski. Pleased to meet you. I'm amazed how much Ellie resembles you."

"It's the smile. People say we can pass for sisters," Mom said proudly. "Ellie says you live on Huron Street?" which she pronounced Urine Street, which embarrassed me even more.

"I do," he answered. Our eyes met and he gave me an understanding smile.

I made introductions all around. He stuffed his cap into his pocket and worked his way around the table, shaking hands and making polite conversation.

"Cold hands, warm heart," said Aunt Mary Louise.

"You look *Eyetalian*," said Aunt Maxine.

"My mother's Italian," Duke said.

"Terrific gal you got here. Take care of her," Uncle Frank said, winking man-to-man.

"Is Danny Dukaschewski your little brother?" Father Ben asked.

"He is," Duke answered proudly.

"Talented basketball player. I've been coaching him."

When Duke reached the head of the table, Dad stood up to shake his hand, but he stepped so close to him I thought he was going to plant a kiss on his cheek. How ludicrous it would have been for my father to kiss Duke before I did. I knew what he was doing though. He wanted to get a good look at Duke's face. Lately, I'd observed him studying the details of everything very closely—faces, views out the window, even small objects like his car keys, his dinner fork, even knickknacks—memorizing them all so he could remember them later.

Unsure of what was up, Duke took a small step backwards.

"Just want to see you, son," Dad said. "Ellie's a talker. I'm sure she'll fill you in later."

CHAPTER EIGHT

⌒⌒

*O*utside, the cool dry air was a relief.

"I hope they didn't embarrass you," I said.

"You should see *my* relatives," Duke said.

I wrapped my arms around my chest and we walked beneath the awning of the imposing *Klub Kultury* and headed down the block. Headlights of passing cars and triangles of light slanting out of storefronts illuminated the sidewalk. Neon signs buzzed in the shop windows advertising Miller High Life, Coca-Cola, Vienna Sausage. The fuzzy ball on top of my navy blue cap bobbled in the wind.

"You're shivering," Duke said.

For a moment I thought he'd put his arm around me, but he was a gentleman and didn't. We continued walking toward Milwaukee Avenue, occasionally bumping arms, which I liked the feel of.

He held the door of Woolworth's open and followed me to a booth in the soda fountain section in the back where we slid into red vinyl seats facing each other.

We examined the menu, then he looked at me and asked,

"So what did your dad mean when he said you'd tell me later?" I had no choice but to tell him about Dad's retinopathy and how worried I was because he was going blind. "Do you believe it? I'm the one with the rotten eyesight and he's the one going blind."

"Sometimes life throws you a curveball," he said, shaking his head.

"We've all be praying to the patron saint of the blind, Saint Lu—"

"St. Lucy," he said along with me.

"How do you know that?"

"It's Donna's middle name. She has this holy picture of St. Lucy tucked into the corner of her bedroom mirror. On it she's holding an olive branch in one hand and a plate that looks like a candy dish in the other with two eyeballs in it."

"No!"

"Yeah, really!"

"What color are the eyeballs?"

"You wanna know their color? I don't believe you!" he laughed.

As I ate my tulip sundae, he told me about his extended family, stressing all their eccentricities to make me feel more comfortable about my oddball relatives. His Uncle Ludwig V. Dukaschewski (he emphasized the V) lost his leg to cancer as a teenager. "He never wanted to upset us about the cancer, so he'd make up preposterous stories about how he lost his leg—fighting the Bolsheviks, defending his wife's honor—stuff like that. Whenever we go to visit my grandparents' graves at St. Adalbert's Cemetery, we stop to visit Uncle Ludwig's leg."

"Holy cow!"

"And don't ask me if it's his right or left leg, because I don't know."

We talked about politics, basketball, and books. He'd just read *Advise and Consent*; I had just finished *The Ugly American*. We talked about Communism—I thought it was a threat; he disagreed. "Americans needs to simmer down about it. It's human nature to want to be free."

He told me how he loved the Loyola Ramblers, the Chicago skyline, and those little red pizza trucks from Angelino's that zipped through our neighborhoods with spinning lights on top that played *O Solo Mio*. He laughed at his own jokes and mine, and his laugh was infectious. I loved how his eyes smiled when something amused him, how determined he looked when he argued a point, how calmly and confidently he made his arguments—a trait I still struggle to emulate. I also liked how a curl of dark hair fell over his forehead, how one of his front teeth slightly overlapped the other, and how his strong swimmer's hands gripped the fluted ice cream dish and tipped it sideways so he could spoon out every last strawberry from the bottom. From the start we were easy together.

In looking back to my teenage years, that may be the evening I'd most like to relive if I had the chance. It was there in that red vinyl booth at Woolworth's, across a Formica tabletop scratched with hearts and initials that I fell in love with Duke. I remember how my teenage imagination cartwheeled into summer. I pictured myself sitting on a blanket in the warm sand outside the Boathouse at North Avenue Beach in a skimpy two-piece bathing suit I'd buy at Marshall Field's, watching him through my oversized Jackie prescription sunglasses. I imagined him on his lifeguard's perch, standing on legs as muscular as Michelangelo's David's, peering through his binoculars, blowing his whistle at some kids bobbing too close to the swimming ropes.

Years later I asked Duke what he thought of me on our first date. "I liked your earrings. Those little tigers, they looked good on your ears."

"Is that all you remember?" I laughed. "Oh yeah, I wanted to rip your glasses off and give you a big kiss."

Most dates I've had said goodnight in front of the funeral home for obvious reasons, all associated with fear, but that night Duke insisted on walking me upstairs. We were laughing up a storm when we reached the landing outside Nina's apartment.

I had been so caught up in the moment that I hadn't immediately noticed Nina sitting on the flight of stairs leading to our flat. I saw her tan pointy-toe pumps first. Then beside her shoes, two wider black shoes—loafers, with black socks rising to meet two black trouser cuffs. She and Father Ben were wearing the glazed expressions of a couple interrupted in deep conversation.

"Hi," I said, feeling as if I'd just barged in on a priest hearing a confession. The thought had actually crossed my mind that Father Ben might have been hearing Nina's confession. That's how naïve I was then.

"Good evening," Duke said.

Nina stood up. "You two are home early."

I checked my watch. "It's almost eleven."

"Already? We must have lost track of the time. We were talking about your dad, Ellie. He seemed to be in good spirits tonight, considering."

"He was," I said. I introduced Duke to Nina, and Nina shook Duke's hand.

"Are you feeling better, Nina?" I asked.

"Yeah, I guess so," she said, glancing at Father Ben.

There was an awkward silence that Father Ben broke. "Actually, I better get going. Early morning tomorrow." He rose from the steps to his full height, smoothed the creases in his black trousers, and said, "I enjoyed our conversation earlier, Ellie." He shook Duke's hand. "It was a pleasure meeting you, and tell Danny I'll see him at practice Thursday after school." I smelled the festive scent of wine on his breath.

For a moment, the four of us just grinned stupidly at one another, adjusting our stances, but then Duke spoke up. "I better get Ellie upstairs."

We stepped around Nina and Father Ben and made our way to my door. In our building the hallway lights stayed on all night so the stairs were well lit. Duke pecked me on the cheek and said maybe we could go out next weekend and see *Bye Bye Birdie* that would still be playing downtown.

Our apartment was dark and quiet, and the scent of smoke and food from the party lingered in the air. I was grateful to be alone with my thoughts.

It was a moonless night; the windows were dark as blackboards. I didn't turn the lights on because the dark was comforting. I felt for the kitchen table. My fingertips followed its edge to the corner, and I took four steps into the family room. It occurred to me that my father would finger his way along this path if he became totally blind, but I quickly dismissed the thought, preferring to savor my time with Duke, to make my lovely evening last longer. I touched the cheek he had just kissed and felt it puff when I smiled.

The room was already chilly. At ten every evening, our furnace shut down. During the six heatless hours that followed, until the thermostat clicked on at five and the water heater began belching and clanking steam into our radiators, we were forced to rely upon down comforters, flannel pajamas, and sweat socks to keep warm. The family room was pitch black, and as I stepped forward I had the sensation that I was out of my body—a shapeless, formless, colorless entity powered by touch and instinct alone. For a moment I felt so detached from reality that I couldn't remember what I was wearing; so I fingered the nap of my leopard collar for a clue.

I felt for the rocking chair.

"Ellcha!" my father mumbled.

"You're still up, Dad?" I said, startled. I touched the curved teak corner of the chair and felt the wool of his cardigan sweater beneath it. "You're in the dark," I said, instantly regretting my choice of words.

"I was waiting for you. Must have nodded off."

"You don't have to wait up. I'm a big girl now."

"I know. But things can happen. Ya never know."

I flopped down on the sofa across from him.

"Nice young man you've got there, Ellcha. Firm handshake. Seems solid." Solid was the greatest compliment my father could give a man.

I nodded, and then realized that in the dark I needed to use words. "Yeah, I think so too."

"Do you like him?"

"I really do."

Dad was quiet for a moment. All I heard was the back and forth squeak of his rocker on the linoleum. My eyes had grown accustomed to the darkness and I detected the silhouette of his head and broad shoulders against the back of the rocking chair. I wondered how much he could see of me.

"So, what's he like?"

I felt for the throw pillow I knew was on the couch,

grabbed its corner, pressed it into my stomach and hugged it with both arms. "I like him. He has a corny sense of humor." I told Dad about Uncle Ludwig's leg.

"Hmm . . . the Dukaschewski leg? I've buried a lot of legs, but I don't think I buried that one. Where does the family live?"

"St. John's Parish."

"That's Old Man Slowacki's territory." Joe Slowacki was an undertaker in St. John's neighborhood.

Although things were changing then, in my parents' minds, the business of life was still pretty much divided up by parish. If you were born in one parish, that's where you went to school, married, and died. If you're born in another, you stuck close to it. When I was a kid, some of the old timers called our neighborhood *Cazimierzowo*, Casimir town, and the next neighborhood over, *Stanislawowo*, Stanislaus town. How strange, I thought, this provincial attitude coming from the same people who journeyed across the ocean to make their home in America. Maybe a soul could take only so much travel before settling down and making his world small again.

"What do you think of Father Ben?" I asked.

"Good man. Has the human touch. He's someone I can talk to about losing my vision. Not that he can cure me or anything, but maybe he could help me find some peace. Right now, I'm just damn angry, excuse my French."

"I don't blame you, Dad."

"Ya know, Ellcha, earlier today I had a frank talk with The Man Upstairs. I said to him, 'Je-sus Christ, what are ya, nuts?'" His voice started to crack. "'Don'tcha know I make my livelihood by driving a car? Would it be so hard to just let me be?'"

"I know, Dad."

"Things are changing, Ellie. You're going to have to learn to drive the limo to help me out."

"Of course, Dad. Whatever you like."

We sat in silence for a moment. Sadness is sadder in the dark—something I learned much more about later in life. That evening, the silence shattered by the pain in Dad's voice was almost too much to bear. He'd always been there to solve my problems, but I couldn't do a thing about his. I wanted to say the right thing, but words felt wrong and advice seemed empty. I thought of the kid's game we used to play: If you had three wishes, what would they be? That night all three of my wishes would have been the same.

"I'm sorry," I said. "I wish I could change things."

"Ellcha, Ellcha, ya never know what the good Lord is going to give ya, so enjoy life while you can. You have a young man there who makes you happy, so keep company with him and have a good time, but not too good, if you know what I mean. I'm going to tell Janina tomorrow to get out more. Spending her evenings alone downstairs . . . those four walls are closing in on her."

I thought about the lonely bed Nina slept in downstairs, the bed she once shared with Al. During the daytime she covered it with a white chenille bedspread and three square pillows, two pink and one gray, that she always set tips pointing up. Since Al's death she had taken to unfolding only half the bedspread and using half the sheets. When I think about it now, I realize how lonely Nina was that year, returning every evening to a tomblike apartment that once was alive with laughter, with two hearts bursting with dreams for a houseful of kids.

That evening I thought of Nina and her heartache, of

Dad and his problems, of the fun I had with Duke. I felt guilty for being happy when they had so much to worry about. Dad would need help driving, writing obituaries, arranging funerals. There'd be additional medical expenses and our family's savings would be stretched, and, under the circumstances, there was no way I could be first in line with my hand out for college. So, as much as it hurt, I started to rethink my college plans.

In church the following morning, Marta rushed to sit with her class, and Nina, Mom, and I hurried into a center pew. The altar bells jingled and Father Ben, enveloped in a shimmering emerald vestment, genuflected and stepped up to the white marble altar. He held his arms out to his sides in praise. "*In nomine Patris, et Filii, et Spiritus Sancti.*"

"Amen," the acolytes responded.

"*Introibo ad altare Dei,*" he said. I will go to the altar of God.

The ritual of the Mass never changed—it was basically the same as it was hundreds of years ago when the early Christians said Mass in the catacombs—but during my teenage years I found myself changing in how I perceived it. Sometimes I took solace in the rhythm of the Latin words, taught to me by years of repetition. Usually I felt elevated by the music and the sound of our voices raised in song. But other times, I resented the obligation of having to go to church every Sunday, feeling bored with the Mass, like a movie I'd seen too often.

That morning I wasn't bored. I had a lot to pray for. I prayed for Dad. I prayed for a miracle. I prayed for Duke to like me not a little but a lot. *Please. Please. Please.*

Then my attention shifted to the altar. I found it difficult to reconcile my perception of Father Ben the priest, consecrating bread and wine at the altar, with Father Ben the man, who hours ago was sitting at our dining room table drinking Chianti, laughing at funeral home jokes, and talking to Nina on the hallway steps.

"*Judica me, Deus, et discerne causam meam de gente non sancta: ab homine iniquo et doloso erue me,*" Father Ben implored, his hands folded in prayer. Do me justice, O God, and fight my fight against an unholy people, rescue me from the wicked and deceitful man."

There are many ways a priest can praise God, I remember telling myself.

CHAPTER NINE

Back in the '60s, the trend in the funeral business was to build fancy chapels with pillars, verandahs, and porticos that looked like mansions straight out of *Gone with the Wind*. Dad subscribed to a trade magazine called *Casket and Sunnyside*—which in my book was the ultimate oxymoron—that showed pictures of those sprawling, multi-winged behemoths. Inside there were enough viewing rooms to wake a small town, casket display rooms, accessory rooms where vaults and urns were on display, and preparation rooms with enough stainless steel to rival the operating suites of our nation's finest hospitals. Some of those fancy establishments even had coffee machines, which in my father's mind was crass commercialization. "We're not a concession stand at Wrigley Field," he'd say in his cranky way.

Our place was nothing like that.

Manikowski's was a simple mom and pop operation housed in a narrow three story redbrick building with an unassuming white stone façade. A thick double door opened into the funeral home, and a smaller single door off to the side opened into a staircase that led to our apartments. There was an awning above the entrance that we cranked open with a long metal pole. On the scalloped edge of the awning were the words: Manikowski & Sons.

When you passed through the double doors, you were in Dad's office that served as a reception room. Facing his desk were two Chippendale green chairs upholstered in a subdued leafy print. That was where the bereaved sat when they made funeral arrangements.

In the corner was a Chippendale armoire that used to belong to Grandpa Bronislaw. Inside it we kept appropriate reading material: a Bible, prayer books in English and Polish, and my favorite, *The Lives of the Saints*. Back then I figured you could never have too many of them on your side when you had a problem. It was like having an army of aunts and uncles out there interceding for you.

The funeral chapel was one long room that extended some sixty feet from beyond Dad's office to a hallway that led to the restrooms, a supply room, and a music room that housed a record-player from where we could pipe in melodies like *Beautiful Dreamer, Good Night Irene,* or Tchaikovsky's *Sleeping Beauty Waltz*. At the end of that hallway was the door to the morgue that was always kept closed. The morgue was off-limits—forbidden territory to everyone except my father; my uncles; our embalmer, Vincent Neuger; and Marcie, the hairdresser.

When Grandpa Bronislaw bought the building in the 1930s it was much smaller, but he expanded it deeper into our lot, adding restrooms, the music room, the morgue, and a garage off the alley large enough to accommodate a funeral car. Of course, we had become the beneficiaries of that addition, since we were able to use the flat roof above the new section of the building as a patio. Nina's entry to the patio was directly off her family room. Ours was also, but we had to walk down fifteen steps to reach it. When I was five, Dad had staked a metal swing set out there for me. In the years following, we supplemented it with a barbecue grill, six fire engine red metal rocking chairs, two chaise lounges outfitted with red flowered cushions, a cedar cross-legged picnic table, and redwood flower boxes mounted on top of the brick railings in which every May we planted flaming red geraniums and garlands of ivy that cascaded over the sides of the building. For folks living above a funeral home smack-dab in the city, we had quite an urban patio extravaganza going on there.

It was on that rooftop patio that I decided to throw a party. I planned it for the Saturday after school let out, the first week of June. Since Duke and I had been dating for two months then, and were almost going steady, I asked him to help. He removed the attachments from the swing set—the swings, the ladder, and teeter totter that balanced on the ladder—stored them under the steps, and hung several strings of Christmas tree lights on the barren swing set frame, and tucked them into a couple dozen cheap Chinese paper lanterns I'd bought at Monarch's Novelties on Division Street. He also rounded up enough coolers from his beach buddies (he passed his lifeguard test and was assigned to the Boathouse at North Avenue Beach for the summer) and filled them with blocks of ice and bottles of soda. Mom invited Mrs. Dusza to chaperone, and she was thrilled to be included. She promised to bring apricot *kołaczki* and dill pickles. Joy said that if her mother came, she wouldn't. "Ma just wants to spy on me and Andy," she'd claimed. But she promised to provide tunes from Dick Biondi's Top 40 on her reel-to-reel tape recorder anyway.

The day before the party, Marta, who was still wearing her school uniform to celebrate her last day of school, stood up at the dinner table like a grownup. She smoothed the skirt of her blue plaid jumper. "I have an announcement to make." That surprised us because that was the kind of thing an adult in our family said when they were announcing a life-changing event like an engagement, a new baby on the way, or a surprise trip to the Illinois State Fair.

"Yes, Marty?" Dad asked.

"I've invited Father Ben Bo to our party," she said smiling, showing off two halfway grown-in front teeth.

"What?" I cried. "It's my party."

"Well you need music and Joy isn't coming, so I asked him to bring his accordion."

"Are you crazy? We don't want a priest with an accordion."

Dad piped in. "Ellcha, that's not so bad, is it? It'll be an honor to have Father Ben with us. Marta says he plays pretty good. So what's done is done, right?"

"Right," Mom said. "What's done is done."

Father Ben arrived early dressed in a short-sleeved blue and yellow plaid shirt that looked like he borrowed it from a senior citizen in Florida, a pair of wash pants, and a red paisley cowboy neckerchief right out of *Hee Haw*. He seemed genuinely happy to be there. After he greeted the family he pulled up a red metal lawn chair, sat down and fastened the wide tan canvas straps of his accordion around his chest. Listening to him tune up was like being privy to a violent case of flatulence. Eventually, the squeezing sounds passed, and he fanned out the bellows and moved into a robust rendition of

Edelweiss. I tromped past them shaking my head, and they both gave me bouncy, party nods.

A good crowd showed up. Wanda Dusza appeared on the scene, carrying *kołaczki* and a crock of dill pickles in one hand and Joy's enormous tape recorder with her straw handbag shaped like a parrot in another. I grabbed the tape recorder, returned the parrot, and practically kissed Mrs. Dusza for bringing popular music.

"Enjoy the dill pickles, sweetheart," she said. "They're garlicky."

"I'm sure they are, Mrs. Dusza. Thanks."

When Father Ben wore himself out and took a break, I got the tape recorder going and Elvis Presley began to croon *Love Me Tender*. After the crowd downed enough grilled *kiełbasa*, potato salad, dill pickles and *kołaczki* to feed a small village in Poland, the serious dancing began.

I was relieved to see that the adults had respectfully taken their places on the patio chairs near the door to Nina's flat, about twenty feet away from the dance floor, and before long they were huddled in conversation. Sitting with her knees crossed, Wanda Dusza looked like a Copacabana chorus girl in her yellow skirt with turquoise parrots and lime green branches imprinted on it. Nina and Mom both wore pedal pushers and platform wedges. Mom had dressed in red to match the patio furniture. Nina's hair was looking blonder from either the sun or the peroxide bottle. She had it tied up in a high ponytail that swayed from side to side when she walked, and she was unusually bubbly that evening. Dad was in a serious mood, rocking in his patio chair, working his lips around a cigar, his eyes closed.

That night Father Ben came prepared with a joke. "Stan, did you hear the one about the accordion?" he asked.

"Nope." Dad opened his eyes.

"Why do accordion players make good politicians?" he asked.

"Why?"

"Because they're used to playing both ends against the middle." Father Ben let out a husky laugh at his own cornball joke—a laugh that started in his throat and got deeper as it moved down. When he really got to laughing, Dad joined in, and I was sorry I had made such a fuss about inviting him. He was good company for Dad, and he was thoroughly enjoying himself. In the absence of having a family of his own nearby, he seemed to fit in well with ours.

I was surprised to see Andy at the party. I thought out of loyalty to Joy he might not show, but after a while I realized what I'd suspected all along: he was hardly the loyal type. He was dancing with a girl in our class, Millie Rugalski, who was known as the kissing slut because she had a new guy every week. Millie's head was buried in the crook of Andy's neck and their bodies were barely moving. He couldn't keep his eyes off Millie's breasts that were pushing out of the ruffled neckline of her peasant blouse.

Mrs. Dusza was watching them too.

While Duke restocked the coolers, I danced with Barney Gogolinski, a junior at Holy Trinity, the boy's school across the street from Holy Family. Barney was tall and gangly, and his red hair was squared off into a crew cut that stood up a good two inches above his scalp. Barney was a terrific guy, but quirky. He was sensitive to climatic changes and always happened to know exactly what the temperature was, indoors or out, and he always came prepared—with an umbrella, earmuffs, suntan lotion—for whatever Mother Nature might dump on him. That's how Barney was. There's one more thing about him that's important to know: Barney was madly in love with Joy.

"Aren't Andy and Joy still going together?"

"Far as I know."

"Then he's a cheating bastard," Barney mumbled in my ear. "Joy should dump him."

"No kiddin'," I said.

When the sun slipped behind our building, I flipped the switch on the Chinese lanterns and the rooftop sparkled. For the next hour, Duke and I danced and every once in a while he gave me a discreet peck on the cheek. The adults were watching, so we were more restrained than usual.

A couple of weeks earlier, when Mrs. Dusza had gone to visit her sister in South Bend with a hernia, Joy had a bash at her house. Their apartment was dark, except for the light of a fluorescent tube above the burners of the Hotpoint stove in their kitchen, and for a floor lamp in the front room over which Joy had draped two red silk scarves to give it a brothel, piano-bar ambiance. Duke and I had claimed a vinyl Barcalounger in the corner and spent most of the night in it, necking. That was the first time we had French kissed.

But my party was different, and there were rules— rules that had to do with respect for our parents and the embarrassment of getting caught. It was okay to neck in private when we could get away with it, but not in front of our parents and especially not in front of a priest who would blame you and shame you into never wanting to touch a guy again.

Yet Andy and Millie didn't care. That night they slow-danced brazenly in and out of the shadows kissing up a storm with the Christmas tree lights flickering through paper

Chinese lanterns onto his shiny DA and her teased-up hairdo. The adults were watching us. I didn't know how much Dad saw. The red tip of Wanda's cigarette bobbed up and down, and the fatter tip of Dad's cigar glowed like a giant firefly jitterbugging in the dark.

As we danced, Duke pressed his thigh against mine and I let it linger there, and being the smart guy he was, he got the message. "Let's get out of here," he whispered against my cheek.

I led him by the hand off the dance floor. I didn't know where we were going, but we wanted to get away. No one was watching us, so we ducked behind a group of guys and snuck down the rear staircase into the small courtyard between the funeral home and our garage.

The garage door was open. I motioned Duke inside, grabbed the car keys from a nail on the wall and unlocked the back door to Dad's limousine. I crawled inside the dark, airless space and Duke followed me in. We cranked down the windows, shucked our glasses, flopped into the plush velvety seat and start grabbing for each other. *Theme from a Summer Place* by Percy Faith was playing upstairs. His lips were firm, his tongue was moist, and I slipped into a romantic paradise where I was aware of every breath and every touch. His fingers inched up toward my breasts and I felt of every incremental movement of them, and I wondered how far up they were going to go. I knew we should stop, but I didn't want to.

"Is this okay?" he breathed, working his fingers underneath my blouse.

"It's okay." I moaned. But when I felt myself falling onto the plush seat with his weight on top of me, I thought better of it and pushed back. "We better not," I said.

He groaned, "Why?"

"Because my parents and Father Ben are upstairs."

"Aw, Ellie, that's the point. They're upstairs and we're down here. They can't see us," he moaned back. Duke was always a very pragmatic person.

"Well, okay." But then I changed my mind again. "We can't." No matter how hard I tried to relax, I couldn't.

"O-kaay." His voice was a prolonged sigh. He slid his hand under my back and helped me into an upright position.

I buttoned the two buttons on my blouse that had come undone, smoothed my Bermuda shorts, put on my glasses, and centered my pearls. (Nina had said you could never go wrong with pearls.) There was a pack of cigarettes on the seat—a pack of Kools some passenger had left in the limo. "Mind if I snag one?" he asked.

"Sure, go ahead."

He slid a book of matches out from the cellophane. When he struck a match, I saw in the flare of white light the frustration in his eyes, and I knew I had caused it.

He took a long drag, and then coughed. "Wanna smoke?"

"No thanks."

He held the cigarette out and looked at it. "Actually, neither do I. These things can't be good for you." He snuffed it out in the ashtray in the armrest on his side of the car, and then looked at me kind of funny over his shoulder. "Okay, how'd you get so interested in saints?"

"Saints?"

"Yeah, saints."

"After what we were doing, you ask about saints?"

"Yeah, I'm not ready to go upstairs yet," he said, looking down at his crotch.

"Okay." I took a deep breath to recalibrate myself.

"I guess because they stand for something. Their lives are full of tips on how to become a better person. Like Saint Vincent de Paul who cared for the poor, and Mother Cabrini who ministered to the immigrants, and St. Casimir who lead an army." Purposely, I hadn't mention Saint Maria Goretti, the patron saint of purity, who was stabbed something like sixteen times for not giving up her virginity.

That was also the evening Duke told me about his Plan. "I have a plan," he said, emphasizing the word like it was an architect's blueprint for a grand cathedral. "I'm going to be a doctor . . . what kind I don't know . . . maybe a cardiologist or a pediatrician . . . and I'm going to go to Loyola's Stritch School of Medicine because it's the best. Then I want to practice in Chicago and live right in the city. No suburbs for me."

Very impressive, I thought. While I was dreaming of the Amazon one day and Africa the next, Duke, so confident and self-assured, had his life all figured out. As I learned later, Duke was not a person who would easily deviate from his plan. That was not his way. There would be only one time much later in our lives when, for my sake, he would deviate.

Back upstairs Andy and Millie were still going at it. Millie's arms were locked around Andy's neck. His mouth was holding a cigarette and his hands were clamped around her so tightly that her crinoline pouffed out from beneath her full skirt. A slow song—*Many a Tear Has to Fall* by Tommy Edwards—was playing on Joy's reel-to-reel tape recorder, and Andy and Millie were swaying their hips steamily to the beat.

I made eye contact with Father Ben. "Ellie, come here a second," he said signaling me with his thumb over to a private space beneath the overhang of Nina's door. My heart leapt into my throat. I was sure he had caught me and Duke.

"Ellie, would you like me to talk to those two?" he said, gesturing to the dance floor.

"If you think so, Father," I stammered.

"I don't want to embarrass you, so go tell them I'd like to have a private word with them right here. Your dad's aware of what's going on. He's unsure of himself in the dark, so he asked me to handle it."

"Okay, Father," I said, feeling like a hypocrite for my own behavior. I looked into his priestly gray eyes and imagined that because of the Sacrament of Holy Orders they were like X-rays that could see into my soul. I crossed my arms over my chest so he couldn't see the wrinkles in my cotton blouse.

But before I had a chance to do anything, a piercing, all-too-familiar voice came shrieking across the patio.

"Andy Klimaszewski, what the hell are you doing?"

The dancing stopped, and all eyes turned toward Joy who was standing at top of the steps pointing a finger at Andy. "Dammit, Andy, what kind of two-timer are you?"

Joy loped down the steps three at a time, her full skirt flaring, her hair whipping like a black flag in a storm. She flew past Father Ben and me, kicked her tape recorder a good one—so good that Tommy Edwards shuddered and stopped singing—and on the way leapt over an open Coca-Cola cooler. One of her sandals caught on the edge of a bottle cap and flew off.

It was the sight of Joy's fragile sandal sailing through the air that did it. Mrs. Dusza gripped the arms of her chair, and in a single motion sprung up like a Slinky and grabbed her straw handbag from the floor. In a flash of turquoise and chartreuse she sprinted after Joy. *"Jezus Marija,* Jesus Mary," she cried.

"Andy, you rotten cheat!" Joy said in a loud, low voice. "I knew it!"

About six couples backed away and formed a half circle around Andy, who by that time had let go of Millie. He dropped his cigarette and stomped it out with his foot.

Joy glared at him.

Until then I had no sympathy for Andy, but at that moment I felt a twinge of compassion for him. I wouldn't have wished it upon anyone to have to tangle with Joy and Wanda Dusza at the same time.

Joy poked two fingers into his rumpled white shirt. "All those things you said to me, and now you're carrying on with Millie." She glared at Millie. "And you, I thought you were my friend." Millie, with her teased-up dandelion hair, cowered behind Felicia Dombrowski who had even bigger hair.

Mrs. Dusza pushed herself between Joy and Andy and stood nose to nose with him, sputtering in Polish. The only word I understood was *dupek*, asshole. Andy protested in English and broken Polish, but Mrs. Dusza wasn't listening. She pulled her parrot handbag off her arm and started whacking him with it.

Joy stood helplessly on the sidelines. "Ma! Stop!"

Mrs. Dusza turned and wagged her finger at Joy. "That's enough, Joasia. I told you Andrzej Klimaszewski was trouble. But did you listen to the mother who gave you life? No! Don't think I don't hear you tiptoeing soft like a toe dancer past my bedroom door." She was on her tiptoes strutting around. "I look at my clock and it's one in the morning when you come home!"

"Ma, you're embarrassing me," Joy whimpered. She

scanned the stunned faces of our friends and tears welled up in her eyes. "I'm so embarrassed."

That's when Father Ben stepped in. He was gentle with Mrs. Dusza. He moved slowly toward her, put his hands on her shoulders and spoke softly. Because he was a priest and because he was speaking Polish, she calmed down and nodded up at him like a humbled child.

Joy sank to the ground and folded in upon herself, cross-legged on the floor. She dropped her head into her hands. I crouched beside her and patted her knee.

When I think about that moment now—sitting beside Joy, watching her head tremble in her hands—I feel Joy's heartbreak all over again. Joy trusted Andy. She had planned her future around him. She had given herself to him, and the house of dreams she'd built around her collapsed like a house of rain. It was only much later that I would understand that Joy's devastation was rooted in the death of her own father, and that Andy's betrayal only strengthened her belief that men weren't worth investing in. They'd always leave her, she believed.

Mom, wearing her compassionate dental assistant face, took over calming Mrs. Dusza. She held her elbow and guided her toward Nina's flat. Nina was waiting for them in a cone of light beneath the overhang of her doorway, holding her screen door open with her foot, swatting at mosquitoes with both hands.

Father Ben had turned his attention to Andy. He treated him with the same kindness he had shown Mrs. Dusza. Andy's arms were folded across his chest and he was nodding at Father Ben. The last I saw of him was his greasy head bobbing down the back stairs with Father Ben a step behind him.

Since then I realized that Andy wasn't such a bad kid—no worse than any of us. He just got carried away by his own coolness and hormones. *Hormoneous*, my kids would have said. I never did have much contact with him after that. Then in the early '70s, I heard he had been killed in Viet Nam. Bien Hoa. Friendly fire, someone said. Every so often I think of Andy and pray that he hadn't carried the embarrassment of that evening around with him until the end. For heaven's sakes, he was kid. Only nineteen.

Anyway, that night Barney joined us and knelt at Joy's other side. He fished a handkerchief out of the pocket of his yellow bowling shirt and handed her the perfectly pressed white cotton square. "Blow. Don't worry about messing it up. It's yours."

Joy blew hard.

"You did the right thing," he said, looking down at her fists balled up tightly in her lap, but not touching her or assuming intimacies other than friendship. That's when I saw a gallantry in Barney I hadn't seen before.

Joy stared straight ahead. Her eyes weren't blinking. "My ma's crazy."

"You're blaming the wrong person," I said, even though back then I thought Mrs. Dusza was a little bit crazy.

"I have to apologize to Andy."

"Apologize? You have nothing to apologize for," Duke said firmly. "He's not right for you. He doesn't deserve you."

Barney was staring at her in starry admiration. "Joy, you had spunk out there."

For the next few minutes no one spoke. Joy was sniffling. Duke reached for my hand and held it between us. Barney swatted at mosquitoes, and I listened to the hum of traffic and the air brakes of the Southport/Clark bus angling into the bus stop out front, wishing I were on it. I looked up and saw that everyone had left and we were alone, a pathetic foursome crouched beneath the flickering pink and green paper Chinese lanterns.

Dad yelled, "Kids, come on inside. The mosquitoes are going to eatcha alive and you'll be scratching yourselves raw all night." At the door Dad spread his arm around my shoulder. "It was a good party up until, wasn't it, Ellcha?"

"Yeah, up until."

Father Ben's accordion was sitting at Nina's doorstep. "He forgot it," I said.

Dad lifted it by its canvas strap. "I'll carry it inside to Nina's. If we leave it out, it's going to get warped by the humidity."

"Then no more *Edelweiss*," I whispered to Duke.

That night I couldn't sleep. My mind was reliving the details of the evening—Father Ben's accordion music, me and Duke necking in the Cadillac, Mrs. Dusza's Oscar-worthy performance, Joy's humiliation, the things I could have done to avert disaster.

The only light in my room came from the glow-in-the-dark face of the alarm clock on the windowsill near my bed and from the dim ceiling light in the hallway that entered through the window near Marta's bed. The clock was ticking loudly. The first time I looked at it, it was two o'clock. Then two-twenty, then two-forty. I wanted to smash that clock.

At three o'clock, I slid out of bed, slipped on my glasses and paddled toward the door, past Marta who was snoring like a Cocker Spaniel. On my way I stopped at Marta's window where I could see across a window well directly into our hallway, and on the floor below into the hallway outside

Nina's apartment. The low wattage light bulb in the ceiling fixture stayed on all night, casting familiar shadows of the balusters onto the walls. Everything there was still.

I flicked the bathroom light on and the fluorescent rod above the mirror hummed and blasted sharp light into my eyes. I opened my eyes slowly and studied my reflection in the glass. My hair was a disheveled mess with spikes still holding hairspray sticking out in a dozen directions; my cotton nightgown was open in a V at the neckline, exposing the fleshy part above one of my breasts; my eyes were bloodshot from rubbing them. I drank a glass of water. I dampened a washcloth and dabbed my face and neck. I flipped off the light and headed back into the bedroom.

I passed the window and heard a sound. The metallic sound of a doorknob turning. I stopped and looked out the window again. The landing outside our front door was empty. Then I heard muffled voices. I looked downstairs to the landing outside Nina's door. A figure stepped out of Nina's apartment. I blinked my eyes to make sure that what I saw was real. There was no mistake of it. It was Father Ben. I recognized his blue and yellow plaid shirt. Nina's hand was resting on his arm. Father Ben turned and I saw his profile, his strong, straight nose and the shadowy stubble on his cheeks. Nina's hair hung loosely around her shoulders now. His hand brushed a strand away from her eyes and continued slowly down her cheek. She leaned into him, as if into a lover on a gently lit dance floor, and they swayed in the stillness of their silence. Then suddenly, he turned and disappeared down the steps.

I smile when I think of that scene now—the two of them framed in the window like impassioned lovers in an old-time movie. It was a hallowed interlude in their lives that only God and I were privy to. But I did not see it that way when I was seventeen and had definite ideas about who was allowed to love whom. All that registered then was shock and confusion.

My entire body began to burn. My cells were millions of flashbulbs popping inside of me. I stood at the window for a long time staring at the landing, bathed in yellow light, then emptied of the two images I least expected to see there. It wasn't possible. There must be an explanation. But then my rational mind took over. *Don't be a fool, Eleanor. He's the one.*

The next morning I lied to my parents. I told them I was going to Mass at St. John's with Duke, but instead I went to the Super Cup around the corner and sat alone at the counter drinking bitter coffee for an hour. There was no way I could watch Father Ben say Mass at that altar. At that time, perched atop my high horse of self-righteousness, I had an elevated idea of what priests should be. Of course Father Ben was human, but he was supposed to be a spiritual cut or two above the rest of us. He was supposed to be out baptizing babies, handing out rosaries, walking down Milwaukee Avenue looking like a dignitary in his black suit and notched collar, shaking hands with people like Father Flanagan in Boy's Town—not sneaking out of Aunt Nina's apartment in the wee hours of the morning. What did he think he was doing?

And Nina. Where was her self-control? Wasn't she the one who told Joy not to mess with priests? She could pass out all kinds of advice she didn't follow herself.

CHAPTER TEN

*T*he following week I was in a rotten mood, but it was nothing compared to Joy's. She spent most of her time in my room lying on my bed rehashing the events of the party. The best I could do was keep her supplied with Kleenex and listen. Her emotions ran the gamut. She hated Andy. She loved him. She was glad to see him go. She missed him. She wished he'd get struck by lightning. She wished he'd get stuck with Millie. She was so distraught over her own problems that even if I considered telling her mine—which I wasn't ready to do—I knew I couldn't get in a word in edgewise. So I watched her pull tissue after tissue out of the Kleenex box that she balanced on her stomach; watched the box rise and fall as she gulped air and exhaled it with agonizing sighs; watched her dab her eyes, blow her nose and crumple damp tissues into tight little orbs that she flung toward a trash can, always missing.

If the week wasn't going badly enough, at supper on Friday my father flung another humdinger at me.

"Ellcha," he said, stabbing a crumb-coated fish stick,

"I've talked to Mrs. Dusza and we agreed. Joy's going to be working at WW Wagner's this summer. I arranged it."

"What? You arranged a job for Joy without asking her? Didn't she have anything to say about it?"

"The two of you have been lollygagging around the house long enough. Joy doesn't have a father to set her straight, so I'm stepping in. It's only right. Mrs. Dusza was grateful and you should be grateful too."

I smashed the limp fish stick on my plate with my fork. "What is this? Punishment?"

"No. It's progress. Joy's been wallowing in self-pity for long enough. Now she'll be working for Marisol Wing."

"Maxine's creepy sister?"

"She runs the whole personnel department at Wagner's. Don't you know, Wagner's is the nation's foremost distributor of industrial supplies . . . flanges and jackhammers and hoists," he went on. The gizmos he rattled off meant nothing to me and I was sure they'd mean even less to Joy. "Joy should consider it an honor to have Marisol take her under her wing, no pun intended."

"Geeze!" I glared at him. "I suppose I'll be working there too?"

"You, young lady, are going to be working for me. Good pay, a buck fifty an hour, fifteen cents more than minimum wage."

And so began Joy's summer at WW Wagner's and my summer as an undertaker's apprentice.

Every evening Joy would call me and report in excruciating detail the saga of her day. She'd tell me about the smelly, overcrowded bus she rode, the red-brick Wagner Building on Halsted Avenue with its crumbling iron fire escapes and belching smokestacks, the windowless office where she worked as a file clerk ("the damn A to M files") with a metal light fixture beaming harsh fluorescent light onto her head and a humungous clock on the wall with hands like swords that "ticked off the damn minutes."

She'd tell me about Marisol Wing and the chunky gold timepiece that dangled from a chain between the wide lapels of her polyester jackets, her kinky red hair that fluffed around her face like a Brillo pad, and her annoying habit of accentuating her verbs: "'You will *punch* in no later than nine and *punch* out no earlier than five. You will be *docked* for being late. There will be two fifteen minute breaks, one in the morning at ten o'clock, the other at three o'clock, and buzzers will *sound* at the start of the work day, before and after each break, before and after lunch, and at quitting time.'" Joy did a hilarious imitation of Marisol.

That first week Uncle Bruno taught me to drive and the second week he took me to the DMV for my road test, which by the grace of God and a miracle I passed. I don't think there was a more unqualified driver on the road, but that's where I found myself—on the road, behind the wheel of my dad's intimidating limo, honking and weaving and lurching between cars and trucks on the Northwest Expressway, heavy-footing the gas, slamming on the breaks, driving Dad—his hand pressed to the dashboard in a death grip—helplessly mad. "Jesus Christ, God Almighty, you want to kill us on the way to our funeral home?" he'd say. I'd drive him there for funerals and meetings, to the Board of Health to pick up death certificates, to cemeteries to help bereaved families select graves. It got so that I knew my way around the Catholic cemeteries of Chicago—St. Adalbert's, Mount Carmel, St. Joseph's, Maryhill, Queen of Heaven—the way other kids knew their way around the bars of Old Town.

As part of my education in the funeral business, I'd polish that limo to a blinding sheen in our garage. I'd sit in on meetings with casket salesmen who'd push the top of the line bronze and mahogany caskets and downplay their lower-priced fabric models. I'd order slippers and gowns from funeral supply catalogues to replenish our inventory. I'd politely dismiss novelty salesmen who hawked cheesy giveaway items such as combs, pens, rain bonnets, and matchbooks, which my Dad put in the same "crass commercialization" category as coffee machines. To him, funerals were something you didn't advertise. Families came to you in their moments of great sadness because of your reputation for honesty and compassion. Dad was highly respected in our community. To him, our family's reputation was golden, and he wasn't about to tarnish it by handing out worthless plastic rain bonnets.

Although I didn't appreciate it until much later, I learned a lot about my dad that summer. I saw how he'd never take advantage of a bereaved family, how he'd always steer families toward the lower priced funerals they could afford, how he never came after them for payment. "There's no place for greed in any business," he'd say, "especially in our business."

When I had downtime, I'd ponder my own life and ask myself the big questions: What in the heck am I doing here? Where am I headed? Is this what Dad expects me to do with my life?

But most of the time I'd think about the most immediate problem facing me: Sex.

As it turned out, Duke was nothing like I thought he'd be on our first date. Oh yeah, he was handsome and witty, self-confident and ambitious, but he was also one big horn dog, and after a slow start, I had become a horn dog too. I was an undertaker's apprentice by day, a horn dog by night.

That summer, sex was on my mind all the time, even when I was helping Dad show cemetery lots. I thought about how Duke and I should put the brakes on things—practice self control, as the nuns taught us—yet I didn't want to. I was in love him, and I wanted him to love me. I wanted to have sex, but I didn't want to end up dumped like Joy, or worse, PG like Connie Ostrowski who left school in her freshman year and was shuttled off to a home for unwed mothers in the tundra of Minnesota. I couldn't talk to Joy about it because it would only remind her of Andy and what she was missing. I wouldn't talk to Nina for obvious reasons, and I wouldn't dare mention it to my mother.

One particular afternoon, when business was slow and I had a day off, I ventured into my parents' bedroom, which was their private place, a room Marta and I never entered without invitation. I sat down on their squeaky double bed, the bed I was probably conceived upon. It was covered with a shiny polyester bedspread with huge red poppies and two fringed throw pillows. I ran my fingers over the hump of Mom's pillow and up the smooth surface of their varnished mahogany headboard. Centered on the wall above the headboard was the papal blessing they had received from the Vatican after their marriage in 1942. It was printed on parchment paper and protected under glass in a gilded frame. Pope Pius XII's picture was surrounded by fancy scrollwork, and below were the words:

Most Holy Father,
Veronica and Stanley Manikowski
Humbly prostrated at the feet of Your Holiness,
beg the Apostolic Benediction on the occasion of their marriage.

Prostrated at the feet? That was 1942! Another time. Another place. I remember thinking that I'd never hang such a thing above my marital bed—that it would be like having ménage à trois with the Pope.

I looked around the room for more secular clues to their lives as a married couple. On the dresser, upon a mirrored tray, were three perfume bottles, nearly full, and a comb and hairbrush set trimmed with mother of pearl. Nothing there.

I pulled open the small drawer of their bedside table. In a sliding tray near the front were a crystal rosary, a bobby pin, and a religious medal taped to a card with a prayer for the blind, a card Dad could no longer read. I moved the tray to the other side and beneath it was a round jewelry box with a mother of pearl lid, decorated with a geometric art deco design. I lifted the lid and inside was a rubber disk, flesh-colored, with a dome in the middle. It took me a second to realize that it was my mother's diaphragm, and when I did I almost fainted. A dozen inappropriate images flashed through my mind. I slammed the lid on the box, shut the drawer, fluffed up the bed, avoided eye contact with the Pope on the wall, and got the heck out of there. That was my first lesson that everyone's sex life is private.

Unfortunately, as circumstances would later reveal, it took me much longer to learn that lesson completely.

During my downtime on the job I also thought about Joy and how she was coping with the loss of Andy. What helped, Joy said, was that she had been meeting with Father Ben. At first she started pouring her heart out to him in the confessional, but when she realized she was taking too long and holding up the line, she started meeting him in the rectory every Wednesday after work. "You'll never know what a relief it is to take my sweet time talking to him," she said about their meetings. "He's not like most priests. He understands. He's human."

Too human.

My mind went wild, and I worried about Father Ben making a pass at Joy too, but then I told myself, fat chance. How much trouble could a person get into in a rectory full of crucifixes, statues, and portraits of popes and saints?

I thought about how Nina had let me down. I'd respected her. I poured my heart out to her. I went to her for advice and mostly took it. Now I needed to talk to her about sex, but I couldn't. Nina's the one I would have gone to, but now she was the problem.

But then, on the other hand, maybe I misinterpreted what I saw. Maybe Nina and Father Ben were just talking. What if I confided in Joy or Duke and then found out what I saw was completely innocent? I knew my friends could keep confidences, but what if they slipped? What if the story reached St. Casimir's and Nina got fired? What if rumors got started and hurt Dad's business? What if it wrecked Father Ben's reputation? Then all the good that he did in our parish would be for naught. I considered telling Dad, but dismissed it. He didn't need more problems, and in the state of mind he was in, he would have exploded like a truckload of bottle rockets. Definitely, it was information I had to keep to myself.

Then, to amuse myself while waiting in traffic or waiting for Dad, I'd fantasize about Jackie. Even my fantasies were about sex and they doubled back on my problem with Nina:

"Mrs. Kennedy, were you nervous when you had sex the first time?"

"Ah, Ellie," she whispers. "You're the only one I'd tell this to . . . it's so very personal. Yes, I had enormous

trepidations over my first sexual experience. I believe all women do. But before you proceed, you must ask yourself some important questions: Do you love this young man? Do you trust him? Then she looks at me with those hazel wide-spaced eyes. "You must remember that one of the most important decisions you'll ever make is who you give your body to."

"What if I love him?"

"Then the rest is easy. You must select a romantic spot for this first liaison. A balmy summer evening on the shore would do nicely. Light music would be simply sublime . . . flutes, violins, no ghastly tubas or accordions. And, my dear, by all means, be mysterious. Wear something tastefully revealing. Dump the glasses, eschew polka dots, and allow yourself to be a bit naughty."

Then she looks at me askance. "You appear a trifle distraught today, Eleanor. Is there something else on your mind?"

So I spill my guts about catching Father Ben and his accordion leaving Nina's apartment in the middle of the night, and I tell her I'm afraid they're having an affair. "What should I do?"

"Why, Eleanor," she whispers, "just between you and me, if you're so terribly concerned about your aunt," which she pronounces the refined way that rhymes with haunt, "you must simply approach her and tactfully inquire about her imbroglio."

"And what if she admits it?"

Jackie waves a slim hand serenely past her face. "Perish the thought, my dear."

Then it was back to my real world.

As an undertaker's apprentice, my evenings were as busy as my days. After supper I'd take wake duty downstairs. In a black sheath, pearls, and a teased bouffant, I'd follow Dad to his office and sit beside him on a straight-backed chair behind his desk. I'd whisper the names of the mourners who entered through the front door so he could acknowledge them. I'd make sure the holy cards and ballpoint pens were stocked in the lectern above the guest book. I'd carry flower arrangements of roses and gladiolas that were larger than I was into the chapel and set them at the head and foot of the casket with their white sympathy cards peeking out so the names of the donors were visible. I'd flick dust off the lapels or collars of the deceased. I'd discreetly slip keepsake items under their tufted satin pillows—religious medals, photos, letters, kid's drawings, a mini bottle of vodka, a Cub's cap—all requests of the family. (The strangest item was foot powder. I never asked why.)

I'd crank open the frosted windows for air, dim the lights, raise or lower the volume of the music, empty ashtrays, be ready with smelling salts and tissues. I'd soothe bewildered children and hug widows whose bodies shook like empty packages in my arms. "I never expected this to happen to me," they'd invariably say. I'd sit with them as long as I felt was right, and then I'd give them the privacy to be alone. Sometimes I'd escort family members upstairs where Mom would serve them a cup of chamomile tea and a plate of homemade cookies on her finest china with cloth napkins to momentarily take their minds off their sorrow. If they weren't teetotalers, Dad would serve them a stiff whiskey. Sometime there'd even be laughter. People would often tell humorous stories about the family member they lost. We didn't have psychology books then telling us that laughter was a healthy way to relieve stress, but intuitively it felt like the right thing to do.

As I sat beside Dad listening to widows, widowers, parents, and children tell their stories, eventually the bodies lying in caskets became people who once had lives and secrets and stories. One evening I listened to a father describe how he lost his little girl, Beverly, in the fire at Our Lady of the Angel's school that rocked Chicago a few years earlier. Dad had buried Beverly and another one of the ninety-two kids who died in that blaze. The man reached over Dad's desk and showed me a photo of her in his wallet—a smiling blonde girl in her lacy Communion dress and veil. "She'll be fourteen next month," he said, speaking as if she were still alive. Without thinking, I put my hand on top of his and started to cry. I remembered the images that were on TV the day of that horrible fire, of kids jumping out of second-story windows, their bodies falling through the air like lit candles. Immediately I was embarrassed because, in my position sitting next to my father, wasn't I was supposed to be strong? I tried to stifle my emotions, but Dad heard my sniffling and patted my knee. "You never get used to it, honey," he whispered in my ear.

Those summer evenings, the hardest thing I had to do was welcome Father Ben into our midst. By that time he had become a regular at our wakes. Because he spoke "a good Polish" Dad had arranged for him to stop by and recite the rosary—in English or Polish, the family's choice. "Thank you for coming, Father Borowczyk," I'd say leaping from my chair to greet him at the door, as I was instructed to do. "The family will be honored to see you." And the families were honored. A handshake, a kind word, a hug from a priest—especially someone as young and educated and handsome as Father Ben in his dignified black suit and notched collar, seemed to assuage their pain and lift their pride that their loved ones were worthy of such attention.

His appearance always caused a flutter in the room, like the flap a movie star creates at a film debut. People would gather around him. He'd hug them, squeeze their hands, pat their backs, and look them in the eye as he promised his prayers. Then he'd invite them to kneel with him around the casket and recite the rosary. From Dad's office I could hear his priestly voice, deep and reassuring, rise and fall as he repeated the final words of the Hail Mary: "Pray for us sinners, now and at the hour of our death. Amen." Or in Polish: "*Teraz i w godzinę śmierci naszej, Amen.*"

Afterwards, I'd keep my eye on him to make sure he left the building, which he always seemed to. Of course, it was none of my business. Even then I knew I had no control over whether he'd sneak back into Nina's apartment later, but in my black and white bubble of self-righteousness, I had rigid feelings about what a priest should and shouldn't be doing. To me he was a fraud.

That summer I didn't mind helping Dad because it was my responsibility, and while I developed a new respect for my dad's work, I knew it wasn't the right career for me. Death was too sad, too final. I wanted to work with people who had a future.

Invariably, someone at the wake would say, "Stan, how fortunate you are to have such a capable (or helpful, or compassionate or considerate or willing) daughter." And Dad would say, "Yeah, Ellie's become my eyes and ears. I don't know what I'd do without her."

I'd smile and accept the compliment, but inside I'd grimace. Every time Dad said that, I'd feel more and more trapped—

like a bird squeezed by over-eager hands. I'd imagine myself growing old in our third floor walkup on Ashland Avenue, taking wake duty, wearing a black suit and a chauffeur's cap, leading endless funeral processions, cooking *kiełbasa* and boiled potatoes in our kitchen, and weeping for the life I could have had if some microscopic blood vessels hadn't ruptured and clotted deep inside my dad's eyes.

When I'd look at Dad's prideful face, when I'd sense his pleasure in having me beside him, I'd feel like a block of clay slowly being molded into someone else's dream. That's when I would recall Grandpa Bronislaw's words: "This is a family business."

CHAPTER ELEVEN

That August a heat wave enveloped Chicago and we slept with our windows wide open, hoping for an occasional breeze to blow in through the screens. The window beside my bed faced the windows of the four-story red brick apartment building next door, and our communal snores, belches, grunts, and much more co-mingled in the dank air of the gangway. Sometimes I thought I heard sounds coming from Nina's bedroom, directly beneath mine. One night I heard a burst of husky laughter that could have been Father Ben's, followed by a "shh," that could have been Nina's. Several times I heard water running and a toilet flushing more often than usual. I thought I heard her front door opening, but by the time I reached the window across the room to check, the landing outside her front door was empty.

Then, two weeks before Labor Day, the suspicious sounds abruptly stopped. I awoke in the night and heard nothing but the normal hum of traffic, a snort I could attribute to a neighbor, the screech of alley cats out back. That's when I convinced myself that my suspicions were groundless, that there was nothing to worry about, and everything I thought I heard or saw were figments of my overactive imagination. That's when I allowed myself to relax and sleep.

In mid-August I stopped complaining about my job. What really got me to take stock of myself was the sad shape Jerzy Pilarski was in when he stopped over after work. Jerzy had been my dad's best friend for years. He bundled newspapers at the *Dziennik Chicagoski.* Six days a week he worked in a sweltering pressroom, and then loaded the delivery trucks in the hot sun or frigid Chicago winters.

For a few extra bucks, Jerzy helped Dad by taking telephone duty when our entire family had to go out together. Every day on his way home he dropped off a stack of Polish and English newspapers so Dad, with our assistance, could check the obituaries we had called in.

That afternoon I entered the kitchen from our rooftop patio where I had been sunbathing on a chaise lounge. I was slathered in Coppertone, happily sun-dizzy, wearing my huge Jackie sunglasses and a cover-up imprinted with a giant magenta hibiscus. When Jerzy staggered past, huffing and puffing, I noticed a pancake-sized patch of perspiration on the back of his blue work shirt. Instantly I felt ashamed that the most serious things on my mind were the book I was reading and my suntan.

"Hi Ellie, that's some book ya got there. Whatcha reading?"

"*Advise and Consent.*"

"Well, keep up the good work." I could have said, *Peyton Place*, and Jerzy would have said the same thing. Keep up the good work. Our conversations were about the same every day.

"Ya tinking about your future yet, kid? Your dad says you have a knack for the business."

"I'm thinking about college, then the Peace Corps," I said, mostly to get a reaction out of Mom. She was standing at the counter meticulously lining up slices of pound cake on a plate. Every afternoon, because Jerzy was a hardworking guy, she prepared him a snack. Her hands stopped in mid-assembly.

"Ellie has these highfalutin ideas. She wants to live in a dorm-i-tor-y like some debutante when she has a perfectly good bed down the hall. Just listen to her. She thinks she's Jackie Kennedy or something."

"I do not, Mother."

But that day Mom was on a roll. "Who'd want to be Jackie Kennedy anyway? She doesn't have a perfect life. Far be it for me to criticize, but Jackie Kennedy's own father was a roaring drunk who got so sauced he was unable to walk her down the aisle. And John Kennedy . . . they say he's a womanizer like his old man. You never know what goes on behind closed doors. There are a lot of secrets in that family, if you ask me."

I shook my head, regretting a weak moment last year when I told her about my dreams for the future. Now she was using them against me.

"You live in a dream world, Ellie."

"I don't think so, Mom."

What I didn't tell my mother—I wouldn't give her the satisfaction—was that I was already writing a new future for myself. I'd probably stay in Chicago and go to Loyola. It wasn't what I dreamed of—it was just going to be more of the same, riding buses to school and back, helping Dad out downstairs—but it wasn't a catastrophe either. At least I'd be close to Duke.

Mom fanned out the last piece of pound cake on the plate and sighed. "Our Ellie . . . she just sees what she wants to see."

"I see more than I want to see, Mom," I snapped. "You don't have a clue."

Jerzy dropped the thick stack of newspapers he was carrying under his arm onto the table. The front page of the top one stuck to his skin, and he peeled it off like a wet label from a jar.

"You look bushed, Jerz. Have a seat. Make yourself at home."

Jerzy nearly collapsed into a chair. "Tanks, Vera. Don't mind if I make myself *homely*."

I was swallowing a glass of water, and when Jerzy said *homely*, I nearly spit the water out of my nose. Jerzy was always coming out with stuff like that. Once, we were listening to an opera singer on TV and he said she must be "a metro soprano or something."

Mom frowned at me. "I'll have some lemonade ready in a second, Jerz." She grabbed a handful of lemons out of the refrigerator.

Jerzy grinned obliviously, pulled a crumpled pack of Lucky Strikes out of the pocket of his work shirt, shook a cigarette out, tapped it on the table, shoved it between his lips. Jerzy's face was a roadmap of wrinkles that crept from his cheeks to his ears and down the peninsulas of his earlobes. His hooked nose supported wire-rimmed eyeglasses that were always dusty. His stubble was in full bloom by late afternoon. No one minded though, even finicky Mom. "Tanks, Vera." He clicked his lighter with a thumb calloused from years of twisting rope.

I stomped off to the bathroom. Through the closed door I could hear Mom cracking ice cubes out of the metal tray and dumping them into a pitcher, stirring the lemonade with a spoon, pouring it into glasses. Jerzy's voice was as loud as a foghorn on Lake Michigan—so I heard every word he said.

"Vera, ya gotta gimme this recipe for Lydia, will ya?"

"I'm sure Lydia knows how to make lemonade, Jerzy, but I'll write it down for you anyway. So, you and Lydia are going strong?"

"We're like this," he said. I imagined Jerzy crossing his fingers. "She's my gal."

I pulled the straps of my bathing suit down to check my tan in the mirror. The thought of Jerzy and Lydia together made me smile. Jerzy Pilarski had been a widower since his wife Mary died years ago. He raised his kids himself—Joe and Madeline—in a small third floor rental down the block.

Jerzy was courting Lydia, a spinster from our parish. Lydia was a career woman—we called them that in the '60s— who worked as a teller at the bank at the corner. Sometimes I'd see her, perfectly turned-out, strutting down the avenue in her fitted suits, her bleached blond hair pulled back in a tight chignon, a slim clutch purse tucked efficiently under her arm. You wouldn't believe what a surprise it was when I heard that in her off-hours she was a championship, trophy-winning polka dancer.

At the mention of Father Ben's name, I tuned back into the conversation in the kitchen.

"Looks like I'm going to have to eat my words, Vera. I didn't tink da guy was going to last, but he's a hit."

"We think highly of him."

"He sure beats da pastor, ol' Leo Walenski, who I'd like to give a good kick in the keister."

"Father Walenski?"

"He's a lush. The guy likes his Jim Beam."

"Well, you like your Jim Beam, Jerzy."

"Yeah, but I don't drink it before Mass like dat guy does. Cripe, he walks out der and ya can tell the guy's three coins in the fountain. I'll be glad when dat new guy gets back. He went up north someplace."

"I didn't know Father Ben was gone."

"Yeah, yeah, Vera. That's why Walenski's been saying all the Masses last week. I thought ya knew dat. The young guy's at his ma's place in Wisconsin. He'll be back around Labor Day."

"Father Ben's probably a fisherman, Jerzy," I remember Mom saying in her know-it-all tone. That was just like my mom. She didn't know a thing about Father Ben, but forevermore he'd be a fisherman in her mind, just because she said so.

Fisherman my fanny.

That evening, lying in bed, I decided I'd had enough. I was tired of not getting any sleep. I was tired of pressing my ear to the floor and hanging my head out the bedroom window to match sounds to their sources. I was done with keeping everything to myself, and letting my mind go wild, blowing everything out of proportion. I was tired of being nervous in front of Nina. I decided to stop being a coward. I would tell Nina what I heard and saw, and I'd let her do the explaining.

The following Friday I had my chance. Nina was dashing down the stairs, I was heading up, and we met in the middle. I studied her face for signs of guilt, but there were none. She'd become a mystery woman to me.

"Nina, I need to talk."

She gave me a concerned look. "What's going on, sweetie? I'm all ears."

"Not here, Nina. It's personal."

"Mother problems?"

"Father problems," I said too quickly.

"Okay. I've got an appointment tonight, but I can cancel."

"No, it can wait."

"Dinner tomorrow evening?"

"Can't. We're having a beach party."

"Sunday then?

"Sunday's fine. It'll keep till then."

CHAPTER TWELVE

I'd never been overly sentimental about my friendships. They'd always come easily to me, and I'd never been one to get into fights the way some girls did, weaving in and out of alliances like automobiles passing on the expressway. But the evening of the beach party, as I slipped my shorts and red sleeveless top on over my two-piece turquoise bathing suit, I realized how fortunate I was to have close friends like Joy, Duke, and Barney—friends I could be myself with.

Joy had been recovering slowly from her breakup with Andy. The evening of my party, after Joy had left with Mrs. Dusza, Nina had given me some good advice. "Joy will be down in the dumps for a while, so the best thing you can do is keep her busy." As a result, Duke and I included her in many of our activities.

Once, we went to the King Pin on Division Street to bowl a few lines and we ran into Barney who was working there that summer. Joy had just thrown a strike and sent the pins crashing to the sides when from the machine room behind the pins a familiar voice called out, "Looking good, Joy Dusza…

huh, huh, huh, that a-way!" Barney pulled up the curtain, and there he was crouched behind the pinsetter, waving and grinning. At his break he came out and joined us. Fat navy blue earmuffs, the furry winter kind, cuffed his ears.

"What's with the earmuffs, buddy?" Duke teased him.

"A guy can go deaf back there!"

"Ever hear of earplugs?"

"What? Oh yeah, got 'em in too," he said, pointing at his ear.

The four of us spent an hour at the snack bar. Barney took a longer break than he should have to do some serious flirting with Joy, directing every statement to her, listening to every word she uttered as if she were the most engaging conversationalist in Chicagoland.

Joy: "Did you know, Barney, that WW Wagner distributes more than a hundred thousand products?"

Barney: "Like what?"

Joy: "Air compressors, rivets, hoists . . . every kind of motor you can imagine."

Barney: "You really have a mind for industry, Joy."

Spare me!

Later, when I told her Barney was crazy about her, she came back with a "Hell, Ellie, we're just friends." But that same afternoon Barney had Joy paged at Wagner's and after a few more phone calls, the four of us decided on the beach party. Joy, Barney and I agreed to meet Duke at the North Avenue Boathouse on Saturday after his shift ended at six o'clock. We'd swim, cook burgers on the hibachi the lifeguards kept in a locker, and when it got dark, Duke and I'd agreed we'd go for a romantic walk alone.

By that time I had made up my mind. The beach was the perfect setting for romance, so what was I waiting for?

If Nina could have sex with a priest, I could have sex with a normal guy I was madly in love with. Of course, I wasn't about to be stupid. If Duke wasn't prepared, I mean, if he didn't have condoms with him—I'd be prepared.

Later that day, I jumped in the Cadillac and drove to a Walgreen's about ten miles away in a run-down neighborhood where nobody knew me. I took a deep breath, collected my courage, and marched to the pharmacy counter in the back of the store. A tan-skinned girl with overdone eye makeup and a matching attitude looked me over like I was trespassing on her turf. In my baby blue seersucker suit, white pumps and polka-dot headband, I guess I was.

"Whatdaya want?" she asked.

I lowered my voice two octaves. "Condoms."

She glared at me and stood up taller. "Lube, non-lube, latex, non-latex, extra strong, average, large, six-pack, twelve-pack?" Then she smirked.

If there's one thing I hate, it's smirkers. I slowly took off my glasses, slipped them into my straw handbag, leaned over the counter and looked her dead in the eye. "Large, lubricated, latex," I said in a voice lush with alliteration.

She raised her chin and her voice. "Quantity?"

"What?"

"How many, honey?"

"Five dozen, please."

Her eyes widened. She turned and picked five bright blue boxes off the shelf behind her and stacked them in front of me, one on top of another like children's blocks. "Sure ya got anough?"

It was my turn to smirk. "It's going to be a big night, honey." I paid her, hopped in the black Caddy limousine out front, gunned it, and drove off.

Chicago's lakefront is magical, especially at night, with the waves lapping the shore, the cool smell of Lake Michigan, and the majestic vista of lights twinkling on the skyscrapers overlooking Lincoln Park and the water. As a kid, I used to dream about living in one of those elegant high-rise apartment buildings with turrets, wrought iron balconies, and rococo facades; about having a doorman who knew my name and carried my shopping bags from Bonwit Teller and Peck & Peck into the elevator, a newspaper boy who dropped the *Tribune* at my door, a concierge who ordered my symphony tickets. I imagined having a view of the lake from the twenty-fifth floor and hearing the foghorns in the middle of the night blaring their plaintive *whoo-oos*, reminding me when I drifted off to sleep, wrapped in my husband's arms, that I was among Chicago's most privileged. Those apartments on Lake Shore Drive and on the streets branching off them, with names like Astor, Aldine, Scott, and Pearson, are where the doctors, lawyers, bankers, and corporate officers who breathe more expensive air than the rest of us live.

That evening we spread our blankets on a section of sand between the Boathouse and the lake. We played volleyball and swam and walked to the rocks at Oak Street Beach, about a quarter mile south. The guys dived off the rocks into the deep water. Barney always wore those flesh-colored nose clips that pinched your nostrils together, but that evening he wasn't wearing them. I watched him inhale a full measure of sun-warmed air into his lungs, hold it there, and spring himself off the edge like a champ. Of course, Barney's pale, bony body was no match for Duke's suntanned, muscular physique, but his effort was impressive.

Joy and I sat behind the guys on the warm concrete

cheering them on. At one point, I joined the guys and Joy sauntered off and perched on a wide stone embankment behind us. From time to time I glanced over at her. Just a few years ago she was a clumsy package of limbs that never seemed to move in concert, and angles that appeared severe rather than exotic. But that night, in her black bathing suit flecked with silver threads that shimmered in the dusky flakes of sunshine, and with her knees drawn up to her chin, a breeze ruffling her hair, and a faraway look in her sea green eyes, she looked like a goddess perched on the cliffs of Mykonos.

Back at the Boathouse we polished off a burger and a beer apiece and tossed around the Frisbee. When the sun dipped behind the skyscrapers, we stretched out on our blankets and stared up at the arabesque of stars flickering above us. An airplane blinked across the dark sky, but its motor was stilled by the rhythmic *sa-woosh* of the waves slapping the sand. In the eastern sky, a full moon hung over the lake like a giant communion wafer. To the northwest, thousands of lights twinkled from the skyscrapers that arced the lakefront like a diamond necklace. I glanced at my friends. Duke was lying beside me with his eyes closed. A breeze was picking up, so I'd thrown a beach blanket over us. Joy was lying next to me staring into the heavens, and Barney was on his back tapping his full belly, humming the song that played on his transistor radio, *Blue Moon*.

I took off my glasses and set them on the blanket. "You guys, what do you want out of life?" I asked.

"She's getting philosophical on us," Joy said in a monotone.

"Good question," Barney said.

"Big question," Duke said.

"No, seriously, we're like blank slates. Life's barely made

an imprint on us. Oh yeah, we have some history, but our futures are there for us to decide."

There was a long silence. Beneath the blanket Duke's hand found my leg. "I know what I want," he said playfully. His fingers crept up my thigh. He traced the edge of my bathing suit with his finger. "Let's go for a walk," he whispered in my ear.

"In a minute," I said under my breath. When I recall that moment now, I know I was scared to death and was stalling for time.

"As you were saying, Duke?" Barney asked.

"Actually, I've been thinking about it," Duke said calmly. He slid his fingers beneath the elastic of my bathing suit. "Sitting on that lifeguard perch watching the petals on swim caps, listening to the waves roll in, all kinds of thoughts come into a guy's head."

"So what are you thinking, big man?"

Duke's fingers kept moving. "I have a plan. I'm going to finish up at Loyola," he said, rubbing my skin in small circles. "Then med school, internship, practice in Chicago, give something back."

"I know what you mean," Barney said. "You know, man, we have it so good and some folks have so little. I've been thinking about how Kennedy's inspiring us to make the world better. Our parents' generation cleaned up the mess in Europe. Now it's our turn. Kennedy's telling us to aim high. He's telling us to get the country moving again . . . explore new frontiers."

"New frontiers," Duke whispered in my ear. "He's my kind of man."

"Ask not what your country can do for you . . ." Barney said.

" . . . but what you can do for your country," Duke, Joy and I (in a nervous voice) finished the quote. It was amazing how a whole generation of us had memorized that one line. To the thousands of our generation who joined the Peace Corps, marched for civil rights, signed up for Viet Nam, those words had become our mantra.

Duke slipped his leg out from beneath the blanket, signaling me to get going. In the moonlight the fine hairs on his calf and the grains of sand that had dried between them, glistened. "How 'bout you, Barn?" he said quickly, trying to hurry him up.

"Maybe I'll give the space program a try."

"You're going to be an astronaut?"

Barney sat up. He was wearing a crushed fishing hat to keep his head warm. "Nah, I wouldn't make it through the training, especially in that centrifugal force machine with all that spinning. I'm thinking the research side of things. Like figuring out what happens to our muscles at high altitudes because, you know, in a few years we're gunna be going to the moon. That's what Kennedy said."

"How about you?" Duke asked me. "Wanna go to the moon?" By that time his entire hand was under my bathing suit.

"Stop it," I whispered.

"Ellie, I hear you want to be an undertaker," Barney said. Everyone laughed.

"Are you kidding? I want to go far away from here . . . the Peace Corps, you know that."

"Ellie wants to be Jackie Kennedy!" Joy piped in.

"I do not," I said, adjusting my swimsuit and pushing Duke's hand away.

Joy popped up from her blanket, tightened the rubber

band on her ponytail. "Don't be embarrassed, Ellie. I think it's sweet how you admire Jackie."

"My mother was ga ga over Bess Truman," Barney said.

It wasn't fair. After stirring things up, Joy had settled herself back down on the blanket and was lying there like a saint in beatific repose. Her eyes were closed, which gave me a whole new perspective on the smudged arcs of black eyeliner she applied with a miniature brush that fit in the little bottle she kept in her purse. She had eyelashes to die for.

Barney was staring at her too. "Hey, Joy, you never told us what you're going to do in this wonderful world. We've got a doctor, a scientist, and a Peace Corps socialite in our midst. How about you?"

Joy took a deep breath and her chest rose and fell beneath the Marilyn Monroe beach towel she'd covered herself with. Her hands were folded across Marilyn's smile. On her finger was the amethyst ring her mother gave her for her eighteenth birthday, which until then she had never worn because she was hoping Andy would see her bare finger and give her a diamond.

"Do you really want to know? Truthfully?" Her voice floated across our bodies.

"Truthfully," Barney said.

"You won't laugh?"

"Nope, promise," he said. "I'd never laugh at you."

Duke's swimmer's hand was back in action under my swimsuit and I was about ready to leap out of my skin. I shifted positions and squeezed Duke's hand to signal that I was ready for us to go off alone. Earlier, when I went to the restroom, I had tucked two condoms into the bra of my bathing suit. One was pressed to each breast, so we were definitely prepared.

"I'm going to become a nun."

"What?" Barney cried.

"I'm going to become a nun," Joy repeated.

"Joy!" I nearly shot up from under the blanket. And just then Duke's busy hand had caught religion, and he pulled his arm away. Later he told me that he felt like a nun had just slapped his dick with a ruler. As for me, I felt like I'd just gotten sprayed with a garden hose.

I was about to make a wisecrack, but I looked at Joy and I knew she was serious. I watched her breathe in and out, her fingers entwined across Marilyn Monroe's white teeth, waiting for our responses. Barney's smile stiffened, and he gawked at her with comic book eyes that looked like they could pop out of their sockets. I put my blouse and shorts back on and sat up. I kept hoping Joy would start laughing and say, "just kidding," but she didn't. In the moonlight a tear glistened in the corner of her eye, a translucent pearl clinging to her long painted eyelashes. I felt like an intruder and looked away before it slid down her temple. Some moments were meant to be private.

"It may seem sudden to all of you, but I've been thinking about it for a long time," she said. "Father Ben is the only one who knows."

We were unusually quiet on the bus ride home. We were the only passengers aboard the North Avenue bus and because no one was waiting at the bus stops, the driver pressed pedal to metal and sped us toward our neighborhood. The harsh white light inside the bus was blinding. Once we were seated—Joy and Barney on a bench seat across from Duke and me—we each got lost in our separate thoughts. Duke's hand was resting on my bare knee. Barney's arm was around Joy's shoulder in a brotherly, protective way. I rode the vibrations and listened to the *ba-bump* of the bus tires. It was then that the magnitude of Joy's announcement sunk in. I was ticked off about the convent and miffed that she didn't tell me first. It was Father Ben who had influenced her.

"Why didn't you tell me?" I asked from across the aisle.

"Because I wasn't ready to."

"Why not? We tell each other everything."

"Dammit, Ellie, I just wasn't ready to."

"But you told Father Ben."

"That's different."

"What's so different about it," I snapped.

"Not tonight, Ellie," she said, holding up her palm.

Barney looked at me with eyes that said, drop it.

"I'm not dropping this, Joy. You hurt my feelings."

"It's okay," Barney said nodding at me but patting Joy's hand. Duke yanked the cord above the window that signaled the driver to let us off.

In the aftermath of Joy's announcement, groping each other outside my front door just didn't seem like the right thing for Duke and I to do.

"You looked beautiful in the moonlight this evening, and as you could tell, I couldn't keep my hands off of you."

"Sorry we never got to take our walk." I reached under my blouse and pulled one of the condoms out from my bra. "I came prepared though."

"I see you did. I brought some too."

I told him about my trip to Walgreens. "I had all these condoms and I didn't know where to hide them."

"So what'd you do with them?"

"At first I thought about stuffing them into the lining of a casket so they'd get buried, but I couldn't do that. So I ended up hiding them in the closet, in a Candy Land game no one ever plays."

"Good move. Keep them for later," he laughed.

"Joy would make a horrible nun, don't you think?"

"Give her time. Andy broke her heart and she's running away. She'll change her mind." He touched my lips with his fingertip. "Just give me a kiss."

My heart melted.

He pulled me close and held me in silence for a long time. Finally, he whispered, "Ellie, I can't leave without telling you something I've been thinking about all summer."

"What's that?" I whispered back.

"I love you."

I stepped back and looked at him. His face was glazed with moonlight. "You love me? How could you love me? I was so tough on Joy tonight."

"I love everything about you, Ellie. Your smile, your tender eyes behind those glasses, the way you want what's right for Joy."

"I love—" I started to say back.

"Ellie," he wrapped his arms around me. "You don't have to say it back until you're one hundred percent sure. That's not why I told you."

"I love you too, Duke," I whispered.

With our bodies pressed together I felt the rapid beating of his heart. I felt like electricity was prickling through me, like my emotions could come bursting out of my pores any second. It was a different feeling than the groping we were doing under the blanket, different than the grabbing and clutching and fumbling that marked the horny landscape of our summer. We'd said the words that made the difference. I glanced at my watch. It was ten minutes past eleven.

There were many things that confused me that summer—Nina and Father Ben, and Joy's surprise decision—but there in the moonlight, in the hallway above the funeral home, I tucked them into a back pocket of my mind and concentrated on Duke, the sandy scent of his hair, the hazy quality of the light caressing his face, the way he looked at me, his smile holding his heart. Our love was the one thing I was sure of.

Even now, thirtysome years later, when I look at my wristwatch and it's ten past eleven, I remember that night outside my door, the way he looked at me in the hazy night, and the tenderness in his voice when he said he loved me. Those are words a woman never forgets.

CHAPTER THIRTEEN

*C*razy old sentimental lady sitting on a bench reliving her past. Is this what my life's come to? I chuckled out loud.

Two teenagers came bouncing out of the taqueria munching corn chips from the same bag. They reminded me of Joy and me sharing pastries from the Polonia Bakery that used to be around the corner. The aroma of chilies, fried tortillas, and salsa wafted out the door behind them, reminding me I hadn't eaten since breakfast. Famished, I went in and ordered myself a massive taco-to-go and grabbed a Snickers bar on the way out for Ranjit.

I walked to Ranjit's cab and peeked inside. I thought he might want a half of my taco, for I definitely overbought. But his head was tilted back and he was asleep, his turban serving as a pillow. An anatomy book, open to a diagram of the human heart, lay in a pool of sunlight in his lap. His finger was still pointing to the place where he fell asleep, the superior vena cava.

There was a strip of photos taped to Ranjit's dashboard,

the kind of photos taken in one of those old-fashioned photo booths you still see at shopping malls. I craned my neck to take closer look. They were close-ups of Ranjit and a pretty Indian girl mugging for the camera—he kissing her cheek, she covering her face with her hands, he ruffling her messy black hair, both of them trying to be serious but failing, their noses looking large close to the camera.

Abruptly, Ranjit shifted and changed positions. His knee knocked an empty Tupperware container off the seat and onto the floor where it landed beside a wadded up ball of aluminum foil, an empty bag of potato chips, and a browning apple core. That kid'll never be anorexic, I thought. A pair of running shoes with worn laces and socks stuffed inside lay on the floor. My motherly instincts clicked in and I wanted to knock on the window, "Ranjit. Clean up your room." But he seemed so peaceful with his chest rising and falling and a soft snore coming from between his parted lips that I couldn't bother him. Let him have his dreams.

I placed the Snickers bar on the windshield and jaywalked across Ashland Avenue to our old funeral home. I looked up at the sad building, then stepped over to the front door and peeked in through what used to be a stained glass window. It had been replaced by an inexpensive piece of plate glass covered on the inside by a dingy piece of fabric. At the side door I checked out the names taped to the rusty bell box: G. Gonzales, Hernandez, Arriaga.

Suddenly, the door flew open. A middle-aged fellow with dark eyes, rumpled sweatpants and a Bull's cap stood in my face. "Ya looking for someone?" he asked, defiantly.

"I used to live here when I was a kid," I tried to explain. "I was just remembering." His gruff look softened and he held the door open for me.

"Ya wanna take a look?"

"Sure," I said, leaping at the chance.

"No one's home . . . apartments are locked, but if you want to see the hallway and look around, be my guest." Then he added, "Wait a minute, you're not one of those holy rollers, are ya?" I shook my head no. "Good. We don't want any of them religious flyers to sweep up. No catalogs or phone books either. Just let yourself out when you're done. I'll be back in a flash. Just getting some cash," he smiled at his own corny poetry and pointed to the bank at the corner.

Thanking him, I stepped inside and let the door close behind me.

It was quiet as a vault inside. No voices. No music. Nothing. A shabby veneer door, dented in as if someone had kicked it, had replaced the polished wood door that once led to my dad's office. A tarnished metal Number One was nailed to its chipped finish. Our funeral chapel was now an apartment. Crazy. I couldn't believe that a family now lived in that space.

Clutching my taco, I walked up the stairs, counting each step. Still twenty to the second floor. The hallway seemed narrower, the walls felt closed-in, but the handrails and banisters, though scarred and worn, were the same dark wood I remember. I stopped on Nina's landing and looked around. I remembered the sight of Nina and Father Ben sitting on those steps, and the pandemonium that occurred in that hallway the night of the beach party. A metal Number Two was nailed to Nina's old door, and below was taped a kid's coloring book drawing of an Easter bunny with yellow and green crayon scribbled outside the lines. It was signed by Jesus. *Hey Sus, where were you when we needed you then?*

I climbed the stairs to the top floor—the same sixteen

steps I climbed and counted as a kid. Outside our door was a scruffy welcome mat and to its right an umbrella and a jumble of shoes, some of them with the backs flattened in like teenagers do when they're in a hurry. I looked out of the smudged window to my left into the window across the window well that used to be my bedroom. My window was covered with white curtains, gathered in the middle and tied with a cord. On the wall was a poster of Hulk Hogan or Mr. T, I couldn't tell which. A glittery vase of fake flowers, a row of assorted plastic containers, and a cardboard Kleenex box sat on the windowsill. My mother would have been appalled.

I looked down at my high-heeled black boots. I was standing on the same hardwood floor that Duke and I had stood on so many years ago. I leaned against the banister the way I did back then, closed my eyes and imagined Duke leaning into me. I pictured him as he was that summer: his flushed cheeks, a curl of dark hair flopped over his forehead. For a moment I could almost feel his presence. We were so young then, so much in love—fumbling with our clothes, planning our futures, and even naming our children. How could we have been so certain that we could take care of each other? That life would take care of us?

As much as I wanted to be in that building five minutes ago, that's how much I wanted to leave now. I had to get out of there. I was a voyeur, an interloper, a taco-holding trespasser searching for something inside someone else's world that no longer existed in mine. I was in a place full of the artifacts of other people's lives. But more than that, it was the tidal wave of memories that washed over me, one, then another on its wake, that stirred up feelings inside me that for years had been dormant. I felt myself sliding too deeply into the cheerless territory of the past.

I took one last look at the door to my old apartment. The metal Number Three nailed to the wood was crooked. I reached up and straightened it, thinking of Mom as I fussed to set it just right. Then, wiping my tears away with my scarf, I ran down the stairs and out the building.

CHAPTER FOURTEEN

1961

I returned to the plastic bench outside the taqueria, set the uneaten taco on the seat beside me, and settled back into my thoughts.

That night. That night.

That night after the beach party I dreamed that Duke and I were strolling hand in hand on the beach, dashing in and out of the surf that left scalloped fringes of froth on the sand. The sun warmed our shoulders. Our laughter felt like music. We cupped water in our hands and splashed each other's tanned bodies. It was a dream I never wanted to end.

There was a bell ringing. Iron upon iron. Deep and resonate. *Bong-Bong. Bong-Bong.* Then there were more bells—all the neighborhood church bells were clanging at once in a wild cacophony of sound. Their clanging became banging, and suddenly I was no longer on the beach. I opened my eyes. My clock on the windowsill read two-thirty. The banging was coming from somewhere inside our house. I sat up and looked straight ahead through the window near Marta's bed. There was a blurry figure on the landing in the hallway. Someone was pounding on our front door. I sprang out of bed, put on my glasses, and dashed to the window. It was Nina. She was banging so hard I thought the door would fly off its hinges if someone didn't open it immediately.

I sprinted past Marta and out the bedroom. Dad reached the door first and pulled it open. Through the space between the door and the doorjamb I saw the corner of Nina's blue chenille bathrobe and the tips of her bare toes, but not her face.

"Stan! Stanley!" she screamed.

"Janina, what's the matter?"

Nina was blubbering unintelligibly.

"Now, now Janina. What's going on?" he asked, trying to calm her down. His hair was mussed up. He was wearing his white boxer shorts and was bare-chested and barefooted.

Nina tugged at his arm. "Help me. Come downstairs. Help me."

"What's the matter, Janina?"

"C-C-Come down! I need you, Stan."

By this time Mom and I were beside him, she in a silky nightgown, struggling to fit her arms into the armholes of her robe, me in a baby doll nightie that barely covered my thighs. She turned on the dining room light and the first thing I noticed when I looked down was the sand between my toes; I hadn't showered because I didn't want to wake anybody up. Dad dashed into the hallway and followed Nina. He knew the count and curve of our hallway steps and the feel of the handrail as well as he knew his own body, so with whatever sight he had left—sight aided by instinct and memory—he flew down the stairs behind her.

"I'm going down too," Mom said. "He needs me, Ellie. You stay with Marta. Lock the door behind me."

I turned the deadbolt and for about thirty seconds, everything was eerily quiet. Then I heard raised voices and Nina sobbing in her bedroom. She was sputtering, trying to say something, but through the floor all I heard were gasps and guttural syllables.

I ran back to bed and leaned my ear against the window screen.

"Oh my God," I heard Mom say twice.

Then Dad's deep voice. "Jesus Christ! What are you nuts, Janina?"

"Do something. Do something, Stan," Nina pleaded.

"Call the pulmotor!" Mom cried.

Nina screamed. "Make him breathe, Stan."

"Shh, Nina."

But Nina was not quiet. She was howling like a wounded animal.

I knew who was down there. There was no question in my mind. I pictured Nina and my parents gathered around Father Ben, shouting. "Breathe." "Look at me." "Open your eyes."

"Mommy!" Marta whimpered from her bed.

"Shh, Marta. Go back to sleep," I whispered.

"Mommy, I hear noises."

I crossed the room to tend to her. Her eyelids fluttered.

"It's okay, Marta."

"Ellie, there's noise."

"It's okay, sweetie. Aunt Nina's sick and Mommy and Daddy are downstairs giving her medicine. She'll be okay. Just go back to sleep. Please Marta, please. Go to sleep."

"I'm thirsty."

"Okay, I'll get you water. Close your eyes." I crossed the hall to the bathroom, turned on the tap, held a plastic drinking cup beneath it. The cup trembled in my hand.

When I returned, Marta was sitting up in bed. "Nina's crying. I can hear her."

"Here, drink this." I held the cup to her lips. "She's going to be fine." I tried to keep my hand steady but the water was spilling. "Go to sleep, Marta. Everything's going to be fine." She gulped and gulped and gulped, and I wanted her to stop. She slid down between her sheets. I brushed her sweaty bangs with my fingertips and tucked the cotton blanket around her gently, the way Mom did. "Sleep, Marta." I sat with her until her breathing slowed.

When I rushed back to the window, I could hear Nina sobbing louder. Dad's low voice said, "There's nothing I can do. I'm not God! There's no pulse. He's gone."

Nina screamed a soul-wrenching scream. "No!" she wailed, and the wailing didn't stop.

"*Psiakrew cholera*," my father cursed. "Stop it, Nina. You're gonna wake the dead," which was obviously a bad choice of words because that was exactly what Nina was trying to do. Then he shouted, "Vera, get Bruno and Frank on the phone and call Jerzy!"

Someone slammed the window shut and the voices became faint. I lay down on the floor and pressed my ear into the hardwood, trying to hear through the layers of wood, plaster, paint, and air that separated me from them. All I heard were muffled voices and rapid footsteps. I checked on Marta. She was sound asleep, so I dashed to the front door, unlocked it and made my way down the steps.

Nina's door was open and I tiptoed down the dim hallway of her apartment into the kitchen. The kitchen was dark except for a shaft of light beaming out from Nina's half opened bedroom door. Ambient light illuminated a powder blue sweater slung over the back of a chrome kitchen chair that had been pushed away from the table as if someone vacated it quickly. Two empty wine glasses sat on the table, and between them a half full bottle of wine. On the floor, in a wedge of light just outside her bedroom door, was a pair of men's shoes.

I was frozen in place. I couldn't have moved if I wanted to. All of my energy was fixed upon those black shoes. My mind was a camera with a wide-open aperture madly clicking photo after photo of those shoes. One lay on its side, the other was pointed outward. The leather across both toes was creased from walking. The heels were worn down on the insides. My mind was not working right to be dwelling on shoes then. How I hated those shoes.

Nina was sobbing.

"Dammit, Nina. Hold it down, for cryin' out loud," Dad said.

"Shh, Nina. Stan's on the phone," Mom said.

I imagined her, a lesion of sadness, trembling as she did on Inauguration Day in our family room. I felt the same confusion and helplessness I felt then—when there was nothing I could do but let Mom take over.

"Maxine, let me talk to Frank. No, it's not old man Pistanowicz . . . someone else . . . just give me Frank." There was a pause. "Frankie, I'm down at Nina's. Wake Bruno up and get over here in the hearse, with a gurney, will ya? Pull into the alley. Na, the family's okay, but we got a problem, Frankie. I'll tell you when you get here. Hurry up."

I heard the short and long ticks of the telephone dial spinning. I could tell by the three short ticks in the middle that Mom was dialing Jerzy.

"Lydia, it's Stan. Lemme talk to Jerz." *Pause.* "Jerzy,

sorry to call you in the middle of the night, but get over here quick, will ya. No, we're all okay. Just get over here now. There's something we gotta do."

Dad slammed the receiver into its cradle and didn't get it right. "Seven a bitch," he cursed. "I can't even hang up a damn telephone!"

In the bedroom, Nina was howling. "No, no, Ben, no."

"Shut up, Janina. Don't let me hear that damn priest's name again."

"Easy, Stan, you're going to give yourself a stroke."

"Hell, Vera, I'm blind, but all my other parts work. Don't censor me." Then he said in a quieter tone, "Vera, get Father Walenski on the line."

"Stan, it's three in the morning. Can't it wait? He'll be up for Mass soon enough."

"Hell no. It'll be light in two hours."

"What are you going to do?" cried Nina.

"Janina, just be quiet and let me handle it. You caused enough problems. God, Nina, didn't you know what you were doing?"

"Stan, calm down," Mom said in a voice that was anything but calm.

"I am calm," he snapped. "You women sit still and let me handle this. Vera, call the rectory. Get Father Walenski on the line. We're going to get this guy out of here and wash our hands of him."

"Stanley," Nina sobbed.

Again, the sound of dialing. Mom knew all the numbers by heart because she dialed them so often for Dad. "It's ringing, Stan."

I heard my father pacing around the room. "Pick up the receiver, you drunken bastard. The old fart's asleep when he should be up watching his priests."

"He's on the line," Mom whispered.

Dad simmered down and sounded as if he was making a typical business call in the middle of the day. "Leo, Stan Manikowski. Sorry to disturb you, but it's an emergency," he said flatly. He started speaking in choppy Polish, most of which I couldn't understand. They talked for a while. Everything he said was in Polish except for a few words he couldn't think of the Polish words for: "hearse," "back door of the rectory," and "forty-five minutes."

He hung up and began shouting orders. "Vera, get Nina dressed. Get him dressed. No, don't you touch him. Frank and Bruno will do that. I'm going upstairs to put my pants on."

When I heard Dad heading out of the bedroom, I dashed into the dark bathroom where he wouldn't run into me. I was inches away from him when he flew past. "That damn seven a bitch," he swore. Dad always said son of a bitch that way.

I sat on the cool edge of the porcelain tub, lowered my head into my hands and started to cry. I was breathing quickly, trembling. I wrapped my arms around myself. They were ice cold.

The bathroom door opened and Mom stepped in. The light switch clicked and a split second later the fluorescent rod above Nina's sink flickered and flooded the room with light so white it was painful.

"My God, Eleanor, what are you doing here?"

I knew from the look on her face that she knew I heard everything. Color had drained out of her cheeks. Her wavy shoulder-length hair was disheveled, with a flat patch on the side from the pillow. In the harsh light the small wrinkles around her eyes looked like gouges. We stared at each other.

"He died in bed with Nina. Didn't he?"

She closed her eyes and nodded. "I came for Nina's hair brush, but I guess there's no hurry." She sat beside me on the edge of the tub.

"I hate him, Mom. I hate her too. I hate them both!" My arms were folded across my breasts. I was shaking and couldn't stop. Even my knees were clapping together.

Mom wrapped her arm around me. "Oh, honey, honey."

"What in the heck were they thinking, Mom? He's a priest."

"I don't know what to say, Ellie. You shouldn't be here. You're too young . . . but now that you are . . . well, I guess it's part of growing up and seeing things for what they are. Your precious Aunt Nina is flesh and blood. She's just human and maybe she thought . . . dammit, I can't answer for her. I don't know what she was thinking, Ellie. I don't know what to say. I don't know anything anymore. Excuse me. I'm just babbling."

"I hate them," I blubbered.

"I know. I know," she said, patting my shoulder.

"Mommy, what's going to happen?" I can't believe I called her Mommy—like I did when I was five.

She slid her arms down and held my hands to stop them from shaking, but her hands were trembling as much as mine. She reached for a bath towel from the top of the radiator and draped it over my shoulders. I stared at my shaking knees.

"I could lie to you, Ellie, but I won't. Jerzy and your uncles will be here any minute. They'll be taking Father Ben back to the rectory in the hearse. It can't get out that he died here. Father Walenski will find him in his bed tomorrow morning."

I looked up at her. "God, a cover-up."

"Tomorrow we're going to carry on like none of this happened."

"But Mom, we'll know it happened."

"But we don't have to announce it to the world either. It's about handling grown-up problems, Eleanor. One of these days you're going to know how many secrets there are in this world."

Her stare dug into me. Her chapped lips were slightly parted, as if she were holding words in her mouth she couldn't speak. When she let them out, her breath had a nighttime sourness to it. "Ellie, you must promise. Not a word to anyone." She tapped her bare foot on Nina's fuzzy blue bath mat to emphasize every requirement of the secrecy agreement she was imposing on me. "What happens within our four walls stays within our four walls. You will mention nothing to Joy or Duke or Mrs. Dusza, or anyone." As if I'd run and tell Mrs. Dusza anyway.

"I won't tell Joy," I said firmly. At that time, I thought I'd never tell her. Why would I? It would be like firing a bullet into her heart.

"Here's what you need to do. When you hear your dad come down, and when he's in the bedroom, go upstairs. I don't want you here when they carry the body out."

The body. Less than an hour ago Father Ben was a person. Now he was a body.

"I'll be up when it's over." Mom stood up and put her hand on my shoulder. I looked straight ahead into the fluffy ties of her bathrobe, one hanging lower than the other. One of the ties was badly frayed. She needed a new bathrobe. Why was I noticing that?

"I don't want you to leave."

"It's going to be fine, honey. It's going to be fine."

"It can't be fine," I cried.

"It will be." She bent over and hugged me.

"Don't leave me, Mom."

"I don't want to leave, Ellie, but I have to get some clothes on before the men get here," she said. "First I've got to get back to Nina. She wanted time alone with him. She's frightened, the poor thing."

After Mom left, I looked around the bathroom. Everything was illuminated. I saw vibrant colors I hadn't seen before. Each square of yellow ceramic tile on the wall was defined by the white grout surrounding it; every wrinkle and water spot on the clear plastic shower curtain leapt out at me for attention; the creamy bar of Camay rested in the soap dish like the smooth top of a child's hand. The chrome fixtures reflected the blues and yellows of the towels. I was seeing everything anew, but there were mysteries in this room. On top of a stack of two blue towels on a glass shelf above the toilet tank was a leather toiletry kit, a new kit without creases or mars. Its zipper was open and a tube of Ipana toothpaste poked out. I snooped into the bag. Inside were a red toothbrush, an aerosol deodorant, a metal razor, and a small plastic prescription bottle with a white screw-on cap. The kit also held a brown plastic short-bristled hairbrush that gripped strands of Father Ben's curly brown hairs—strands the Lord, in charge of things grand and small, allowed to be plucked from his scalp as a preamble to taking all of him. I didn't know whether to cherish that kit of toiletries or fling it across the room, pray to the Lord or curse Him, console Nina or crucify her. I didn't know anything any more. So I turned the light off and waited in the dark until I heard Dad storm back into Nina's room. Then I snuck out.

The next hour was a flurry of activity. From upstairs I heard doors opening and closing and familiar voices in the hallway speaking in take-charge tones, giving orders, pointing out directions. They were doing what men did: solve problems, protect their reputations and those of their women, sweep under the rug what must be concealed—all to keep the untarnished Manikowski name in sterling repute.

I picked up snatches of conversation.

"Watch the doorway . . ."

"Careful with his head . . ."

"Jesus Christ, Bruno . . ."

Then I freaked out. Where was Nina when her apartment was being cleansed of the evidence? When wine was being dumped down the drain? When someone was dressing him in his underwear, bagging his personal belongings? I imagined her cowering in the harbor of Mom's arms on the sofa, the two of them huddled together like the Madonna and Mary Magdalen.

After Father Ben had dinner at our house that time, I'd gone to the library and found a picture of the sculpture of Mary Magdalen that he described to me, and now Nina was that Mary Magdalen: a blighted frame of a woman, shard upon shard of wood. She had torn apart everything we held true, destroyed everything we'd built, ruined our family's name. There would be hell to pay for Nina. I knew how Dad would behave, but I had no idea what I'd do when I'd see her face-to-face. In my teenage mind, where everything was black or white, where people were either on the holy road to canonization or the bullet train to perdition, I didn't know if I could ever trust her again.

Once Father Ben's body had been removed, the men

returned to Nina's apartment. I heard their hushed, serious voices downstairs.

Dawn was approaching. I stepped over to the family room window and in the distant sky watched strands of pink light rise above the range of tired rooftops and ascend behind the bell tower of St. Casimir's in a violet and golden prelude to a new day. I wondered if my uncles and Jerzy saw it too. The sky brightened and cast a tawny glow over St. Casimir's. Slowly the glow crept closer, washing over rooftops, garages, and porches. I wondered if that soft light would engulf our building as well, or whether in some grand heavenly reprimand it would stop at our threshold, the site where one of the Lord's most revered had fallen from grace.

An hour or so later, Mom returned upstairs.

"I gave Nina two sleeping pills she had from when Al died. When Marta gets up, tell her Nina has the flu and she'll be in bed for a few days." Her voice was weary.

Dad was already at the kitchen table in his suit, ready for Mass. "Jerzy's coming back at eight-thirty so the four of us can walk to church together," he said.

Waiting at the door, Dad fumbled with the knot in his tie. With his chin buried in his clavicle, he hemmed and hawed and sputtered, "Ellcha, I know . . . I know . . . you know what happened . . . a tragedy. Let me repeat what your mother said. No one outside these walls is to know the truth . . . not a word to Marta either." His face was ashen. The muscles around his mouth and eyes held a worried deposit of tension.

"I promised Mom," was all I said.

"Good. Just so you understand."

He slipped his arm around my shoulder. "One more thing, Ellcha. You don't have to help out in the funeral home for a while."

CHAPTER FIFTEEN

That morning we walked to church in a fog. Every church in our neighborhood had a nine o'clock Mass, so discordant bells pealed from all directions. Joy would be in church with her mother. Lately, they'd been sitting in the pew in front of us. I thought of the few peaceful minutes she still had, and how hearing the news would change her day, her week, her life.

Cars rolled past us. Even they had a measured pace on Sunday mornings. As we advanced block after block, Mom whispered the names of the people walking toward us so that when they greeted Dad, he could acknowledge them by name. Mom's arm was hitched in the crook of his elbow. I was linked to his other arm. Marta skipped ahead. I used to be proud to walk down the street with my parents. I used to be proud to be a Manikowski, but that day I wasn't proud at all. I felt like an accomplice to a crime, although none had been committed.

I was relieved that we didn't run into Joy on the way. She could read me like a recipe—one look would have told her something was wrong. I was also grateful that Duke was a member of St. John's. The news would travel to him fast enough.

The altar bells tinkled three times and Mass began. Father Walenski hobbled out from the sacristy behind two acolytes, and we rose. He stepped up to the altar and set his missal, a giant book of church liturgy, on the altar top. But rather than open it to begin the Mass, he shuffled toward the pulpit, hunched over like a laborer pushing a plow. The microphone picked up the sound of his shoes climbing the steps to the top of the pulpit. The acolytes took their places on high-backed chairs against the sacristy wall.

Father Walenski's breath was labored. With both hands he adjusted the arched stem of the microphone that cut the bridge of his metal-rimmed glasses in two.

"My friends, I have an announcement. Kindly be seated."

There was a flurry of sound: shoes shuffling against floor, hands brushing against fabric, throats clearing, coughing.

Father Walenski had a halting voice that on an average day made me impatient because he couldn't get the words out quickly enough. That day, with horrible news waiting to be told, I longed to push his words back down his throat rather than pull them out.

"My friends . . . boys and girls. I'm sure you expected to see Father Benedict back this morning, refreshed from his vacation. But, due to an unforeseen event, he will not be with us."

Unforeseen event. He made it sound like Father Ben got stuck in traffic.

"It is with a heavy heart that I must tell you that Father Benedict Borowczyk, the Lord's faithful and trusted servant, passed away this morning."

During the split second it took for sound to become meaning, all was silent. All I heard was the quick *tick-tick, tick-tick* of Mom's Timex. Then a gasp shot through the nave and up into the balcony and choir, and the communal gasp twisted into a soulful groan.

"What?" Joy cried. "No!"

"My God," I said feeling duplicitous as I leaned forward and placed my hand on her shoulder.

There was murmuring and then slow quiet. Everyone was holding his breath, waiting for more information.

"When Father Benedict didn't come to the kitchen this morning for his usual cup of coffee, our housekeeper Mrs. Olitzka, checked on him and found him expired in his bed."

Expired. Dead. What's the difference?

Mom's knuckles were white from squeezing Dad's hand.

Father Walenski's voice quavered. "He died in his sleep of a massive heart attack, peacefully in the arms of the Lord."

"Holy smoke!" I whispered into Dad's collar.

My father nudged me. "Shh."

"Shh," Mom hissed.

"When I approached his bed, I saw an amazing sight. Father Ben had a saintly smile on his face, as if in the moment of his death he was gifted with a glimpse of heaven." Father Walenski's voice trailed off into a barely audible babble. "We should all be so blessed as to have such a wonderful passage into paradise."

Mom's profile was fixed, as if chiseled out of stone. Dad's was equally as rigid, only his dark eyes, no longer bespectacled, bugged out. Joy was slumped over with her head in her hands. Leaning forward, I placed my hands on her arms. "I'm so sorry, Joy," I whispered into the back of her neck. She just shook her head. She was weeping softly as were so many others. Being with family when you hear devastating news is one thing, but hearing it in a crowd is another. I remember thinking of the three-way mirrors in department stores and how when they're positioned just right you can see reflections of yourself indefinitely. We were like that that morning, seeing ourselves and our grief multiplied in the reflections of everyone else.

"Although Father Benedict was only with us for a short time, he had made an unforgettable impression on our community. He loved this church and he loved all of you." Father Walenski then spoke to the children. "I'm sure one of the things you were looking forward to back at school was having Father Benedict visit your classrooms . . . play his music."

Some children were whimpering so hard that their nuns had to leave their pews to comfort them. One of the first grade nuns walked a girl with yellow pigtails back to her pew and sat her on her lap. Another third grade nun joined some of her children in their pew. Marta turned around with a look of horror on her face.

Father Walenski saw what was happening. "Boys and girls, if any of you would like to sit with your parents while we celebrate the holy sacrifice of the Mass, please feel free to do so."

I could tell that Marta was considering coming back to sit with us, but she remained in her pew. She was a fourth grader then, a big girl, and I gave her credit for staying with her class.

"Father Benedict's family has been notified. At the request of Father Benedict's mother, the Manikowski Brothers will make the funeral arrangements. I believe the internment will take place on Tuesday. There will be a notice in tomorrow's

Dziennik and also in the *Trib* with the details, or you can call Manikowskis."

His family knew about us. I wasn't surprised. It dawned at me that at that very minute my uncles were probably transporting Father Ben's body back to our funeral home for embalming.

Father Walenski nervously shuffled the papers on the lectern. I felt sorry for him.

"Let us now pray for the repose of the soul of God's faithful servant, Father Benedict Borowczyk."

Kneelers thunked to the floor, sending an echo throughout the church, and our stricken bodies slid off the pews onto the kneelers.

Wanda Dusza inched closer to Joy. She wrapped her arm around Joy's back and consoled her, "Shh, my Joasia." The yellow rosary beads Wanda had coordinated to the color of her summer suit were threaded so tightly through her fingers that the wire links looked ready to snap. Leaning into her, Joy, dressed in her usual black, was grimly appropriate.

"Grant eternal rest to him, O Lord, and let perpetual light shine upon him. May his soul and the souls of all the faithful departed rest in peace. Amen."

Faithful departed. What a sham. Father Benedict Borowczyk was a man who spoke of faith, who influenced others to be faithful, but in the end had not kept the faith himself. He had taken the priestly vows of poverty, chastity, and obedience, but in the end had made a mockery of them.

"Let us dedicate this Mass to Father Benedict."

Most of the Mass was a blur, a slow unfolding of familiar words trumped by unfamiliar feelings. At Communion time, I slipped ahead of my parents and walked to the altar rail behind Joy, who knew I was there because I patted her arm.

We knelt on the plush red velvet kneeler and with shoulders touching waited for Father Walenski to give us Communion. Through the corner of my eye I saw him sidestepping closer. His trembling thumb and forefinger pinched host after host out of the gleaming chalice and lay it upon the extended pink tongues of communicants. His cheeks were networks of broken blood vessels. His nose was bulbous, almost purple. When he approached me, there was a flicker of recognition in his eyes. He knew who I was, and he knew I knew the truth. He set a white host on my tongue and recited the mysterious Latin words: "*Corpus Domini nostri Jesu Christi custodiat animam tuam in vitam aeternam.*" May the Body of our Lord Jesus Christ preserve your soul unto everlasting life.

After Mass, parishioners huddled in small groups outside the church exchanging superficial platitudes, all of them interchangeable given minor word substitutions for age and cause of death.

"The man was a saint."

"So young . . . so much to offer."

"He died all alone . . ."

"In the arms of the Lord."

Bullshit. He died in the arms of my Aunt Nina.

Jerzy sat behind Dad's desk, setting the telephone receiver into its cradle when we returned home. As soon as the connection broke, the phone rang again.

"Already the damn ting's ringing off the hook," he griped. He picked up the receiver and switched to his less gruff, businesslike voice. "Manikowski Funeral Home." He gripped the phone with one hand, listened, then gave Mom an okay sign. "The funeral Mass will be Tuesday at ten, visitation at St. Casimir's tomorrow evening." *Pause.*

"Yeah, the Manikowskis confirmed the arrangements fifteen minutes ago."

Mom sent Marta and me upstairs while she and Dad stopped to check on Nina. In the kitchen, Marta couldn't stop jabbering, but I let her talk because she needed to. Her face was as pink as the watermelon slices on her sleeveless summer dress. To keep her occupied, I asked her to peel some potatoes. She was quiet as she rummaged through the utensil drawer looking for the potato peeler. The profile of her moon face was too serious for a kid her age.

"Father Ben Bo liked show tunes. Did you know that? He played them for us all the time." The set of her lower lip reminded me of Mom.

"No, I didn't."

"Yup. *Carousel . . . The Sound of Music . . . Camelot.* Let's play a record for him."

The last thing I wanted to hear were show tunes, even though on a normal Sunday after Mass, I'd be the one who'd put them on. "We'll wake Nina downstairs."

"Not if we keep it low. Please?"

I didn't have the heart to refuse. For Marta's sake it was important to keep everything as normal as possible.

She set a half-peeled potato on the rubber drain board, wiped her hands in a dishcloth and trotted over to the stereo. She slipped a vinyl record out of its jacket, held it by its edges, set it on the turntable and watched the arm of the needle lift and drop. "Is Father Ben Bo downstairs?"

"I think so."

"That's creepy."

She watched the record spin. I could tell she was trying to sort out all that happened in the past few hours. "The only good thing is that he's with God, don't you think so, Ellie?"

I didn't respond. The phone rang again and someone, probably Jerzy, picked it up downstairs. A few minutes later it rang again. That darn telephone was going to ring incessantly until Father Ben was buried.

The opening music of *Carousel* filled the room, a flowery medley of calliope, piano, and violin. With Marta occupied, I picked up the phone and dialed Duke's number. It rang twice and Donna answered.

"Hi, Donna, I suppose you heard the news?"

"Yeah. How sad." Her voice was clear, like we were standing eyeball to eyeball, which felt way too close for comfort. "I'd met Father Ben at Danny's basketball practice. He looked so healthy, I can't imagine him gone." She asked me a zillion questions about how he died, whether there was any history of coronary disease in his family (as if I'd know), and how his family is coping with the news. She blathered on about how God has a plan for each of our lives, that it's the not the time you have but what you put into the time, and how, as a priest, he was probably more prepared to meet God than the rest of us, which is exactly the kind of lecture I didn't want to hear. When I said the funeral was going to be on Tuesday, our first day of school, she suggested we get time off and go together along with Joy and Millie; and to shut her up, I agreed. She would have yammered on all day if she could, but I got a break when Duke grabbed the phone.

"Sorry 'bout that. Donna thinks every call is for her." There was some shuffling, then the sound of a door closing. "I just pulled the phone into the pantry where it's private. You okay, Ellie?"

"Yeah."

"And Nina?"

At first I was stunned he asked that, but then he quickly

added, "She seemed to know him pretty well, from the parish and all."

I lied. I told him the first lie I'd ever told him. "I'm not sure Nina even knows yet. She's been in bed all morning with the flu."

"Anyway, it's a shock. And Joy, how's she?"

"All broken up."

"Do you remember what I told you last night?"

My voice softened. "Yeah, and do you remember what I told you?"

"How could I forget?" He whispered so I could barely hear, "I love you."

"Me too," I said louder because Marta had just turned the volume up and *June is Bustin' Out all Over* was ricocheting through our rooms like air blasting out of a party balloon.

More than anything, I wanted to be close to Duke. Even though it was summer and he was probably wearing Bermuda shorts and a short-sleeved shirt, I imagined him in a huge quilted parka that he'd open against the cold and wrap around me. It must have been ninety degrees out, but I was shivering as if it were winter.

CHAPTER SIXTEEN

Joy called that afternoon to say she needed a bus ride, so I ran downstairs and waited for her at the front door. While I waited, Mr. Neuger, my dad's embalmer, pulled up and parked his lugubrious black Ford Fairlane at the curb. Mr. Neuger was a gentleman in his sixties; thin as a pipe cleaner, with an ashen face and sparse gray hair slicked straight back on his narrow head. The window on the passenger side was down and his spidery white fingers crept across the upholstery searching for something. He climbed out of the car, unwrapping a roll of Life Savers, tossed one into his mouth, stuck the roll in his pants pocket, and opened the trunk of his car. His black trousers hung on his frame and his white short-sleeved shirt needed a pressing. His skin was bone white, except for a suntanned triangle of his left arm, the arm he leaned out the car window when driving. He lugged his two black satchels of embalming equipment toward our door. I pulled open the door to help him in. He smelled like cherries.

"Ah, good afternoon, Ellie."

"Good afternoon, sir. Dad's in the back waiting for you."

He nodded and trudged into the dim funeral chapel, following the path toward the morgue that my dad had walked minutes ago. Dad passed me without even acknowledging my presence, and it wasn't because he didn't know I was there. When I said "hi," he just grumbled.

Long ago, Dad had told us when he knew the person he was burying, he sometimes went into the morgue before Mr. Neuger arrived, when the body was still as close to its natural state as possible, and he talked to it. "Sometimes I reminisce about old times. I tell the guy a story I forgot to tell him. Sometimes I tell him a joke. I know he can't hear me, but I have to believe he's listening." I'm sure Dad wasn't back there telling Father Ben a joke that day.

"Ah, the mortuary princesses," Charlie said as we boarded the Southport/Clark bus. "Long time no see."

"Afternoon, Charlie," I said.

"Why so sad, you two? Looks like you lost your best friend."

"Yeah, almost," Joy replied.

I wanted to be with Joy because she was in a bad way, but I was nervous about spending time with her. What if she sensed I was keeping something from her? What if I said something I shouldn't? I told myself to act normally. But what was normal when a priest died in your house having sex with your aunt, and you had a pretty good idea of what was happening and you did nothing?

Joy slid into our regular seat over the wheel well and wrapped her arms around her stomach looking like she just took a belly punch. I folded in after her. The skin beneath her bloodshot eyes was as sheer as tracing paper. "Not a cheery trip today," she said in a thin voice.

"Nope," I agreed, staring blankly out the window.

"Holy shit. I can't believe it. Father Ben is gone," she said, stressing every word.

I fished out a miniature packet of Kleenex from the pocket of my Bermuda shorts, offered her one, took one for myself, and set the cellophane pack on my bare knee. "Neither can I."

She blew her nose. "How's Nina doing?"

"I don't know." The lie again. "She's got the flu and I'm not sure she knows yet."

"Yeah. I didn't see her in church this morning." She looked me straight in the eye. "Crap. I think those two had a mutual admiration society. If only he wasn't a priest, I could have seen them together."

"Crap is right."

"Ya know, Ellie," she whispered, reaching for another tissue, "Father Ben never mentioned he had a heart problem, but then again, I shouldn't have expected him to tell me about his health. That's something old folks do with each other—complain about their bowels and bladders. But he wasn't old, dammit, he was thirty-five!" She crossed her knees and bobbed her foot the way she did when she was angry. "There's so much I wanted to know about him, but I guess I never will, and so much I wanted to say to him."

"Me too."

"He was like a father to me, excuse the pun, and now he's gone. What is it about me that takes men away? My father. Andy. Father Ben. They've all abandoned me. I must be cursed."

"You're not cursed," I said, patting her knee.

Joy had never known her own father, Michal Dusza. All she had of him was a sepia-toned portrait that she kept in a tan plastic frame beside her bed. In the photo Mr. Dusza was a young man, but his serious expression belied his youth. I knew Mr. Dusza had died in the war, but I didn't know the details until a month or so after her breakup with Andy when we were sitting on the edge of her bed, and she picked up the picture frame. She ran her finger over the glass and started talking about him.

"My dad was an accountant, but when the Germans invaded Poland, everything went crazy and he joined the Polish Underground."

"Was it dangerous?" I'd asked.

"Well, yeah," she said, looking at me like I was an idiot—a look I deserved. "He and Ma had to move from town to town where partisans sheltered them while he ran his secret missions."

"How did he die?"

Tears welled up in her eyes, and I was sorry I'd asked. "You don't have to tell me if you don't want to," I said.

"It's okay, Ellie. It happened long ago," she said, setting the framed picture back on the table. "One night we were in Kielce, a town near Kraków, and a troop of SS butchers stormed into our hiding place. Ma was pregnant with me . . . nine months pregnant . . . ready to deliver." I remember how Joy held a rounded palm inches in front of her stomach, and how her fingers tapped the air the way a pregnant woman taps her belly. "They were huddled in the dark under the stairs . . . behind a bunch of crates, beneath a wooden table. But the Nazis rammed through the wood, clubbed their way through the crates, and dragged them out. One Nazi bastard held a gun to Ma's stomach, and my dad dove in and another goddamn bastard shot him point blank in the chest. Then they took off, leaving my ma shrieking and going crazy."

"Oh my God, Joy!"

I didn't raise the subject of Joy's father again because I knew how much it hurt her to remember. But I thought about it a lot. Her father died for her. I also thought about Mrs. Dusza and how it had traumatized her. I understood then why she went nuts at my party. She would put herself between Joy and anyone who threatened her.

"The last time I saw Father Ben was two days before he left for Wisconsin. Joy sighed. "That was when I told him about the convent."

"What did he say?" I held my breath waiting for an answer, fearing he was like one of those priests or nuns who tried to entice us into their way of life. I thought of our English teacher, Sister Theodora, who we called Sister Teddy. You never wanted to look too pious in her presence, because if she saw any hint of a religious vocation in you, she'd pull you over to ask if you had a "little calling from God."

"He didn't say anything at first. We were sitting in the parlor of the rectory. There was this big crucifix on the wall, one of those realistic ones with Jesus' chin hanging into His chest. Finally, he said, 'being a nun means giving up a lot.'"

"He's right," I said.

We were quiet for a few minutes, both of us staring blankly out the window. I thought about all Joy would have to give up. Nuns were allowed only a few family visits a year and weren't allowed to go home for birthdays, anniversaries, even weddings. Only funerals. How could she want that?

"He said I've got to want to become a nun more than I want anything else in the world, and I've got to want it for longer than a week or a month. I've got to want it for a lifetime."

"A lifetime could be a long time," I said, thinking about some of the shriveled up nuns I've known who'd spent their final days doing exactly what they'd done for the past seventy years—fingering their rosary beads, praying for a world they weren't part of. "Is that what you want?"

"I want security."

"What about kids and a husband?"

"I can teach kids."

"Don't you want a husband?"

"Men are way too much trouble."

"Not all guys are like Andy."

"I don't want to hear his name."

"Are you sure Father Ben didn't over-influence you?" I asked gently.

Joy gave me an annoyed sigh.

"Well, I have the feeling he did. You two spent a lot of time together, so I'm thinking he might have."

"This is bullshit, Ellie. Andy's a creep and I don't want to talk about him, and Father Ben's dead, so don't criticize him. And no, he did not over-influence me. If anything, he tried to talk me out of it. He reminded me I'm only nineteen and said I should give it time before I decide. I think he was testing me."

"Maybe you should listen to him."

"I am listening," she sniffled. "If I could lead half the kind of life he's led, that would be good." She looked me in the eyes. "You know, Ellie, you're really bugging me now."

"I'm bugging you? Why didn't you tell me about the convent earlier?"

"You want to know? You really want to know, honestly?"

"Yeah."

"Because I knew you'd try to talk me out of it. I waited 'til I was sure. You mad?"

"Uh uh. I was yesterday, but I'm not today," which was the truth. How could I have been mad at Joy for not confiding in me when I was keeping the Holy Grail of secrets from her?

"Thanks, I don't want you to be mad at me."

"Okay, so we're friends?"

"Yeah."

"Good."

"Does your ma know about the convent?"

"Nope, and I'm not going to tell her for a while. She's going to crap! If there's anything in this life she wants more than a husband for herself, it's a good Polish Catholic husband for me so she can have good Polish Catholic grandchildren." Joy tapped her foot on the tire hump of the bus and said, emphasizing each word, "She's going to really crap!"

I chuckled.

"Maybe I won't tell her 'til a week before I leave," she said, half crying, half laughing.

"Yeah, there's a plan. I can just picture it." I spread my hands out in front of me, flattening the air with my palms and making this dramatic stuffing motion. "Your suitcase is wide open on the bed, and you're packing it full of jeans and tight sweaters they won't let you wear, and your ma's asking, 'Where you going, Joy?' and you're saying, 'I'm taking a trip. A long trip.'" I tapped Joy's knee three quick times. "What's that train from Chicago to Denver? The one Barney's grandparents took to Pike's Peak?"

"The Denver Zephyr?"

"Yeah. You'll tell her you're taking the Zephyr to heaven."

A minute ago we were crying and fighting. Now we were laughing so hard that heads in the front of the bus turned around. One old man winked, a few others begrudged us half-smiles, and there were a few smirkers in the group, which is just how life is.

Joy gulped too much air, snorted, and we both laughed.

"Hey, this is good, Ellie. He'd like to see us laughing."

She pressed her forehead into the window glass and lost herself in thought for a moment. Then she turned to me and started nodding her headstrong *I've-made-a-decision* nod. "You know, I'm going to cry my heart out for the next three days. Then I'm going to clean up my damn act and live in a way that would make him proud."

CHAPTER SEVENTEEN

Dad wasn't laughing when I got home. He'd just come upstairs from Nina's and was pacing between the kitchen and the family room. I leaned against the tiled wall and listened to his tirade.

"She's like a statue," he said to Mom who was thumbing tinfoil around the edges of a plastic container of food for Nina. "She won't talk about it. I said to her, I said, 'Janina, did your common sense fly out the window?' Talking to her is like talking to a wall." He paced. He waved his arms. "And him. We invite him into our home, fed him our food. What's that you cooked for him that night, Vera, filet mignon? A good cut of meat. And what does he do? He blasts through our family like a wrecking ball. How do you like that, Vera?"

"I know, Stan."

"I should have thrown him out on his keister."

"You didn't know, Stan. None of us did."

But I did.

The phone rang.

I hated that menacing ring and its intrusion. I wanted to

grab that phone and shout into the mouthpiece, "Don't bother us. Read the death notice if you want to know what's going on!" But instead, I picked up the receiver and answered in my practiced funeral home voice. "Good morning, Manikowski Funeral Home."

When I hung up, Mom gave me a sympathetic half-smile and Dad started in again. "This happened under my roof, and where was I?" he asked, stabbing his fingers into his chest like a fork. "If I didn't have this retinopathy problem, maybe I would have seen some clues? But these damn eyes don't work."

"I have eyes and I didn't see it, Stan," Mom said.

But I saw and I did nothing. I could have told Dad. He would have listened. But he also would have stormed downstairs and accused Nina of all kinds of things I wasn't a hundred percent sure she was guilty of. Instead I chose to trust Nina's judgment, to hope for the best.

"This damn family is going to hell in a hand basket!"

"Shh, Stanley, Marta's in the bedroom."

"Ah, she's got that music on so loud the stove could explode and she'd never hear. Isn't she too young for Elvis Presley?" He circled the table and did this little Elvis shift with his hips that on any other day would have been comical.

"When she sat in that pew staring at him up at the altar, didn't she get it? Didn't she see that he was forbidden fruit? Didn't it register with her that he took a vow to keep his pants on?"

Dad thought in waves of fixation. When a thought rolled in, it spun in his head like a whirlwind and flew out of his mouth. Then he simmered down—until he got going again.

Mom had had enough. She wiped a film of sweat off her forehead, glared at him and set her hands on her hips. She was wearing a mint green polyester housedress that hung lower on the right side when she tilted.

"Stan, he's a man and she's a woman. Not that it's okay or anything, but these things happen. Remember how Father Zimorovich ran off with the Mexican cook at the rectory? And how Helga What's-Her-Name, who worked the cash register at Continental Clothing, was out cavorting with some priest from St. John's? And how—"

"— Janina's not some cha cha cook. She's my sister. Those things don't happen under this roof," he said pointing at the light fixture on the ceiling. "My father would have packed her bags and tossed them on the sidewalk. She's lucky our dad's in his grave. He's probably spinning down there right now!"

I couldn't help but chuckle. The image of Grandpa Bronislaw spinning like a Vienna sausage on one of those cooking rollers they have at the confection stands of movie theaters flashed into my mind.

"It's not funny, Eleanor!" he snapped.

"Sorry, Dad." I didn't know what came over me.

One thing I did know was that Dad was never going to forgive Nina, and that for that one act she was always going to be the black sheep of the family. I thought of the conversation Nina and I'd had about limitations, and I knew that as long as Nina lived in this house my father would set some major limitations for her. He'd be watching her every move, and what he couldn't see with his eyes he'd invent in his mind.

Part of me hated Nina for what she'd done, but part of me felt sorry for her. No matter what, she was still Nina. All the love she showered on me, all the fun we had, all the sound advice she gave me—flashed through my mind. No.

There was no contest. On the scale of good and bad, the good outweighed the bad.

"I'm going downstairs," I announced, pushing myself up from the table.

Dad knocked his fist on the table with such force that an apple rolled out of the fruit bowl and fell to the floor. "You stay right here, young lady!" he barked.

I sat back down.

"Stanley, don't be so hard on her."

"She doesn't need to go downstairs. That's no place for her."

"Ellie, your father's right. Leave Nina be. Furthermore, she doesn't want to see anyone but me," Mom said in that superior tone of hers, as if she were Nina's great protector. She picked up the apple, wiped it in her housedress, and meticulously repositioned it in the fruit bowl.

I'd had enough. I headed toward our bedroom. When I opened the door, I was assaulted by the pounding rhythm of Chubby Checker. Marta was standing on a chair twisting her plump body in front of the dresser mirror, studying her moves. She caught me watching her and her cheeks flushed, but when I turned up the volume on her record player, her self-consciousness faded.

I threw myself across my bed, buried my face in the pillow part of my quilted bedspread and started to cry, muffling myself so Marta wouldn't hear. Was everyone nuts around here? Our house was full of crazy people with Father Ben lying dead on the first floor, Nina in quarantine on the second, and us acting like lunatics on the third. "Don't they know I have a life too," I cried into my pillow. "I don't care if he's dead. I don't give a shit. I just want to get out of here."

CHAPTER EIGHTEEN

The following afternoon I was sitting on the metal radiator cover in our front room staring out our window, when Father Ben's mother, Stella Borowczyk, arrived. She, her younger son and his family, and a cousin, had driven down from Wisconsin to view Father Ben's body before it would be transported to St. Casimir's where it would lie in state that evening.

A tall, suntanned man with blond hair, who appeared to be in his thirties, helped her out of the passenger seat of a bright blue Mercury station wagon. He buttoned his gray summer suit jacket. He was probably the cousin. It was two o'clock; they'd been on the road in that stifling car since after breakfast.

Mrs. Borowczyk was a buxom woman with close-cropped salt and pepper hair. She carried a boxy handbag that matched her practical shoes with stacked heels. She brushed the wrinkles out of her skirt and buttoned the black fitted jacket that accentuated her ample hips. Her lips were pursed, the muscles in her face constricted.

Another stockier, dark-haired man who resembled Father Ben helped a younger woman and two children out of the back seat. The children, both girls, were twins of about five. They were the same height, had the same blunt, no-nonsense haircuts, and were both wearing identical rainbow sherbet-colored dresses with full skirts, smocked bodices and bows tied around their waists, and patent leather Mary Janes, probably their Easter clothes. One girl wobbled from foot to foot as if she had to go to the bathroom. The other stared at the sky while her mother fluffed her skirt and dabbed a hankie on her cheek that she'd wet with her own saliva. The child appeared lost in her new surroundings, and I could hardly blame her. How frightening it must have been for a kid accustomed to the rolling green hills and pristine red barns of Wisconsin to be deposited in one of Chicago's busiest neighborhoods amidst brick buildings, bus exhaust, screeching breaks, car horns.

Dad and Mom were outside waiting for them. Mom had her arm around Dad's waist, guiding him unobtrusively. Dad hated being dependent, and it broke my heart to see him that way—the man who was always the leader being the follower. There were solemn introductions and nervous handshakes before they all moved under the awning, out of my field of vision into the funeral home.

I couldn't imagine what Nina was feeling, closed up in the crypt of her apartment. Nor could I imagine her not wanting to see me. No matter what, I still loved her. On a whim, I ran downstairs.

I wasn't sure what was going to happen. I didn't know what I was going to say when we met face to face, but I trusted that the right words would come. Perhaps we'd embrace;

perhaps we'd keep each other at arm's length. I didn't know. I turned the doorknob to her apartment, but the door was locked. I knocked, but there was no answer. I knocked harder and heard footsteps on the linoleum in her hallway, then the softer sound of slippers scuffling on her dining room carpet.

"Is that you, Vera?" she whispered in a voice as frail as the voice of a hundred-year-old woman.

"It's me, Ellie." My stomach was churning.

"Ellie, no."

"Can I come in?"

"No. Go away, please."

"Nina, I love you."

"I love you too, Ellie, but I can't now."

My heart sank. I didn't move and I didn't hear movement from her either. I imagined her standing on the other side of the door—with inches that could have been continents separating us—in her bathrobe and slippers, hollow-eyed, paralyzed by grief and shame. Maybe if I gave her time.

Coming from Dad's office downstairs, I heard the murmur of serious adult voices and then the lighter voices of children, who were unaware of the thicket of emotions into which they had been thrust.

When I heard the floor creak and Nina shuffling back toward her kitchen, I returned to our apartment.

"Change your clothes Ellie. We're going to church tonight. To the wake. We have to make an appearance." Mom had just put away the last plate after drying the supper dishes and was straightening the lace doily beneath a wicker basket of fruit on the center of the table.

"Is everything about appearances, Mom?"

We locked eyes. "Don't sass me, young lady."

"All you care about is that we look like a perfect family, everyone present and properly dressed. All you care about," I sputtered, "is that your *nice* fruit basket is centered perfectly on the table. You even shine up the lemons!" Anger, critical and ugly, rose up from inside of me. I could almost taste it in my mouth. I knew I'd crossed the line, but I didn't stop. "And Dad, all he cares about is this family's sacred reputation. Do you think a family decides to give us business because Marta and I are well mannered and perfect? I don't think so, Mother."

"It's not all about appearances," Mom snapped, brushing nonexistent crumbs off the flared skirt of her housedress. "If it was, do you think I'd be taking care of Nina the way I am? Do you think I'd be fixing special meals for your dad all these years, helping him control his diabetes?"

"Yes, you would be," I said weakly, turning my back on her.

"Then you don't know a thing. You're selfish, Ellie. The only person you think about is yourself. Your clothes. Your parties. Your trotting off to college. Your high-minded talk about the Peace Corps and saving the world. Don't you know that service begins at home?"

I pointed my finger at her. "I help you out around here, but you don't see it, Mom. I take wake duty downstairs. I drive Dad around. I order underwear for dead people. You never acknowledge what I do. You never say thank you. Did you ever think I have my own life? I don't think you've ever considered that. You want me to be a carbon copy of you, but I don't want to turn out like you. I want to go to college and do something important." I turned to walk away, but she grabbed my arm and spun me around. We stared at each other, matching and mirroring each other's rage. Her eyes teared up and she pressed her lips together. I'll never forget the pained look on her face, and although I had no desire to take my words back then, I'll always regret saying them. *I don't want to turn out like you.*

She shut her eyes to hold back the tears, but she didn't give an inch. "And, by the way, Eleanor, our family reputation is important . . . it's what puts food on our table. Just be glad your father's at church now and can't hear you because he'd put you in your place. Can't you see, young lady, circumstances have changed and you better get used to it. Now get yourself dressed and wear something appropriate."

Jerzy showed up at six-fifteen to take telephone duty while we went to church. I was leaning against the kitchen counter dressed in a tight sleeveless black dress with a three-inch red patent leather belt I'd buckled defiantly around my waist. "Not so good an evening, huh, Ellie?" He did a double take at the charcoal eyeliner I'd circled my eyes with, and at the clumpy layers of mascara I'd brushed on my lashes.

He was a conspirator and I refused to acknowledge him.

Mom appeared in the doorway, stuffing a perfectly pressed handkerchief with crocheted corners into her black clutch bag. She frowned at the sight of me.

"We'll be back after the rosary, Jerzy. There's some *nice* ice cream in the freezer. Neapolitan. Help yourself." Marta and I followed Mom down the stairs, Marta prancing like a fancy poodle; me plodding behind like a bulldog.

What should have been a summer evening of gaiety in our neighborhood, with people wearing Bermuda shorts and licking ice cream cones, turned into a grim pageant of sober souls trudging to church. The heat of the day had not dissipated. If anything, it had become more concentrated, settling into the aggregate of the concrete sidewalk. I felt the heat through the thin soles of my skinny too-high heels.

Halfway to the church, Suzie Siemianowski was selling red hots from a cart outside her cafe. A rotund woman, she had tied a white cotton bib apron so tightly over her chest that it flattened her bosom into a pillowy mound. When we walked past, she was slathering mustard the color of her hair on a line of red hots for a family returning from the wake. Although she was doing her job, she was not her jovial self—hawking hot dogs to passersby, chattering about Chicago politics, giving everyone a serving of lighthearted humor. *"Didya hear the one about?"* That night she was somberly going through the motions of plucking buns out of her steamer, plopping red hots inside them, slathering them with piccalilli, wrapping them in waxed paper. She made eye contact with Mom and lifted her plastic mustard bottle in salute. The aroma of steamy wieners and yeasty poppy seed buns was jarringly out of place with the heaviness of mourning in the air.

We cut through Kosciuszko Park where a softball game was in progress. A bat cracked and the crowd cried, "Run!" as the batter flung his bat aside and dashed to first base like the fate of the free world depended upon it, and then slid cleats first into second, kicking up a gritty blanket of dust. Spectators sprung up from the benches and shouted, "Safe!" adding still another contradiction to an evening where nothing felt safe.

Inside the vestibule of St. Casimir's, I inhaled the heavy churchy fragrance, the sum of generations of melted candle wax, varnish, and incense embedded within the pores of every wall, statue, and pew. The altar was ablaze with more candles than I could count. Dozens of beeswax tapers rose from the branches of ornate golden candelabras.

I followed Mom and Marta down the aisle, inside a long queue of mourners. There was no music. Only the sounds of footsteps slapping, shuffling along the marble floor, an occasional cough or sniffle, and the intermittent slam of a kneeler to the floor.

We inched forward and I could see the foot of Father Ben's casket. It was positioned between the Communion railing and the pews, beneath the dome featuring Thaddeus Zukotynski's *błękitny* sky. If Father Ben could have opened his eyes, he would have been staring right into it.

Dad and Uncle Bruno stood near the casket ushering people forward. Uncle Frank guided people away. They were the funeral directors—the ones who directed the orderly flow of traffic among people who, for the most part, needed direction when death made no sense at all. I wondered what were they were thinking as they stood guard over the body of the man whose secret they kept?

It was the bottoms of Father Ben's shoes I saw first—new, out-of-the-box shoes with no scuff marks that might suggest he walked the secular byways of this world. The toes of his shoes pointed straight up and the inside edges of the soles looked like they had been glued together. I followed his feet up to the hem of his black trousers, which I assumed wasn't the pair my parents found balled up on Nina's bedroom carpet. Draping over them just below his knees was the rounded edge of his vestment that rose past his folded hands and fingers entwined with dull black rosary beads. The rich moiré pattern on the vestment shimmered in the light of two additional candles that rose from elaborately carved golden candlesticks that flanked the casket. The inside of the casket lid was upholstered in tufted ivory satin. Attached to its center was a palm-sized gold crucifix with an elaborately carved image of the suffering Jesus.

It occurred to me that evening how completely Father Ben, who seemed so secular, was owned by the Catholic Church. The word vestment said it all. He was the church's investment. The church groomed him in Rome where they educated their finest; read him the vows of poverty, chastity, and obedience that he willingly accepted; and upon his death dressed him in his princely, priestly vestments. As part of the pact they'd made, he was theirs. He belonged to the church as much as the elaborate gold crucifix atop the altar, the ornamental chalice inside the tabernacle, the murals on the walls, the chandeliers, the rose windows. That night the church had, with its lavish display of ritual, made its final, undisputable claim on him.

I hesitated to look at his face, but I was standing directly above him and had no choice. His lips were sealed together in a straight pink line. His skin was powdery, the texture of pink flannel. Some people stepped past the casket quickly. Others loitered, gawked, and knelt.

As we rounded the casket, I spotted Father Ben's family in the front pew. I made eye contact with Mrs. Borowczyk and although she didn't know me, she offered me a tristful smile. She was cuddling a sleepy little girl on her lap, one of the twins I saw earlier. The child's eyelids were heavy, and a droopy Raggedy Ann doll was ready to slip from between her limp fingers. Mrs. Borowczyk's round silver-gray eyes— Father Ben's eyes—followed me as I passed. I was no different than she. We were both picking up our share of the pieces.

CHAPTER NINETEEN

⌐∽◯⌐

Tuesday was my first day of school as a senior.

Sister Mary Joseph, who had been principal of Holy Family for twenty years and had presided over the first day of school for as many Septembers, stood like an icon framed by the arch of the varnished double doors that were flung wide open, welcoming us. Bound by tradition, she made it a point to greet us by our first names. She wished us a "stellar academic year." She commented on the freshness of our navy blue gabardine uniforms, the shininess of our shoes, and on our suntans—which she did to demonstrate she was worldly and aware of such things. To me she said, "Welcome back Eleanor. Stop in the lavatory, my dear, and wipe off that makeup."

I didn't need more troubles, so I headed for the john.

Surprise registered on Sister's face when she saw the four of us—Donna, me, Joy and Millie—sitting on the sturdy maple bench outside her office, the bench where many a rule-breaker quivered awaiting discipline. How ridiculous we must have looked. Unintentionally, we had arranged ourselves by size: Donna, me, Joy and petite Millie. Joy had reconciled with Millie, which in my book was a major accomplishment in forgiveness. Of course, Millie had made forgiveness especially easy by telling us how Andy dumped her for another hot dish named Patrice who went to the public high school and according to Joy, "probably put out more," which, at the time, I didn't understand. Once you give it all away, how could you give more?

"Ladies, to what do we owe the honor?" With an imperious flick of her index finger Sister Mary Joseph motioned us into the sanctum of her office. She took quick, efficient steps that Joy in front of me mimicked. Ordinarily I would have laughed, but that day there was nothing to laugh at because Joy's imitation was sadly prophetic. Sister stepped behind her desk and slipped into a high-backed chair upholstered with paisley hopsacking. Neatly organized on her desk were stacks of papers, a black telephone, and a Blessed Virgin Mary coffee cup filled with freshly sharpened pencils, points aimed heavenward. She set her folded hands on the desk and stared at each of us in turn with pearly blue eyes. She had one of those clean, scrubbed, high-gloss nun faces that never aged. I tried to replace her image with Joy's, and the result gave me the heebie-jeebies.

"Ladies, what can I do for you? Have you a complaint already?"

"No Sister," we answered in unison.

"Sister please, we need time off for a funeral," Joy blurted. "Here's the obit to prove it, Sister." She handed the nun a clipping from the *Dziennik Chicagoski*, which she had carefully trimmed on four sides with the pinking shears she'd bought for sewing class when we were freshmen because she preferred zigzagged edges to straight ones. Sister lifted the reading glasses that hung on a chain around her neck, set them on the bridge of her nose, and began to read the Polish words. "Mercy me. The priest at St. Casimir's. I heard about this. It's unusual for such a young man to die."

She had no idea of how unusual. I imagined myself telling her the whole story. Sister Joseph couldn't get past the image of Nina and Father Ben sitting on our dimly lit hallway steps without fainting, much less hearing my account of his toiletry kit perched on top of the stack of towels in Nina's bathroom, which would literally have flipped her over the edge.

"Ladies, how are the four of you acquainted with Father Borowczyk?"

"He's was a friend of our family," I said.

"He was my confessor," Joy said with downcast eyes.

"He coached my little brother in basketball," Donna said.

"I went to a party with him once," Millie said stupidly.

Fortunately, Sister Mary Joseph had stopped listening after Joy. "How much time will you require, ladies?"

Joy moved to the edge of her chair. "We'll be back in time for lunch."

"Then Miss Dusza, you and your friends go, and ladies, say a prayer for me, will you? Thirty-five is much too young to die."

CHAPTER TWENTY

The main floor of the church was packed with people crowded into pews elbow to elbow. Jerzy, who had taken time off work to usher, greeted us somberly in the vestibule, and sent us up to the balcony. He was in his officious mode, suited in black, stroking his diagonally striped gray necktie. That day he smelled like soap and cologne. "There's room upstairs for ya girls. Ya watch yourselves climbing dem steps in dem heels," he said, not noticing that all four of us were wearing the regulation black flats we wore with our uniforms.

We took our seats in the second row of the balcony. Behind us, light filtered in through an enormous rose window, casting swirling patterns of scarlet, cobalt, and emerald upon our shoulders. Looking down into the somber sea of black dresses and suits below, my eye was drawn to Father Walenski who stood in the transept swinging an ornate golden censer of purifying incense around the casket. *Ka-clink. Ka-clink. Ka-clink.* I waited for the puffs of white smoke to disperse and for the spicy scent of myrrh to rise into the balcony.

I spotted Mom in a pew toward the front with Aunt

Maxine and Aunt Mary Louise. Jerzy strutted past them with latecomer Lydia hooked on his arm, towering over him in her spiky high heels. He negotiated a choice seat for her in an already overcrowded pew in front of my mother and aunts. He tapped the top of her hand and strutted off. A few minutes later he appeared again, this time escorting Nina, who slid into the pew beside Mom.

I recognized Nina's black hat. I was with her when she bought that hat, a satin headband covered with overlapping silk petals, with a short fishnet veil. The long-ago memory of Nina sitting in front of a white French provincial dresser in the millinery department of Marshall Field's came to mind. When the sales clerk had lowered the hat onto her head with the solemnity of a coronation, Nina raised her eyebrows and struck a haughty-lady pose that made me laugh. She rattled off all the reasons for not buying it—that it cost twenty dollars, that it was too extravagant, too avant-garde, that she'd never have a place to wear it—but she bought it anyway. We had such a gay afternoon shopping together. And then, a few months later, she wore the hat to Al's funeral.

"God," I mumbled.

"Shh," Donna said, leaning out from behind Joy. She fished in her oversized handbag, pulled out a jumbo box of Kleenex and passed it around. Joy took a few sheets and I passed the box to Millie who noisily pulled out enough tissues to supply everyone on the balcony. Donna, the goody-goody, shushed us again.

Throughout the service I couldn't take my eyes off Nina. My stare was so intense I wondered if she could feel it searing into her. How brave and stupid and brazen and courageous and shameless she was. I drew a mental circle around her, a red circle, a ring of fire. Then I drew the same circle around all the other people in church who knew the truth: Mom and Dad, Uncle Frank and Maxine, Uncle Bruno and Mary Louise, Father Walenski, Jerzy, and also Lydia because of pillow talk. Nina's circle blazed the brightest. I watched to see if the heat of it stung her, but she didn't flinch. She was a model of Requiem Mass etiquette, sitting and kneeling and standing straight-backed at the appropriate times.

From my aerie in the church balcony, I felt like a voyeur, a critic, a protective angel. I wanted to mourn, but I couldn't. Even when the a cappella choir sang the mellifluent *Panis Angelicus* I couldn't cry. Next to me Joy was honking; next to her Donna was sobbing out the Latin words, dabbing her eyes with a tissue; and to my right, Millie was weeping as if her own father had died. The *Panis Angelicus* was one of those moving songs that always made my skin tingle, made me feel the presence of God among us; but that day I felt empty. Everyone in the church but me seemed to be transfixed by its words and melody: *fit panis hominum; Dat panis coelicus figuris terminum: O res mirabilis!* What kind of person couldn't cry at the *Panis Angelicus*? Couldn't cry at a funeral?

I wanted everything to be right. But there was nothing I could do to make things right. The singing stopped. The echoes receded into the planes of stone, murals, and stained glass where they would remain locked forever. In the silence I imagined myself standing up and shouting out the truth, loud enough for the deafest ear to hear: "Father Ben Borowczyk died in Nina Krasznik's bed. Deal with him accordingly!" But I couldn't do that because certain truths are meant to remain secret forever.

CHAPTER TWENTY-ONE

*F*or most people a new year begins in January, but I'd always felt the swell of new beginnings in September. Part of it was conditioning: The new school year started then, accompanied by a new uniform, teachers, and textbooks smelling like ink and glue, fresh from the bindery. Also, my birthday is in September, which that year marked another milestone on my dubious path to adulthood.

Everyone in our family had been on their best behavior those days. Nina, with her heart and conscience in repair, was back working at the parish office. Dad had an appointment with Doctor Kowalski who confirmed that his proliferative retinopathy had taken its toll, that the buildup of scar tissue blocking his vision was permanent. This time Doctor Kowalski did use the word, blind.

Somehow we all knew what was coming so we braced ourselves for the worst. While Mom and I expected Dad to take the news hard, he surprised us by saying, "I knew it," in a breath of resignation at the dinner table that evening. "It didn't take Doc Kowalski to tell me what I already knew.

Anyway, I've got other things on my mind now."

As for Mom, she was back to her housecleaning and to being Dad's eyes. It had become a full time job for her.

The rest of the characters in the Manikowski drama were carrying on. Jerzy was Jerzy. Stoic and hardworking. Uncle Frank was back to being the consummate businessman, organized, unruffled, attentive to details. Uncle Bruno, the family storyteller, had returned to normal as well, having filed the Borowczyk incident away in his private chest of funeral anecdotes marked Confidential.

Each of us held memories of that night within the taut cellophane wrappers of our minds. Even then, from time to time the residue would squish out and Dad would resort to his old vitriol, "What was the guy, nuts?" But then, like a tired train chugging into the station, he'd sputter, "Heck, the past is the past, so we gotta leave it there. Ya can't unboil an onion, can ya?"

As for me, I was a high school senior by day and an undertaker's apprentice by night. More wake duty. More chauffeuring Dad in the limo, more funeral processions on Saturdays. More listening to other people's heartbreaking stories. More catering to their requests for Mass cards, chairs, holy pictures, toilet paper. "Yes, Mrs. Dombrowski . . . Of course, Mr. Rostenkowski . . . I'd be pleased to, Mr. Graczyk . . . I'll see that it gets done, Mrs. Plishka . . . I'll check with my father, Mrs. Jablonowski." Although the work was the same, my attitude had changed. I'd become short, impatient, and resentful.

Things came to a head when Mom suggested I enroll in a Polish language class at the *Klub Kultury* so I could be more conversant with our clientele. When I think back at that now, I wasted an opportunity. I should have jumped at the chance to learn another language, and Polish would have been a fine language to learn. But back then it felt like another entrapment in the life I longed to break out of. "It's an ugly language. People spit when they speak Polish," I remember telling her in a demeaning tone. "I want to learn Italian."

Everything was catching up with me.

As for Nina, since the day she dismissed me, I hadn't had the courage to visit her. We'd exchange pleasantries in passing. Sometimes we'd laugh. But it as nothing like it was before when I'd be down there all the time chatting about my love life, grabbing cookies from the blue tin in her pantry, pouring out all my secrets.

And Joy? Well, Joy was acting like she had a lobotomy. She was no longer sneaking out of class to smoke in the john. She gave up chasing guys and swearing (except for occasional lapses) and wearing gobs of makeup. And to boot, she joined the Sodality of the Blessed Virgin, an organization of holy-holy girls who she once would have deemed too saintly, too cheerful, too Catholic. If that wasn't enough, she was spending a nauseating amount of time in tête-à-têtes with Sister Teddy, the vocation maven, and all of it made me want to puke.

Trying to bolster my spirits, Mom suggested I invite a few friends for dinner for my eighteenth birthday. At first I objected because I was hardly in a party mood, but in the end I ended up going along with it.

I invited Duke, Joy and Barney, and Donna and her boyfriend, Mike Adamski. Mom had insisted we dine like adults at our dining room. She unfolded a hot pink tablecloth and set it with our fine china and stemware complete with wine glasses for sparkling cider. She pressed two ivory tapers into her treasured silver candlesticks and set them on either side of a silver bowl overflowing with white carnations.

Nina was also trying to regain my favor and had offered to bake a dessert. She asked my preference—fully expecting me to say, "chocolate birthday cake, please"— but I threw her a curve ball. "Napoleons, if it's not too much trouble," which, of course, it was. I was getting back at her.

On the evening of the party, my friends showed up with gifts. I greeted them at the door and managed to do the required squeezing of packages and shrieking over the festive gift-wrappings, but I was definitely not in my peak party mood. I felt like I was coming out of anesthesia— groggy, grumpy, not quite right. It didn't help that Mom had taken on the production of my party with the zest of a society matron planning a debutante ball. The instant she heard us squealing, she dashed to the stereo and turned on the Broadway production of *My Fair Lady*, and chirpy music that constituted her ideal of eighteenth birthday party perfection flittered through the rooms.

My friends scampered into the front room and plopped themselves on the sofa and side chairs that for the occasion were shorn of their protective plastic slipcovers.

"Ellie, open your presents," Donna cried.

"Hold everything!" Joy raised her hand. "I brought Ma's camera."

"Don't, Joy," I muttered.

"You're going to thank me fifty years from now." She held the camera at waist height and squinted through the viewfinder. "Smile, birthday girl. You look so pretty." *Click*.

I could imagine how I looked: A scowling girl wearing way too much foundation, blush, and eyeliner. Even makeup couldn't hide the foul mood I was in.

I forced a smile and opened my presents. Donna and Mike chipped in and bought me a hardbound copy of *To Kill a Mockingbird* signed by Harper Lee who was at Marshall Field's a week earlier autographing books. Duke gave me my favorite perfume, Youth Dew by Estee Lauder; and Joy and Barney put their screwball heads together and filled a shoebox with products intended for graceful aging: Fungi Rex for athlete's foot, dandruff treatment shampoo, cod liver oil, and a pair of support hose. I held up the support hose that unfolded from their cardboard and hung in front of my face like empty sausage casings.

Click. A flashbulb blasted a shot of light into my eyes. "Geeze, Joy, must you?" I groused.

"Ellieee," Duke whispered.

"Thanks, everyone," I said, trying to recover. I moved around the room passing out hugs. These were the people who meant the most to me, but all I wanted was for them to go home.

Mom served us appetizers on a silver tray. Cheez Whiz on sesame thins with julienne cuts of pimento, and Smoky Links on toothpicks with cellophane frizzies on their tops. She was wearing a pristine white organza apron over her black sheath. As she bent slightly in front of each of us, holding out the tray and offering us starched cocktail napkins from the stack she held beneath the tray, I noted how much she looked like a waitress at the Palmer House. I vowed again never to be like her, always catering to people, cleaning up their messes.

Dinner was prime rib on large china plates along with a leafy green salad, a fluffy spinach soufflé, and parkerhouse rolls. My friends were duly impressed. They unfolded their linen napkins on their laps, nervously eyed the assortment of silverware and crystal before them and held their spines rigid.

When Mom left, we all relaxed.

"This is like the Ritz," Barney said.

"Yeah, wouldn't it be great if we could fly to New York?" Donna chimed in.

"Considering I've only been to Wisconsin, New York would be an improvement," I said, hearing the whininess in my voice.

Duke wrinkled his brow. Everyone was watching me.

"Okay, guys," Donna chirped. "Our birthday girl has raised an interesting topic. How about if we go around the table and everyone tell the farthest place they've traveled." As class president Donna was used to being the boss. It didn't help that she looked spectacular in a brand new apricot sweater that showed off her creamy skin and her short black bob. It didn't help that she just got her application off to Northwestern. Tonight she was running my birthday party as if it were a meeting of the Student Council. "Joy, you go first."

Joy set her dinner fork diagonally on her plate. "No contest, guys. Before Chicago, I lived in Poland, Germany, and Buffalo. Top that!"

Our eyes connected across the white carnations and she cheerfully acknowledged my fake smile.

"Can you be more specific?" Donna was pushing it, and I was starting to think I wanted to punch her out cold.

"I was born in Poland, in Staszow, near Krakow," Joy continued. My dad was in the Polish Underground and we hid out in so many towns that even Ma doesn't remember their names. After the war, the Allies sent us to Trillkewerke, a displaced persons' camp in Hildesheim, not far from Hannover, Germany in the foothills of the Harz Mountains." Joy spit out the names of Polish and German towns like a native. "A cousin in Buffalo sponsored my *Ciocia* Danuta and Ma and me to America, and we sailed on a Liberty ship."

Donna cupped her chin in her palm and nodded as if she were listening to the most fascinating travelogue in the world. I'd heard Joy's story at least a dozen times and I wasn't interested in a replay.

All at once I was resenting Joy. While I was carrying around one sopping sandbag of a secret, she was bubbling around snapping photos and talking about World War II like the wartime reporter, Marguerite Higgins. It bugged me that she was proud of her heritage. It bugged me that she had suddenly dumped her dreary black clothes and was looking ravishing in a creamy ivory A-line. What kind of friend resented her best friend for looking great and for telling her story about immigrating to the United States after wartime atrocities? And what kind of daughter was so unappreciative of a mother trying to do her best? I felt like a jealous, selfish brat, but I couldn't control myself.

"How about you, Barney?" Donna asked.

Joy popped up from her chair, camera in hand, and found Barney in the viewfinder. "Don't mind me. Just keep talking."

"I haven't started yet." Barney winked at her. "Cleveland's the farthest I've been."

Click. Flash.

"How about you, big man?" Barney asked Duke.

"Wisconsin. Boy Scout camp three years in a row." He gave Joy a three-finger salute.

"Same here," Donna said. "Wisconsin. Counselor last summer at Camp Anokajig on Little Elkhart Lake near Glenbeulah." Joy ejected her old flashbulb and inserted a new one. Donna saw Joy aiming at her in the viewfinder. She lifted her chin and struck a pose of authority.

Click. Flash.

"And you, Ellie?"

"I told you already. Milwaukee."

Duke rolled his eyes.

"How about you, Mike?" Donna asked gently.

Mike Adamski was a hard guy to figure out. He was unsure of himself and seemed content to listen to the rest of us talk. I'd often wondered what Donna saw in him, but she said that someday he was going to come into his own, and we had to give him a chance.

"Paris," Mike said.

"Paris?" we said together, impressed.

"Yeah, Paris, Tennessee."

I gulped.

A flashbulb popped, but Mike didn't react.

"Tell them about it," Donna urged him on.

"You guys don't want to hear this."

"We do," we all said, sort of enthusiastically. Donna was nodding and encouraging him. She had a way of building confidence in people. Emboldened, Mike took a deep breath and began.

"A bunch of years ago we went to Tennessee to visit my dad's cousins. You think it's hot in Chicago in August, but it's hell down there. At a rest stop I went over to this water fountain, and I was bending over to take a drink when this fat white arm cut me off. The guy pointed to a sign above my head that said Colored. 'This here is where the Negroes drink.' Except, he didn't say Negroes. 'Your water's over there, white boy.'"

"My God!" Joy said, staring at the line of burnt out flash bulbs next to her dinner plate.

"You gotta see it to believe it. Down there everything's

separate—bathrooms, lunch counters, movie theatres—and what the colored people have is falling apart."

As we pierced the crusts of Nina's perfect napoleons and forked custard and drippy chocolate into our mouths, we discussed segregation, Rosa Parks's bravery in refusing to move to the back of the bus, and Martin Luther King leading marches in the South.

"When I get to Northwestern, I'm going to join SNICK," Donna said.

"SNICK?" we all asked.

"The Student Non-Violent Coordinating Committee. A protest group," Donna answered, because she knew everything.

"You're going to miss out," Barney said to Joy with a hangdog face.

"I don't think so," Joy laughed, passing him half her dessert, as if that was all it would take to make him feel better. "While you're out marching, I'll be praying for the world."

As we teased Joy, new layers of sadness built up inside me. On top of everything else, I realized that my time with her was running out. I sank into my chair, folded my arms across my chest, glowered at her. She was animated and full of life. Definitely not nun material.

"Why so glum, Ellie? What's the matter?" Joy asked from across the table.

"Nothing's the matter."

"You ought to see yourself."

"Mind your own business, Joy."

"You're mad because I'm leaving, aren't you?"

"I don't care if you go or not," I snapped.

Joy's smile faded and her eyes widened in disbelief. She

looked at me like a wounded swan. The chatter around the table stopped. Time stood still and silent. The judgment of ten eyes stung me, and I knew I was getting exactly what I deserved.

After everyone left and Duke and I were alone, I put an Elvis Presley album on the stereo. We necked a little, but my heart wasn't in it. My rotten behavior sat like a pile of dirty underwear between us, undiscussed and invisible.

To make matters worse, every fifteen minutes Dad came paddling down the hall to make his presence known. He poured himself a glass of water, crunched on a piece of celery, used the toilet, then moseyed into the family room and hung around looking goofy in his plaid bathrobe that was open just enough to show hairy legs rising out of tan socks and fur-lined felt slippers that had seen better days. He ignored my annoyed sighs and made small talk with Duke.

"Ya still swimming at the Y?"

"Ya think Roger Maris is going to tie the Babe's record?"

To his credit, Duke was polite and engaged him in conversation, but when Dad was out of earshot, he said, "Your dad's acting odd tonight, Ellie. Have you noticed?"

"He's driving me crazy," I groaned.

I slouched into the sofa. Duke didn't know the half of it. I was too embarrassed to tell him Dad had taken to patrolling the house at night. At least twice every evening he'd walk out of our flat and down the steps to the landing outside Nina's door where he'd linger. Then he'd go down to the chapel. He said he was checking on things.

"Maybe he doesn't trust me," Duke pondered out loud.

"He doesn't trust anyone."

Duke took a deep breath and put his glasses back on.

"Ellie," he said, looking at me, "We've got to talk. This is all about Joy going into the convent, right?" He put his arm around me, but I pulled away.

"No. Even though I think she's crazy."

"Then what's bugging you?" he asked.

I shrugged. "I don't know."

"Well, something is. You're changing right before my eyes. Look how you just pushed me away. You've been doing that since the beach party." His eyes appeared larger through the lenses of his glasses, and his stare bore into me.

"What are you looking at?"

"Just you, Ellie." He offered me a handkerchief.

I wiped my eyes behind my glasses and black streaks of mascara, eyeliner, rouge and flesh-colored foundation rubbed off onto the white cotton. Duke's gaze bounced between the Maybelline mess on my face and the streaks ground into the fibers of his handkerchief.

"I'm sick of everyone telling me what to think, what to feel, what to be, when to smile for the camera."

"I'm not telling you what to do."

"You're pressuring me for sex."

"Wait a minute, I'm pressuring you?" he said indignantly. "You were sure ready that night at the beach. If you remember, you're the one who went shopping for condoms. All summer you were giving me signals, and now look at you. You're acting like you don't even want us to be together."

"Well, maybe I don't."

Just then Dad came shuffling down the hall.

"I've had enough of this. I'm out of here," Duke whispered.

"Kids, what Mass are you going to in the morning?"

Neither of us answered. Duke pushed himself off the sofa and stomped toward the door, me tagging behind. Undaunted,

Dad opened and closed the refrigerator door and flicked the light above the kitchen sink on and off for our benefit.

When we were alone, Duke turned and faced me. The muscles in his face were taut and he spit out the words, "So what is it you want, Ellie?"

Thoughts piled up in my mind like out-of-control cars on black ice. Then a little voice poked up out of the wreckage: Be honest for a change. Speak your mind. I looked him square in the eyes and said, "I want some time to think about my life and I want to be alone."

His expression tottered between anger and rejection.

"Is that what you want? Is that what you really want?"

I nodded.

"You want to be alone?"

"For now I do."

"Then you've got it," he said, definitively. "And don't come running back until you figure yourself out."

"Duke, I didn't mean it."

"Ellie, you meant every word you said, just like you meant every word you said to Joy. You keep treating people this way and you're going to end up alone. One day you're hot. Then you're cold. You tell me you love me, and then you push me away like I don't count. Just remember that whatever you do or wherever you go, you're going to be taking yourself with you . . . your same screwed-up personality." He stuffed his hands in his pockets, turned his back on me and headed down the stairs. I watched him descend in jerky motions and disappear around the corner; I listened until his heavy footfalls become distant.

"Duke! I'm sorry. Don't leave that way."

"Happy birthday!" he shouted from the bottom of the stairs.

It all happened too quickly. Dumbstruck, I clutched the handrail and stared into the vacant air until the echo of his voice faded and the funeral home door slammed behind him.

That night I tossed and turned and flipped my pillow, trying to find a cool spot. My eyes burned and swelled with tears. I probably looked like a blobfish. But who cared? I didn't need to be pretty.

In the grainy darkness I traced the outline of my typewriter on my desk, its metal carriage centered above the keyboard, and above it the campaign button of Jackie pinned to my bulletin board.

Jackie'd understand. Her life hasn't been a perfect fruit basket. Her mother could be a pill. Her parents went through a contentious divorce that devastated her. Her father died of cancer. She's suffered miscarriages. What would she have said if she saw me wallowing in my puny pond of self-pity? She'd tell me to quit feeling sorry for myself. "Get back up on your feet. Forget what happened and move on. You're not a spineless amoeba." That's what Jackie would say—or something like it.

CHAPTER TWENTY-TWO

*T*hat year autumn encroached—not with the brilliant burst of color we'd see on wall calendars—but with horrendous rains that pelted our windows, and swirling winds that forced us to switch from sweaters to jackets to woolen coats within a week. The seasons seemed as impatient to move on as we were.

When I was a kid, autumn seemed to take its time, lingering like a comfortable guest. Those days, when Dad could drive, he'd pile us in the limo—Mom, Marta, me, Joy, Aunt Nina, and Uncle Al—and we'd head to the Forest Preserve to take in the change of color. Sometimes we'd drive up to Wisconsin, listening to the radio, swapping jokes, reading Burma-Shave signs as they revealed their slogans phrase by phrase every quarter of a mile or so. *"Don't pass cars/ On curve or hill/ If the cops don't get you/ The morticians will/ Burma-Shave."*

That autumn we spent our evenings occupied by the fall lineup of TV shows. NBC's new doctor programs, Doctor Kildare and Ben Casey, did nothing but remind me of Duke, who hadn't called since we broke up. Marta was all hepped up about Mr. Ed, a talking horse. Dad said he probably wasn't missing much and that Newton Minnow got it right when he called TV "the vast wasteland." He carried his transistor radio with him everywhere—it had become a plastic appendage linking him to the world.

October 1 was a banner day for Dad and Jerzy, when in the fourth inning against the Boston Red Sox, Roger Maris broke Babe Ruth's thirty-four-year-old record. Dad and Jerzy listened to Phil Rizzuto do the play by play: "Two balls, no strikes on Roger Maris. Here's the windup. Fastball, hit deep to right! This could be it! Way back there! Holy cow, he did it! Sixty-one for Maris!"

Aside from baseball Dad found a lot to complain about, and for the most part, I saw his point. Every other day you'd read about the Russians exploding nuclear tests in the Arctic Ocean. Then we countered with nuclear tests in Nevada, and President Kennedy told us to build fallout shelters to protect ourselves from atomic fallout in case of an attack by the Russians. "Bullshit," Dad said. "Then whatawegonnabe? One Nation Under Ground?"

During the past few months Mom had rarely criticized Jackie. I think she even admired her efforts to restore the White House. An article in the issue of *LIFE* that I left on the table was what turned her around.

That time I didn't say a word about politics, or Jackie, or the antiques she was unearthing from her "spelunking" missions, as she called them, in the White House basement. I didn't preach or try to convince her. I just left *LIFE* opened on the kitchen table. In one photo, Jackie was helping a workman hang a candelabrum on a wall. In another, she was lifting a cardboard box with printed block letters on the side that read, "Special cornish hen; frozen chicken; keep away from heat." That brown box did the trick. At the supper table Mom surprised me by saying, "Any first lady who can clean her own house is okay with me."

As for Nina, she was doing her penance. Not only was she baking me napoleons, but also she was babysitting Maxine's and Mary Louise's brood of ten at least every other weekend, spoon-feeding them butterscotch pudding, chasing after them like a zookeeper rounding up chimpanzees. Whenever we had wakes downstairs, she volunteered to help. But Dad always turned down her offer. "Ellcha's got it covered," he'd say.

Mom, of course, fussed over Nina like a solicitous handmaiden. Every evening before we sat down to dinner, she portioned out servings of meat, potatoes, vegetables, and a dessert for her, wrapped the plate in tin foil and carried it downstairs. And every evening Dad said the same thing: "Whatdoesshethinkthisis, room service at the Holiday Inn?"

Those days I stopped in and visited Nina, but I didn't share confidences with her. I'd never told her that Duke said he loved me, and I never told her why we broke up. A part of my life had come and gone without her knowing the details.

I still didn't know what I was feeling about Duke. Guilt? Definitely. Regret? Of course. Self-righteousness? Sometimes. I was a muddle of emotions. Several times I reached for the phone, but always I stopped myself at the last minute.

I remember clipping an article out of TIME and underlining a few lines where Jackie was talking about her teenage years. She talked about enjoying the parties and the dances in Newport, but she said she didn't want to spend the rest of her life there, married to any of the young men she grew up with. "I was just floundering," she said.

Maybe that's what I was doing—floundering.

Joy and I had patched things up, as I knew we would. We never stayed mad for long. I wanted to confide in her about Duke, and I knew she'd listen. But I also knew she'd agree with him about my moodiness and probe for the reasons. Then one thing would to lead to another, and because all my problems were tangled up like a skein of yarn a cat had gotten into, I couldn't risk it. At school, I even found myself turning corners to avoid Donna, feeling embarrassed and wondering what Duke had told her about me.

It took Dad until Thanksgiving to soften towards Nina. When we returned home from Uncle Bruno's and Aunt Mary Louise's—holding our overfed stomachs in our hands—he fell into his rocking chair, and in the bounteous spirit of the holiday declared his personal détente with Nina.

"Vera, it's time I forgive her."

"Yes, it is, Stanley."

"Everyone makes mistakes because we're human."

"So true." I was helping Mom stack containers of leftovers in the refrigerator, while Dad waxed sentimental.

"Ya know, I was sitting at that table with the family, smelling that turkey, and I'm thinking about Janina and all our Thanksgivings, and the tiffs we've had, how we all slip up from time to time, and how I can't let this thing with the hotpants priest come between me and Janina. I said to myself, 'Stanley Manikowski, you gotta remember that women have urges just like men, and Janina's womanly urges overcame her.' She made one mistake, and who am I to hold it against her? I gotta be bigger than that."

"That's right, Stan." Mom heaved a sigh of relief.

"So I've been thinking, Vera."

"Thinking what?"

"I've been thinking that Janina needs a man."

I was heading to the bathroom to take a bath, and I stopped in my tracks.

Mom dropped something. "Aw shit," she cursed.

"What was that, Vera?"

"Mashed potatoes I dropped."

"So I'll repeat myself, Vera. Janina needs a man. A healthy man with good years left on him . . . and not a priest . . . and I'm going to help her find one."

My mother whispered, "*Matka Boska*," Mother of God.

"They're just potatoes, Vera. Use a paper towel."

Mom was on her knees scooping up potatoes with her hands. "What am I supposed to do with him?" she whispered under her breath.

"Stop him. Somebody's got to," I whispered back.

She stood up and recovered her composure. "Stan, that's a thoughtful thing for you to say, and I know you have Nina's best interests at heart because that's the kind of well-meaning guy you are, but maybe you should let her find her own man."

"Very diplomatic," I whispered.

Mom furrowed her eyebrows. "Shh, Ellie."

"Heck, Vera, the last time she did that, look what happened?"

"It's too soon, Stan. Let her regain her footing."

"Vera, you're talking like she's a ballerina who slipped on the stage or something." He rocked in his chair faster. "Janina is sort of like a ballerina. But ballerinas can't dance forever. She's running out of time. How old is she now? Thirty-one?"

"Give it a rest, Stanley."

One afternoon in mid-December, Jerzy walked in and Dad called to him from his rocking chair. "Hey Jerz, I've got something to ask you man-to-man."

"Ask away, Stan." He plopped himself on the sofa across from Dad. He shook a Lucky Strike out of the pack in his shirt pocket, tapped it on his knee and lit it. Dad had forgotten I was there, and Jerzy didn't care.

"How'd you find Lydia, Jerz?"

"She found me," he said proudly.

"She's good at finding people then?"

"Yeah, Stan, but what's your point?"

"I'm looking for a man for Janina. I'm thinking maybe your Lydia has some old flames, some names in that address book of hers? All women have address books."

Jerzy took a few short puffs on his cigarette and squinted behind his eyeglasses. He got up and started to pace. "Aw, you're treadin' on some icy sidewalks dere, Stan. Ya tink I'm gunna go snooping through Lydia's personal belongings looking for old flames? Naw, I ain't one of dem guys who does that." He paced a little more. "Howdaya tink I'm gonna feel if I find some names? I'd feel like I'd want to kill dem guys, and I could be wrong about them. They might be da names of her plumber or that doc she goes to for female problems."

"I get it, Jerz." But then in his next breath Dad said, "Is her doctor married?"

"Cripe, Stan, I ain't gonna spy on Lydia or butt into her affairs."

"Jerz, I'm not asking you to do anything that's going to put you in the doghouse."

"I'll give you this much, Stan. I'll tink about it."

Later that week Dad got me to dial Marisol Wing's number, and when he got her on the line, he asked if she knew any single executives at WW Wagner who might be looking for an attractive wife. When she said no, he asked,

"How about widowers?"

Dad's own question gave him the brainstorm of all brainstorms. Suddenly he had the look on his face you get when you realize all seven of your Scrabble tiles make a word. He was Stanley Manikowski, a man with connections.

"Vera, go downstairs and bring up the funeral records from the past five years. If anyone should know how to find a widower, it's me."

"No, Stanley. You're not going to—"

"Get me those records. Read me off the names."

Mom had had enough. She was in the middle of sewing sequins on a Christmas tree skirt and she held a needle in her hand, which she perilously jabbed in the air. Five jabs. One for each word: "OVER. MY. DEAD. BODY. STANLEY."

I could have applauded.

Later that evening, I heard them arguing in their bedroom. "What do you have, a screw lose or something, Stan? That's a cockamamie idea." When Mom returned to the kitchen with victory in her stride, I was sure she had put the kibosh on Dad's ridiculous matchmaking scheme.

CHAPTER TWENTY-THREE

*I*n our neighborhood, on the day after Thanksgiving, it was like a shot went off and everyone started sprinting toward Christmas. Overnight, the arched lampposts were transformed into giant candy canes, the mannequins in the shop windows were surrounded by miniature trains that chugged smoking circles around their plaster feet, and the revolving doors of Wieboldt's were spinning with kids hurrying inside to visit Santa Claus.

In our funeral home, the only concession to the holidays was a tasteful arrangement of pinecones that Mom set atop Grandpa Bronislaw's Chippendale armoire. In the foyer of our other more spacious funeral home the decorations were more elaborate. In the huge picture window overlooking Milwaukee Avenue my uncles assembled a twelve-foot Evergleam aluminum tree with a red, green, yellow, and blue color wheel rotating beneath it. Beside the color wheel Aunt Maxine set up a Nativity scene complete with ceramic characters of the essential Jesus, Mary, and Joseph, a sizable flock of sheep, three wise men, and camels. Each year she reminded us that the figures were very expensive when she bought them on sale in the basement of Marshall Fields. "Two bucks apiece I paid for the people and camels, and a buck each for the sheep and Baby Jesus."

That year Maxine hosted our Christmas party in grand style with a ham and a turkey.

Joy and Wanda were supposed to have spent the holidays with Wanda's sister, Danuta, in South Bend, but because of a blizzard that hit Indiana they decided to stay in Chicago. So naturally, we invited them to our Christmas.

"Your family's a gift from the angels," Joy gushed into the telephone minutes after Mom called to invite them. "I'm glad we'll be spending Christmas with you. Ma is glad too."

"We're all glad," I said sincerely. I told her that Marisol Wing and her husband, Wally Wing, were going to be there, as well as Gertrude and Otto Saragusa, Maxine and Marisol's parents. Gertrude had worked keypunch at Wagner's before she retired.

"Swell! One big happy Wagner reunion," Joy said.

After Mass on Christmas day, we drove to Aunt Maxine's and Uncle Frank's with Nina at the wheel of the Cadillac. Jerzy and his kids were at Lydia's and there was no one available to stay and listen for the telephones. "We're going to risk it this year. If someone dies, they can figure things out and call us at the other place," Dad had announced.

Go for broke, Dad.

We walked in, our arms laden with Christmas gifts wrapped in shiny paper and stick-on bows. Aunt Maxine greeted us with two gigantic plastic antlers on her head that would have gouged the ceiling had her stiletto heels been a half-inch higher.

That year Maxine and Mary Louise got together on dressing the kids. The girls were wearing red velvet dresses, anklets cuffed with red lace, black patent leather Mary Janes, and red plastic barrettes clipped to the fine strands of their fresh Buster Brown haircuts. The boys were miniature men in their flannel trousers, plaid suit jackets and bow ties, already askew. They were all brandishing sticky candy canes that had been sucked to dangerous points.

We always began our Christmases with cocktails—Manhattans and Old Fashioneds premixed by Uncle Frank who funneled them back into old Jim Beam bottles so that when guests arrived, all he had to do was pour; and with *opłatki* which are Christmas wafers that taste like Communion, but are not consecrated. Our *opłatki* were pink wafers the size of a holiday card, embossed with the Nativity scene, that came three sheets to a package for a dollar at St. Casimir's.

Aunt Maxine flittered around on her stilettos distributing half a wafer to everyone. The Polish tradition is to make the rounds among the guests, break off a piece of each person's wafer, make a wish, then eat the chips to seal the deal. There are hugs and kisses, and sometimes tears because it's also a time when grievances are forgiven and grudges forgotten, at least for the remainder of the day.

Just as we were beginning, Joy pranced into the room carrying two highball glasses of what looked like grape soda.

"Mogen David," she whispered, handing me one. "Blackberry. Twenty per cent alcohol. I read the bottle."

"Good girl. We're going to need these."

Gertrude Saragusa was at the piano playing *kolendy*, traditional Polish Christmas carols. A large Slavic woman with a wide face, high cheekbones, and a braid of white hair coiled around the dome of her head, she was rocking on the bench, feeling the emotion of every note. Her black oxfords pumped the pedals. Her graceful arms raised and fell in the air, her wrists arched like a virtuoso's as she pinged the notes to *Lulajze Jezuniu*, a nostalgic lullaby to the Baby Jesus. It was a tender, simple tune, a delicate musical treasure. As a kid, I never understood why *kolendy* brought tears to adults' eyes, but that year with soft musical notes flooding the air, I found myself tearing up as well. I stared into the purple moiré of wine in my glass and took a gulp.

"We'll share later," Joy said quickly, waving her pink *opłatek* in the air. "Ma would kill me if she wasn't first." Her dark hair swayed like a postulant's veil as she dashed across the room toward her mother.

Dad was leaning against the wall, *opłatek* in hand, waiting for one of us to approach him. It was sad to see him waiting. Usually he was the first off the *opłatki* starting block, leaping toward us. Infused with family and tradition, Christmas was the biggest day of the year for him.

I wended through the crowd. "Hi Dad, want to exchange?"

"I'd be honored, Ellcha."

I snipped off three pieces of his wafer and wished him what I wished him every year: "Health . . . happiness . . . a long life." I gulped more wine. He wished me, "good grades . . . good friends . . . the best of luck when you go off to college."

"What?"

"College. When you go off to college."

My jaw dropped.

"I'm proud of you, Ellcha," he said softly. "For helping me out in the business, for keeping your grades up, for handling everything as best you could. And I'm sorry."

"Sorry for what?" I took his hand.

"You saw the worst of me this year." His eyes were tearing up.

"That's okay, Dad."

"When you leave home, remember the good times, will ya?"

"You mean I can go away?"

"Definitely. Just don't go too far away."

I was speechless.

"What are you drinking there?"

"Mogen David."

"Give me a sip, just a sip, will ya? Every once in a while I want to remember the taste of it." I held the glass up to his lips and he took the smallest amount a person could sip and still taste something. "Umm."

"Dad," I blurted. "I'd be glad to stay at home if it would help you out."

"Heck no, Ellcha. You go out into the world. What do you think we've been saving for? There are enough women in this house to keep me in line, and I can cope better than you think. Jerzy will take wake duty and he'll learn to drive." He pulled a handkerchief out of his trouser pocket and wiped his failed eyes.

"Really?"

"Your mom and I talked it over, and I talked some sense into her. I have to admit, for a while I had hopes that the business would click with you, but I know you better than you think. It wouldn't be a good environment for you, especially now after Father Ben. So it's settled."

"Dad," I said.

"What is it, Ellcha? You don't sound happy."

"Dad, I know I should be dancing around the room right

now, but—"

"—Then dance, honey."

The wine was muddling my thoughts and something that felt like obligation was gnawing at me—obligation deep as a birthmark. Maybe I'd been listening to my mother for so long. "Are you sure, Dad?"

"You've earned it, young lady. We want you to be the first girl in our family to go to college," he said, reaching his arms out for a hug. "You go and live your life. It's yours," he said.

Live your life. It's yours. I'll never forget those words.

"Okay," I whispered in his ear. "Thank you, Dad."

I started to pull away, but he held on to my hand. "But don't have too many experiences when you go out into the world, if you know what I mean, Ellcha. Stay away from those Beatniks. They're up to no good."

Mom was heading toward me waving her *opłatek.* "Ellie," she called. I gulped more wine to fortify myself.

I wrapped my arms around Mom and thanked her for going along with Dad. She said she was proud of me too. Then she cracked off about half of my wafer, but she wasn't really listening to me because Dad and Nina were a few feet away and we heard Dad say, "Janina, it's been a tough year for us both."

"I know, Stan." Nina chipped off pieces of his wafer. *Crack.* "I wish you peace of mind." *Crack.* "Patience." *Crack.* "Understanding."

Mom and I listened shamelessly.

"I wish you happiness, Janina, and . . ." *Crack* . . . "I pray you find a good man."

Nina's eyes opened wider. It was Dad's sly smile that I saw through the corner of my eye that started me worrying all over again. When he and Nina finished, Mom grabbed

Nina's elbow, mumbled something about Aunt Maxine's yummy Kaukauna Club cheese ball and moved her toward the appetizer table across the room.

For the next half hour, I exchanged *opłatki* with my aunts and uncles and sipped my Mogen David. Magically, when my glass was empty, Joy appeared with a refill.

"Our turn," she said, helping herself to the remainder of my wafer, by then the size of a Chicklet. "I hope you and Duke patch things up."

I took a big gulp of wine. "Fat chance. He's probably got a new girlfriend by now." All of a sudden, the reality of losing him me hit me like a boxer's wallop. "I know I asked for it," I said to Joy. "I told him I wanted time alone, but he went ahead and DUMPED me. And now you're leaving and I'm going to be alone."

"You'll be okay, Ellie."

"Look at those kids," I said. I flailed an unsteady arm at my cousins who were zigzagging across the room like red and green bumper cars. "Even though they're sticky and loud and in-cor-ri-gible little buggers, I do want kids like that, and you want kids like that, and I want us to have kids like that together."

"Sounds like you're proposing to me!"

"I am pro-pro-posing that you stay out of the convent."

"You're drunk," she said, wrapping her arms around me.

Suddenly, Marisol Wing popped up out of nowhere, an amber Manhattan with two maraschino cherries on stems swishing in her glass. "What *are* the two of you in cahoots about? You must be *plotting* something," she said, accentuating her verbs and waving an orange cheese cube on a toothpick in front of our noses.

"Ellie'd like to work at Wagners too, Mrs. Wing," Joy

said, releasing me. "In fact, she was just saying how much she'd love a job there after graduation."

"Bullshit," Marisol said. "What makes you think I'm going to *believe* that crap?" Marisol threw her head back and laughed so heartily that I could see her tonsils, two little balls bobbing up and down in the dark cove of her throat. "But if there's ever anything I can *do* for either of you when you *need* a real job someday, I'd be glad to *help* you out," she said, her eyes darting above my head. "Excuse me, girls, while I *find* my Wally!" She lifted herself up on tiptoes and waved across the room. "Over here, sugar!" she waved to a guy with a paunch and a red and green bow tie.

She clomped off and we both cracked up.

Back at home, walking up the stairs, Dad invited Nina to our flat for a nightcap. She pleaded exhaustion, but he talked her into it.

"I'm turning in," I said.

"Good. Sleep it off, Eleanor," Mom said.

"No, Ellcha. I want you here too," Dad said.

I collapsed into the chair kitty-corner from Nina with a Mogen David headache that had only worsened on the ride home. While Mom was in the kitchen pouring us drinks, I stared at the front window that was black except for the circle of miniature white lights blinking on the evergreen wreath beneath the window shade. I studied Dad's reflection in the glass. He was cheerful and animated, tightening his tie, squaring his shoulders, adjusting his gold cuff links that twinkled in the dark glass. For so late in the day, he seems to be just getting started.

"Put some music on, Vera," he called to Mom in the kitchen.

"Haven't you heard enough of that today?" she called back.

"I want this day to continue as long as it can. It's been a good day with the family and it's not over yet." Mom put on a Bing Crosby record and turned up the volume. A minute later she entered the front room carrying a silver tray of tall glasses filled with disgusting orange soda for the ladies and club soda for Dad.

Marta was sprawled out asleep on the sofa. Nina was stroking her hair and gazing down at her tenderly. I was headachy and dizzy and I wanted to throw up.

"Janina, how ya doing?" Dad asked jovially.

Nina looked up and yawned. "Fine, Stan. Just sleepy."

"Well, in that case, I won't dawdle. I have a surprise for you. The women here tell me it's a surprise you may not want, but I'm your big brother, and I know you best, and what I'm doing I'm doing for your own good."

Nina sat up in her chair.

Mom, who had taken a seat at Marta's feet, grimaced.

My eyes opened wider.

Dad continued, "I figure it's time you put the past aside, Janina, and get on with life."

"—Stanley!" my mother said.

"—Quiet, Vera, this is between Janina and me."

Nina's eyes were wide open.

"Janina, I've arranged for a date for you for tomorrow night."

"—Stanley!" my mother cried. She was squinting a warning at him.

"—Vera, don't censor me."

Nina had a look of horror on her face that Dad couldn't see.

There is so much he couldn't see.

"Janina," he said tenderly, "I've arranged for you to meet a fine gentleman named Peter Rumza. He owns Rumza's Windows in Park Ridge. Casements, double hungs, storm windows. He has a home of his own where he just finished remodeling his basement with a full bar and parquet dance floor."

Nina stopped stroking Marta's hair.

"He's a widower with three sons, and he's looking forward to meeting you. I sent him your picture." My father's crescent-shaped smile made his chunky cheeks puff and his eyes narrow. He was thoroughly delighted with himself, like a boy who had just assembled all the wooden poles, connectors, and windmill flaps of his Tinker Toy set and was standing back admiring his creation. "Stanley," Mom begged. She grabbed his elbow, but he moved away.

"Stanley, you did what?"

"Aw, your voice is cracking, Janina. I knew you'd be touched. This is no time for tears. A heartfelt thank you will do."

It was so embarrassing. I'd never believed Dad would go this far, and from the bug-eyed look on Mom's face, neither did she. All the while I thought he was downstairs checking on things, he was making phone calls from his office. He had trained himself to memorize the alphabetical/numerical coordinates on the telephone dial well enough to dial any number, and he probably enlisted the help of the operator to get the numbers of the gentlemen he wanted to reach.

I could hear it in my head. "Good evening, Peter. This is Stanley Manikowski . . . I was just thinking of you and thought I'd call to see how you're doing . . . Great . . . You still

in the window business? . . . How are the kids? . . . Great . . .
You haven't remarried, have you? . . . Well, I've been thinking
. . . Stop me if I'm off base on this, but I have this sister."

"He'll be picking you up tomorrow at six-thirty for
dinner."

Nina's face was bright red and her mouth was frozen
open.

"Well, there you have it," Dad chuckled.

There was no reply. Even though the windows were
closed, we could hear the steady stream of traffic whizzing
past our building, an occasional honk of a car, and the skid
of a vehicle as it hit a patch of ice and screeched to break.
Triangles of frost had built up in the corners of the windows,
and in the glass my father was framed like a photo in a
scrapbook. It was snowing outside, our first snowfall of the
season. We were in for a frigid winter.

"Janina, you're speechless!"

Nina was hugging her stomach. My mother moved beside
her. She slid her hand into Nina's and squeezed it.

"Nina, if you have other plans, tell me so I can call Peter
and reschedule. He's flexible. His oldest son is sixteen and
can watch the other boys, so he's covered on the home front.
I told him it's time he starts dating. His wife, Agnes, God
rest her soul, died of an aneurysm about four years ago . .
. left him with three little guys . . . we buried her from St.
Hedwigs. They used to live in the neighborhood in the flat
above her mother's, but Peter said that wasn't working out,
ya know, mother-in-law problems, and they had to leave."

Nina took a deep breath that I thought would go on
forever. *I'm Dreaming of a White Christmas* wafted in from
the family room and Marta was snoring. Nina stopped
stroking Marta's hair.

"Janina, you still there?"

"Yeah, Stan."

"Then say something."

Nina licked her lips and took another deep breath. "I can't go Stan."

"You can go, Nina," he pleaded. "I've thought about it. Ellcha's going to college. It's time for you to be getting out too. Everyone has to take the plunge into new territory some time."

"I'm plunging into new territory, Stanley. I'm pregnant."

My mother squeezed Nina's hand harder. She knew it all along.

The rest of us were stunned, except for Marta who was off in dreamland, which was a preferable land to be in then.

Of course it was Mom who broke the silence. "Nina, we're going to work this out."

Nina's high heels were lying on the floor where she kicked them off. In her stocking feet with her arms wrapped around her she looked as pathetic as *The Little Match Girl* in Hans Christian Andersen's Christmas story. "What are you looking at me that way for, Stan? I loved Ben and he died. Don't you get it? If anyone should know about loss, it should be you."

"Don't tell me about loss," Dad said, pulling a handkerchief out of his pocket and rubbing his eyes. "I've lost my eyesight. You've lost a priest you shouldn't have been with in the first place. And now you're having his baby. Holy cripe!"

Tears were flowing down Nina's cheeks and her hands were trembling and reaching in the air for something she couldn't quite grasp. "That's it. I've had enough. I'm leaving."

"Then leave, Janina. Go downstairs and hide out from the world."

"You don't get it, Stan. I'm moving out. Nina was

sniffling and stepping nervously in a small circle. She grabbed her shoes from the floor and headed toward the door. "I've had it," she shouted. Then she looked at me. "I'm sorry Ellie. I didn't know how to tell you." The door slammed and she was gone.

"Your sister has to find her own way, Stan," Mom said softly.

Dad was speechless. Within five minutes the boyish look of elation on his face had changed to bewilderment, to rage, and then to the haggard look you'd see on the face of an old man who had run out of dreams.

I stared into the empty space Nina left and then at the mahogany table in the dining room. In the middle of the table, on a white crocheted doily, sat a small pine tree with tiny red and green glass bulbs. My gaze fixed on the chair that Father Ben had sat on at dinner many months ago when he described the sculpture of Mary Magdalen in the Baptistry in Florence. Nina was the Mary Magdalen. Her face was like a melting candle; her waxy skin was sliding off her bones, puddling at her feet.

All I could think about was how Nina, whom I had confided in, who was like a big sister to me, had betrayed me; how everything the Church had taught me was a sham; how my head was throbbing. Tears swelled up behind my eyes. "She's having a priest's baby?" I shrieked.

I sprung out of my chair and ran to the bathroom clutching my stomach. Sickening sweet blackberry wine rose up in my throat.

CHAPTER TWENTY-FOUR

*T*he following morning, I got up before everyone else. I pulled on my jeans, a red mohair sweater, woolen socks, my car coat with the root-beer barrel buttons, and the multicolored hat and mittens Mrs. Dusza knitted for me. I tugged my fur-topped galoshes on over my saddle shoes and grabbed my black faux leather purse. Definitely, I didn't have the Jackie look down yet.

Mom met me at the door wearing the huge peacock blue bathrobe we gave her for Christmas. Actually, she'd bought it herself, wrapped it and put our names on the tag, which sounds crass, but that's what she had been doing for years. It was her practical way of avoiding exchanges.

"Where do you think you're going so early in this weather? It's been snowing all night." Her cheeks looked blotchy from crying.

"Out."

"Did you have breakfast?"

I shook my head.

She tied the thick terry cloth belt around her waist. "You shouldn't leave the house without a good breakfast. I'll fix you eggs. Scrambled. We have leftover *babka* from Maxine's."

"I can't eat." I waved her off.

"Then take a *nice* banana." She hustled to the kitchen and returned with an overripe banana.

I stuffed it into my purse. "See you later," I said, stomping out.

"Ellie, I'm going to worry about you," she called down the stairs.

I had no idea where I was going, but I definitely was going to be gone for a long time, or at least until my Christmas money ran out. Outside, I looked for a sign that might point me in the right direction—a gust of wind pushing me one way, a ray of sunshine beckoning me the other. But there were no signs. It was a dreary morning and I was on my own. Snowplows had shoveled the streets and dumped several feet of dirty snow alongside the curbs. Next door, the custodian at the *Klub Kultury*, a bareheaded man in floppy unbuckled rubber boots, was scraping the sidewalk in quick, sharp motions, tossing shovelfuls of snow onto the snow bank. Other shopkeepers down the line were also out shoveling. Together they created a walkable path toward Milwaukee Avenue, so that's where I headed.

At the corner I headed for the Super Cup where I'd been hiding out on Sunday mornings instead of going to church. Behind the picture window decorated with sickly pink Glass Wax stencils of Santas and reindeer, customers were hunched over chrome tables reading newspapers. I'd become an indiscriminate coffee drinker, and that day I needed to shake off my nasty hangover.

A new waitress in a starched yellow uniform with a nametag that said "Kasia" was working the counter. I climbed onto a cracked red vinyl stool where no one was sitting beside me. Kasia's over-bleached blond hair was so lacquered with hair spray that a pudgy pigeon could perch on top of it without her feeling it. Cheerful and efficient, she moved in quick steps juggling steaming plates of *kiełbasa*, eggs and coffee cake, bouncing from conversation to conversation, bantering in Polish and English with the short order cook working the grill and a lineup of patrons.

"Whatdayahave, *pani*?" Kasia addressed me like an old Polish woman.

"Coffee," I said joylessly.

"No *kiełbasa*?" she asked, offended. "Fresh today."

"No thanks."

"Ten cents," she said, pouring the coffee without looking. She knew exactly when to stop. Her attention was already on a new customer at the end of the counter. "Be witcha in a minute," she called over to the gent.

"*Dziękuje*," I said, speaking one of the dozen Polish words I knew.

I tipped her a nickel and reached for sugar and cream to mask the coffee's bitterness.

I picked up a *Chicago Sun Times* someone had left on the stool beside me. A train wreck in Italy had killed seventy people two days before Christmas. Adolph Eichmann was sentenced to die for his part in the Jewish holocaust. Fidel Castro agreed to release 1,113 prisoners from the failed Bay of Pigs Invasion for $62 million worth of food and medical supplies. Sadness had silenced Christmas for so many, but in my family no one had died and there was going to be a birth. So why was I wallowing around like a lost soul?

The traffic light at the intersection changed and I crossed the street. A green and ivory Milwaukee/Downtown bus was waiting at the bus stop with its door open. Through his side mirror, the driver saw me and waited.

I leapt over a snow bank, through a cloud of diesel exhaust, and hopped on the bus. The vehicle was nearly full. The day after Christmas was one of the busiest shopping days of the year.

A double seat in the middle was empty and I claimed it. The bus jerked, hissed and we were off. Heat was pumping in. I loosened my scarf and yanked off my mittens and woolen hat, feeling the tingle of static electricity that made my hair sizzle like Einstein's. The dry heat, the rhythmic motion of the bus, and the cadence of conversation, broken Polish, and then English the farther we got away from my neighborhood, lulled me to sleep.

I rested my head against the window, closed my eyes, and dozed.

Dreams are funny. The dream I dreamt on the bus that day seemed real, yet it was hazy and like most dreams, I could never reconstruct it exactly after waking up. In the passage of time I'm sure I've embellished it, but honest to God it went something like this:

A woman hops aboard the bus. She's wearing a fashionable beige coat with cloth buttons the size of vanilla cookies, and she's carrying a stack of Christmas presents wrapped in paper so reflective I had to squint.

The bus driver spins the steering wheel with one finger. It spins like a child's pinwheel and calliope music starts playing. The classy woman glides down the aisle and stops at my seat.

"May I sit hee-ah?" she asks in a soft New York accent.

"Most certainly. I'm Ellie Manikowski," I say, offering her my hand.

"I'm Jacque-lene Kennedy," she says in a deep Lauren Bacall voice. A pillbox sits cockeyed on top of her bouffant. Her handshake is light. Her nose is upturned and patrician, and the freckles on her cheeks glitter like gold dust. When she crosses her knees, I notice she is wearing multi-colored high-heeled bowling shoes that blink colors when she moves— red, green, yellow, and blue. She taps the packages on her lap with a gloved hand and whispers, "I've come to Chicago to drop these off at Sarge Shriver's. He's the director of the Peace Corps, you know. Foot powder."

"Oooh," I say.

"Enough of that. Tell me about yourself, Ellie."

"Mrs. Kennedy, I'm not great today."

"Call me Jacque-lene, si vous plait." Her brown eyes light up, her freckles sparkle, and I feel I could tell her anything. So I jump right in.

"Jacque-lene, I have this Aunt Nina . . ." I give her the full story about how Uncle Al kerplunked down the elevator shaft and how Nina was using only half her sheets, and how she slipped up and slept with Father Ben who died in her bed leaving her PG, and when I mention Mr. Rumza, the window salesman, I use the word, fenestration, to impress her because she's French.

"Heavens, that's quite a story," Jackie says. "And PG no less. I know it's against the rules, but didn't they ever consider condoms?"

Just then a parrot flies in through the window. It flaps its wings like a geisha fanning herself, and a woman who resembles Nikita Khrushchev in a bearlike fur hat snatches the parrot mid-air and hands it to Jackie.

"The poor thing must be simply devastated," Jackie says.

"I'm simply devastated too. I knew what was going on

between Nina and Father Ben, yet I didn't do a thing to stop it."

"Don't be hard on yourself, Ellie," she says, stroking the parrot's belly. You never know. Nina's flying the coop may be a blessing in disguise. Things change."

"I hope you're right. But Father Ben was a priest."

"Ha Ha Ha! He was a man, Ellie. That's how men are."

The Nikita Khrushchev lady turns around and smirks. Jackie leans forward, places both her hands firmly on the earflaps of the lady's fur hat, and centers her head. "Au revoir," she says, and POOF, the Khrushchev lady disappears.

The bus jerks and I lose track of what Jackie is saying.

The next thing you know, Jackie and I are flying over the rooftops of Chicago and I know it's her bowling shoes that are powering us because of the primary-colored vapor trails that puff out of her stiletto heels. We swoop over the playground of Kosciuszko Park and she looks at me and says, "May I ask you a personal question?"

"Jacque-lene, I'm not pregnant," I say.

"Oh, no, my dear, I did not mean to insinuate, for heaven's sakes. What I meant to ask is, do you have a beau?"

"I did, but we broke up. His name is David."

"Terribly strong name."

"We call him Duke."

"I adore nicknames. Jack for John, Duke for David. Why did you break up?"

"He dumped me."

"Oh, Ellie. He broke your heart."

"I had it coming. I was keeping secrets from him—you know, about Nina and Father Ben—and whenever I lied to him, I felt guilty, and I pushed him away."

"It's hard to live with lies, my dear, isn't it?"

"Yeah."

"And secrets."

Right there in the air I open my coat and show her my heart. A pulsing pink burlap sack. "This secret feels like I'm carrying sandbags inside my chest."

"Secrets feel like sandbags. Would you like to reconcile with your young man?"

"Yeah."

"Then stop being scared, Eleanor. Go to him. Tell him the truth, and listen to what he has to say."

Suddenly, I'm sitting in a makeup chair at the Hazel Bishop counter in Marshall Field's and a woman who looks like Joy, but her name is Lolly, is brushing powder on my cheeks and lining my eyes with a pointy black pencil. "This new lipstick, Peach-Me-Perfect, is absolutely transformative!" She's also breathing kiełbasa breath on my face. Jackie is perched on a stool beside me, the high heels of her bowling shoes hooked on a metal rung of the chair. "How do I look?" I ask Jackie. "FAN-tastic!" she says.

I look in the mirror and scream. My peachy lips are puffed up like smoky links and my eyes have thick black rings around them like corrections on two mistakes. Jackie guides me toward the ladies room to scrub them off. "I just said fantastic because I didn't want to embarrass Lolly, but all that makeup is not you. Always remember, Ellie, don't imitate me or anyone else. Be authentic, always use moisturizer, and buy yourself some contact lenses."

"End of the line, ladies and gents! Everybody off the bus," the driver called out.

I strained to open my eyes and tried to remember where I was. My neck had a crick in it and my head was resting on the raccoon collar of a heavyset woman with jowls like Khrushchev.

"You were out like a light, dearie. I thought I was going to have to give you a shake," she said with *kiełbasa* breath. She reached for her shopping bag and hoisted herself off the seat. I scooted out behind her. The trapezoids of sunshine beating in through the smudged bus windows were disorienting as I staggered down the aisle.

The brisk Chicago air woke me up. I joined ranks with the crowd and after marching some fifty feet, made an agile left turn under the landmark Marshall Field's clock, through a revolving door into the store. With the acumen of a practiced shopper, I wended my way through jewelry and gloves, through handbags and corsets to cosmetics. At the Hazel Bishop counter there was no Lolly, and sadly, no Jackie. I rode the escalator up to the second floor. I stepped off, rounded the corner and stepped onto another escalator, continuing up to the third floor, and just then a white-jacketed maintenance man pushing a cart heaped with the body parts of naked plaster mannequins—wigless heads, legs with arched shoeless feet, busty torsos—trudged past the escalator, and that's when I started to giggle. The lady on the escalator beside me glanced at me as if I were a nutcase, but I didn't care. Jackie had told me exactly what I needed to hear. "Thanks, Jackie," I said out loud, which caused the lady to clutch her clutchbag tighter and step down a step. I knew full well I was thanking myself, for wasn't I responsible for my own dream?

I knew exactly where I was heading. I got off on the fifth floor and marched into the book department where I found *Dr. Spock's Child and Baby Care*, which I picked up and didn't even thumb through because if you couldn't trust Dr.

Spock, who could you trust? On the cover was a photo of a bright-eyed baby propped up on its elbows, nestled in a fluffy white blanket. Hard to think we all started out that happy.

I asked the clerk to please put the book in a box and give me a receipt because I intended to have it giftwrapped on the main floor. I did the same in the Infant's department on six, where I purchased a lacy white christening gown and a matching lace-trimmed cap, small as a teacup. Downstairs in Giftwrap, a chatty clerk carefully folded several plies of white tissue paper around the book, wrapped the christening gown, and placed the whole regalia in a forest green Marshall Field's box.

"For a special someone?" she chirped.

"My aunt's having a baby."

The whole extravagance sets me back fifteen bucks, but it was worth it.

I headed back upstairs to the luggage department and stopped at a display of the most amazing luggage I'd had my eye on for myself, the most perfect luggage on earth, the Samsonite Silhouette in white. Hard shell. Rounded corners. Snap locks that receded into the top. I asked the clerk to put my giftwrapped box into the largest suitcase, a twenty-five incher—and wrap it up. Five minutes later I was back on the escalator carrying my jumbo treasure by a white handle that popped up through the cardboard box. Samsonite Silhouette was printed diagonally across the gigantic box, and I felt proud to be carrying a product of such quality.

On the way out of Marshall Field's, I stopped in the lobby and stared at a public telephone mounted on the wall. I set my suitcase down and stood frozen.

The night before, when Joy and I were staggering to the car, drunk, with our arms around each other for support, I finally broke down. "I just want to tell you . . . I just want to say, that all of this talk about wanting to be like Jackie Kennedy . . . well it's my in-se-cur-ity talking. If I try something big and fall on my face, I'll dis-appoint EVERYONE." Tears rolled down my cheeks and I was blubbering, "You're the only person I'd tell this to, Joy. I'm afraid of EVERYTHING. Now that I know I can go away to col-lege, I'm even afraid of that. If I go to Northwestern, the kids there are going to have more money and fancier clothes than I do. If I join the Peace Corps, I'll probably get scurvy and my bones will rot. Even if I got back together with Duke, I'd probably screw THAT up too."

Joy didn't laugh. She said she understood. "It's our age. Father Ben said so," she slurred back. "I think you should give the Duke a break and call him. You miss him and he probably misses you." That's when Aunt Nina opened the back door of the Cadillac, handed me her hankie, and gently eased us both inside.

Funny how Joy and Jackie said the same thing.

I stepped into the revolving door and spun around, but when the cold air hit me, I didn't exit. My humongous Samsonite and I spun around another time, and then I stepped back into the store's lobby. The phone was not in use—a good omen. Nervously, I dialed Duke's number. It was almost noon. He swam in the morning, but he should be home by now, I thought.

The phone rang twice and someone picked it up. In the half second it took for a voice to say hello, my stomach plunged as if I were on a rollercoaster.

"Dukaschewskis," Duke answered.

"Hi, it's Ellie." My voice came from a high place in my throat.

"This is unexpected."

"Merry Christmas."

"Likewise," he said flatly.

"May I come over?"

"I can barely hear you. Where are you, Ellie?"

"Crowd noise," I shouted. "I'm downtown and this Salvation Army guy is ringing his bell three feet away from me."

"You okay?"

"I'm fine. But I need to talk. Is it a good time?"

"Mom and Donna went to Wieboldt's for the sales and Dad's out shooting baskets with Danny in the gym. I guess you could come over."

CHAPTER TWENTY-FIVE

❧

I walked from the bus to Duke's on Huron Street, my stomach churning, my Samsonite knocking against my calf. Duke hadn't sounded friendly on the phone.

I was surprised to see him waiting in the hallway outside the door of their second-floor flat. The door was open and steam was rising from the spout of the stainless steel teakettle on their stove. The air smelled like chocolate and dry evergreen, which calmed me down a notch.

"I was watching for you out the window."

The Dukaschewskis lived on the top floor of a brick building they owned. After his grandparents died, they rented the first floor to a young couple just starting out, nice kids who both worked at Walgreens. In exchange for rent, Kenny, the husband, did odd jobs around the house. He was shoveling snow then and had a rhythm going, scraping the sidewalk, dumping, scraping, dumping. It was snowing softly and the new snow was laying a carpet as fine as tissue paper upon the path he had just shoveled.

My knees were shaking. I set the Samsonite on the floor.

Duke kept his distance, a good three feet away from me. He looked at my suitcase. "You leaving town? What, did you come to say goodbye?"

"Oh, this? It's not mine. I'll tell you about it later."

"Well, come on in." His face was rigid.

I tossed my coat, hat, and scarf on a chair and yanked off my galoshes and shoes, which brought instant relief to my aching feet. He pulled out a kitchen chair and I sat down and nervously started tracing my finger around the border of a Santa Claus face on the oilcloth table covering. Duke poured us cups of hot chocolate and set mine on top of Santa's goofy smile. He plopped into the chair across from me.

"So, what's up?"

"I want to clear the air."

He let my words hang. "What does that mean?"

"It means I've been keeping secrets from you and I need to come clean."

Every muscle in his face tensed up. "You're dating someone else, right?"

"No, nothing like that." My cup was trembling in my hand. "It's something else."

"What?"

I looked into my lap and at my stocking feet that were planted on the floor a foot away from his black high-tops, and I started at the beginning. I told him about Nina and Father Ben's affair, from my earliest suspicions to the events of that night, to the cover up.

He didn't take his eyes off me, nor did he register surprise. "It happened after the beach party? Why didn't you tell me?"

"I wanted to . . . you were the only one I could talk to. But my father made me promise not to tell anyone."

His eyes were wide and unblinking. I tried to read his

expression, but I couldn't. As much as I thought I knew him, he was a mystery to me. Two months had passed. He probably didn't want anything to do with me, and who could blame him?

"My God, Ellie, you poor thing," he said softly. Then in the next breath he said, "So, why are you telling me this now?"

"Because I realized that being secretive made me turn away from you. And at the same time you were encouraging me to go to college, Mom was calling me selfish for wanting to go, and Dad was acting goofy . . . you saw him. On top of it, we were this far from having sex," I said, holding almost no space between my thumb and index finger. "I didn't know how to handle it. I was taking all my frustrations out on you, and I just—"

"Bolted."

"I made you bolt. I'm sorry."

"I'm sorry too, Ellie."

"I'm sorry for not talking about things." I reached across the table for his hand. His eyes followed my hand, but he didn't take it.

"I love you, Duke."

"I love you too," he said flatly," but I have to be with someone who'll be honest with me so things don't go crazy like this."

"I will from now on, if you'll give me another chance."

His eyes meet mine. We stared through our glasses at each other, but still he didn't reach for my hand. I wanted him to forgive me. I wanted him to touch me.

"If you found someone else, I wouldn't blame you," I said.

"No. I'm not out looking." Finally, he slid his hand across the table and touched my fingertips. "Okay, so I've had a few dates, but I guess I was waiting for you."

I took a deep breath of relief and felt my eyes well up with tears. "I don't think I'm ready for sex. I'm scared."

Duke got up and walked behind me. He circled his arms around my chest and kissed the top of my head. "It's okay. We'll take our time."

I stared into the front room where the Dukaschewski's Christmas tree half filled the room. The lights, little bubbles with liquid that squiggled inside when warm, were turned off, but the sun softly entering the front room window behind the tree made the strands of tinsel flicker like icicles. Heat was pumping in through the radiators. Unwrapped toys and games surrounded the small ceramic Nativity scene beneath the tree. I stared at the infant in the manger and wondered how I was going to tell Duke the rest.

So I just said it. "Nina's pregnant."

He swallowed hard. "Wow!"

I nodded. "I'm sure my father wouldn't want me to be telling you, but heck, it's not something that's going to be a secret forever."

"Gosh. I know it's none of my business, Ellie, but is Father Ben—?"

"—It's Father Ben."

Duke's face registered sadness but not surprise.

"You're not shocked?"

"No."

"How come?"

"Because I'm putting two and two together. Remember the night we saw Nina and Father Ben on the steps talking? They looked pretty cozy. Then a few months later, my mom said she saw them downtown at Berghoffs having dinner. She said they looked chummy, drinking wine, laughing."

He saw my jaw drop. "Don't worry, Ellie, my folks aren't gossips. I didn't tell you then because I didn't want to worry you. You can understand that, can't you?"

"Of course."

"Nina said she's moving out. I don't want her to go, especially now, but heck, maybe it's time for her to be off on her own."

Duke swallowed again.

"So I bought her the luggage," I said.

His eyes softened behind his glasses. His hands squeezed my shoulders gently. "Just like you, Ellie." He walked me into the front room, turned on the Christmas tree lights, and we sunk into the sofa.

The couch had puffy cushions and side pillows to snuggle against. The pattern on the sofa was of pink and red roses, some buds, some open in full bloom, some singles, others in clusters. Magically, there were no thorns visible, just sleek smooth stems that never pricked. I felt protected on that flowery sofa, and I felt safe in the warmth of Duke's arms.

That afternoon in the Dukaschewski's apartment was really the turning point in our relationship. In thinking back, I learned a lot about honesty that day. I learned you couldn't have intimacy without it. A major secret's like a supercharged electric fence that separates you and the person you're keeping it from, and although the secret doesn't change, its sting becomes more intense. You can't talk honestly with that fence between you, zapping you with fresh currents of caution and guilt.

From that day on, Duke and I started talking about everything—sex, responsibility, college, and the possibility of being apart if I chose to leave home. We talked well into many a night about our goals and where they meshed or didn't mesh at all, about our fears of not being good enough, disappointing our parents, disappointing each other, disappointing ourselves. But we also talked about our dreams: of doing good in the world, of having children, of traveling, and how we wanted to do these things together. In opening our souls to each other we discovered a deeper love that connected us in ways we never thought possible.

We didn't always agree, not by a long shot.

One afternoon, sitting on that same rosy sofa in his living room, this time on a spring day with the windows wide open and the broad leaves of the oak tree out front brushing the screens, we had a serious talk about me leaving home. His arm was around me, and even though we were alone in his apartment we found ourselves whispering.

"I feel like there's something inside me that's scratching to get out," I said, looking up at him. "Maybe it's because I've been around the funeral business too long, but I know how fleeting life is and I want to cram everything into it, and I can't do that if I stay put. There's so much I'd be missing out on if I stayed in one place."

"Did you ever think that if you were somewhere else, you'd want to be somewhere else?"

"Well, maybe."

"Well, just think about it."

"I have a lot of goals inside me too," Duke said, "but I don't have to travel across the world to reach them. I'm different than you are, Ellie. I want to see the world as a tourist, but my work . . . I can do that right here." He gestured to the window. "I see people out there all the time who could use help and I don't have to go to Africa to do it."

You sound like my mother, I thought. But I didn't say it.

"I probably sound like your mother," he said, and we

both laughed.

"But she's not me, and you're not me," I said seriously.

We were quiet for a long time.

"What are you thinking?" I finally whispered.

"I'm thinking about what you said earlier . . . about not wanting to miss out on anything. Sometimes I think that I'm good enough for you for now, Ellie, but that eventually you're going to find some guy with a case of wanderlust and a fancy T-Bird, and I'm afraid I'm going to be left behind. I don't want that to happen."

I remember moving away and staring at him. I felt sad because he was sad. His feelings mattered to me. He was opening his heart to me in a way he hadn't before. He was telling me he was afraid, and his fears weren't something I could abuse or trivialize. My mouth must have been wide open. In addition to making himself vulnerable, he was making me think. He was really making me question myself. Is that what I was doing? I didn't think so, but if it was, it wasn't fair to him and I knew it.

"Am I right?" he asked.

"Ya never know what's going to happen," I said, truthfully. "That could happen. I guess anything could happen. Then again, you might find someone better than me right here in Chicago. I think about that too sometimes . . . I think about what if you stopped loving me. But I guess we've got to trust what we have now and hold on to it."

"Holding on to it might mean you staying right here," he said firmly.

"I don't think I can promise that, Duke."

I remember how we sat there staring at each other in troubled silence, how his arm slipped off my shoulders and settled on his knee, and then how—after we both had a chance to process the gumbo of thoughts swirling around in our minds—his arm found its way back across my shoulders. "Well, I guess I have no choice then," he said softly. "I guess you're going to do what you're going to do, and I'm going to do what I have to do, and we'll see what happens."

"It'll be fine, Duke," I said, knowing I sounded a lot like my mother.

"Just give me a kiss," he said, pulling me closer.

Those were our innocent days, when our love, disagreements, and plans were new, when we thought we were different than every other couple in love, when we felt sprinkled with gold dust and charmed with good fortune, when we believed we could overcome any obstacle, when we could word our way out of any hypothetical problem. It was easy to talk about compromises as long as we didn't have to make them—easy then to believe that our own little Camelot would last forever.

CHAPTER TWENTY-SIX

MAY 20, 1994

I stood up and stretched, walked over to Ranjit's taxi and peeked through the window he had cracked for air. He had loosened his tie and opened his shirt collar and was leaning against the inside of the door on the passenger side, his long legs stretched across the bench seat. He was still studying the heart, this time reading a page of dense text.

He was beginning his long journey.

I thought about the heart, that magical, life-giving pump made up of muscle tissue; that poetic center of what makes us human; that romantic keeper of love and loss. The heart. We protect it, break it, mend it, open it, lose it, trust it, deny it, change it, abandon it, soften it, romanticize it, paint it, draw it, cut it, glue it, fold it, give it away. We stress it, time it, race it, shock it, massage it, diagnose it, monitor it, bypass it, regulate it, replace it.

Just as I was walking off, he turned around and caught my eye. In a strange way—it might have been his intense concentration, or the set of his jaw, or how his dark eyes held the light—he reminded me of Duke.

"Do you mind if I take a little longer, Ranjit?" I laughed because I found myself whispering respectfully, as if I were in a library.

"Be my guest, lay-dee. I have all afternoon," he whispered back.

"You can call me Ellie," I said softly.

"El-eee," he repeated my name with a lilt in his voice that rekindled more memories, even sadder ones. There was a door in my life I seldom opened, and I was unprepared for the intensity and immediacy of my reaction to such a simple thing—hearing my name pronounced with that certain inflection. "El-eee."

He must have seen my face change.

"You okay, lay-dee, I mean Ellie?" This time he pronounced it with an American accent.

I bit my lip and nodded. "I'm just fine." I looked down at my wristwatch to hide the tears forming behind my eyelids. "It's two-thirty now, Ranjit. I know I'm taking a lot of your time. Are we still good?"

"We're excellent," he said, flashing his broad smile. "I've got to learn this stuff by next week," he said, flipping a page of his textbook. I smiled. "You'll learn it, believe me." But not by next week.

"By the way, Ranjit, why do you want to become a doctor?

"It's my duty to my family," he said. "My father is a physician. To him, a physician is good. Anything else, not so good."

"I completely understand," I said.

"Thanks for the Snickers, Ellie. Brain food," he chuckled, tapping his turban.

CHAPTER TWENTY-SEVEN

1961

*I*t was late that afternoon when I had returned home from Duke's. When I opened the weighty funeral home door, a sinking feeling gripped my stomach. I hadn't known what to expect.

Dad's office was bathed in warm light. I remember that there was a calm about the funeral parlor that was interrupted by two muted voices coming from the morgue in the back. Dad was there with Mr. Neuger. A black sign with white letters on the wall told me our new houseguest was Helen Dulski. It was always sad to see a new name on that board, another life ended, another baby grown as far as life would take it, and then the growing stopped.

I held my breath as I climbed the first flight of stairs. I tried to put myself in Nina's place. I imagined the shame she must have been feeling. If I were pregnant, I would have been terrified to tell my parents. I would have been seeing their disappointment in every nod and gesture, even in their acts of kindness. I was afraid for Nina. What had her day been like?

I imagined her sitting on her sofa staring into the air with my father harrumphing around her, spewing out his wrath, saying hateful things.

Nina's door faced me, as ominous as a mountain. I contemplated knocking, but that just didn't feel right, so I turned the knob and walked in. I left the Samsonite in her front room.

Her apartment was quiet. "Nina!" I called.

"Come on in, Ellie."

Nina was standing behind her ironing board, carefully pressing wrinkles out of a peach-colored blouse. The aluminum board squeaked with the push and pull of her iron. She looked up, and then down again, skillfully poking the tip of the steam iron between the buttons, pressing the Peter Pan collar into a perfect plane of smooth cotton. The iron hissed as she set it upright on the end of the board. She turned it off.

"Well, this is a surprise."

"It's been a while, hasn't it?"

"Yeah, and I thought it would be a while longer."

"I'm sorry, Nina. I've been a jerk. I just don't know how to handle this."

She smiled. "You're doing fine."

"I don't want you to leave, Nina. Are you still leaving?"

"Are you hungry?" she asked.

"Well, yeah, but don't go through any trouble."

"Tomato soup?"

"Thanks."

I sat down at the table. She stood over the stove, stirred the soup with a wooden spoon and poured it into a ceramic bowl. She unwrapped a fresh package of saltines and fanned them out on a plate. As she worked, I stared at the hardly detectable bulge beneath her wool sweater and tried to imagine the pink fetus learning to live inside of her. I thought of the many hours I'd spent as a kid at the Museum of Science and Industry staring wide-eyed at the display on human gestation that included graduating-sized jars that contained preserved specimens of embryos and fetuses, staged from conception until delivery. While those specimens were rather disturbing to look at because they came from pathology labs, the fetus inside Nina was pulsing with life. At four months gestation, her baby had a heartbeat of its own, fingers and toes that were more than nubbins, distinct physical characteristics, and a brain that would soon respond to the love or disapproval we chose to give it. I wondered if she'd felt movement yet.

Everything had changed. Everything was changing. As Nina worked, I imagined how empty our house would be without her. The floorboards creaked upstairs; Mom was hustling around in the kitchen. I'm sure that's how Mom felt about me wanting to leave home. Empty.

"I do plan to leave, Ellie. I've been thinking about it for a while now. I didn't intend for it to come out yesterday the way it did, but your Dad pushed me."

Nina slid into the chair across the table and reached for a cracker. "If I stay, I'll always be the wild card of the family, the unwed mother, the one who'll need watching. At work, with Father Walenski knowing what happened, I'd never be able to relax. It's best this way."

I slurped my soup and let her do the talking.

"Today was an emotional day. Your dad and I had a talk. This morning he came downstairs, sat down where you're sitting now . . ."

I set down my spoon, prepared for the worst.

She saw the look on my face. "It wasn't bad. He apologized and said he wanted me to stay, but if I needed to leave, he'd understand and he'd be glad to help me out."

I sat back in my chair, relieved. *Let's help her out.* I could hear Dad's words. That's the way he was. Many times when families in our neighborhood ran into tough times, my father would say, "Vera, we gotta help them out. Write them a check. . . . Slip them an envelope when you see them at Mass." *Help them out.*

"Then we drove over and told the family."

"My God! You didn't."

"It was the hardest thing I've ever had to do, Ellie."

"How did it go?"

Nina took a deep breath. "You know Maxine. She tittered and wrung her hands. She couldn't stop talking about options and alternatives and adoption and the girls she knew who had babies out of wedlock. Finally, Frank told her to shut up and she stomped off into the kitchen."

Nina reached for another paper napkin and blew her nose. "Mary Louise sat there with her jaw hanging down, cuddling little Sarah. And Frank and Bruno . . . you know them . . . they take their lead from your dad. Your dad was so kind. He said there's a lot of love in our family, enough for one more. Frank said that business is good and they could afford to help me out with whatever I need."

Nina took a deep breath. "Enough of that. So how was your day, Ellie?"

"You won't believe it." I told her about my dream, which made her laugh, especially the part about my makeover at the Hazel Bishop counter.

"I've been meaning to talk to you about that makeup, but Jackie beat me to it."

"Just a minute," I said. I ran into the front room, grabbed the luggage and carried it in.

"This is for you."

"For me?" Nina slid the suitcase out of the box and gushed over its features.

"Open it."

Fumbling with the green bow on the first Marshall Field's giftbox, Nina's watery blue eyes peered up at me. "By the way," she smiled impishly, "What was Jackie wearing?"

I laughed. "The same outfit she wore to the inauguration. The beige coat with the fur collar, the one with the big buttons, you know," I said making a circle with my fingers in front of my chest.

"Hah! She's no different than the rest of us. She buys an outfit for special, then, before you know it, she's wearing it for everyday . . . with her bowling shoes."

Nina got bleary eyed at the sight of the lacy christening gown, which she held up to admire. She laughed at the *Dr. Spock's Baby and Child Care* and said she'd sure need it, and in no time we were giggling and blubbering together—an emotional, hormonal bundle of tears and mangled paper napkins.

Just as I was ready to leave, I remembered there was something else I had to tell her. "Nina, you know Duke and I broke up, but you don't know the details. Anyway, you don't have to because we got back together again. He said he loves me."

"My God, I'm so happy for you. Your heart must be dancing, sweetie. Do you love him?"

"With all my heart."

She scurried around the table and hugged me.

CHAPTER TWENTY-EIGHT

1962

*I*n the serenity after the storm, our life at home had settled into a routine. Mom busied herself with taking down the Christmas decorations, which every year she made into a daylong production because she insisted on wrapping each ornament separately in its own fresh square of tissue paper, recycling every strand of tinsel, and coiling every strand of lights into a perfectly formed loop. Then she layered the whole shebang in a timeworn brown box marked "X-Mass Decs" that she ceremoniously carried upstairs into the attic to await the razzle-dazzle of next year.

On our first day back at school, we compared notes on how we spent New Year's Eve. That year I was able to report that Duke and I, and Joy and Barney, went bar hopping on Rush Street using the fake IDs that Barney and Joy had given us for Christmas. The two of them had scavenged through their families' various identification cards—expired drivers' licenses, insurance cards, even Joy's mother's membership card from the *Klub Kultury*—and artfully forged birth dates.

One bar turned us away, but the others let us in. When

we let loose dancing and downing beers—we each nursed three all evening—and screamed and hugged at midnight, not much else mattered than the four of us being together.

Once we were back at school and dipped our feet into the shallowest waters of 1962, it became clear to me that I had to seriously dig into my schoolwork. I had a mid-term paper on Carl Sandburg's poetry due by the middle of January, a paper that half my grade depended on. I'd been working on it in fits and starts and hadn't ventured deeper than Sandburg's most popular poem, *Chicago*, the "Hog Butcher for the World, Tool Maker, Stacker of Wheat . . . City of the Big Shoulders" poem that every Chicago kid can recite in her sleep.

After class one day, Sister Teddy, the vocation maven who was also our English teacher, had called me aside and suggested I read all of Sandburg's *Chicago Poems*. She said I might want to pay particular attention to one called *Mamie* because it was about a dissatisfied Chicago girl who was always looking for what was around the next corner. What I didn't tell the old busybody was that she might want to pay less attention to Joy, whose life she was royally screwing up those days.

The snow abated, so I decided to head to the public library to work on my paper.

As I dashed down the stairs, it occurred to me the poems I needed might be right under our roof in Nina's bookcase. Nina had a marvelous collection of books, especially when it came to literature and poetry.

I twisted the doorknob and walked right in. It was a huge relief to be able to visit Nina's again, unannounced, even when she wasn't home. That night she had gone to the rectory to tell Father Walenski she was resigning. I was sure the old priest would put the pieces together.

I flipped on the lights, first in the front room, and then in the kitchen, and then the overhead light in her family room that illuminated the floor-to-ceiling bookcase against the wall. There was an open box of Fannie May candy on the middle shelf and I helped myself to a piece and ate it in small bites as I cocked my head and scanned the spines of her eclectic collection: *Introduction to Logic*, which I questioned whether she'd read; and *The Spirit and the Flesh*, a novel based upon the life of Isadora Duncan, which I was sure she'd read. On the second shelf, next to *Fiction of the Fifties*, I found the book I was looking for: *Carl Sandburg, Chicago Poems*. There were about fifty-five poems I'd have to read. I slapped the book shut and slipped it under my arm. Just as I was about to leave, another book caught my eye. I turned my head sideways and read the title: *The Best Loved Poems of the American People*.

I flipped through the pages and an envelope fell to the floor. It was a thick white envelope the size of a Hallmark card. I bent down and turned it over. In a bold hand, written in pen and ink, it was addressed to Mrs. Janina Krasznik. The return address read: B. Borowczyk, 125 Hidden Lake Road, Green Lake, Wisc.

I should have done what was right—slip the envelope back into the book and put the book back where it came from, but I didn't. My shoes felt like gargantuan suction cups pinning me to the floor. I was conscious of my breathing and the white pressure spot in the center of my thumbnail on the corner of the envelope. After what seemed like an eternity, I stepped over to the floor lamp behind me. I pulled the beaded chain on the lamp and held the envelope in the crescent of light beneath the bulb. The postmark was a faint circle with

Aug. 26 stamped inside. Father Ben mailed it the week before he died.

I checked my wristwatch. I had at least a good hour of privacy. I lowered myself into Nina's reading chair and lifted the flap of the envelope. It was a letter. I counted six pages, written on both sides. No one condoned reading someone else's mail. But my curiosity overcame me and I read it anyway. In fact, I read it a dozen times, pretty much committing it to memory.

Thursday, August 24, 1961
My Dearest Nina,

Here I am violating our agreement not to call or write until I return from Green Lake, but I know you'll forgive me. It's a promise I can keep no more than pledging to hold my breath for a week or promising to keep my heart from beating. So here I am, at six o'clock in the morning sitting in the screened-in sun porch at Mom's, watching the blazing red sky turn golden, wanting desperately to hold you but knowing that before I have the right to do so, there is some unresolved business I must attend to.

All night long I've been writing this letter to you in my mind. I've been telling you all that's in my heart, even wondering if at the same time you were awake thinking of me. So at the first light of morning, I pulled on my Bermuda shorts and T-shirt, and dashed down to the kitchen to make coffee.

I'm sitting in an overstuffed wicker chaise lounge with a pad of paper propped up against my knees. In the spirit of full disclosure, let me also add that I'm drinking from a cup that says "Grandma Stella" in faded red script, and that I've just pulled a red, white, and blue afghan over my bare legs to ward off the morning chill. "Too much information," I can hear you saying. But I want to tell you everything.

Today begins my seventh day here. It's been a great week, if I can manage to have a great week without you. My brother Doug, and my cousin Steve and I are almost finished winterizing this sprawling old lake house for Mom. We've been scraping layers of paint off the clapboards, painting and installing new double-pane windows, replacing boards on the redwood deck outside this sun porch that has taken a beating from the seasons.

Although I had reservations about Mom living here full time—the isolation, the upkeep, she leaving her friends— I'm glad she sold the family house in Minneapolis. What's happened since is that others in the family are also feeling the gravitational pull of the lake. Even Steve is toying with the idea of moving his law practice to Green Lake as soon as he can convince his fiancé, Dolores, to leave St. Paul. He's the kind of guy who likes to keep things basic. Give him a grocery store and friends, a golf course and a good woman, and he's happy.

Lord, I love this place. Every room is full of memories. Even the sounds of the floorboards creaking remind me of the summers we had here as children, sneaking food out of the kitchen at night, listening for footfalls of Mom or Dad coming downstairs to tell us to pipe down. In the sun porch that surrounds the back and sides of the house are four square wooden tables (the size of card tables) that each have at least five coats of paint on them by now. They started out white, became yellow, then an ugly orange, and now they're pale blue, the color of the sky. Our summers have revolved around those tables. When we put them together we have one long table that stretches across the whole porch to accommodate the entire family, kids and all; when we separate them, they're perfect for Scrabble or Michigan Rummy. We don't have television and probably never will, if Mom has anything to say about it.

What I'm trying to say, darling Nina, is that I can hardly wait to bring you here to meet my family. I know they'll treasure you as much as I do.

Which brings me to the heart of the matter. I think I've known subconsciously from the start that I'd be leaving the priesthood to be with you. I knew it from our first meeting in the parish office. It was then that I began to see in you a wise and intelligent woman with whom I wanted to spend time. I was attracted to you, but I told myself, "Ben, you're a priest. Don't get involved." And, of course, you tried to discourage me by keeping our meetings all business. I even tried to deny my feelings, but like the still and deep water beneath the surface of the ocean, they lay there waiting to be ruffled. I felt the stir of them whenever I'd see you dashing across the schoolyard in those impossibly high heels. I felt drawn to you when you'd wave at me from behind your desk. Sometimes I'd hear you laughing with the parishioners who'd stop in and I'd want to be part of the fun, marveling at your ability to make everyone, including me, feel better in your presence. The truth is I had fallen in love with you, Nina.

Yet I was a priest, and as a priest I tried to keep my distance. I prayed for guidance. I meditated. Last week on my way up to Green Lake I stopped in Milwaukee to visit with Father Al Morrissey, a wise old priest who had been my mentor in the seminary. He is a person who would never be afraid to confront me if he felt I was heading in the wrong direction. So I poured out my story to him. He listened carefully, asked a few questions, and considered everything I *had to say. Then we prayed. He left me with a final thought: "Ben, did you ever consider that you are no longer meant to be a priest, and that the Lord is actually guiding you, not away from the Church, but toward Nina? Your faith in God and your love for Nina are not mutually exclusive." Suddenly, I felt as if a weight had been lifted from my shoulders, and at that moment, my path became luminously clear.*

Last evening after supper, Mom and I took a walk. There's a mile long gravel road that leads from our front door to the main road. It's sheltered on both sides by towering blue spruce that perfume the air with what must be the fragrance of heaven. There's a break between the trees that leads to a path that crosses a field overgrown with milkweed. I followed her onto this path. The flies and bees were buzzing. The gravel crunched beneath our sandals. The sparrows were chattering, desperate to get their last chirps out before darkness fell.

When I told Mom I was leaving the priesthood, a graceful starling swooped across the meadow and perched on a fencepost not far from us. He was bobbing his head in agreement, which made me chuckle. Then he flew away.

"Benedict, I just knew there was something on your mind. I sensed it all week," Mom said. "I knew you would tell me when the time was right." Then she asked, "Is there a woman?"

"There is," I told her.

"Then good, Ben, you won't be alone."

She was walking ahead of me. When she turned around, there were tears in her eyes.

"If you are giving up everything you've worked for, she must be a fine person."

"Mom, she's a treasure," I said. I told her about you and your family—about Stan and Vera and Ellie and little Marta—

and I don't think I stopped talking for twenty minutes. My mom, who has a particular fondness for daughters because she has raised only sons, was especially charmed by my description of Ellie. I borrowed your words: "A remarkable girl who's waiting in line, impatient to buy a plane ticket, destination unclear."

I pray that one of these days Mom will get to know you, Nina, and be able to lavish her attentions on you as well. I know one of the sadnesses in your life is having lost your mother when you were fifteen. My mother can never replace yours, but she's a good one to share.

Back to my story. The prairie path leads to an inlet of Green Lake and to another path that winds down to the beach. The two of us sat down on a fallen tree trunk and watched a rowboat of teenagers splash their way across the lake. In the gaiety of their laughter, we talked about the past and about my decision to enter the priesthood. Mom told me she never felt such loss as she did the afternoon I told her about the seminary. She said she wanted nothing more than to tell me to wait, to experience more of life first.

"Then why did you bite your tongue?" I asked her. "I thought you wanted me to become a priest."

"I didn't feel I had the right," she said. "I felt God has spoken to you and who was I to contradict Him? Would it have made a difference?"

"Probably not," I said, not really sure of my answer. As we continued our walk, I tried to remember what I felt like when I was eighteen. I guess I was like any other kid: set on doing exactly what I wanted to do and stubborn enough not to change my mind.

I told Mom that the past years were good ones and never would I take them back, and that the priesthood had given me more than I'd given in return—which is the truth. I've been privileged to share in parishioners' moments of great joy and deep sorrow, including birth, marriage, sickness, and death. I pray that in some other capacity I may continue to do so.

The practice of celibacy is another story. While I have a deep respect for men who can be celibate, it's a discipline I no longer choose for myself. I've been faithful to my vows for seventeen years. But through prayer and reflection I've concluded that I am not meant to be celibate, and that with you I must live my life honestly and fully. One day I'd like to see the Catholic Church allow priests to marry. But I know that's not going to happen for a long time.

I've written to the Superior General requesting dispensation from my vows. I mailed that letter yesterday, with a copy to Father Walenski who deserves to know my intentions. Yes, as you say, "he is an odd duck," but he has been kind to me and has been nothing but generous in allowing me to assume many of his responsibilities. There will be a waiting period, but after that time, my dearest, I am yours if you'll have me.

I cling to the memory of our talk after dinner a few weeks ago at the Como Inn, when we sat across from each other in the velvet curtained booth, when we both let down our defenses and spoke of our love for each other and our desire to spend the rest of our lives together. I look out into the stillness of Green Lake, and in the mist above the glassy water I can see your face as I saw it that evening illuminated by candlelight. Your right eyebrow was arched like an acute accent on a French word. Your lips were trembling as you spoke words that caused my heart to dance. Every night I fall asleep hearing you say the words you said then, "I love you,

Ben, and I will love you forever."

During the past week, work has been my savior. Wrapped up in the small tasks of pounding and lifting and painting, I've been able to let my mind wander into the nooks and crannies of thought. I was the producer of my very own MovieTone movie that reeled through my mind. Of course, you were my heroine and I created new unborn characters as well. When a motorboat zipped by pulling water skiers, I imagined us zipping through the water pulling our own children on skis, hearing their laughter. I imagined us all going to the Field Museum to see the dinosaurs, and I saw us eating French fries with catsup at McDonald's, and checking out store windows downtown at Christmas, and I imagined our kids playing the accordion. "Heavens, no, not that," I can hear you say.

After my mother and I returned from our walk last night, and after Marcie and the girls had gone to bed, I had a beer with Doug and Steve. Both of them were more than supportive of my decision; in fact, they were enthusiastic. Doug joked, "Now we can go to Sharkey's and have a Leinenkugel and I won't be feeling like I'm leading you into a den of iniquity." But Steve, the deeper thinker, was a lot more philosophical: "Hey, Ben, now you can sleep late on Sunday mornings like the rest of us."

After they went to bed I paged through some old photo albums, the kind with the brittle black pages and silver corners holding the photos. You would have laughed to see me then. In one photo, taken when I was twelve or thirteen, I was a scrawny kid with no shoulders, and hands and feet too big for my body, standing up in a rowboat behind Steve, who was at the oars shouting to me not to rock the boat. It seems like since the day I was born Steve has looked out for me like an older brother. There has always been an unexplainable bond between us. In another photo, taken when I was eighteen, I was standing outside our house with my mother and father the morning they dropped me off at the seminary. My mom and dad looked solemn; I looked sure of myself, even cocky. I was a posturing like a grown man. Today I realize how little I knew at eighteen.

Which reminds me, Nina, there is a young woman who wants to become a nun whom I need to talk to before you share any of this with your family, especially with Ellie. She's an impressionable, idealistic young woman who reminds me a lot of myself as a young man. I would like to spend some time alone with Ellie and Marta as well.

Well, my darling, the sun is a bright ivory ball now, hovering over the lake. A fishing boat is out already. A fishing rod is barely visible at its stern. I smell the aroma of bacon wafting in from the kitchen, hear it sizzling in the pan. Soon Mom will discover I'm out here and she'll join me. Then Steve and Doug and Marcie and the girls will trickle in. After breakfast Mom will put us to work. We have only three more double-pane windows to paint and install, a few more odd jobs to tackle, and then the house will be tight for many winters. Then I'll be coming home.

Home. For the past seventeen years my home has been a seminary or a parish, and after an absence, I've always returned there refreshed and eager to be back at work. But now, it's different, my dearest Nina. Now my home is with you. I have no doubt about this, no hesitancy whatsoever. I pray you have none either.

All my love,
Ben

CHAPTER TWENTY-NINE

I slid the letter back into the envelope.

Sitting in the shadows, listening to the steady hiss of steam entering through the baseboard registers, a hundred thoughts rushed through my mind. Father Ben loved Nina and was planning to leave the priesthood for her. He would have wanted the baby. Yes, he was a priest, but more importantly he was a man. A man with a heart full of courage and hope. And me, I was so busy judging them that I never considered that they might truly love each other.

God, what were you thinking? Couldn't you have passed over Father Ben? Couldn't you have let Nina be happy? I wondered if Nina had been in touch with the Borowczyks. I wondered if they knew about the baby. "Please Lord, protect Nina and her baby," I said out loud. "Keep us from judging her harshly."

I read the letter again and again, then folded it, tucked the envelope between the pages of the book, and wedged the book back into the shadowed sliver of space on the shelf where it belonged. I turned off the lights. I slipped off my coat and eased myself into Nina's chair. In the darkness I waited.

The sky outside the window was slate gray. Wispy membranes of silvery clouds glided into the frame, trailed by the curved edge of the moon, then the whole moon. Suspended in the sky, the moon was glorious at its distance of two hundred thirty-nine thousand, eight hundred and fifty-seven miles, a statistic Barney had taught me. Sweet Barney who had his mind in the heavens and his heart in Joy's hands.

Joy. What about Joy?

The clock on the wall ticked out the seconds. Nina would be home soon. I flicked the lamp back on because I didn't want to frighten her. The last thing Nina needed was to think some pervert with a pantyhose head was lurking in the shadows. I waited for her because I had no choice. Only a coward would run. I listened and waited to hear the metallic crank of the garage door opening, to hear her footsteps.

"Ellie!"

Nina was surprised to see me. Her voice was hoarse. Her cheeks were red and her lips were chapped from the wind. She probably wanted nothing more than solitude, a hot bath, and sleep. I should have waited until tomorrow, but I was afraid I'd have lost my courage by then.

"Hi Nina. How did it go?"

"Father Walenski thinks I should leave now." She lifted her eyes at me and her face registered concern. "Are you okay, Ellie? What's the matter?" She pulled her fur-lined leather gloves off, tossed them on the table and draped her tweed coat over the back of a chair. "You look like death warmed over," she said, studying my face. She knelt beside me and began to rub my hands that were knotted tightly on my lap.

Her fingers were ice cold. "What's the matter, sweetie? Did you have a fight with your mom?"

"No. Nothing like that." Every instinct pulsing through my body said, stand up and leave. But I couldn't leave.

"Nina—"

"What's the matter, sweetie?"

"Nina, you're going to kill me."

"Don't be silly. I'd never do that." Her voice was soothing.

"You might for what I did."

She's started to look nervous. "What did you do?"

I was seconds away from making the hardest confession I'd ever made. I felt the words rise to my tongue. Then they slipped back and I swallowed them. Finally, I looked straight into her eyes and from a high point in my throat I blurted out, "I read the letter. I didn't intend to. I was heading to the library to get p-p-poems by Carl Sandburg . . . but I thought you might have them and—"

"I see you found the book," she said looking in my lap. My fingers pressed onto Carl Sandburg's white flyaway hair on the photo on the cover.

"Yeah, but after I found it, I saw another book of poetry that looked in-in-interesting. I opened it, and the letter was inside. I didn't come down here to snoop, Nina, I didn't." I was blubbering and stuttering and leapfrogging over my words.

Nina wasn't smiling. "That was my private letter, Ellie. It's all I have left of him."

"I know. I'm sorry."

Nina took a deep breath and sighed. Her jaw was fixed. Illuminated by lamplight, her skin looked stretched and transparent. I had stripped her of her secrets.

"Nina?"

"What?"

"I shouldn't have read it."

Her eyes softened. "Oh, it's okay, Ellie. I know you didn't come down here to pry. It could have happened to anyone. If I were in your position, you never know, I might have read it too." Her voice was weary, resigned. She offered me the slightest smile, which made me feel even worse.

"His letter," she said more to herself than to me. "I read it again last night, probably for the hundredth time. I must know it by heart."

"I'm sorry."

"I shouldn't have left it in the book," she said shaking her head. "Ben gave me that book.

"If it's any consolation, the letter helped me understand."

"That night when you and Duke caught us sitting on the steps . . . that night, I wanted him to stay there with me forever. I wanted him to choose me rather than God, and I felt ashamed for wanting that. This may be my punishment."

"No, Nina, no."

"Anyway, now you know everything."

We were silent for a moment—she on her knees in front me like a penitent in a confessional, me bowing into her so our hair almost touched. I took her hand and squeezed it.

I told Nina I knew whom Father Ben was referring to when he wrote about having to talk to a young lady. "It was Joy. He was counseling her."

"I thought so."

I told her how much Father Ben had influenced Joy and how it was because of him that she was going into the convent. I told her how I wanted to stop her, but how I didn't have any right to. Then it occurred to me that maybe knowing Father Ben's decision to leave the priesthood might affect

Joy's decision. "Nina, we've got to tell her."

"I'll leave that up to you. You know Joy better than anyone else, except maybe Ben. So I'll leave it up to you."

Tears streamed down my cheeks. "I p-promise you one thing. Joy can keep confidences better than anyone I know."

Nina sat back on her legs and exhaled, like a rag doll slumped over.

I stood up and gave her my hand. "Why don't you get into your bathrobe while I run your bath water and fix you a cup of mint tea. Are you taking your vitamins?"

"By the handfuls," she sighed. "I'm eating them like popcorn."

CHAPTER THIRTY

I set Carl Sandburg's *Chicago Poems* aside for still another evening. Thank God that as far as academics went, I've always been at my best with a deadline, when my butt was close to the fire, when I could hear the guillotine blade rattling above my head. I was counting on that happening again.

After supper on Friday, I picked up the phone and dialed Joy.

"Hi, it's me. What are you doing?"

"Knitting."

"Good God, Joy." I pictured her knitting a black scarf for the convent or some thick black socks she could wear when the heat went off and her roommate opened the windows because she was having hot flashes.

"Ma's teaching me. Actually I'm doing pretty well. Wanna learn? She'll teach you too?"

"I'd like nothing more," I said sarcastically. "Then maybe the three of us could play some Lawrence Welk records and mix a pot of Ovaltine." I figured if I humiliated her I'd have a better chance of getting her out of the house. Shame had its place.

"Give me fifteen minutes. I'll meet you at your house."

"Sounds good."

That was easy. The next part would be hard.

I paid the fare for both of us.

"My idea. My treat," I said, leading her down the aisle of the bus.

Wouldn't you know, the bus was crowded. Polka dancers, whom I knew would be getting off at the Midnight Inn on Diversey Avenue, occupied almost every seat. You could tell they were polka dancers by the women's ribboned, starched skirts that practically took up a whole bus seat. Some of them were balancing Tupperware containers on their laps. Some were gripping baking dishes thumb-sealed with tin foil.

"What's with the food?" Joy asked no one in particular.

"Friday night. Polka Potluck!" a pretty young girl trilled in a Polish accent. A number of people smiled. The folks on the bus were jabbering among themselves, linked as they were by ribbons, crinolines, boutonnieres, happiness, and hot dishes.

In a seat on the right, I spotted Jerzy and Lydia. They must have gotten on at the stop near Lydia's house. Her starched crinoline was sticking out into the aisle and I made an effort not to smash it, with the bus jostling us. Some bus drivers like Charlie were conscientious of women carrying babies and casseroles, but the driver that evening, a young guy with a tattoo on his forearm, seemed not to care.

"Ellie! Long time no see!" Jerzy joked. Three hours ago he was over delivering our newspapers. Now he was all gussied up with a red carnation poking out of the buttonhole of his lapel, looking like Groucho Marx out on the town.

"Long time no see, Mr. Pilarski."

Lydia was gripping both edges of a tray of *mazurek*, a dense almond cake layered with preserves and topped with marzipan, candied orange peel, and drizzled with angelica. Already cut into squares, the confections were neatly lined up on a paper doily and protected under cellophane.

"Looks yummy," I said pointing at one with my pinkie.

"Good evening, Mr. Pilarski and Mrs. Wagodzinska." Politely, Joy didn't call Lydia "Miss," which was technically accurate, but would sound like she was rubbing it in that Lydia was a spinster. She also added the feminine "a" on the back of her name that she pronounced, Va-go-JEEN-ska.

"*Mazurek*. Help yourselves, girls," Lydia said, unfolding a corner of cellophane.

"Gee thanks," we said in unison. I slid a square out, took a bite and gave the rest to Joy. A whole piece would have been wasted on me, given my nervous stomach.

"Joy," Lydia said, "Tell your mom to come to the Polka Potlucks on Fridays. "She'd enjoy herself." Then she added in a voice loud enough to be heard three rows back. "You know, Gregory Duda's a good dancer and he's looking for a partner. Ain't that right, Gregory?" She turned around to face Mr. Duda. Gregory Duda was a stout man with a thick neck and a walrus mustache that hung like an awning over his lips. He was also a tad hard of hearing.

"I'm what?" he called back, cupping his hand over his ear.

"A good dancer! I said you're a good dancer!"

"I am," he shouted back.

"And you're looking for a partner!"

"Who ya got in mind?"

"Joy's mother, Wanda. Wanda Dusza needs to kick her heels up a little."

"Fine by me," he said a little flustered. "I'd kick up my heels with Wanda any day." Gregory Duda had been the head usher at our church as long as I can remember. There was gossip about him being a gambler.

"I'll tell my ma," Joy said sincerely.

The bus jerked and Joy fell into me, and it took all the agility I had to keep us from both tumbling into Lydia's lap. "Well, thanks for the *mazurek*, Mrs. Wagodzinska, and the invitation for my ma, Mr. Duda." She gave them a finger wave. "I'll tell her about the opportunity."

"You do that, young lady." Mr. Duda was beaming with the rest of them.

I remember thinking about how love in one's life, or even the promise of it could brighten one's spirits.

The polka dancers got off at Diversey Avenue. Through the window we watched them laughing and hanging on to each other—trying not to slip on the icy sidewalk, struggling to keep their trays and Tupperware containers upright. Above them the garish marquee of the Midnight Inn, which used to be a movie theater, glowed in eye-popping neon. The crooked black letters on the marquee read, "Every Fri. Nite: Polka Pot Luck, 8 p.m."

Joy and I made our way to the back of the bus and scooted into our usual seats. The bus pulled back into traffic and my stomach tightened. The polka dancers had been a distraction; now the silence was painful. I felt like I was tottering on the edge of a high diving board and the only way down was to jump.

"Joy?" I said seriously.

"Ellie?" she laughed.

"No really Joy, I've got to tell you something important, but first I have to say something. You know I don't want you to go into the convent."

"I know."

"But you also have to know if you do it, I'll miss you every day."

"I know Ellie. But it's still a long way off. Let's just enjoy the moment, okay?"

Then she got introspective on me. "Ever since Father Ben died, I realize how important every moment is. Once, he tried to tell me this. I was sitting across the table from him in his office, and I was wishing out loud for time to pass so I could get over Andy, so I could get a better job, so Ma would stop nagging me, so I could graduate and go into the convent where I wouldn't have to worry about being loved because in the convent God would always love me. Father Ben shook his head and said that that was a fallacy because . . . because . . ." Her voice trailed off and she gulped a breath of air.

"Because why?" I asked.

"Because God's always going to love me no matter what I do in the future," she said quickly, with embarrassment. "And then, bingo!" she snapped her fingers. "He goes and dies in his sleep, and he's the one without a future." She looked me in the eye. "So what have you got to tell me?"

"I'm going to tell you something in the strictest of confidences, Joy, because I think it's something you should know."

"Ellie, I never tell any of your secrets."

"I know. But still, you have to promise."

"Okay, okay, I promise."

My voice caught in my throat. "Nina and Father Ben were having an affair." I said softly.

"What?"

"Remember that phone call I told you about . . . on Inauguration Day?"

"Yeah."

"She was talking to him."

"No."

"It's true. But it wasn't what you think."

"Oh yeah, right!"

"He was in love with her and she was in love with him."

Joy's eyes widened. I wanted more than anything to stop right there, but I couldn't.

"And she's pregnant. It's Father Ben's baby," I said, hearing my voice break.

"What?"

In that split second, in the time it took for the information to register, I could feel the spirit drain out of Joy.

"Not Father Ben. Nina's lying," Joy said.

"No, it's the truth." Then I told her everything—about my suspicions early on, about how I didn't tell her because I knew how she admired him, about the horrible night when Father Ben died and how he died, about the letter, about how he wrote it a week before he died and then how he came back and they made love for the first time.

"He was planning to leave the priesthood to marry her. He had written for dispensation from his vows. In the letter, he said there was a young woman he needed to talk to before anyone else found out. That woman was you."

"Now wasn't that considerate!" she said sarcastically. "The guy was having an affair with Nina, and he knocks her up and he wanted to tell me."

"I know. I know."

It would take time for Joy to understand. For me, all this had unfolded like a seven course meal eaten over a long evening; for Joy, the news was like force feeding her five pounds of *kiełbasa* on a fifteen-minute lunch break. So, I tried to remember everything Father Ben wrote in that letter and to repeat it using his words. As I spoke—as gently and lovingly as I could, emulating the way Aunt Nina spoke to me—I noticed Joy inching away from me on the bus seat, which I understood. She looked stiff and gray, as if someone had poured cement into the shell of her body and it was hardening.

We rode in silence, Joy not moving a muscle, me staring through the bus window at the rooftops of the Fords, Chevies, and Dodges passing us. Occasionally, I made eye contact with a person in a passenger seat who looked up as I looked down. My usual behavior would have been to smile and wave, but that evening I didn't have it in me.

Joy jolted me back into reality. "I had an appointment with Father Ben on the Wednesday after he died. I wonder if he was going to tell me?"

"Probably." Then I asked, "If he had told you about leaving the priesthood for Nina, what would you have said?"

"Ellie, if he told me exactly what you told me tonight, I would have understood. Really."

"Then what's so different now?"

She closed her eyes. "Because he's dead. I'm ticked off he died, dammit. He was in love. They made a baby. What kind of God would let that happen?"

"That I can't begin to answer."

I wanted to give Joy privacy, so I stared at the snowflakes splattering against the bus window, melting and stretching oblong tears on the glass. Only once I glanced at her hands folded on her lap and at her profile, which seemed to be getting more beautiful every day—another cruel joke for someone who was going to a place where looks didn't matter.

At the end of the line, I followed Joy down the aisle and out the door. The bus door shut with a pneumatic *whoosh*, sending us into the cold. We stood alone on the sidewalk; neither of us ready to move. The bus accelerated, kicked up slush and pulled away, belching gaseous clouds of diesel exhaust into the air around our legs. The rectangular yellow lights of the bus windows grew smaller, and we would have been standing in the dark were it not for the overhead streetlights beaming cones of white light upon us.

Across Milwaukee Avenue were a row of commercial storefronts: A vacant Christmas tree lot with a For Lease sign tacked on the chain-linked fence fronting it; the Milwaukee Devon Put-Put, boarded up for winter; and the End of the Liner Diner with a red neon sign blinking, Open-Open-Open.

The bus driver headed a half-block farther, swerved into a turnabout and parked. When he flipped the lights off, it looked like the bus had disappeared. Seconds later, the driver jaywalked diagonally across the street toward the cafe. Earlier he seemed insensitive, but now with the wind pushing at his back and his black busman's shoes clomping through the slush, he seemed vulnerable. I tried to remember his face, but I hadn't taken a close enough look when we boarded. All of a sudden, it was important that I knew. He was a man inside that CTA uniform, perhaps a father with responsibilities, a student working for tuition money, or another lost soul trying to find his way. One thing I knew for sure was that he was more than I could see of him; more than my snap judgments had made him out to be. Weren't we all that way?

"Hungry?" I asked.

"Nope."

"Cold?"

"Hell yeah," she said, sliding her hands into her coat pockets.

"Me too."

What finally got us moving was the sight of the bus driver, clutching a paper cup of coffee and a brown bag that probably contained a sandwich or a doughnut or a banana, hustling across the street, sidestepping between cars, returning to his bus. On the way, I told Joy that Nina had been corresponding with Stella Borowczyk and that after a number of letters and telephone calls, Mrs. B suggested that Nina have the baby with her in Green Lake, if that would make things easier for our family. "So that's what she's going to do."

"Does Marta know?" Joy asked.

"Marta thinks that Nina is going to Wisconsin because she's been sick and she needs to breathe cleaner air. When the baby comes, they'll tell her about that, and then more, in small doses. Nina's leaving next week."

"Let's go home," Joy whispered.

We dashed across the street toward the bus stop where the same driver would pick us up. I was shivering; Joy's teeth were chattering like a chorus line of tap shoes. Snow was heaped high at the curb. With my arms extended for balance, I stomped through a knee-high snow bank, carving a fresh path of my own; Joy found a safer one that had been carved by other people's galoshes. When we met on the sidewalk, she offered me a supportive half-smile and hitched her arm to mine, and from then on we walked in step with each other.

CHAPTER THIRTY-ONE

*O*ur family comedian Uncle Bruno understood timing: The critical match of joke to audience, the elevated inflection, the theatrical sideways glance, the pause that beckons the listeners' brain cells to connect and anticipate. He knew all of this. "Timing is something that bubbles up in your blood," he'd say. "It's intuitive, but you must learn it. It's spontaneous, but you must practice it."

I'd watched Marta struggle for timing as she'd fling her silver baton in the air and tap her foot to the beat of a John Philip Sousa march as the baton twirled end-over-end against the clear blue sky. Sometimes she'd catch it; more often she'd miss. Then, out of sync with the music, she'd chase after it, retrieve it and try again. Marta would have said timing was something she had to practice. What she didn't know then was that it was something she had to feel.

No matter how you cut it, my dad had the worst timing of any of us Manikowskis. He was usually a step ahead or behind everyone else. I remember when I was in grade school—when my ego was even more fragile than it was as a teenager—how he'd bring leftover funeral flowers to my classroom. He'd walk into the room carrying this monster wreath of withering roses on a wobbly wire tripod. "To set in front of the Blessed Virgin," he'd tell the nun. Then he'd make a big production of setting the flowers in front of the life-sized statue of Mary that stood on a pedestal in the corner (every classroom had one), and invariably the nun would say, "Ellie, come up here and thank your father," and Dad would crouch down and lean into me for a kiss, and I'd reluctantly have to peck his cheek in front of the whole class, and on his way out the door Dad would wink at me like Father of the Year.

As for my own timing, all in all, it was improving, considering where I started out. At my party that summer, I couldn't even tell Andy and Millie to cool it. I had to wait for Father Ben to offer. And my timing was definitely off in confronting Nina. I was operating in a different time zone—a minute off here, a day off there. So okay, no one was going to crucify me for misplacing a stinking minute, but I'd have bet you money that Jackie Kennedy never had that problem. With her finely honed instincts and her social secretary Letitia Baldrige by her side, she was always in the right place at the right time, speaking the right words in the right language. You were never going to find her clock a minute off.

Although I never thought I'd admit it, Mom had the best timing of any of us. She intuitively knew what had to be done. After Nina decided to leave, Mom started sewing Nina a wardrobe for her new life, a suitcase full of maternity clothes from Simplicity patterns.

Although I vowed I'd never again lift a needle after the torment of a sewing class I had to endure during my freshman year, I ended up coming home after school and helping

Mom. While she sewed the zippers and set-in the sleeves—the difficult work that required patience and skill—I ran the straight seams through her Singer—contributions I couldn't screw up. I worked carefully, trying to make those tops and skirts with elastic waistbands perfect, because I figured Nina needed a generous dose of something excellent in her life.

Those afternoons, Mom and I sewed companionably beneath the window in the family room, at first in silence, listening to the rhythm of the motor of the sewing machine, grinding, then racing its steely needle across lengths of fabric. We passed pieces of crisp cotton and soft wool from hand to hand; we threaded needles and tied knots for each other; we passed scissors back and forth, lengths of thread and straight pins that we both had the bad habit of holding between our lips. Then gradually, as we became more trusting of each other's presence, we allowed easy conversation to enter our world.

One afternoon, I said out of the blue, "I know she loved him, Mom."

The motor growled, hummed, raced.

"And he loved her," she said when the motor stopped. After a silence, she added, "Maybe I shouldn't be telling you this, but they planned on getting married."

I didn't tell Mom I knew, nor did I mention the letter. That was between Nina and me. "Does Dad know?" I asked.

"I told him on Christmas evening after everyone went to bed. If you could have seen him, Ellie, he was inconsolable, and I couldn't let him believe that Ben took advantage of Nina. I'm one to keep confidences, but in this case, I had to tell him. Nina was fine with it. Actually she was grateful because it gave your dad a night to think things over. Your dad's the kind of man who'll try to change things until he runs into a situation he can't change. Then, eventually, he accepts reality. You know, he could never deny a baby."

"Dad's courageous."

"I had no idea how courageous when we met. He's taught me a lot."

"Was he always that way?"

"I think so," she said, folding a swath of leftover moss green wool. "Your father today is just more of what he once was," she said, smiling. "I remember how we met. He saw me on the avenue and followed me to Dr. Kruk's. I can see him in that dental chair with Doctor Kruk's big hand in his mouth allowing himself to be vulnerable in order to get to know me. He did the same thing with you, Ellie, making you work for him so you'd learn what hard work felt like. Then he went out on a limb for Nina, and we know how that turned out. What he lacks in style, he possesses in good intentions."

"And you're just more of what you once were?" I teased.

"I guess you could say that. For better or worse," she laughed.

Every few years our bodies recreate themselves down to the very last atom. We become more educated, more experienced, more at ease in the world. Yet, our characters remain basically the same. I'd always been fascinated by those Russian nesting dolls that twist open at the waist. The smallest doll, no larger than a thumbnail, is a miniature version of the largest but painted with considerably less definition and color, with fewer brush strokes. Perhaps Mom was on to something when she said that we become more of what we were when we were young.

Mom slowly lifted the pressure foot off the fabric. "I guess I've always been afraid of my own shadow, afraid of not making a good enough impression, afraid of stepping out into the world, afraid of not being good enough. I'm like your grandma was. Afraid of life."

"Oh, Mom—"

"No, Ellie, let me finish. She and your grandpa came to this country not speaking English, and like most immigrants they worked at simple jobs. Grandma made salads in a cafeteria. Grandpa worked as a machinist. I remember many a time they'd come home in tears because people laughed at them for their broken English, for their old-fashioned clothes, for misunderstanding directions. So they took comfort in sticking with their own. 'Stick with your own,' they'd tell me again and again. And I guess that's what I've been telling you . . . in a million different ways."

Mom turned to look at me. "I've just been trying to protect you, Ellie. But you're different than I am, honey. You don't need my protection. You're ready to face the world. You're smart and you work hard and you deserve an education. Your dad has helped me understand that."

"I don't always feel ready to face the world, Mom, but I hope I am." I wrapped my arms around her and gave her a big hug. I couldn't remember the last time I did that.

After we finished working, I dropped the sewing machine into its housing and folded one maple leaf over another until the machine took on the appearance of a simple desk.

As I set a lamp and candy dish on top of it, I looked out the picture window at the urban mountain range of garages and simple frame homes that extended block after block into the distance. The homes were narrow and deep with two or three stories. Most had peaked roofs and chimneys that huffed plumes of smoke into the sky, and wooden back porches that held metal lawn chairs, potted geraniums, and laundry drying on lines in the summertime; snow shovels, overshoes, and used-up Christmas trees in the winter. In the background, hovering over us was the mighty steeple of St. Casimir's. If our church had arms, they'd be enveloping us. If it had fingers, they'd be scolding us. This view from our window was as familiar to me as the image of my own face in the mirror. I didn't own this neighborhood, yet it belonged to me—and I belonged to it.

There was a pulse to our neighborhood, a heartbeat, a history. I heard it in the honk of the horns and the hum of traffic, heavy in the mornings and evenings, lighter at night; I smelled it in the diesel exhaust and sour aroma of cabbage wafting through the gangways; I tasted it in the grit of the air and the garlic of *kiełbasa*. It was my neighborhood. I'd been seasoned by its traditions, comforted by its habits, protected by its mores and rules. It was a place where family mattered more than refinement, heart mattered more than money, and shared history mattered more than status. It is where life was solid, familiar, and safe.

There were years when I wanted nothing more than to leave it—because of its provincialism, but also because of its familiarity. Yet when the time came, it was hard for me to think about picking a college and leaving.

I'd wanted it both ways. I wanted the familiarity of my neighborhood, but the novelty of someplace new; the safety of my city blocks, but the adventure of other vistas; the security of my life with my parents and friends, but the opportunity to make my own way. I wanted to hold back the hands of the clock and keep things as they were. I wanted the clock to spin, racing me into the future. I wanted a big life, but as I stood on the edge of adulthood, I was afraid of that too.

CHAPTER THIRTY-TWO

On Valentine's Day, at seven o'clock, I turned on the TV. Jackie Kennedy was giving a tour of the White House, and I'd been anticipating it for weeks.

From a distance the camera panned into the White House on Pennsylvania Avenue. In the lower left corner of the screen, a male figure strode toward the entrance.

"He's Charles Collingwood," I said. "From CBS. He's the host."

My mother called from the kitchen, "Wasn't he the host on the *Today Show*?"

"Yeah, until Hugh Downs booted him off," I called back.

"I love Hugh Downs," she said.

"I count at least twenty-one windows in the front alone," Barney quipped. "How would you like to wash those windows, Mrs. M?" he called into the kitchen.

"Uggh," Mom groaned.

"Is this going to be like a fashion show?" Duke asked.

"Shut up you guys and watch," I said.

Joy was in the kitchen with Mom and Nina. The automatic can opener whirred.

"Shh!" I said.

"Well you want ice cream sundaes, don't you? Isn't that what you requested, princess Eleanor?" my mother asked in her high and mighty tone.

"We can't open the can of syrup with our teeth," Joy groused.

On the screen, Jackie was gliding down a long colonnade with a series of small arched windows on one side and large rectangular windows on the other. She was slim, poised, and dressed in a long-sleeved two-piece outfit, surely red for Valentine's Day. The camera zoomed onto her face. She was wearing a triple strand of pearls, slightly tucked inside her collarless dress. Ceremonial music played in the background; the kind of music that I imagined always played softly throughout the rooms of the White House. Charles Collingwood said something about Jackie being the third youngest of the twenty-nine first ladies to live there, but I missed a few words because of the clinking of spoons and bowls as Joy passed out our sundaes.

Charles Collingwood asked Jackie about her plan for the White House.

"I really don't have one because I think this house will always grow, and should. It seemed to me such a shame when we came here to find hardly anything of the past in the house, hardly anything before 1902." Then she said something about how everything in the White House should be the best.

"Where'd she get that voice?" Mom asked.

"It's a little girl's voice," Barney said.

"It sounds like she sucked in a helium balloon," Joy said.

"It's a refined voice," I said. But if I were being perfectly honest, I would have had to agree. Jackie's voice was nothing like the womanly Lauren Bacall voice I'd imagined. It was wispy and breathy and very New York, with a hint of a Southern drawl because she had spent some of her childhood in Virginia. She pronounced china, *chiner,* and Jefferson, *Jeffason.* But it was also a shy voice, as if the cameras and limelight frightened her. That's something I understood— something I still can.

For the next forty-five minutes we listened in relative silence. Jackie talked about the history of the White House and how Abigail Adams complained about the dampness and the cold. "Mrs. Adams kept the White House habitable only by building fires in every room. The British added to the flames by burning the White House." She told how, until Herbert Hoover's presidency, the White House was opened to the public every New Year's Day so anyone could stop by and shake the President's hand. In a bubbly voice she explained how during the Truman Administration, the White House had to be almost completely reconstructed because it was unsafe to live in.

Mom, scraping her spoon against the side of her ice cream bowl, oohed and ahhed over the Monroe pier table, a pair of one-hundred-and-sixty-year-old wing chairs from New England that Mamie Eisenhower had recovered, and in the East Room, a larger-than-life size portrait of George Washington painted by Gilbert Stuart, one of many portraits Stuart painted of him.

"This painting is the oldest thing in the White House, the only thing that was here from the very beginning," Jackie explained. "And then Dolly Madison, when the White House was burned by the British in 1814, managed to save it along with a cart load of furniture and documents that have been invaluable to us in our research."

When Jackie welcomed us into the State Dining Room, Mom floated into another world. "Imagine being able to serve one hundred and two people at one seating! Such grandeur. I wish we had color TV," she said.

Dad shuffled into the room making a commotion. He planted himself in front of me, blocking my view of the television set. He coughed, pulled his handkerchief out of his pocket, wiped his mouth, and rocked impatiently from foot to foot.

"Sit down, Dad. Listen to the program with us," I said tactfully.

"I'm leaving. Too many knickknacks," he muttered.

Duke nudged me and nodded agreement.

"President Theodore Roosevelt hung deer heads with antlers on the walls of the State Dining Room, Dad. That's manly."

Dad shook his head and walked into the kitchen.

On the screen, Jackie was leading Charles Collingwood toward the fireplace.

"Mrs. Kennedy, on the fireplace under the mantle is an inscription that I find to be one of the most moving things in the White House."

"Yes," Jackie said in her breathy voice. "It was taken from the very first letter written from the White House by President John Adams to his wife Abigail, dated November 2, 1800, when he had only been here two days." The camera zoomed in to the fireplace as Jackie read the inscription:

"I pray to Heaven to Bestow
the Best of Blessings on
THIS HOUSE

and on All that shall hereafter
Inhabit it. May none but
Honest and Wise Men ever rule under This Roof."

The camera cut to Jackie's exquisite, wide-eyed expression. "Franklin Delano Roosevelt loved that prayer and had it put under the mantle," Jackie said, beaming.

As I studied the faces in our family room, I realized that we wouldn't have many impromptu gatherings like this again. Some of us would be moving on. Whether it was the White House or our house on Ashland, we were all temporary caretakers on this earth.

I'd give anything to be back in that room again, seeing Dad in his wash pants and cardigan sweater, Mom staring star struck at the TV, Marta not giving a darn, Barney counting windows, Joy licking her ice cream spoon, and Duke and I, snuggling Valentine's Day close, feeling the brush of each others' arms.

Many years later, my small family returned to the Midwest to ride in an annual bike ride across Iowa. It was a weeklong event that started in western Iowa and finished at the Mississippi River. You could ride the entire distance—580 miles as we did—or join for a day and slip away. Pedaling along under a blistering sun one afternoon, my butt aching from days on a bike seat that I swear was imbedded with thorns, I thought of how the bike ride was like life. We began as a core group, a family of sorts that stayed together until we were no longer together. New riders entered. Some traveled the distance. Others set off on their own paths. A few disappeared completely. Our gears shifted and our wheels kept spinning until they stopped spinning.

On that Valentine's Day, lulled by the optimism of youth,

I had no idea of how our lives would play out. I had no way of knowing that within fifteen years—two presidents and first ladies later—our neighborhood would change, I would experience the heartbreak of my life, that Dad would succumb to cancer (Oh, how empty our world became without him), that Jerzy and Lydia would take off for a planned retirement community in Florida, and a string of new families— some honest and wise; others not so—would occupy our flats. There was no way I could have predicted that for the remainder of Mom's long life that she would become a tireless jetsetter, traveling between my family's home in California and Marta's apartment in New York City where she'd help me raise my children and help Marta run a chain of popular Polish fast-food restaurants cleverly called "Marta's."

Looking back to that Valentine's Day today, I can still see Dad's dwindling image moving down the hallway, and I can still hear his irascible voice saying loud enough for us to hear, "I'm not sure about Jackie, but that FDR had it right."

CHAPTER THIRTY-THREE

A week after graduation, Joy left for Des Plaines so the good Sisters could begin molding her into a nun. Barney, Duke, Mrs. Dusza, and I took her to the Greyhound Bus Terminal, a grimly appropriate word given our mission. I remember how Joy looked that afternoon swinging her suitcase as casually as if she were a kid heading off to summer camp. A one-way ticket poked out of the pocket of the flared skirt of the yellow shirtwaist that her mother had bought her at J.C. Penney's. What struck me—in addition to Joy's incomprehensible good cheer—was how few material things she'd need for rest of her life.

The day before, I had helped her pack.

"Bring only the necessities, the rest will be provided," the instruction form from the convent read. It was a single sheet, mimeographed in liturgical purple ink. For the most part, Joy followed the instructions. She packed a brand new toothbrush, deodorant, and hairbrush. Her "edifying" religious texts (as the form prescribed) included her prayer book and my *Lives of the Saints*, copped from the funeral home. Beneath a meager stack of underwear, she tucked in a locket Barney had given her with their second grade pictures inside (Joy in pigtails threaded with red ribbons; Barney with eyeglasses and an overbite), and a packet of photos, including the framed sepia photograph of her father.

The bus arrived in a dark cloud of diesel and rolled into its stall. A pneumatic door opened with an all-too-familiar *whoosh*, and the bus driver, a jolly sort, hopped out. He fished a loop of keys out of his pocket and flung open the cavernous luggage compartment beneath the bus windows. Passengers bound for summer vacations with overstuffed luggage, pumped-up inner tubes, and golf clubs, hugged their loved ones and casually bid their goodbyes.

"Well, Joy," I said, trying to maintain my composure.

"Write me everyday," Barney said, getting choked up.

"Go easy on the nuns," Duke said.

Joy studied us with such intensity that I knew she was memorizing our faces. I hoped she knew how much we loved her.

Mrs. Dusza, who until then had kept her composure, fell apart. She blubbered and carried on and wrapped her arms around Joy like she was never going to see her again. She squeezed her black rosary so hard that the bones of her knuckles looked ready to pop out. Then, within her misery she found her words.

"From the start Josia, it was just you and me. To America we came. To St. Casimir's we go, every Sunday, you and me. I send you to the nuns to teach you in school, and now you go to live with them. Maybe too much church I gave you?" She studied her daughter with soulful eyes. "Next time I see you, you will be nun," she said, pounding her chest with her rosary fist. "And no grandchildren."

"No, Ma . . . don't think of it that way. I'll think of you every day and I'll pray for you." She reached for her mother and pulled her close. "Thanks for everything, Ma. You're a great mother."

At the sound of the luggage compartment slamming closed, Joy ran over, hugged me a final time, and slipped me an envelope. "I knew this would happen," she whispered in my ear. "Take Ma out for *pierogi* at The White Eagle . . . all you can eat. Buy her wine. My treat."

"I will," I promised.

I studied Joy, wanting to remember her as she was: curly black hair, pink skin, prim shirtwaist over her shapely body. I knew I'd see her again, but it would be different. Then she'd be wearing a dowdy black habit. A veil would hide her shorn hair, and she'd be one of them, speaking in measured tones and taking small sacred steps across the glassy marble convent floor. I'd bring her gifts and she'd unwrap them, careful not to rip the paper. She'd smooth out the ribbons and coil them into a frugal ball for reuse the ways nuns do.

The driver was checking tickets. As each passenger disappeared into the bus, the four of us inched up closer to the door with Joy. "Watch your step, Missy," the driver said as she set her shoe on the first metal step.

I remember staring at Joy's shoes, ugly black rubber-soled nun shoes with thick laces that she had to buy at a clerical supply store downtown. Couldn't the convent at least pop for a pair of shoes? If I'd learned one thing about myself over the years, it was that in stressful situations I had a tendency to fixate on footwear.

The four of us, lined up like mourners at a wake, watched the yellow image of Joy in her too sunny shirtwaist, pass behind the line of windows and stop at the seat in the back, above the hump. She lifted her single bag into the overhead rack and fell into her seat. Just as the bus began to move, she tapped the window and waved. Our eyes met. Tears were streaming down our cheeks.

Since we were fourteen, Joy and I had taken zillions of bus rides together. Every time we'd left together and returned together. Suddenly, the enormity of what was happening hit me. This was a bus trip Joy had to take alone.

CHAPTER THIRTY-FOUR

*T*he first wedding I'd ever attended was the wedding of Dad's third cousin, Robert. His bride was an older woman—she must have been in her forties. She was heavier than most brides whom you'd expect to be svelte enough to fit in a champagne flute, an hourglass, or a drinking straw. Third cousin Robert (my father always took pains to emphasize third) was an odd duck with a long neck, sparse blond hair, and a nervous smile. Even though I was only eight, I had the impression something was amiss with that marriage.

"Why aren't they dancing close?" I asked my mom. "Why are they smiling only for the cameras?"

Mom gave me the kind of adult answer that answered nothing. "Don't be so quick to judge, Eleanor. You never know who you're going to end up with." So I smiled when the flash bulbs popped in my direction and I ate their bland vanilla wedding cake.

This marriage lasted only three months before the Church annulled it. But it left an impression on me. I had begun to learn one of life's most important lessons: Trust your gut.

So there I was, on a flawless autumn afternoon some twelve years later, preparing for yet another wedding.

I clipped on my dangly earrings, sprayed a final film of hair spray on my carefully teased flip, smoothed the skirt of my orange and gold flower-patterned taffeta bridesmaid gown, grabbed my beaded handbag, dashed down the stairs. Uncle Frank, looking paunchy and prosperous in his black suit and starched white shirt, was waiting for us in the limousine parked at the curb. Once he deposited us at the door of St. Casimir's, he'd come back to pick up the bridal couple.

Marta was already scrunched in the back seat of the limo between Mom and Aunt Maxine. Also a bridesmaid, Marta was wearing a ballerina-length skirt made of the same taffeta as my floor-length number. She was fluffing up the skirt to keep it from crushing. I wedged myself into the pull-up seat next to Mary Louise and Mom. Dad, handsome in a tuxedo, was smashed between my uncles in the front seat. He was sporting sunglasses that he had taken to wearing, not as an affectation but as a shield, because he was self-conscious about his inability to focus on the faces of the people he was talking to. Ironically, what was medicine to him had become mystique to others.

"Ya look like a Hollywood star in those shades," quipped Aunt Maxine, who was also wearing sunglasses. Hers had pointed corners studded with rhinestones. A flicker of sunshine flashed off her lenses and disappeared.

As we veered into traffic, Uncle Bruno said, "Ya got the ring, Stan?"

"Right here," Dad answered, tapping his breast pocket. "Ya think I'd forget the ring? Jerzy'd kill me."

The previous May, Dad had called me at school to say Jerzy had given Lydia a "half-carat sparkler."

A few days later, Jerzy called and got right to the point. "Ellie, I'm calling you up because me and Lydia are getting hitched and Lydia doesn't have a sister or girl cousins, so the two of us were wondering if you'd be a bridesmaid along with Marta and my Madeline. The three of you are the prettiest girls we know. Wouldya stand up for us?" His voice was formal and nervous, as if he had rehearsed what he was going to say and was trying hard to get it right. I felt sorry for him because he was doing something he wasn't accustomed to doing. He was asking me a favor. *Stand up for me. Be there for me.*

"I'd be honored, Mr. Pilarski."

The lofty melody of Debussy filled the church. Marta, Madeline and I had already processed single-file down the aisle and were standing shoulder to shoulder in the sanctuary on the bride's side facing the congregation. Up close, the altar looked like a wedding cake. Lush bouquets of white chrysanthemums in glass urns graced its marble tiers, and dozens of ivory candles glittered in golden candelabras on both sides of the tabernacle. At the foot of the altar, a starched white carpet flowed through the open gate of the Communion rail and down the center aisle into the vestibule where Lydia was waiting.

Our new priest, Father Witek, a recent immigrant from Poland, stood stiffly at the altar. He was an odd gentleman who had a dachshund look about him that I'm sure worked to his advantage in landing him a position at our parish after what happened between Nina and the handsome Father Ben. The groomsmen, Joe Pilarski, and Lydia's teenage nephews,

Marek and Casey Wagodzinski, stood opposite us, as did Jerzy and Dad who was leaning ever so slightly against Jerzy for balance. A volunteer from the Chicago Foundation for the Blind, who'd been delivering Dad books on tape, told him that a cane planted firmly on the ground would help him orient himself to a particular spot. Dad knew this and started to use a white cane outdoors, but he had not yet overcome his pride enough to use it at Jerzy's wedding.

I observed the congregation. Mom was kneeling in a pew near the front, her elbows resting on the pew in front of her, her hands folded beneath her chin. She had that earnest, beseeching look on her face that people get when they're praying so hard they can feel it. She knew things about marriage that I didn't have a clue about at that time.

Nina was in the pew behind her. We'd hugged briefly in the vestibule, but there wasn't time to talk. I could only imagine the memories that flashed through her mind as she stared at that magnificent altar upon which she had once laid her dreams.

We were taught to believe that God could change whatever He wanted to change. In a blink He could shatter a person's world and reconfigure it. He could stop a heart from beating, bring about a change of heart, or send a new heartthrob onto the bewildering stage of one's life.

Since Father Ben's death, the God we believed in had an absolute field day with Nina. As suddenly as misfortune showered upon her, that's how quickly good fortune resurrected her from the depths.

When Nina was about five months pregnant, she and I had said our goodbyes at the curb in front of the burgundy Pontiac Catalina that Uncle Frank had found for her at a bargain price. Nina tried to put on a brave front. "I'm going to miss you, sweetie," she blubbered. She felt like a fragile bird in my arms when we hugged.

My first inkling about what had begun to transpire happened about two months later when I had gone up to Green Lake for a casual weekend at Nina and Mrs. Borowczyk's invitation. That Friday, Father Ben's cousin, Steve, who the Borowczyks had raised, had also come to Green Lake to meet with a client who wanted to set up a trust, and, of course, he spent the night at the house. To make a long story short, it took about ten minutes after he entered the door for Nina's wild craving for pizza to come face to face with Steve's certitude that he was the best deep-dish pizza maker north of the Illinois border. With a surname like Hansen— his father was Norwegian—I was surprised that he was so passionate about pizza. But as I learned later, it was Nina he was attracted to.

When Mrs. B mentioned Nina's hankering for pizza, Steve rolled up his shirtsleeves, loosened his tie, and with dramatic flair began pulling cheeses, tomatoes, olives, and a mélange of other ingredients out of the refrigerator. Then he enlisted a very pregnant Nina's help.

Throughout it all, I sat on a stool sipping red wine, watching Steve and Nina reach across each other for utensils and ingredients, slide past each other in comfortable ease, and banter back and forth like friends who'd known each other forever. With a deft hand he sautéed garlic and onions, stirred in heaps of chopped Roma tomatoes, fresh basil and a pinch of hot pepper for the sauce; and with matching skill, she kneaded a yellow cornmeal dough to its perfect texture and coaxed it into a humongous pizza pan.

As I watched Steve work, I searched for a hint of Ben in him, but there was none. Although their mothers were sisters,

Steve resembled his Nordic father. He was taller and fairer complexioned than Ben, and his hair was a light sandy color. It fell over his forehead as he worked, and he made no effort to brush it aside. He had a crooked smile that made his face look slightly lopsided, in a boyishly handsome way.

During dinner, I could tell that Steve was attracted to Nina by the way his eyes rested on her a little too long when we raised our wine glasses, and by how interested he was to hear her viewpoints on every topic of discussion. Later when we were alone, I said, "He was flirting with you."

Nina looked down at her melon belly and insisted, "No man in his right mind would be interested in a pregnant woman who isn't his wife, and besides," she reminded me sternly, "Steve has a lovely fiancé at home." I told her, "You're full of baloney because I know what I saw." And I was right.

Two weeks later, Nina slyly snuck it into a phone conversation that Steve had broken up with Delores and had decided to move his law practice to Green Lake. In a later conversation, she prattled on about the competitive Scrabble matches the two of them were playing. It was then that I noticed that laughter had returned to her voice. More than Scrabble was going on between them, but out of respect for Nina and the upcoming birth of her baby, I decided to drop the subject.

Right around her due date, Nina mentioned that Steve asked whether he could be with her in the hospital.

"How do you feel about that?"

"I want him there. I broke down and cried when he offered."

So when the day came, Steve held Nina's hand throughout her labor, and when beautiful little Christina was born, he was the first to rock the swaddled bundle in his arms. Since then, they had become an inseparable threesome.

When baby Christina was four months old, Nina and Steve were married in a simple ceremony at Our Lady of the Shores. All the Manikowskis drove to Green Lake; I took the Greyhound Bus up from Madison, traveling a route that I had come to know well, the route that tethered me from my dormitory at the University of Wisconsin to Green Lake, where I had become a frequent visitor. Duke drove up for the wedding and we stayed together in the downstairs guest room of the two-story bungalow that Steven and Nina bought on the opposite side of lake from the Borowczyk home. Steven and Nina were open-minded in a way that my parents (who knew nothing about our sleeping arrangements) and Stella were not.

The first time Duke and I had made love was in the blackish brown VW van (Duke called it Old Meconium) that he bought in a used car lot on Division Street. The romantic guy he was, he outfitted the back with a mattress and sleeping bags, and hung manly curtains with patterns of Mallard ducks in the windows that we could roll down at night. We folded together in that cozy space like pages of a love letter. When he came to visit me at college, that van became our motel on wheels.

On Nina's wedding day, the jabbering band of us hurried to the church, crunching through the dried red maple leaves blanketing the sidewalks, savoring the warmth of the waning autumn sun. I remember thinking it was Ben's approving hand on our backs that afternoon, blessing us.

They were married in a chapel off the main altar in an alcove replete with frescoes depicting some of Catholicism's more congenial saints—St. Cecilia strumming a harp, St. Francis feeding a gentle deer, and St. Dominic, the patron saint of astronomers, gazing dreamily into the sky. A tall leaded-glass window was open enough to admit the singsong rhyme of kids playing Red Rover in the schoolyard. "Red rover, red rover, let Stevie come over," one childlike voice sang out above the rest. It occurred to me then, that in some heavenly changing of the guard, Nina's Steve was stepping in to raise Christina just as Ben's parents had stepped in to raise him. Little did we know that by then Nina had officially joined the Manikowski breeding race, and that she and Steve would go on to have their own pew-full of children: Christina, Stephen, Stephanie, Sara, and Benedict. And little did we know that their sprawling home at Green Lake would become the center of many lively Thanksgivings, Christmases, and glorious summers with our families on the beach.

And little did I know then that eighteen years later Christina Hansen would also read her father's letter.

My thoughts turned to a particular June morning in 1980 when we were in Green Lake. It was the day after we had celebrated Christina's eighteenth birthday. I had slept late that morning and was alone in bed. The door opened and I could hear the tap of Christina's footsteps on the hardwood floor.

"Are you awake, Ellie?"

"I'm all ears," I mumbled.

"Good, cuz I want to tell you something." She leapt into my bed with a bounce. "Sure you're awake?"

"I am now," I said. By that time I had learned that when adolescents are ready to share any kind of information or confidence or confession, the worse thing an adult can do is shut them down.

"Mom and I stayed up late last night and talked," she

said. "We got talking about my real father and she let me read the letter. She said you read it when you were my age."

"It wasn't my finest moment. I shouldn't have done that," I said.

I can still picture how Christina looked that morning stretched out beside me in an Iron Maiden nightshirt, tall, lithe as a willow branch, with Ben's dark curly hair and gray eyes studying my every reaction. She was lying on her side facing me. Her silver-ringed fingers rested on my pillow, her randomly chopped bangs were streaked with swords of fuchsia. As a child Christina had danced like a curly-headed elf to music in her head. During the summer of her eighteenth year she was the drummer in a local rock band called Green Lightning.

"That's okay, Ellie. I've done some stuff that I'm not really proud of either—with guys, with booze. But I don't want to talk about my moral degradation right now."

I chuckled, the way Nina had chuckled so long ago with me.

"I've been thinking about that letter all night," she said pensively. "My dad's been a great dad . . . you know how amazing Steve is. But all my life my real dad's been a mystery to me. Oh, yeah, I've heard stories about him. I've seen photos . . . I know he was a priest . . . I even have his accordion . . . but he never seemed real to me until I read that letter." She rolled over on her back and stared at the ceiling fan twirling the lazy morning air above us.

"He never seemed real to you?"

"Not really, Ellie. You've been to his grave. You've seen it. He's buried in the priest's section of St. Adalbert's. He has a stone chalice on his grave. And his tombstone says, "Rev. Benedict Borowczyk . . . sort of hard to get close to that, huh?"

"You've got a point there," I said.

"Now that I've read the letter, I know how much he loved Mom and how much he would have loved me if he got a chance to know me."

I remember how she ran her fingers through the air, stroking it as if she were stroking his face. "When I touched his handwriting on the paper, I felt like I was touching him." Tears glazed her eyes. "Now I have someone to miss, Ellie."

"I know," I said.

She gave the mattress a little bounce. "Holy shit, Ellie, when he was a kid, he probably slept right here in this bed we're in right now, and he probably looked at these same funky red roses on the wallpaper that Grandma refuses to change."

I nodded.

"Now I really, really miss him."

"You're a lot like him, you know," I said, touching her cheek.

"That's a good thing, huh?"

"An extraordinary thing, sweetie."

Our organist, Adele Pawlowa, hit the first deep note of Mendelssohn's Bridal March and jogged me back to Jerzy and Lydia's wedding. I made eye contact with Nina. By then I had gotten contact lenses and my view was clear and unobstructed. Her smile told me that all was well. She reached for Steve's hand. He leaned into her and whispered. She smiled, pressed her lips together and nodded.

The congregation stood. My eyes traveled above the flowered hats of the women, the mostly gray heads of the men and above the swath of sunshine streaming through the main entrance. I looked up, beyond the teardrop chandeliers into the balcony, where more people were standing. Still higher in the choir loft, Adele Pawlowa was pumping out the regal melody her fingers had memorized. Her broad back and thick arms swayed as jubilant tones floated through the church.

Lydia stood in the vestibule at the edge of the white carpet ready to take her first step down the aisle.

"She looks like a queen," Marta whispered to me.

"She is a queen today," I replied.

I would have thought Lydia would have opted for a sedate ivory suit and a wisp of a veil, as the bridal magazines say a woman of a certain age should wear. But after having waited decades for the opportunity, Lydia went all out for the full bridal regalia. Her skirt, fashioned of yards of organza, flared out beyond the edges of the white carpet; the V of her neckline was edged with appliqués of pearls. Her hair was teased into a tall, meringue-like twist sprinkled with pearls that glimmered as she glided beneath the chandeliers, smiling, blowing air kisses, waving to her public. I swallowed hard when Jerzy stepped forward and offered her his arm.

There must have been two-dozen sleek, chromed-up Cadillacs, Oldsmobiles, Pontiacs, and Chevies caravanning from the church to the reception that day, with all of us honking our horns. The limousine carrying Lydia and Jerzy slid into a space directly in front of the *Klub Kultury*. The rest of us pulled into a vacant lot across the street. Car doors slammed and women in their spikiest heels and mink stoles smelling like mothballs, accompanied by men decked out in tuxedos and spit-polished wing tips, jaywalked between the Saturday afternoon traffic, waving and calling out to one another. Duke and I ran behind Nina and Steve, hooting and carrying on as if the world belonged to us. We stopped breathlessly beneath the scalloped green canopy of the *Klub Kultury* and waited our turn to pass through the carved oak doors.

"You okay, honey?" Steve asked Nina.

"Good as gold," Nina replied, hardly out of breath. It was only when the wind blew the loose bodice of her lacy two-piece dress into her body that I could see the mound in her stomach. As we waited, I caught Steve staring with a faraway look in his eyes at our funeral home next door. It was how he looked two years ago when he and his family had come to view Ben's body.

His sadness made me realize how much I missed Joy.

For the first few months after she left for the convent, I prayed like crazy that she'd be a short-timer. There are no saints in charge of springing someone from the convent, so I had to improvise. At first I prayed to St. Rita, the patron saint of desperate cases, and when she let me down, I went begging to St. Anthony, the patron saint of lost objects. Again, no dice.

Finally, I took my case directly to Joy, but in retrospect it was embarrassing how I handled it. I wrote her letters about the fun I was having at the University of Wisconsin, hoping that good times would lure her away. I wrote about how they served beer in the Student Union, and about my roommates—Ellen, a Jewish girl from Nashville, who had this cool wardrobe she shared; and Charlotte, a Swede from Sturgeon Bay who played the cello like a dream. Then I appealed to her sense of social justice. I reminded her about Martin Luther King's "I Have a Dream" speech on the steps of the Lincoln Memorial, and I enclosed a photo of me with my hair straight and parted in the center from *The Daily*

Cardinal waving a "Separate Is Not Equal" sign at a UW demonstration.

But the more I wrote, the less difference it made. Joy's letter writing privileges were limited, but when she wrote, it was about the peace she was finding in solitude, the satisfaction she had discovered in performing small tasks mindfully, like baking bread and planting four varieties of lettuce; the difficulty she was having learning Gregorian chant, but the thrill of singing it in a choir of fifty voices that sounded like one. When I had really gotten under her skin, she reminded me in her firmest penmanship that not all of us were called to be activists, and that some of us had to do the behind-the-scenes praying if things were to turn out right in this world. I pictured her sitting at her little desk, ballpoint in hand, nodding her head emphatically the way she did when she had something figured out, and that was that.

Eventually, I had come to realize that it was okay for us to tread different footpaths in life. But it bugged me that she was not allowed to come home for special occasions—not for weddings, anniversaries, or birthdays. Only funerals. And then she wasn't even allowed to spend the night. It wasn't right.

So instead of praying for Joy to leave the convent, I started praying that the Catholic Church would ease up on its rules. Pope John XXIII had called his bishops together in Ecumenical Council to modernize the church, but then he died, and Pope Paul VI took over. At that time I was hopeful because change was everywhere—in the government with President Kennedy at the helm, in world peace with the signing of the nuclear test ban treaty, in the world of fashion with Jackie calling the shots, in civil rights with Martin Luther King making things right. I felt it in my bones. Bigger changes were coming.

But still, I missed Joy.

"Some wing ding," Duke said, when we entered the ballroom. At the far end was a wide stage with an arched proscenium and plush velvet curtains drawn to the sides. Beneath the stage was a long head table, set for the wedding party, and branching off it were four long tables. Sunlight streamed in through the three tall arched windows on the sides of the room, sending flashing patterns on the bronze and crystal chandeliers hanging from the high ceiling, and on the glassware, silver, and china at each place setting. A crowd was congregating around the bar.

"The Polka Knights are playing!" I screeched.

At the back of the stage a serious drum set was set up upon a riser. The Polka Knights' logo, a medieval shield with dancing notes, was imprinted in black and silver letters on the drum and also on the music easels. On a backdrop, T-H-E P-O-L-K-A K-N-I-G-H-T-S in silver letters spread out in staggered formation. Scattered amidst the letters were aluminum cutouts of helmets, swords, shields, and happy notes, dangling from fishing lines attached to the light grid above the stage. A real Polish Camelot.

Duke was at the bar ordering beers. He had just completed his third summer as a lifeguard for the Chicago Park District and had retained his golden suntan. He was wearing his maroon Ramblers tie and cool paisley suspenders. He had ditched his dark rimmed eyeglasses for contact lenses that made him look a lot less scholarly and a lot more fun loving. As the kids today would say, he was a hunk.

At the grand piano in the corner, Adele Pawlowa had

magically reappeared and was playing a sprightly Chopin Polonaise.

Jerzy and Lydia were still by the door welcoming people. I watched Jerzy give Wanda Dusza a smooch and then prime Gregory Duda's hand like a water pump.

"Joy's mom is dating Mr. Duda?" Duke said.

"Yup. I hear they're pretty chummy."

"Looks like your dad's doing well."

"He's great. Just look at him!" I said, pointing the lip of my beer bottle at Dad. Across the ballroom Dad was holding a court of his own, talking to people lined up to pay their respects. Doctor Kowalski and his wife, Greta, were with him. Mom waved me over to say hello.

I excused myself and made my way across the room. I had to laugh because Mom, who never had anything good to say about the Kennedys, had turned into their biggest fan. That day she was wearing a beige silk shantung suit she tailored for herself from a Vogue pattern. It had an A-line skirt and a short jacket with oversized silk shantung buttons. She was lucky to find a tan silk pillbox hat on sale that worked perfectly with the suit, and with it perched on the back of her head atop the new bouffant she was sporting, she looked just like you know who. It's a fad, I said to myself. Hadn't Jackie told me so?

After a traditional Polish dinner of chicken soup, roast beef, *kiełbasa* and vegetables served family style, my father, seated at the head table next to Jerzy, fumbled with his napkin and stood up. As if on cue, Mom lifted her silver butter knife and *ping, ping, pinged* her empty wine glass to get the crowd's attention. She handed Dad a portable microphone that one of the Polka Knights passed to her from behind.

Still wearing his sunglasses, Dad took a deep breath and waited for the guests to quiet down. He lifted the mike to his lips.

"I'm . . ." he began. The microphone reverberated with an ear-deafening electronic buzz, and he held it farther away. "I'm honored to be here with you celebrating the marriage of Jerzy and Lydia Pilarski. Jerzy and I have been friends a long time, so long that today I feel like I'm giving him away."

There was laughter.

"A lot of us have been trying to do that," called out one of Jerzy's cronies from the *Dziennick*. "But I'm giving him to a fine gal," Dad said without missing a beat.

Someone at that same table clinked his glass, which sent a chain reaction of clinking throughout the ballroom, which sent a raucous signal to the bride and groom to kiss, which they did.

Nazdrowies rang out from everywhere.

Dad waited for the clinking to stop. He must have found it disconcerting to be standing in noisy darkness unable to see where the clatter was coming from. But my father was a resourceful man, and within the recesses of his blindness he held memories of similar weddings, where from the head table he had gazed into the blurry-eyed faces of hundreds of people smiling back at him.

He coped with aplomb, patting the air with the palms of his hands. When the clinking receded to a tinkle, he spoke into the microphone again. "As I was going to say, "I'm not going to talk all night. What I'm going to do to get this party going is to lead you in a round of *Sto Lat*." Let's toast Jerzy and Lydia."

Dad had no singing voice at all, and I didn't want him to be embarrassed. The room was quiet, and I squeezed my napkin because I knew it wasn't going to be opera when he opened his mouth.

In a low and off-key voice he began: "*Sto lat, sto lat niech zyje, zyje nam . . .*"

Immediately the crowd joined in. It didn't matter that he was off key. What mattered was that he was singing *Sto Lat* with heart, which he had plenty of. Soon everyone was raising and swaying their glasses and belting out the lively toast that if they were Polish was probably sung to them at their christening and at every celebration thereafter.

"Good health, good cheer, may you live a hundred years," Dad said with a quiver in his voice. "*Nazdrowie.*" He sat down, took his sunglasses off and wiped his damp eyes with his handkerchief. *Sto Lat* was in the category with *kolendy* in its power to turn a Polish heart to mush.

Some guys from the *Dziennik Chicagoski* table started clapping and calling, "Jer-zy! Jer-zy! Jer-zy! Speech!"

Dad handed him the microphone. "It's all your's, Jerz."

Jerzy took a deep breath and found his words. "Up dere at the altar with my Lydia, I was the happiest guy in the neighborhood. She looks like a hundred bucks, don't she?" Everyone, including Lydia, laughed. He leaned forward and glanced at his children, Madeline and Joe, who sat a few chairs down at the head table. "Other than the time I was up there with your ma, God rest her soul." Madeline closed her eyes and gave him an appreciative smile, which she held on her face. "Some of yous older folks were dere when my Mary and I got hitched. We were just kids then, like some of yous younger ones. Mary and I had some happy years. She was a peach, my Mary."

Nina's eyes bugged out of her head. I knew what she was thinking. What in the hell is he doing, talking about his first wife?

Lydia nodded sweetly, and Jerzy recovered. "Well, dose days are done and it's time to make a new speech for my Lydia here, and I'm gonna keep it on the sunny-side-up." He fumbled with his gold cufflinks—cufflinks he got from St. Casimir's for being an usher for twenty-five years. Jerzy was proud of those cufflinks. He always pulled his shirtsleeves down so they'd show.

"On my job I have a lot of time to tink because my work don't take a whole lot of brains to do, not like Stanley here who's tinking all the time, or like Doctor John dere who better be tinking."

Doctor Kowalski was at middle table with his wife Greta. The two of them were grinning like two well-heeled Cheshire cats—he in a tailored three-piece suit, puffing on a cigar, she with enough diamonds on her fingers to signal ships. For all his money and brains Doctor Kowalski was clinging to Jerzy's every word.

"The other day, I was tinking about how life is like a polka. When you're dancing, ya have your ups and downs, and sometimes ya get kicked in the shins and sometimes ya kick the other guy a good one. But the music keeps playing and ya keep dancing and before ya know it, the kicks stop hurting. It's happy, the music. Cripe. How can ya go wrong listening to the Polka Knights," he gestured at the guys in the band at the back table, "when they're playing *She Likes Kiełbasa* or *Wish I Was Single Again*? Ya find yourselves laughing and it keeps ya going."

Glasses clinked again, and Jerzy bent down and gave Lydia another smoocheroo. He was holding the microphone so close to their lips that we heard the full sucking sound of it.

"Wouldya look at my Lydia here! Ain't she a gem?" Then he groused, "Cripe, I just lost my train of thought." He shook his finger at her. "See whacha do to me, Ly-dee-a!"

"You were talking about life being like the polka, Jerz," Dad said.

"Oh yeah. I was gonna say the best part of the polka is having the right partner. Ya gotta have da right partner. There's not a day I don't tank my lucky stars for finding this *illegible* young woman."

The crowd howled.

When the banquet tables were cleared off and pushed aside, the room became a dance floor lit by the golden glow of the dimmed chandelier light. Waiters moved along the perimeter of the room lighting candles in little votive glasses on the tables. On the stage the Polka Knights stood poised at their drums, trumpets, saxophones, concertinas, and a tuba. The bandmaster had donned a glittery Liberace-style topcoat over his silver shirt. He dashed out from the wings like a Las Vegas headliner, yanked the microphone out of its stand and shouted, "What time is it?"

"It's polka time!" we shouted back.

"Then let's get this party going! The first dance is for the bridal couple. Let's hear it for Mr. and Mrs. Jerzy Pilarski!"

The band broke into a polka rendition of *I Love You Truly*, and Jerzy lead Lydia to the center of the polished floor. He slipped his arms around her waist and she stepped up to him like Ginger Rogers slipping into Fred Astaire's embrace, and before you knew it they were circling the dance floor. Jerzy gave me a flirtatious wink as they passed. "Save a dance for me, Ellie." I gave him an A-Okay sign. That evening Jerzy was young again. The grizzled man who'd always settled for a back seat in the auditorium of life was waltzing center stage. The longtime widower was a newlywed again, full of hopes and dreams.

The vocalist, a sparkly brunette with a pixie haircut, slunk up to the microphone and pulled it out of its cradle. Holding it to her lips she began crooning. "I Love You Truly . . . "

It was a tender song that reminded me of couples. Mom and Dad who had weathered every storm. Nina and Al. Nina and Ben. Nina and Steve.

"Let's give them a round of applause," the bandleader shouted. "Now let's have the bridal party join in."

I made small talk with Jerzy's son, Joe, and as we danced awkwardly, I scanned the crowd for Duke. I spotted him sitting at a table in a corner engrossed in conversation with Doctor Kowalski. The next time we circled the room, it was Doctor Kowalski doing the talking and Duke was listening. When the music stopped, Doctor Kowalski was writing something on a napkin.

"Now everyone! Up on your feet and dance!" the bandleader shouted.

The Polka Knights began banging out a peppy version of Elvis Presley's *I Can't Help Falling in Love with You*, and everyone sashayed onto the dance floor.

One memory of that evening sticks tightly in my mind. It's of Mom and Dad dancing to Elvis' new song in an old-fashioned, charming way. They held hands high in the air, palm against palm, their cheeks gently touching. Their bodies were like two puzzle pieces that fit together. She was the eyes, he was the heart. That's how it always was with them.

When Duke cut in on me and Joe, he couldn't wait to

tell me. "Ellie, you'll never believe it. I asked Doctor K for some advice about med schools and we ended up talking for twenty minutes. Did you know he's a diehard Ramblers fan?"

"That's great!"

"Anyway, after we talked basketball he invited me to spend a day at St. Mary's Hospital shadowing him."

"Wow," I said. "That's about the best thing that could happen, sweetie, to get to know Doctor Kowalski. Dad says he's solid."

The dancing continued into the evening. The Polka Knights played the real crowd pleasers first—the *Too Fat Polka*, *You Can't Be True Dear*, and the insufferable *Hokey Pokey*—corny songs we should have known better than to like. But Duke and I danced them all, except for the *Too Fat Polka,* which I saved for Jerzy. Then they punched up the volume and played the pop tunes we'd been waiting for.

We did the swim where I held my nose, wiggled my hips and sunk to the floor. Duke got even crazier, doing the hitchhiker complete with thumb action. When we did the pony, he yanked off his tie and swung it around like a lariat. His suspenders had slipped off his shoulders and hung like giant paisley loops alongside his trousers.

A slow tune started and the vocalist in red began singing a Johnny Mathis tune, *It's Not for Me to Say*. "This is more like it," Duke said, pulling me close. During the past year the warm circle of his arms had become my place. It was where I fit in and felt safe. I breathed in the musty scent of him as our bodies swayed to the music. With my ear pressed against his cheek, I listened to him hum the melody. The intimacy of it made me feel even closer to him. I pulled away and kissed his lips. "It's sweet the way you hum."

"I can't remember the words," he confessed.

Being separated from Duke hadn't been easy for either of us. Leaving home was what I wanted, but heading off to Wisconsin was difficult. I'd applied to Northwestern, Loyola, and the University of Wisconsin, and all of them accepted me. But I chose the University of Wisconsin because Madison was midway between Chicago and Green Lake, and because I'd be on my own there, yet close enough to everyone.

During those first weeks at college I was as homesick as a fledgling flung from the nest. Everything reminded me of Duke—a ticket stub from a movie that I found in a jacket pocket, a whiff of his aftershave, the absence of a hand to grip when I was crossing the street, anything maroon, any mention of a condom. Those were the days when I'd call him up late at night and bemoan how alone I felt in a world where I had no identity, reputation, or history. And he'd bolster me up. "You gotta get out there and meet people, Ellie. It's not going to happen if you sit on your ass." When I did venture out, he was proud of me. And I was proud of him because, although he would have preferred to be away at school, he didn't grouse about living at home the way I would have. He was too busy to complain. In addition to college, he was teaching the lifeguard course at the Y and was delivering pizza for Angelino's—in one of those trucks that played *O Solo Mio*. Duke was working his plan. He was saving money for med school. Most important, he respected me for having made my own decisions.

The band took a break and I headed for the ladies room. On the way back I spotted Nina standing alone near the window sipping a ginger ale. "Having a good time?"

"The best."

"Me too. Cool party."

"The coolest." She signaled me over. "Come here, Ellie, I want you to see something." I walked over to the window and she put her hand on my shoulder and we stood together between the velvet spread of the floor-length drapes swooped to the sides and fastened to the window frame by tasseled cords.

"Hey, look over there," she said, pointing at the window.

At first I saw just a reflection of our own faces in the window glass with the chandeliers glistening above Nina's mounded-up hairdo, my flip, and the motion of people milling about behind us. But as my eyes probed the darkness beyond the window, I saw a rectangle of golden light. It looked like a framed painting suspended in the darkness.

"Across the gangway . . . see your kitchen, Ellie," she said, wrapping her arm around my shoulder. Our kitchen window was about twenty feet away from the ballroom window. "How often we've looked into this ballroom from over there. Now it's the reverse."

"The kitchen looks empty," I said.

"Lonely."

Our cafe curtains were open. Mom had left the light on over the kitchen sink and the room had a golden glow. I studied the tableau in the way I'd study a still life at the Art Institute. The room was appealing in its simplicity, a pleasing composition of curves, lines, and colors. In the foreground above the sink was the steely arc of the faucet. Behind it, a lace doily covered our maple table and at its center sat a fruit bowl heaped with apples, oranges, and a carefully placed banana. Everything was perfectly in place, the way Mom had left it.

"It looks surreal, doesn't it?"

"Like an Edward Hopper painting."

As Nina and I swayed arm-in-arm, I recalled the Saturday evenings I stood in that kitchen watching the activity in this ballroom, transfixed by the music and the elegant couples gliding in a waltz, wondering if I'd ever be sophisticated enough to go to balls, whether I'd ever wear an evening gown and be escorted by a dashing man in a tuxedo. I looked down at my gaudy taffeta bridesmaid's gown. That evening I was hardly Jackie Kennedy, and Duke, with his shirttails hanging out, was hardly Jack, but those were minor glitches in the screenplay of my dreams. Pretty much, my dreams had come true.

"Do you remember long ago, Nina, when we were watching the dancers from our window and you grabbed me and we started waltzing around the kitchen table cheek-to-cheek? We put on those rhinestone tiaras you had from high school and danced our hearts out. Someone in the ballroom saw us and pulled the drapes shut because they thought we were mocking them."

"Party poopers," she said.

Way back then, I'm sure we hadn't been the only ones doing the watching. The people in the ballroom were probably watching us too. To them we were just some oddball American family at home on a Saturday evening opening the refrigerator door during TV commercials, prancing past the window with curlers in our hair, practicing our dance moves. What they saw were snippets of our lives, just as Joy and I saw snippets of other people's lives when we rode the city buses at night. What we never saw were the full pictures of people's joys and sorrows. Only flashes pulled out of context, impressions formed without facts. Like the photos in my scrapbook. Snippets of moments in Jack and Jackie's lives, snatches the cameras clicked and film preserved. Some strikingly candid, others carefully posed to present an image.

Those were the days when the press protected a prominent individual's secrets. There was something comforting then about believing our president was larger than life, that he set a higher standard. Today in the 1990s, for better or worse, every dalliance of a public figure is fair game for scrutiny by the media.

"A lot's happened in that flat," Nina said.

"Yeah."

"Just looking at that room and at my window downstairs brings back memories."

I hesitated for a moment. "Do you ever think of him?"

Nina pointed up at the sky. "I believe he's watching us, sweetie. He always told me to have faith things would work out. He really believed that. I'd like to think he's up there keeping an eye on us. Sometimes I even believe he had a hand in making things happen. Sometimes I think it was part of a grand plan. A grand plan for a very big life, right Ellie?"

"I said that once, didn't I?"

"Still want to join the Peace Corps?"

"Definitely. After college Duke and I will have some decisions to make."

I felt a hand on my shoulder. "What are you two up to?"

It was Mom. She wrapped her arms around us and gave us a squeeze that smashed us even closer together. She smelled sweet and flowery, like the Brandy Alexanders she had been drinking, and a fresh spray of Chanel No. 5.

"We're looking at our empty apartments next door. See over there, Vera," Nina said, pointing out the window. Mom bugged out her eyes. "Our kitchen curtains are crooked."

"Geeze, Mom."

"But the room looks cozy, doesn't it?" She stepped closer to the window and because the three of us were attached, we moved forward as a clumsy unit. "Your flat looks so dark downstairs, Nina," Mom said.

"It won't be dark long. Tomorrow Jerzy and Lydia move in," I said.

Nina looked at Mom and asked the question we'd all been wondering about. "How are you going to take to having a new woman in the house, Vera?"

"It's going to be fine. I'll shape her up."

"Sheesh, Mom," I groaned. "Lydia might shape you up."

Mom cleared her throat. "We'll see about that."

The Polka Knights started up again. A trumpet hit a deep mellow tone, the drummer tapped out a lively cha cha beat, and the accordionist added a little Polish zip. The vocalist in the slinky cinnamon dress shimmied up to the microphone. The dance floor filled up.

"I know that song. What's the name of it?" Mom asked.

Nina and I looked at each other and started cracking up.

"What's so funny?"

"Vera, it's *The Naughty Lady of Shady Lane*," Nina said, accentuating every word.

The vocalist with the pixie hair pulled the microphone out of its cradle. She did a seductive hip shake, lifted her skirt to show a little ankle skin.

"My stars. Well, then the two of you better get out there and dance."

We protested.

"Then we'll all dance," Mom said, pulling us out onto the dance floor.

And that's what we did. The three of us, pregnant Nina, perfect Mom, and me—looking like a wilted arrangement of autumn foliage—strutted and dipped and wiggled our butts to the beat.

Across the room Dad was sitting at a table with Uncle Frank, Uncle Bruno, Uncle Steve, and Duke. All the men except Dad were watching us and laughing. I waved, and Duke and Uncle Steve waved back and grinned. Uncle Bruno gave us a thumbs up. After a few seconds Uncle Frank leaned into my father, pointed to us, and told him what was happening.

Dad sat back in his chair and worked his lips around his cigar. I couldn't tell what he was thinking. Maybe he was glad Mom was kicking up her heels. Maybe he was wishing his eyesight would return long enough for him to capture a fresh image of us in his mind's eye. Maybe he was listening to the lyrics and remembering all that had happened to Nina. Maybe he was even thinking about how Peter Rumza, the fenestration salesman, missed out.

Slowly Dad extinguished his cigar in an ashtray. Then his face lit up into the widest grin I'd seen him grin since his world started wobbling on its axis three years earlier, and he let out a triumphant belly laugh that leapt across the ballroom floor and landed smack inside my dancing heart.

Mom waved to the men. Nina tossed her head back and laughed. I giggled and picked up my step. There was an exciting world out there, and I was going to jump into the fray when I was ready. But that night, I was perfectly happy strutting my stuff in the ballroom of the *Klub Kultury*, whooping it up with my family and Duke and Jerzy and Lydia; and in absentia, Father Ben and Joy.

CHAPTER THIRTY-FIVE

NOVEMBER 22, 1963

I was in History class at the University of Wisconsin when I heard. Professor Gottlieb had just handed me my paper, "Abigail Adams: The Genius Behind John." He nodded and smiled, "Nice work, Miss Manikowski." In the blank space below my name he had written, A- in red ink. An A minus? I'd worked my butt off on that paper. I flipped through the pages to read Gottlieb's remarks. Not a note. Not a comment.

Not cool, I thought. I'd talk to him after class.

Just then a loud burst of static screeched into the room from the PA system above the wall clock. It was a few minutes before 1 p.m. "Ladies and gentlemen, this is George Mellon, Dean of Education. "May I have your attention, please?"

Professor Gottlieb yanked his thick eyeglasses off and scowled up at the speaker box as if an intruder had just barged into our classroom. At the nape of his neck, straggly grayish hairs lapped over his turtleneck; his black jacket was flaked with dandruff.

Head and Shoulders, I thought.

There was more static, the sound of papers rustling near the microphone and then Dean Mellon's voice again. "There has just been a news flash. Three shots were fired at President Kennedy's motorcade in downtown Dallas. CBS reports that our president has been seriously wounded and that he's been rushed to Parkland Memorial Hospital in Dallas, where his condition is unknown."

"What?" I said.

"The President's been shot!" someone else cried out.

"Shh, listen!" A girl in front of me smacked the air for silence.

"We are setting up TVs in Bascom Hall and in the dormitories so you can follow the news. Classes for the rest of the day will be cancelled." Then the PA system went dead.

Professor Gottlieb's hand dropped to his side, slapped his rumpled khaki pants. A stapled paper slipped out from between his fingers and slid beneath a desk, but no one bothered to pick it up. The minute hand on the clock advanced, ticked. A guy in the back said, "Let's get out of here."

Books clapped shut. Students sprang from their desks and metal legs scrapped against the hardwood floor. One girl tugged at another's hand. "Let's go find a TV." Clusters of kids passed through the narrow door, merging into a stream of students and faculty hurrying out of the building.

At my dorm, a crowd had gathered around the TV set in the lounge. Most of the kids were still wearing their coats and hats and clutching books. A boyish reporter named Dan Rather was speaking. "What's going on?" I asked Charlotte, my roommate.

"Kennedy might be dead," she said softly.

I gripped Charlotte's hand. The video switched to Walter Cronkite. He was looking down at a paper, not at the camera. The news could not be good. Slowly he removed his dark-rimmed eyeglasses, put them on again and lifted the paper. "From Dallas the flash is apparently official. President Kennedy died at 1 p.m. Central Standard Time, two o'clock Eastern Standard Time, some thirty-eight minutes ago." He shook his head in disbelief.

There were gasps and painful sighs.

My hand shot up to my mouth. "This can't be happening," I cried, and I burst into tears.

For the next twenty-four hours we hung close to the TV, leaving only for the cafeteria, the bathroom, and the quiet of our rooms. I called Duke and we cried. I called home and cried with Mom. She was watching *As the World Turns* when she heard. I called Nina and we cried more. She was out buying fruit when it happened. I tried to call Joy, but the nun wouldn't let her come to the phone. Dammit. The day passed slowly and heavily, like when I was five and had a tonsillectomy and all I could do was lay in bed and wait for the pain to go away.

The events unfolded before our eyes like a movie, too implausible to be real. Aboard Air Force One, Jackie stood beside the imposing figure of Lyndon Johnson as he raised his huge hand and took the oath of office. She looked dazed and scared and fragile beside him, her lips parted, her bouffant disheveled, her skirt stained with her husband's blood.

Through it all, Jackie stayed close to her husband's body. When the plane landed at Andrews Air Force Base in Washington D.C. that afternoon, she refused to leave his casket even long enough to exit through the passenger ramp. Instead she stayed on the cargo lift that lowered him to the ground. At Bethesda Naval Hospital she left her husband alone only when his body was prepared for burial. Later I learned that at the hospital, Jackie said her farewell with a kiss and slipped her own wedding band on his finger. That evening she rode with the casket to the White House, still wearing the pink suit she had on in Dallas. One reporter called it raspberry—much too cheery a word for that day. Only now it was splattered with his blood. She refused to take it off. "I want them to see what they have done to him," she'd said.

Throughout the evening and the next day every TV station re-ran film of the assassination: the shooting; the chaos at Parkland Hospital; the announcement of Kennedy's death; the arrest of the supposed assassin, Lee Harvey Oswald; the Dallas police strutting around in their ten-gallon hats; and that haunting image of Jackie in that blood-stained skirt— over and over and over again.

It was that bloodstained suit that did it. I couldn't sit in front of that TV another minute watching Jackie's anguish. I had to do more. I had to go to Washington and be there for her.

"What are you, nuts?" Dad said when I called home again, this time to say I was going to Washington.

"I'll be back in three days."

"How you getting there?"

"Greyhound."

"Do you have enough money?"

"Yeah."

I really didn't have enough money. I had the money I was saving for Christmas; enough for a round trip bus ticket and maybe a grilled cheese sandwich, but that was it. I figured

I'd work things out once I got there. Funerals and buses were two things I knew a lot about.

In my dorm room I stuffed some clothes into my suitcase—a change of underwear, a long-sleeved black dress, a pair of black gloves, a fresh package of pantyhose, my pearls, my good black pumps. Church shoes, Mom called them. I tied my hair into a pony tail and left wearing the black sweater and jeans I'd pulled on that morning, replacing my loafers with tall black boots and throwing on the long gray winter coat Mom had bought me at Marshall Field's for more money than we'd ever spent on a coat because she decided I'd need something warm to last through my college years. I checked out of the dorm, saying I was going home for a few days. No one cared. A lot of kids went home that weekend.

For the next twenty-six hours I rolled across the country on Greyhound: through small towns with water towers marking their names, past farms with silver silos, pastures with cows "outstanding in their fields"—as Dad used to say—factories, smokestacks, roadside supper clubs, and a series of Burma-Shave signs. *My job is/ Keeping faces clean/ And nobody knows/ De stubble/ I've seen/ Burma-Shave.* The sun, looking frozen in the sky, faded behind clouds. Rain splattered against the window glass and turned to snow. Snow fell softly, wildly, then softly again. Trucks barreled past and I studied the profiles of the drivers with muscled arms, plaid flannel shirts, hidden thoughts. I used to think people were essentially different in a way that made strangers unapproachable, but that day I learned otherwise. We're all the same—we're all muddling around in this mixed-up world together. A grandmother who sat next to me, riding with her purse on her lap, shared her ham sandwich and *True Story* magazines with me.

"Sad, isn't it," she said with tears in her eyes. "He was just getting started."

At a rest stop in Cleveland I bought a copy of *The Cleveland Plain Dealer*. The headline read: KENNEDY ASSASSINATED; JOHNSON TAKES OATH. A radio with a tinny sound played *Puff the Magic Dragon*.

I slept the broken sleep of a bus ride, the huge tires rolling beneath me, the motor whirring loudly, my head bumping against the window, my arms wrapped around my chest. I had never traveled farther than Wisconsin, and there I was on my first trip riding eight hundred and fifty miles through Elkhart, Indiana; Cleveland Ohio; Hagerstown, Maryland; passing through time zones, threading my way along a route of highways that until then had been no more than black lines and red dots on a Rand McNally roadmap. When evening came, lamps inside of houses flicked on and the gray light of television spread across the country like an electric fog.

I flicked on the overhead light and opened my newspaper. The pages, dense with headlines and photos, captured the same images that ran on TV. The limousine approaching Dealy Plaza. Jackie smiling, clutching a bouquet of roses. The underpass. The president collapsing over Jackie's shoulder. Jackie wearing that bloody suit. I flicked off the light and slid the paper between my seat and the window. I couldn't look any longer. I couldn't read any more. I tried to sleep, but couldn't do that either.

I remembered the only time I saw John Kennedy in real life. It was during his presidential campaign, the day I had bought my campaign buttons. Joy and I had ridden the subway downtown, pushed ourselves through the crowds on

State Street, and claimed a spot behind the police barricades where we waited to see him for three hours. When his motorcade approached, horns honked and people cheered and confetti came falling from the sky, and suddenly there he was—riding atop the back seat of a convertible, suntanned, so alive, grinning and reaching out to shake hands with folks breaking through the barricades. Joy and I went crazy, waving and chanting "JFK! JFK!" at the top of our lungs. Then as quickly as the motorcade arrived, it rolled past, and Kennedy's auburn head disappeared within a barrage of confetti.

I reached for that newspaper and unfolded it. There it was: that photo of Jackie in her bloodstained suit. In the privacy of my small section of the bus, with the highway lights blinking upon the newsprint, the emotions of those days collected in my heart. I wanted to give Jackie strength. I wanted to tell her what Nina went through. I wanted to tell her that the deepest of the pain would pass, that one day she would smile again. That she would waltz at her children's weddings. That she'd find love again. So I pressed that photo to my chest and I told her those things. Tears streamed down my cheeks, and I didn't wipe them away. Then I looked up into the sky and remembered what Father Ben had told us—that suffering and death are mysteries we have to live with until the end, but that love can carry us through.

In the bus station in Washington D.C. I changed into my funeral clothes.

"Which way to St. Matthew's Cathedral?" I asked a black girl at the information counter.

"Downtown. Catch the bus at the corner," she said, pointing to an intersection. "The service ain't open to the public, honey."

I wanted to save on bus fare, so I ran over to Connecticut Avenue and thumbed a ride. The people I passed on the way were somber. Some carried small flags. The only laughter came from children who didn't know any better.

I stuck my thumb out and almost immediately, a greenish Buick pulled to the curb. I bent down to check the driver out. He was an elderly, gray-haired gentleman in a dark overcoat and a diagonally striped tie. Could have been a businessman, a judge, a grandfather. A bobbly statue of St. Christopher on his dashboard told me he probably wasn't a rapist. "Going anywhere near St. Matthew's?" I asked, and he waved me in.

The seat in his car was leather. I had never sat on a leather car seat before. He said his name was Don Hornbacher, and that he was a Republican, but that he was sorry about Kennedy too. "I was not an admirer. Truth is I didn't think he accomplished that much. But I guess he did bring the country together." After riding in silence a bit, he said, "Did you hear that a thug named Jack Ruby, a guy with mafia connections in Chicago, shot Lee Harvey Oswald?"

I hadn't heard.

He looked at my small suitcase. "How long you in town for?"

"Just today."

"Where's home?"

"Chicago. But I came from college. Wisconsin."

He smiled. "You've come why?"

"To pay my respects." I decided not to tell him that I came to be with Jackie because I owed her that much. It was too long a story to tell, and much too personal.

"When you heading home?"

"Tonight."

He shook his head the way Dad did when I confounded him. "Kids today," he said to himself. "What do your folks think of this quick little trip?"

Before I had a chance to answer, a policeman blew his whistle and with a grand gesture waved us off onto a side street. The view changed to storefronts, some with "Closed" signs in their windows. Mr. Hornbacher looked at me out of the corner of his eye. "That's St. Matthew's there," he said, pointing to a rounded dome on top of a compact red brick church. He dropped me off about a block away, the closest he could get. "Thanks for the ride, sir," I said, sliding out of the car, yanking my suitcase behind me.

"Wait a minute, miss," he said. He leaned forward, reached into his pants pocket, pulled out a leather billfold and handed me a twenty-dollar bill. "Take a taxi back to the bus station and get yourself a bite to eat."

"Thank you, sir," I said, feeling tightness in the muscles around my mouth. It felt like a long time since I smiled, although it had only been about seventy-two hours.

He moved his hand to the gearshift and looked through the rear view mirror. A string of cars waited behind us, yet no one honked. That day even the honkers were respectful.

"Sir, may I have your address?" I asked him.

"Why?"

"I want to send you your money back. That's a lot of money you gave me, sir."

He laughed. "No need. Do what you have to do, and be safe."

I remember pushing through the crowds outside St. Matthews and stopping at a spot where I had almost a clear view of the front door, but not a great one. To see better I stood on top of the Samsonite my parents had given me for graduation. The church door was closed, and men in dark suits and walky-talkies were out in front. Secret Service.

"Is the funeral Mass over?" I asked the girl beside me.

"It will be soon," she replied.

Five minutes later the doors opened. A priest in a black vestment and a flag-draped casket carried by eight grim pallbearers passed through the door. Jackie, all in black, and her children, innocent in light blue coats and brown oxfords, followed the coffin.

A grieving Madonna, Jackie held her children's hands as they walked down the steps, the three of them together— Caroline, Jackie and John Jr. She stood stoically with her head bowed. A lace veil fastened to a pillbox hat fell past her shoulders onto the collar of her coat. Through the dark veil she appeared dazed, but strong and dignified. She was only thirty-four. Oh, how she reminded me of Nina.

Little John-John, a bit of a boy with a shaggy brown haircut that glistened in the sunshine, fidgeted and tugged at his mother's hand. She bent down and whispered to him. The boy handed her the small book he held, stepped forward, raised his hand to his forehead and saluted his father's casket. It was his third birthday.

That's when I broke down. Everyone around me was crying. Housewives. Career girls. Businessmen. Cops too tough to cry. Teenagers. We wept openly; our eyes fixed upon the little boy in the double-breasted blue coat who said farewell to the father he would never get to know.

A long black limousine pulled to the curb, Jackie folded herself inside it. The motor purred and the limo pulled away slowly, bound for Arlington Cemetery.

President Kennedy was in office for exactly two years,

eleven months and two days. No matter what he did or didn't do, he gave us something to dream about. In that short time he had changed the world, and in that short time Jackie had changed me.

There was a time when I admired Jackie for her style and grace, and for what I'd dreamt I could become by watching her. But that day I understood the gift and folly of such hero worship. That day I admired her for what really mattered: her courage.

I had come to Washington to pay my respects. Now it was time to go home and to live my own life.

CHAPTER THIRTY-SIX

*R*anjit Kalirai was the first cabdriver I ever hugged. Joy would say it was a California touchy-feely thing, but I'd say it was a hug of gratitude for delivering me safely to the Drake in downtown Chicago, and for his kindness along the way. "Call if I can ever help you out," I said, handing him some extra money and my business card.

> *Dr. Eleanor Manikowski*
> *Adolescent Medicine*
> *Stanford University Medical Center*
> *Palo Alto, California*

"I thought your husband was the doctor?"

"Both of us," I said, waving goodbye.

When I was growing up, being a physician was the last thing on my mind, but it was Duke who led me in that direction. According to plan, he received his degree in internal medicine from the Stritch School of Medicine at Loyola, and he interned at Rush-Presbyterian in Chicago. But he deferred the plum fellowship he was offered in cardiology to accommodate my dream of joining the Peace Corps.

Duke and I were married in a simple service at St. Casimir's. Nothing like the razzle dazzle of Jerzy and Lydia's wedding, but not as sedate as Nina and Steve's. With all the Manikowskis and Dukaschewskis present, plus high school and college friends, sedate was not an option. Our wedding reception was held in the church basement with a romping, stomping Polka band that played *I Love You Truly* and *She Likes Kiełbasa*, and we danced until our feet went numb. But the best part was that Joy, in a sleek magenta gown, was my maid of honor.

According to my prediction, Joy did end up being a short-timer in the convent. On the day of President Kennedy's assassination, at the same time I was trying to call her, she was trying to call me, but the nuns wouldn't allow her to make or accept phone calls. Incensed, as Wanda's story goes, she packed her bags that very afternoon, stormed past Sister Monica, the directress of novitiates, who was trying to talk some sense into her, and ended up finding a pay phone in a nearby tavern where she called her mother, collect. Wanda, in turn, called Gregory Duda who by then was officially her boyfriend, and the two of them sped to Des Plaines to pick up Joy before she changed her mind. By the time they arrived, Joy had downed three Martinis and a beer and was toasting *nazdrowie* to the bartender. In an odd juxtaposition of priorities, the two of them were watching the very public aftermath of President Kennedy's assassination on TV while commiserating over Joy's departure from her very private life in the convent. Wanda and Gregory still tell the story of how Joy was dressed in her novice's habit when they arrived, but by that time had turned her short black veil into a coaster for her lineup of Martini glasses.

Of course, there were a lot of phone calls between Joy and the nuns, and, of course, there was paperwork to fill out, but she was as adamant about leaving the convent as she once was about entering. "If I can't call my friend during a damn national crisis, then the convent isn't the place I want to be."

It took about twelve hours for Joy to reconnect with Barney, who had never given up hope and had gone about his life patiently waiting her out. After finishing college where she majored in Slavic languages, she and Barney got married in the huge Polish wedding Wanda had never stopped saving her pennies for. Barney, now a distinguished and graying professor, teaches physics at the University of Chicago in Hyde Park, where he and Joy live within walking distance of Wanda's three perfect, Polish grandchildren—the aspiring actress, Lilly Gogolinski, and twin sons, Matthew and Maximilian.

Joy's life after the convent has been calm, with the exception of matters having to do with her mother, whose life could never be calm. Gregory Duda, always a sucker for taking chances that included marrying Wanda, struck it rich in the late '70s when, on the way home from ushering at St. Casimir's, he stopped at a 7-11, bought a dollar lottery ticket and triumphantly won $4 million.

His good fortune brought them a front-page interview in the *Chicago Tribune*. "How will your winnings change your life?" the interviewer asked. "We're simple people," Wanda said. "We're going stay in the old neighborhood and I'm going to keep working at Smacycks making the best sandwiches on the northwest side." Gregory and Wanda Dusza Duda are now comfortably and luxuriously situated in a penthouse apartment on Michigan Avenue near Navy Pier with a concierge, a uniformed doorman with an attitude and epaulets, and a breathtaking view of Lake Michigan.

Unlike Joy's, my life has been anything but calm.

The day after our wedding, Duke and I left for our two-year Peace Corps assignment in Madhya Pradesh, the middle province of India. Those years of living with no running water, a hole-in-the-ground latrine, hit-and-miss electricity—those years were our honeymoon. But as we agreed that last week in India, we wouldn't have changed it for the world. Although the people didn't have much, they were eager to share their lives and their customs, and would give you the sandals off their feet. Duke practiced medicine at a Primary Health Center in a village two hours from Jabalpur working to stem the spread of tuberculosis and malaria. The first year I worked on a poultry project introducing chicken and eggs into the diets of the villagers. The second year I was assigned to a family planning team that instructed women to use birth control, which I felt especially qualified to do given my prior condom experience.

Duke and I had just completed our last week in Madhya Pradesh and had already started packing our duffel bags for home, when late one afternoon, at my initiation, we hopped on our bicycles and pedaled to the bazaar some forty-five minutes away to purchase souvenirs. Once we arrived, I ended up lingering too long at the open-air booth of a striking woman named Uma Kumar, whose third eye—a *tilaka*, a dot of vermilion—adorned the center of her forehead. Over the years Uma had become my friend. She had been patient with my faltering Hindi. She had brought me samples of Indian delicacies she'd prepared for her own family. That evening she unrolled bolt after bolt of jeweled fabrics and spread them out on her spacious table for my admiration. The setting sun cast red shadows over the silk threads and made them glitter like precious stones. Rubies. Turquoise. Emeralds. Amethysts.

I took my time making my selections, matching the turquoise to Nina's eyes, the gold to Mom's preference for earth tones, the ruby to the glass in the teardrop chandeliers at St. Casimir's that Marta so admired. I slipped layers of colorful glass bangles over my wrist and held them up to the light, rotating my wrist in graceful half-circles as if doing an Indian dance, watching the speckles of mirrored glass change colors in the light. Being in no particular rush, I matched the bangles to the fabric, then changed my mind and started over again; laughing with Uma as she offered endless choices from the inventory she kept stacked on plastic shelves behind her.

While I shopped, Duke joined in a soccer game with some young boys. I remember the sight of him—longish curly hair, khaki shorts, dusty sandals, his Hindi dictionary peeking out of his back pocket, executing a skillful instep pass to his teammate, a boy of about ten, waving his arms above his head and shouting, "*Shaabaasha*!" when the kid scored.

After Uma and the other merchants closed their booths and the kids dispersed, we hopped on our bikes and pedaled toward home. By then an eerie quiet had settled over the countryside. I remember thinking how the air seemed too still, the birds too hushed, the glare of the setting sun too blinding. Then another odd thing happened. A peacock as large as a swan suddenly appeared before us in the road. We pedaled toward it, but he didn't flinch. Not a flutter of his crown, or a bob of his neck. Then, like an exotic dancer on a luminescent stage, swirling in rouge and crimson lights, he fanned his feathers into a breathtaking aura of blue and green. He remained there, posing, unmoving. The feathers of his plume were studded with what looked like hundreds of unblinking blue-green eyes that watched us advance. It crossed my mind that he was issuing us a warning, but it was a thought I quickly dismissed.

I remember turning to Duke and saying something completely unrelated to my uneasiness. "Nina's going to love the bangles. Blue's her color." Just then we heard a scuffle coming from the bamboo forest, hard running, shouts, then the pop of a gun, and another pop. We veered our bikes to the side of the road and hit the ground. There were more shouts in tribal dialects and random gunfire. Duke sheltered me with his body and held me down, and the gunfire got closer, and there were more pops and his weight collapsed upon me. "My God," he cried, "Ellie."

Those were his last words.

I lay beneath him, his blood streaming down my arm, flowing into the dirt. I reached for his wrist and felt for a pulse. There was none. "Duke!" I whispered. There were more pops and I was too afraid to scream. My cheek was pressed to the ground, my eyes were wide open, I was squeezing his hand and his blood was thick on my skin, and all I could see through the dark curtain of my hair was the peacock's hooked claws prancing past, the bangles and my fabric in the dirt, soaking up my husband's blood like jeweled sponges.

And then there was silence.

"Breathe! Breathe," I remember crying, as I held him. "Duke! Hang on. Stay with me." I thumped his chest. I ran up and down the road yelling like a madwoman for help, waving my bloody hands, sobbing in anguish. But no one came; no one heard me. I ran back to Duke and tried to keep him warm, as if warmth could bring him back to life. And then I prayed. "Hail Mary, full of grace, the Lord is with Thee. Blessed art Thou amongst women, and blessed is the fruit of Thy womb, Jesus. Holy Mary, Mother of God, pray for us sinners, now and at the hour of our death." Over and over I prayed. "Please God, help me."

It was nearly dark when a bullock cart pulled by two oxen clomped up the road. The driver, a wrinkled Punjabi farmer, found me kneeling in the dirt—trembling, praying, sobbing, cradling my husband in my arms. With strong square hands he lifted Duke into the bed of his cart as gently as if he were lifting his own son. He covered me with a blanket and poured me a cup of tepid tea from his beat-up thermos jar.

The Peace Corps officials wanted me to return home immediately, but I stayed in India until arrangements could be made for Duke's passage home. I couldn't leave him. The thirty-hour flight to Chicago was a blur, as was the funeral, the grief-stricken faces of our family and friends, the condolences, the lonely aftermath. I never did find out what the shooting was about or who was responsible.

Those months, living at home with Mom, Dad, and Marta, were the darkest of my life. Although I tried to be strong, had it not been for my family, I might have walked into traffic, overdosed on pills, I don't know what else.

I had no use for church. What kind of God would do this to me? I couldn't abide people and their stupid questions. "Did he have insurance?" Or people who offered ridiculous advice. "You'll snap out of it." As if it was some passing funk I was in. As if snap, crackle, pop, the breakfast food of mourners, everything would be okay.

Not even Nina had the right words.

One afternoon in Green Lake, I was sitting on the sun porch staring into the air and she put her arm around me and said, "You won't understand this now, sweetie, but your life will go on and one day you'll be happy again." I looked at her

314 | ELIZABETH KERN

with disbelief. "My God, Nina, how could you say that?" She just hugged me. "I know," she whispered. "I know."

The nights when I was alone with my thoughts—those nights were the worst. Lying in my narrow childhood bed, turning my wedding band around on my finger, I blamed myself for encouraging Duke to deviate from his own plan to follow mine. "I want to be with you, Ellie," he'd said. "Your dream is important to me." Had he not made that one concession, that one amendment, that one deviation . . . had I not agreed to it, had I not insisted we pedal to the bazaar that evening . . . had I not dallied . . . had I not ignored the peacock's warning . . . had I not . . . had I not . . . I nearly drove myself crazy.

Aside from family, the only friends I saw were Donna, who wept in my arms, and Joy and Barney, whose good cheer held me together, and who, in spite of my sullen, silent moods always brought over something to make me smile—a snow globe of Elvis Presley, a wind-up toy nun brandishing a ruler in her hand, a red hot from Suzie's heaped with piccalilli.

After a year of leaning on others, I finally found a modicum of courage to resume my own life. I couldn't do it in Chicago where there were too many memories, where people were hovering over me as if I were a hopeless invalid. I needed their help. I wanted their help. I accepted their help, but I couldn't stand it anymore. So I packed up Old Meconium and drove west, beginning a two-week odyssey of near self-destruction. I slept on the mattress in back, ate greasy fast food, smoked unfiltered cigarettes, ate Twinkies, cried out obscenities, didn't change my clothes, wore my old horned-rimmed glasses, drove too fast, cursed God and other drivers, listened to Country Western music loud, frowned at happy couples, took wrong turns on purpose, picked up two speeding tickets in Iowa and Oklahoma, saw an X-rated movie in Kansas, had a flat tire in Wyoming and accepted help from a lonely truck driver from North Dakota who bought me a meat loaf dinner, a shot and a beer, and wanted much more. But when I'd burst into tears and told him my whole bloody story, he backed off. He walked me to my van. "Honey, you're a sweet kid, but you're all fucked up." He handed me a joint. "It'll take the edge off." Later that night I smoked the joint overlooking the less than dazzling lights of Chugwater, Wyoming, thus entering—for the first and only time in my life—the hazy world of the stoned. It was by the grace of God and a little pot that I made it to California without hurting myself or anyone else.

For two more years I lived a solitary life in a weathered house in the foggy coastal town of Half Moon Bay, trying to find my footing. I worked at Salamone's bakery selling sourdough bread, focaccia, and cup cakes, worked as a photographers' assistant, walked other people's dogs, cared for other people's children, cleaned other people's houses, took courses in psychology to try to figure myself out.

Then after another year I found a job at a free clinic where I worked side-by-side with a Stanford pediatrician named Jacob Sutter, who ended up mentoring me (the way Dr. Kruk mentored Mom, I hate to admit) and eventually marrying me. Tall and gangly, with angular features, kind eyes, and a balding head, Jake was a man given to running marathons, cycling cross-country, scaling mountains, and leading an all-around healthy life style—an influence I desperately needed. A man of endless energy and unstoppable optimism, he encouraged me when I felt like retreating and over time helped me rediscover the spark I had lost. It was Jake who saw qualities in me that I hadn't seen in myself. It was he who encouraged me to apply to medical school, and it was he who on a walk among a cathedral of redwoods in Muir Woods gave me a biography of Eleanor Roosevelt with this inscription written in his firm hand: "To my favorite Eleanor. Remember the words of Eleanor Roosevelt: 'A woman is like a tea bag. You never know how strong she is until she gets into hot water.' Love Jacob."

But most of all, Jake is the father of our lovely daughter, Amanda, who is now off in Europe finding herself, and our unpredictable, unflappable son, Luke, who is a documentary filmmaker in San Francisco finishing up a film about the Barbary Coast, the city's old red-light district.

As it turned out, I had no time for a nap. As I followed the porter to the elevator, we passed the Palm Court, the lounge where people meet for pre-dinner cocktails, and I saw Joy at a round table sipping a glass of white wine with two women whose backs were toward me.

"Joy!" I said, running to her, but caught myself when I realized that the woman wasn't Joy at all, but her daughter, Lilly, who with her mass of curly hair and green eyes, and her black slacks and form-fitting black sweater was the image of her mother as a young woman. Joy was on her feet by then scurrying toward me with her plump body jiggling inside a colorful caftan, her arms ready to engulf me like eagle wings. "We were worried about you."

"Dad said your flight landed at one-thirty. Where were you, Mom?" I had to do a double take to realize that the young woman who just called me Mom was my Amanda.

"What are you doing here? You were supposed to be in Madagascar or Mozambique or Madrid. I lose track of you, sweetie," I gasped. I threw my arms around her and breathed her in—this girl in the jeans and bulky red sweater was so much my daughter, living out her own dream. "How'd you get here?"

"Dad arranged it."

"He did? Bless him!" I said.

"It's a girl's weekend," Joy beamed.

"Where've you been?" Amanda asked. "You smell like a burrito."

"Well, Jackie Kennedy died yesterday and I needed to spend time in the old neighborhood."

Amanda furrowed her brow and Lilly looked puzzled, but it was Joy who understood. "You did?" she asked softly. I knew she had a pretty good idea of exactly where I had been and why, even the path I took from our house to St. Casimir's, past Suzie's diner and checking out Holy Family along the way.

"Did you go inside St. Casimir's?"

"No. The doors were locked. Security."

"We'll go there on Sunday. Inside it's as beautiful as ever."

"A jewelry box of treasures," I said.

As I looked around the table at the accepting faces of these four special women, I thought of the other courageous women in my life—Mom, Nina, Joy, Wanda, Jackie—who that afternoon danced young again on the stage of my memory; and of the courageous men—Dad, Duke, Father Ben—who with their bluster, their plans and their passions had become my protectors, my teachers. I thought of Jake, who—if chance allowed it and God willed it—would be my lover, my life companion, and the bearer of many birthday surprises throughout our days.

My memory flashed back to that afternoon in Nina's kitchen, when intoxicated by the aroma of freshly baked bread and giddy with adolescent dreams of a big life, I declared that I wanted to experience everything life had to offer—love, adventure, even heartbreak. I pictured myself at seventeen—wide-eyed and effervescent—like a bottle of soda that had been shaken and was ready to explode. And I remember how Nina looked at me, and how her sad smile said what I hadn't understood until many years later: Sweetie, you don't know what you're asking for.

Then the same thought came to mind that I had been mulling over on the last harrowing stretch of my cab ride with Ranjit. It was because of love, adventure, and the lessons taught by heartbreak that I now have a very big life.

$\mathscr{A}$CKNOWLEDGEMENTS

Until now I've been living with the fictitious characters of my story. Now it is my pleasure to thank the real ones who made this book possible.

First, my heartfelt appreciation to the down-to-earth men and women of the Milwaukee, Division, and Ashland neighborhood of Chicago who influenced me as a child; to my parents, Sophie and Harry Brodzinski, who taught me to respect my Polish heritage; and to my extended family of aunts, uncles, and cousins for their love and support. Without their example of what family and faith should be, this book would not have been possible.

Thanks to my treasured group of high school and college girlfriends, the My Ties—Barbara Arendt, Mary Ann Bloom, Christine Dublin, Joan Jareo, Halina Marcinkowski, Diane Mazur, and Jeri Winkles. A special thank you to Halina who was my Polish language consultant throughout this project, and Barbara for her savvy editing and laugh-out-loud marginal notes.

My gratitude to my dear friend, Sandra Sanoski, for designing the cover and interior of this book—and doing so much more—with the kind of grace, love, and creativity Jackie herself would have admired.

I also want to extend appreciation to my fellow writers, the smart and talented members of the finest writing group I could imagine, the Bono Bunch in Petaluma, California. My deepest gratitude to Susan Bono, writing coach extraordinaire; Christine Falcone; Chuck Kensler; Margit Liesche; Dr. Mark Sloan; and Pat Tyler who have lived and laughed with me throughout the creation of Jackie, and who continue to make me a better writer. I am indebted to them as well as to the many others who have read my manuscript and offered sage advice: Winnie Broughan, Kate Campbell, Julie Cartwright (for the story of Uncle Ludwig's leg), Kathy McCabe, Corinne Paquin Meadors, Kriste Kern Michelini, Julia Lord, Cindy Prince, Jordan Rosenfeld, Janet Snyder, Terry Stark, and Amy Meadors Warda.

Of valuable assistance to my research were the archivists at the John F. Kennedy Presidential Library and Museum in Boston, the librarians at the Jean and Charles Schulz Information Center at Sonoma State University, and the media specialists at the Santa Rosa library who helped me muddle through the mysteries of microfiche so I could relive Jackie Kennedy's Camelot years through articles in *LIFE, TIME, McCall's*, and the *Ladies Home Journal*. Also my heartfelt thanks to Mary Ann Bloom of the Field Museum of Chicago, which in 2004-2005 featured the exhibition: *Jacqueline Kennedy: The White House Years*. Mary Ann's explanations of the exhibit helped me deepen my understanding of the careful public image Mrs. Kennedy created for herself, and how she changed the nation's perception of culture, art, and historic preservation.

Finally, hugs to my husband, Lee, who with pencil in hand has read my book more times than I can count, and who is the world's best commentator on the human condition. Hugs also to my children, Amy Meadors Warda and Drew Meadors, who have offered me unwavering support and encouragement throughout my post-corporate career as a writer of fiction.

BIBLIOGRAPHY

Bowles, Hamish; Schlesinger, Arthur Jr.; Mellon, Rachel Lambert. Jacqueline Kennedy: The White House Years. Selections from the John F. Kennedy Library and Museum. New York: Little, Brown and Company, 2001.

Bradford, Sarah. America's Queen, The Life of Jacqueline Kennedy Onassis. New York: Penguin Books, 200l.

Granacki, Victoria. Chicago's Polish Downtown. Arcadia Publishing, 2004.

Hamblin, Dora Jane. "Mrs. Kennedy's Decisions Shaped All The Solemn Pageantry." LIFE. December 6, 1963: 48-49.

Martin, Ralph G. A Hero For Our Time, An Intimate Story of The Kennedy Years. New York: Macmillan Publishing Company, 1983.

Sidey, Hugh. "'Everything must have a reason for being there.'" LIFE. September 1, 1961. 56-65.

"A Tour of the White House with Mrs. John F. Kennedy." The historic 1962 televised broadcast produced by CBS News. (DVD), 2004.

"President Kennedy Is Laid to Rest." LIFE. Vol. 55, No. 23, December 6, 1963. 38-47.

"The First Lady Brings History and Beauty to the White House." LIFE. September 1, 1961. 54-65.

$\mathscr{D}$ISCUSSION GROUP QUESTIONS

1. How are national events used to frame the novel?

2. What role does religion play in the story of the family's values?

3. How does family history and culture color the novel's outcome?

4. What do the middle-class Manikowskis have in common with the Kennedys?

5. Discuss Ellie's relationship with her Aunt Nina, with her parents.

6. Discuss Father Ben's dilemma, his struggle between secularism and spirituality.

7. What is the function of irony in the story?

8. What has Ellie sacrificed, what has she gained during this part of her life?

9. What is important in Ellie's journey toward forgiveness and acceptance?

10. What role do childhood dreams, role models, and heroines play in our lives?

For more information on *Wanting to Be Jackie Kennedy* and Elizabeth Kern, please visit www.elizabethkern.com

ABOUT THE AUTHOR

A native of Chicago, Elizabeth Kern was born and raised in the old Polish neighborhood she writes about. She attended Loyola University and received a degree in Communications from the University of Illinois. After a thirty-year corporate career where she managed employee communications most recently at Apple in Cupertino, California, she received a Masters of Liberal Arts degree at Stanford University. She is the mother of two grown children, Amy Meadors Warda and Drew Meadors. She and her husband, Lee, live in the gentle hills of Sonoma County where vineyards are abundant and the whinny of horses rocks them to sleep at night.

Kern's passion for Chicago's history and people has led her to begin another novel that is set in the Windy City in the 1950s.

3 1125 00765 3551

CPSIA information can be obtained at www.ICGtesting.com
Printed in the USA
LVOW060711180412

278111LV00005B/8/P